THE TALE OF
CASTLE COTTAGE

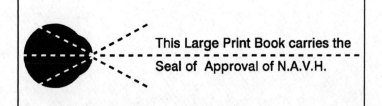

This Large Print Book carries the
Seal of Approval of N.A.V.H.

THE COTTAGE TALES OF
BEATRIX POTTER

THE TALE OF
CASTLE COTTAGE

SUSAN WITTIG ALBERT

WHEELER PUBLISHING
A part of Gale, Cengage Learning

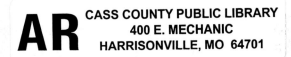

GALE
CENGAGE Learning™

Detroit • New York • San Francisco • New Haven, Conn • Waterville, Maine • London

GALE
CENGAGE Learning

Wheeler Publishing Large Print Hardcover.
The text of this Large Print edition is unabridged.
Other aspects of the book may vary from the original edition.
Set in 16 pt. Plantin.

LIBRARY OF CONGRESS CATALOGING-IN-PUBLICATION DATA

Albert, Susan Wittig.
   The tale of Castle Cottage / by Susan Wittig.
     p. cm. — (The cottage tales of Beatrix Potter)
   ISBN-13: 978-1-4104-4339-7 (hardcover)
   ISBN-10: 1-4104-4339-6 (hardcover)
    1. Potter, Beatrix, 1866-1943—Fiction. 2. Women authors—Fiction. 3. Women artists—Fiction. 4. England—Fiction. 5. Large type books. I. Title.
PS3551.L2637T346 2011b
813'.54—dc23   2011036190

Published in 2011 by arrangement with The Berkley Publishing Group, a member of Penguin Group (USA) Inc.

Printed in the United States of America
1 2 3 4 5 6 7 15 14 13 12 11

*For every reader who has ever loved
Miss Potter's Little Books*

My gentle Reader. I perceive
How patiently you've waited.
And now I fear that you expect
Some tale will be related.
O Reader! had you in your mind
Such stores as silent thought can bring,
O gentle Reader! you would find
A tale in everything.
— WILLIAM WORDSWORTH

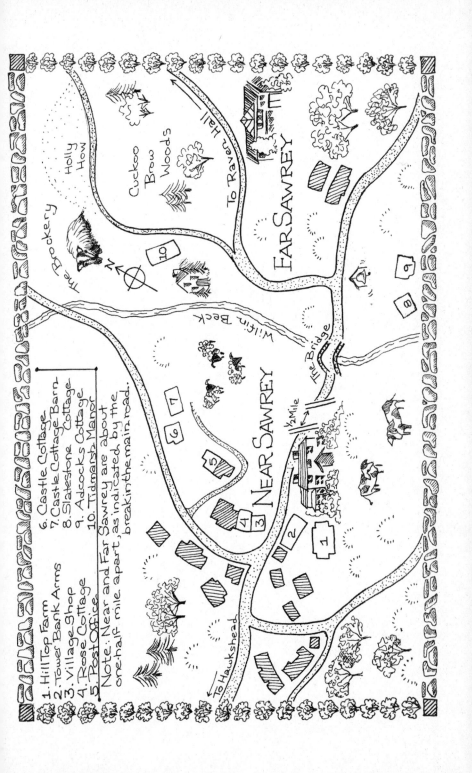

CAST OF CHARACTERS
(* INDICATES AN ACTUAL HISTORICAL PERSON OR CREATURE)

PEOPLE OF THE LAND BETWEEN THE LAKES

*Beatrix Potter** is best known for her children's books, beginning with *The Tale of Peter Rabbit* (1901). Miss Potter lives with her parents, *Helen and Rupert Potter,* at Number Two Bolton Gardens, in South Kensington, London. She spends as much time as possible at Hill Top Farm, in the Lake District village of Near Sawrey. *Mr. and Mrs. Jennings* and their children live in the Hill Top farmhouse and manage the farm while Miss Potter is in London. Her brother, *Bertram Potter,* occasionally visits Hill Top.

*Will Heelis,** a solicitor, lives in the nearby market town of Hawkshead and is a frequent visitor to Near Sawrey. He and Miss Potter became secretly engaged in *The Tale of Applebeck Orchard.*

Captain Miles Woodcock and his wife, *Margaret Nash Woodcock,* live in Tower Bank House. Mrs. Woodcock is the former headmistress of Sawrey School. Captain Woodcock is the justice of the peace for Sawrey District. *Elsa Grape* keeps house for them.

Sarah Barwick operates the Anvil Cottage Bakery in Near Sawrey. She is a modern woman who wears trousers and rides a bicycle to deliver her baked goods.

Jeremy Crosfield, a young artist and amateur botanist, is a teacher at Sawrey School. He and *Deirdre Malone* were married recently and are expecting their first child. They live in Far Sawrey, at Slatestone Cottage. A young woman named *Gilly Harmsworth* is Deirdre's friend.

Reverend Samuel Sackett is the vicar of St. Peter's Church in Far Sawrey. A few months ago, he and *Grace Lythecoe* were married. *Mrs. Hazel Thompson* (a cousin of Agnes Llewellyn) keeps house for him.

John Braithwaite is the constable for both Near and Far Sawrey. He and his wife, *Hannah,* live at Croft End Cottage with their children.

Lester Barrow and his wife, *Frances,* operate the village pub, the Tower Bank Arms, which is located at the bottom of the hill, below Hill Top Farm. *Ruth Safford* helps Mrs. Barrow with housekeeping and waits tables in the pub.

Lydia Dowling runs the village shop at the corner of Kendal Road and Stony Lane. Her niece, *Gladys,* helps out several times a week.

Mrs. Pemberton and her family have moved into Rose Cottage.

Regina Rosier* is an outstanding amateur photographer. (Thanks to the real Regina Rosier for her featured cameo appearance in this book.)

George and *Mathilda Crook* live at Belle Green, where Mrs. Crook takes in boarders. Mr. Crook is the village blacksmith.

Lady Longford lives at Tidmarsh Manor. *Mr. Beever* manages the grounds and her ladyship's horses; *Mrs. Beever* cooks and manages the household staff. *Mr. Depford Darnwell* is an antiquarian whom Lady Longford has invited to appraise her deceased husband's book collection.

Lucy Skead is the village postmistress. She lives with her husband, *Joseph* (the sexton at St. Peter's, in Far Sawrey), at Low Green Gate Cottage.

Mr. Bernard Biddle is a local contractor who manages construction projects for people. Among other workers, he employs *Mr.*

Lewis Adcock, a carpenter who lives in Far Sawrey, and *Mr. Maguire,* who lives near Hawkshead. Mr. Biddle lives at Hazel Crag Farm, where *Mrs. Framley* keeps house for him.

OTHER CREATURES OF THE LAND BETWEEN THE LAKES

Crumpet, a handsome gray tabby, is the new president of the Village Cat Council; she makes her home with Bertha Stubbs. *Tabitha Twitchit* (an elderly calico with an orange and white bib), has recently retired from the position in order to move to the Vicarage with the new Mrs. Sackett. *Felicia Frummety* lives at Hill Top Farm. *Treacle* and her kittens live at High Green Gate. *Max the Manx* lives with Major Ragsdale in Far Sawrey.

Rascal, a Jack Russell terrier, lives with the Crooks at Belle Green but spends his time managing the daily life of the village.

Hyacinth Badger is in charge of The Brockery, a famous animal hostelry on Holly How, and holds the Badger Badge of Authority. Also in residence: *Bosworth Badger XVII,* former holder of the Badge of Authority (now retired); Hyacinth's mother, *Primrose,* chief housekeeper; and *Parsley,* The Brockery's chef.

Bailey Badger lives at Briar Bank, where he maintains an astonishing library. *Thackeray,* a well-read guinea pig, lives there, too. *Thorvaald,* a teenaged dragon, frequently visits his bookish friends but spends much of his time on assignment for the Grand Assembly of Dragons.

Professor Galileo Newton Owl, D.Phil., is a tawny owl who conducts advanced studies in astronomy and applied natural history from his home in a hollow beech in Cuckoo Brow Wood.

Rooker Rat and his evil gang of ratty friends (Jumpin' Jemmy, Firehouse Frank, et al.) have invaded Near Sawrey.

PROLOGUE:
THE REMARKABLE
HISTORY OF A BOOK

In this year, fierce and foreboding omens arose over the land of Northumbria. There were excessive whirlwinds and lightning storms, and fiery dragons were seen flying through the sky. These signs were followed by great famine, and on January 8th the ravaging of heathen men destroyed God's church at Lindisfarne.
— ***The Anglo-Saxon Chronicle***

Our story begins (as do many very good stories) once upon a time and far, far away, in the year of the Lord 793, in a monastery on the Holy Island of Lindisfarne, at the eastern rim of the green and beautiful Britannia. The winter had been stormy and many ominous omens had led the monks to whisper that the hand of God was turned against the world, or their part of it, because they had been misbehaving. They had eaten too well and lain idle too long and enjoyed too much of the fruit of the vine.

The bishop of Lindisfarne, however, was not thinking about the hand of God at this moment. He was crouched behind a stone parapet, clutching his brown woolen cloak with one hand and shielding his eyes with the other.

"Where?" he muttered, peering out across the gray expanse of the North Sea, its waves whipped by an angry wind. "I don't see them. Where are they?"

"There!" the sentry cried, and pointed.

The bishop followed the pointing finger and saw what he had dreaded to see: far away against the horizon, three great Viking longboats riding the wintry tide inward to the island's shores, their square sails colored blood-red. He could not make out the fearful dragon-headed prows, but he knew what they looked like and knew also that when the ships had sailed as close as they could, the commanders would drop the sails and all hands would lay on the oars. The light, lean, shallow boats, manned by expert Viking seamen, could maneuver through shallow surf and river estuaries along the coast with ease. They would be upon the undefended monastery in a matter of hours.

A great fear rose up in the bishop's heart, and he turned to his secretary. "Brother Aelred, sound the alarm and begin the evacuation. The tide will be out soon, which will give our brothers just enough time to cross to the mainland and begin our trek to Norham. Then meet me in the chapel. We must see to the safety of the books."

Three hours brought the invaders' ships very near the shore. But by that time the little procession of refugee monks had safely crossed to the mainland and begun moving swiftly up the narrow lane that led north to Norham, near the Scottish border. They bore on their stooped shoulders their most precious possessions: two carved wooden coffins containing the sacred remains of Cuthbert and Eadfrith, beloved bishops of Lindisfarne, and two smaller and even more beautifully carved boxes enclosing the sacred books that Eadfrith — an artist of unparalleled skill — had made.

The books were a marvel, unlike anything that the monks of Lindisfarne (or anywhere else, for that matter) had ever seen. The first — the Gospels of Matthew, Mark, Luke, and John — was composed of 258 vellum leaves carefully prepared from calfskins, exquisitely lettered and gloriously illuminated and sumptuously bound in leather and decorated with silver and hammered gold and precious gems. Eadfrith had used the same plan for his *Book of the Revelation of John,* except that he had died in the middle of the eighth page, so that was the end of that.

But even though the work was incomplete, all who saw the Lindisfarne Gospels and *Revelation* were breathless with admiration — as were the monks, who treasured this precious legacy and vowed to keep it out of the hands of infidels. They would take it with them wherever they went, even to the ends of the earth.

They didn't have to go quite that far, but almost. The abbot at Norham discovered that it wasn't easy to feed a multitude of monks without a miracle of loaves and fishes, which he couldn't quite manage. So the Lindisfarne crew packed up the bones of Cuthbert and Eadfrith and their beloved books and set off again, wandering through the north of England and having a great many adventures until, as the story goes, they came at last to the shore of the River Wear. They stopped to have a bite of lunch, but when they got up to leave, Cuthbert's coffin had become so heavy that no amount of huffing and puffing would move it. The monks quite rightfully took this as a sign (wouldn't you?) that they were supposed to stay where they were. They cut down a few trees and built a wooden shelter to keep the rain off and prepared to live a lonely life in the woods.

But people will talk, and the tale of that miraculously immobile coffin naturally got around. Soon, pilgrims were arriving from all over northern England, eager to see Cuthbert's coffin and the splendid books created by Eadfrith. It wasn't long before a grand stone church, Durham Cathedral, was erected nearby and the bishops' coffins placed in ornate tombs, where people brought offerings of gold and jewels in hopes that Cuthbert (who by this time was considered a saint) would cure them or save them or give them sons or another piece of property. Eadfrith's books were settled, too, in the cathedral library (where you could see them if you had a library pass), and all was peace and quiet.

It didn't last. Several hundred years later, Henry VIII looked around his kingdom and noticed that the monasteries had accumulated a great deal of gold and property. He was in the mood to go to war with France and needed quite a lot more money than he had, so he ordered the abbots and bishops to hand it over. The vast properties were sold or given to the king's best friends and supporters, and the gold and jewels went straight into the king's capacious pockets.

But the books in the monastic libraries were a different story. Henry had no time for reading (he was more interested in wives) and nobody quite knew what to do with them. So the monastic libraries — among them the library at Durham Cathedral — went to London. There, many books were thrown away or burnt, others were stored in the Tower, and still others were sold. And the man who had his eye on Eadfrith's beautiful books was Sir Robert Cotton.

Sir Robert was seized with the odd (for his time) notion that ancient books were valuable and ought to be preserved for posterity. He shelved his library in cabinets topped with the busts of Roman emperors. Not having access to the Dewey decimal system (which wasn't invented until 1873), he cataloged each of his acquisitions by the emperor's name, the shelf number, and the position.

For example, if you should like to read the great Anglo-Saxon poem *Beowulf* (Sir Robert possessed the only surviving manuscript) you would find it listed in his handy catalog as *Vitellius A.xv.* You would go straightaway to the top shelf under the bust of Vitellius, where you would find what you were looking for fifteen items from the left. On neighboring shelves and quite within reach, you could see not just one but two copies of the Magna Carta, as well as *The Anglo-Saxon Chronicle* (yes, the very same one that reported dragons portending the Viking invasion of 793) and two great fourteenth-century poems, *Pearl* and *Sir Gawain.* Of course, it was quite natural that Sir Robert would want to acquire the Lindisfarne Gospels (even though a thief had already made off with its priceless gold-and-silver cover), as well as the *Revelation of John,* which still had its beautiful cover. So acquire them he did, and put them on the fourth shelf of a cabinet topped by the bust of Nero.

But while Sir Robert might be an admirable collector of the rarest of rare books, he had an unfortunate habit of speaking up often and loudly against the Crown. So Sir Robert was arrested on trumped-up charges of treason, and his library was confiscated. Eventually, however, his extensive collection, including the Magna Carta and *Beowulf* and *The Chronicle* and the Lindisfarne Gospels, became the property of the British Museum.

All but Eadfrith's fabulous, unfinished

Book of the Revelation of John. When Sir Robert's library was moved to the museum, this book was nowhere to be found. The title was in the library catalog, recorded in the neat handwriting of Sir Robert's secretary. But several other important books had gone missing (thankfully, not the Magna Carta or the Gospels), and all that anyone could think was that a malicious thief must have helped himself.

So for several hundred years, what had happened to Eadfrith's beautiful *Revelation* remained a great mystery. Remained a mystery, that is, until Miss Beatrix Potter, herself a well-known and much-admired maker of books, discovered the book, hidden in a —

But now we have reached the point in our story where we must begin to pay attention to small and intimate moments, rather than to the vast sweep of history.

So let us begin.

1
MISS POTTER WORKS UNDER DIFFICULTIES

Hill Top Farm, Near Sawrey, The Lake District
Thursday, July 18, 1913

I enclose 8 [illustrations for *Pigling Bland*]
— probably some of them will want touching up. It is awkward working under difficulties. I fear the drawings may be worse
for it.

— Beatrix Potter to Harold Warne,
July 1913

Beatrix Potter put down her pen, pushed
her chair back, and stood up. Her shoulders
were aching, not a good sign, for she had
lately been ill — seriously ill — with influenza. In fact, Beatrix had spent most of
March and April in bed at Number Two
Bolton Gardens, in Kensington, where she
lived with her parents. But now it was July,
and she was back at her farm in the Lake
District and feeling much better.

The illness had set her back considerably

on the current book project — *The Tale of Pigling Bland* — which was spread across the table in front of the window. They had been miserably tedious months, darkened by her mother's tight-lipped silence and her father's unpredictable angers, and lightened only by letters from friends — especially from Dimity Kittredge and Margaret Woodcock, who had kept her informed with entertaining accounts of the villagers' doings.

The letters had been a blessing, Beatrix thought, and they had made her laugh. No one would ever guess that so many amusingly scandalous bits could be brewed up in such tiny hamlets as Far Sawrey and Near Sawrey (where Beatrix's farm was located). (If you're wondering how these villages came by their names, I can explain it to you very simply: Near Sawrey is nearer the market town of Hawkshead, while Far Sawrey — which is nearer Windermere and the ferry landing — is farther away by a half mile or so. Of course, both Near and Far Sawrey boast a pub and a post office, and each feels itself superior to the other, as I'm sure it is. In the Land Between the Lakes, all hamlets and villages and towns are naturally superior.)

But what had really sustained Beatrix during those wretched months were the letters from Will Heelis, full of details about things that needed to be done at Hill Top and at Castle Farm, along with plans for the purchase of several pieces of land along the shore of Esthwaite Water. The letters, strong and warm and caring, helped to connect Beatrix, far away in London, with all she held dear here in the Land Between the Lakes: her two farms, her Herdwick sheep and cows and pigs and even the silly chickens — and with the letter writer himself. For Will Heelis, Beatrix's solicitor, land agent, and friend, was also her fiancé, a fact that finally, after months of angry arguments followed by equally angry silences, had been accepted by her parents.

But only grudgingly accepted, I am sorry to say, and not yet agreed to, which had been a great part of the reason for the months of ill health Beatrix had suffered. She was not the kind of person who enjoyed rows, and the constant state of near-war at Bolton Gardens sapped her strength. That, and the necessity of remaining in dirty, grimy London, when she would much rather be at her farm, where she could breathe clear air, enjoy her animals, and be near to Will.

Beatrix Potter had bought Hill Top Farm

at what she always thought of as the darkest time of her life, just after the death of her fiancé, Norman Warne. Norman was the editor of Beatrix's little books, beginning with *The Tale of Peter Rabbit*. He and his brothers, Harold and Fruing, worked in the family publishing business: Frederick Warne & Company. The Potters' wealth and social connections, on the other hand, encouraged them to think that they had risen above their own commercial calico-printing beginnings, and they refused Beatrix permission to marry.

But Beatrix knew her own heart, and despite her parents' objections, she accepted Norman's proposal. But a month after their engagement, he was dead — suddenly and shockingly, after the briefest of illnesses. Norman's death allowed Mr. and Mrs. Potter to escape the shameful indignity of a marriage into a commercial publishing family. And if they privately congratulated themselves upon their narrow escape (as I have no doubt they did), I shouldn't be surprised to learn that they also allowed their daughter to see their great relief. There is no record of what they said to her, but I imagine it to have been something on the order of "There, there, dear. Clearly, the good Lord did not mean you to marry this person. You'll get over it."

Beatrix was devastated. But instead of retreating into the black mourning made fashionable by Queen Victoria, she survived by doing something entirely unexpected for a young woman of her social class. She scraped together her earnings from the half-dozen "bunny books" she had written since the phenomenal success of *Peter Rabbit* and used the money to buy a farm.

Not much of a farm, her father had sniffed scornfully, while her mother only pulled down her mouth and grimaced at the thought of her daughter mucking about in the mud and grime of a country farmyard. But the Potters were so relieved by their narrow escape from an unacceptable marriage that they made only a little objection to her purchase and explained to their friends that their daughter's odd little farm was an "investment."

But I daresay that Mr. Potter was probably right: Hill Top wasn't much of a farm. Just over thirty acres, the old place had been in the Preston family for half a century. The livestock had been sold away when Mr. Preston died, the old barn and fences were run down, and the place wore a forlorn look — like Beatrix herself, perhaps. She and the farm needed one another, so (being a practical, down-to-earth woman) she rolled up her sleeves and got to work replacing, repairing, rebuilding, refencing, and restocking. It was a very good thing that her bunny stories were earning so much money and that her editor (Harold Warne had taken over her projects from his dead brother) was delighted to publish two books every year. She plowed every cent of every royalty cheque into the farm.

Beatrix had been new to farming in those days. "Nobbut a reet beginner," the village men liked to say sarcastically, for none had been pleased when a female children's author from London had purchased Hill Top Farm. The women thought she would be far too grand for their little village, while the men were offended by the idea that an off-comer — a spinster who knew less than nothing about sheep and cows and pigs — had bought Hill Top straight out from under their noses. They snickered when they learned that she paid more than they thought the place was worth.

"Took for a reet fool, her was," as George Crook put it. "Her was fleeced."

"Woan't last t' year out," Mr. Llewellyn predicted sagely. "I'll lay a half crown on't."

"Gone by Christmas," put in Clyde

30

Clinder. "And then t' place'll be up fer sale agin."

And all three agreed that when that happened, they would see that a proper farmer bought the farm, someone who could make something of it. "An' he woan't pay wot she paid for it, neither," Lester Barrow said.

But Beatrix outfoxed the lot of them, I am very happy to say. Not only did she stay on, but she succeeded in making Hill Top a model farm. She hired an experienced farmer to manage the livestock and his wife to oversee the garden and dairy. And whilst Mr. Jennings was rebuilding fences and buying the very best sheep and cows and Mrs. Jennings was winning prizes for her butter and cheese at the local fairs, Beatrix got to work on the old farmhouse, turning it into a livable and very beautiful place.

Old? Oh, my dears, yes! When Beatrix bought Hill Top in 1905, the two-story house was already well into its third century and in need of a great deal of help — as I daresay you would be, if you were that old. It was built of Lake District stone in traditional Lake District style, with pebbly gray walls, eight-over-eight mullioned windows, a slate roof and slate-capped chimneys, and a porch constructed of three massive slabs of slate. Some might think it a severely plain, austere little house, but its straightforward simplicity went right to Beatrix's heart and stayed there. For as long as she lived, she would love and treasure Hill Top.

But there were many things to be done. She added an extension to the house to accommodate the farmer's family, built a detached kitchen next to the garden, and remodeled and furnished the rooms that she was keeping for herself — a long process that took the better part of two years. But even when the house was finally finished, Beatrix was never able to spend as much time there as she would like. Her parents demanded her presence in London, where she managed the servants, looked after her mother, tried to keep from annoying her father, and squeezed her writing and drawing into whatever time was left over. I daresay it wasn't a very happy arrangement, and you and I would no doubt have been out of patience with the situation and made no bones about saying so. But Beatrix was a dutiful daughter. She did her best to carry on.

And to the villagers' surprise, she carried on at Hill Top. Their attitudes changed somewhat when they noticed that she was making needful improvements to the neglected farm buildings, and that she was using local labor and local materials and insisting that the work be done in traditional ways. And when they saw her going about the muddy lanes in her wood-and-leather pattens, with sacking over her head and shoulders to keep off the rain, they had to admit that she was, as Bertha Stubbs remarked sagely, "as common as any t' rest of us, an' even more so." Still, whilst they might respect and even like her a little, the villagers knew that Miss Potter would never quite belong in the same way they did, for they were natives and she was still an off-comer, no matter how much time (and money) she might spend in Near Sawrey.

But as the years went on and Beatrix herself began to feel that she belonged to the land (if not to the village), she began to be increasingly disturbed by what was happening to it. As the old farms came up for sale, they were bought by property developers who sold off the livestock, tore down the lovely old houses, and built cheap holiday cottages in their place. It was a concern that she and Will Heelis shared, and whenever land near the village came up for sale, she bought as much as she could. These property transactions largely went unnoticed by the villagers, until — some four years after she bought Hill Top — she bought Castle Farm.

This did not go unnoticed, and occasioned a good deal of grumbling at the pub.

"Snatched it reet out o' t' hands of Lady Longford, who by rights should've had it," Clyde Clinder muttered darkly, which is funny when you come to think about it, because the villagers didn't much like Lady Longford, either.

"Wot's Miss Potter want wi' twa farms is wot I wants to know," wondered Mr. Llewellyn. "One's enough for any person."

"Next ye know, her'll buy up t' whole village," said George Crook dourly, "an' put us all out in t' lane, bag an' baggage."

Beatrix had to laugh when she heard that. She didn't blame the villagers, for she knew how much they hated any sort of change. But she had hoped they might be glad that she had bought Castle Farm and kept it from falling into the hands of a greedy real-estate speculator. He would have built a row of ugly cottages and sold them off to people from the cities who would want to modernize the village. Which in Beatrix's opinion would not do at all, for she loved Near Sawrey (in spite of itself) and wanted to keep it exactly as it was.

The grandfather clock beside the stairs hesitantly cleared its throat, as if begging pardon for interrupting her, and began to chime. Beatrix glanced up in surprise. When she was working the minutes flew past, and she'd no idea that it was so late. It was time she began to think about lunch.

She was clearing a place to put down her plate when she was interrupted by a quick rap-rap at the door. She opened it to Sarah Barwick, who was dressed in her usual blouse and sweater and belted green corduroy trousers, which the villagers still found scandalous. The green bicycle she rode to make her bakery deliveries was leaning against the stone wall, and Sarah's brown hair was mussed from her ride. She was holding a white-paper package.

"Hullo, Bea," she said in her usual gruff way. "I've brought us each a pork pie. Haven't seen you for an eternity and hoped you'd be free for a bite and some talk."

Beatrix opened the door wider and stepped aside. "Well, you're a sight for sore eyes," she said with a laugh. "I was just thinking that I should do something about lunch, and here you are." She gestured toward the littered table. "But I'm afraid I've occupied every possible inch. It's a warm day, and the grass is dry. If you don't mind, let's eat in the garden."

"Exactly what I had in mind," Sarah

35

replied. She slanted a look at Beatrix. "There's something giving me a fair case of the dithers, I'm afraid, and I'd like to talk to you about it. But it can wait until we've had our lunch."

2
SARAH BARWICK ASKS A SERIOUS QUESTION

The chickens are deplorable in the hail & rain — & the last ill-luck is that a rat has taken 10 fine turkey eggs last night. The silly hen was sitting calmly on nothing, Mr. S. Whiskers having tunneled underneath the coop, & removed the eggs down the hole!
— Beatrix Potter to Harold Warne, 1913

A few minutes later, the two friends were sitting on a plaid blanket spread on the grass under an apple tree in the Hill Top orchard, beside the garden. Beatrix had brought out a red tray laden with a square chunk of Mrs. Jennings' yellow farm cheese, a blue earthenware mustard pot, two pretty red apples, and two glasses of fresh milk, as well as plates and knives and forks and napkins. Sarah unwrapped the cold pork pies she had brought, one of the most popular items she sold in her bakery at Anvil Cottage. They ate and chatted, whilst Felicia Frummety (the Jennings' ginger-colored cat) and Crumpet (a smart-looking gray tabby with a tiny gold bell on her red leather collar) watched and listened from their usual vantage point on the nearby stone wall.

"I heard that you'd got back to the village," Sarah remarked, "and I expected to see you out and about." She stole a look at her friend, whose bright blue eyes and fresh color she had always admired. But Beatrix was pale, and she seemed to have lost weight. Sarah, who never hesitated to speak her mind, said bluntly, "You're looking peaky, Bea. You're still not well, after spending the spring flat on your back? Sorry I didn't write," she added ruefully. "Meant to, but the bakery keeps me hopping. There's not much time for writing letters."

Crumpet twitched her sleek gray tail. *That's the truth of it,* she remarked sagely. *"Miss Barwick is even too busy to keep her account books. Or maybe she's just distracted. She has far too much to do."*

If you find it strange that a cat should be aware of the bookkeeping habits of the proprietress of the village bakery, you should know that Crumpet makes it her business to be aware of everything that happens in Sawrey. She was probably perched on the windowsill or underfoot at Miss Barwick's table when the subject of account books came up. Village cats, as you know, are everywhere. And Crumpet happens to be the new president of the Village Cat Council, a position that she has coveted for quite some time. Her predecessor, the much-beloved Tabitha Twitchit, resigned in order to move to the Vicarage with Grace Lythecoe, who has recently become Mrs. Sackett. Tabitha still serves on the Council's Executive Committee, however, and doesn't mind telling Crumpet what she ought to be doing, which is of course no end of annoyance for Crumpet, who wishes that Tabitha would stay at the Vicarage and tend to her mousing.

"Farmer Jennings says that Miss Barwick must be making money hand over fist in that bakery of hers," meowed Felicia Frummety. The other village cats went by such names as Puss or Porridge or Max, so Felicia's name, which had been given to her by Miss Potter, made her think herself a bit better than the rest of them. (This is ironic, of course, because frummety is nothing more elegant than wheat boiled in cow's milk with a little sugar and cinnamon, so Felicia has nothing to feel superior about.)

"I don't see why Miss Barwick's business af-

fairs should be of any concern to Mr. Jennings," Crumpet growled. "Or to you, Felicia. You should be paying attention to the job you're hired to do. Didn't I hear Miss Potter complaining that a rat stole ten fine eggs right out from under the turkey hen the other night? She said he tunneled under the coop and took the eggs down the hole."

"It was the hen's fault entirely," Felicia retorted in a lofty tone. "She slept the whole time, and when she woke up, her eggs were gone. I had nothing at all to do with it. I wasn't even there."

"Precisely my point," Crumpet spat. "You had nothing at all to do with it, when you should have been there with your fangs bared, just waiting for that rat to make his move. Rats are beastly — and where there is one rat, there's a gang. They must be kept at bay, whatever the cost."

Felicia shuddered. She was in charge of rat patrol in the Hill Top barn and dairy, but she found rodents appallingly distasteful and would do almost anything to avoid coming in actual physical contact with one of the horrid creatures. In fact, she was so derelict in her duty that Miss Potter and Mrs. Jennings had once had to bring in a team of more efficient cats to handle the rats, which led to a problem of quite another sort. You might remember this story; it is told in *The Tale of Cuckoo Brow Wood*, where the unlikely hero, stout, mild-tempered Ridley Rattail, arrested and deported (trussed, in a beer barrel) the arrogant Cat Who Walked by Himself.

But Felicia was not inclined to listen to a lecture from Crumpet, whose authority, she thought, ended at the edge of the Hill Top property.

"Oh, hush," she said crossly. *"I want to hear what this is about."* She leant forward to hear the conversation.

"I didn't expect you to write to me, Sarah," Beatrix was saying as she spread a little more mustard on her pork pie. "I know how busy you are at the bakery." Around a mouthful of pie, she added appreciatively, "Really, my dear, this pie is delicious. I'm sure you must be selling hundreds."

"You see?" hissed Felicia. *"What did I tell you? Making money hand over fist."*

"Which is none of your business," retorted Crumpet. *"You should be attending to those beastly rats."*

Beatrix raised her voice. "Crumpet and Felicia, you are interrupting our conversation. Do be quiet."

"I'm happy to say that I'm selling quite a few of these pies," Sarah replied. "You'd be

41

surprised at how many housewives find that a nice pork pie is just the thing for the husband's tea — especially on washday or ironing day, when she's all fagged out. About as fagged out as you look, Bea," she added candidly. She was beginning to be a bit worried by her friend's appearance. Beatrix was always so determinedly cheerful, but she certainly didn't seem so today.

Beatrix sighed. "I suppose I am still a bit under the weather. It's all I can do to go back and forth to Lindeth Howe, where my parents are on holiday. And I'm hurrying to finish a book. I've been pasting galley proofs into the dummy today. I'm dreadfully behindhand with it — the pen-and-inks aren't quite done yet — and the editor is beginning to fret that it won't be finished in time."

Sarah finished her milk and put the glass down. From the beginning of their friendship, she had been impressed by Beatrix's seemingly infinite creativity. She produced dozens of stories and hundreds of drawings — as well as taking care of those demanding parents of hers, and not just one but two farms! Sarah sighed enviously. It was all she could manage to produce a dozen loaves of bread and three or four batches of sticky buns every morning. And the pork pies, of course. She had practically no time for anything else — which was exactly how she had got herself into such a muddle with her accounts.

But that was neither here nor there at the moment. "Another book?" she asked curiously. "What's this one about?"

"Pigs." Beatrix chuckled. "It's called *The Tale of Pigling Bland*."

"Pigs?" Crumpet meowed incredulously. *"Not cats? What can you be thinking, Miss Potter?"*

"I don't know if you remember," Beatrix went on, "but a few years ago, Mr. Jennings bought some pigs from Mr. Townley."

"I remember!" Felicia cried with excitement. *"I was here when they arrived. All but one of them were pedigreed, with papers. Mr. Jennings insists on that — says pigs with papers always fetch a better price when it's time to sell."*

"Mr. Jennings was busy and couldn't get them," Beatrix continued, "so I went to fetch them. When Mr. Townley was loading them into the pony cart, I noticed a tiny one, a perfectly lovely Berkshire girl pig, jet-black, with twinkly eyes and a little turned-up nose. I just had to have her, which annoyed Mr. Jennings no end."

"In fact," Felicia confided cattily to Crum-

pet, *"he said that Miss Potter should have had better sense than to bring her home. She wasn't worth feeding."*

This brought Beatrix to her feet. "Felicia Frummety," she said sternly, going to the wall, "that is enough of that noise." She picked up the cat and deposited her unceremoniously on the ground. "I'm sure that rat who made off with the turkey eggs is hiding somewhere nearby. Go and find him."

"Good enough for you," Crumpet cried triumphantly, as Felicia flicked her tail in annoyance and stalked off.

"You, too, Crumpet," Beatrix said crossly. "Away with both of you, and leave us in peace." She shooed the gray cat off the wall and sat down again to resume her story. "But I fed the little pig and kept her in a basket beside my bed. Aunt Susan, I called her — a lovely pet, quite plump. And a patient model. She used to nibble my boots when I went into her pig sty to draw her."

Sarah smiled. That particular pig had been the talk of the village, for she had a habit of shoving the door open with her pink nose and trotting into the house to beg a bowl of bread and milk. She glanced down at her pie. "You're not put off by eating pork pie while we talk about your pig?"

"Not in the least," Beatrix said, picking up her napkin. "I've always been practical when it comes to such matters as bacon and hams. Anyway, I promised myself I would write a pig book before I was finished, and this is the one. The adventures of Pigling Bland and Pig-wig, the little girl pig he rescues from captivity."

Sarah shot her a surprised glance. "Before you're finished? You're not thinking of quitting, are you?"

Beatrix gave a little shrug. "The publisher doesn't want me to, of course. But the real animals here on the farm are more interesting to me than paper animals. And with the remodeling work on Castle Cottage under way, and my parents at Lindeth Howe —" She sighed. "They seem to *want* to make things harder."

"I'm sorry, Bea." Sarah leaned over and patted her friend's hand. It was unusual for Beatrix to criticize her mother and father. "Why can't they take a holiday house here in the village, so you wouldn't have so far to go?" Lindeth Howe was on the eastern side of Windermere, which meant that Beatrix had a two-and-a-half-mile walk on this side, a half-mile walk on the other, and a ferry ride in the middle. Sarah knew that it must be taxing.

"They won't come here because Mama finds the village society dull," Beatrix replied. "And to tell the truth," she added candidly, "I would rather have them a bit out of the way. If they were closer, we would surely get into rows."

Sarah picked up an apple and bit into it. "And how is the remodeling work at Castle Cottage going?"

"Very slowly, I'm afraid. I can't see why the workmen can't move along a little faster. Mr. Heelis has been keeping an eye on things," Beatrix added. "I'm to meet him there this afternoon." She paused, smiling wistfully. "I shall be very glad to see him, I must admit. We haven't been able to spend any time together for over a fortnight."

Sarah heard the eagerness in her friend's voice and smiled. She very much approved of Beatrix's engagement to William Heelis, which had stunned everyone in the village when news of it had got out some months before. Mr. Heelis, a solicitor from Hawkshead, was handsome, comfortably well-off, a keen sportsman, a nimble-footed folk dancer, and extremely eligible (if exceedingly shy). For years, everyone in the district had wondered whom he would take as his wife. Miss Potter, on the other hand, was an off-comer, eccentric (a *female farmer?*), and sometimes brusque. Their engagement had come as an immense shock, and some of the villagers still weren't over it.

"Doan't believe it meself," proclaimed Bertha Stubbs, when she heard the news.

"Nivver happen," asserted Elsa Grape.

"Ridic'lous," sniffed Agnes Llewellyn, adding pointedly, "Mr. Heelis should be lookin' for a wife who is more of his kind, not an off-comer from London." Agnes had someone in mind, in fact: her young niece, a beautiful girl who would make a perfect wife for a handsome and much-admired solicitor.

Sarah herself had heard all this gossip, for she delivered her baked goods to almost every kitchen in the district and was invited in for countless cups of tea. She never carried tales, of course, but she had heard them all, in a number of versions, most of which were more or less accurate. This in itself is quite remarkable, when you stop to think about it, for village gossip almost never gets anything right.

Miss Potter, it was said, had accepted Mr. Heelis' proposal on the night the Applebeck Farm dairy burnt to the ground. (This, at least, was true, as you can read for yourself in *The Tale of Applebeck Orchard*.) It was further rumored that Miss Potter and Mr.

47

Heelis had attempted to keep the engagement a secret from her tyrannical parents, which was why she wasn't wearing his ring. But they were thwarted when Mr. Heelis' cousin had let the cat out of the bag, resulting in a tremendous family row. Her parents had at last been forced to accept the idea of an engagement, but never, no, never a marriage! At least, not until they were both dead and their daughter was no longer needed to care for them — which would certainly be another decade or two.

And then, to complicate matters still further, it was whispered that if Miss Potter's parents disapproved of Mr. Heelis (he was, after all, merely a country lawyer), Mr. Heelis' family did not approve of Miss Potter, either! The Heelises, it seemed, objected to the Potters' strong connections to commerce, for the Potter money came from the family's Manchester calico business. (I daresay you will find this as ironic as I do, since the Potters forbade their daughter to marry Mr. Warne because he was in the publishing business.)

What was more, the Heelises were high church, and their family tree boasted several Anglican clergymen, rectors, and country parsons. The Potters, on the other hand, were Dissenters (very low church) and Miss

Potter herself was known to favor the Quakers.

And if this weren't enough, Miss Potter was five years older than Mr. Heelis (oh, *dear!*), and more than a bit eccentric besides. One of the Heelis cousins was said to have encountered her in the lane, with pattens on her feet and a woolen shawl over her head, carrying a butter basket filled with roadside flowers. The cousin thought she had met a "common villager" and was astonished when she was told that this was the famous Miss Potter, author, illustrator, and farmer.

All things considered, the Heelises were said to feel that this was *not* a match made in heaven.

And in fact, it didn't seem likely that a wedding date would be announced soon, although the entire village was sure that the coming marriage was the reason that Miss Potter had commissioned several rooms to be built on to Castle Cottage. She and Mr. Heelis must intend to live there, which was why Mr. Heelis had been making frequent trips to see the new construction. Mr. Bernard Biddle, the building contractor who was managing the work, had been heard to grumble that he could not abide interference from anybody, not from Mr. Heelis and most certainly not from Miss Potter.

Sarah folded her napkin with a sigh. Well. Since the subject had come around to Castle Cottage, it was time to speak up. Her visit was not just a friendly drop-in. She had come on a mission, and not a particularly comfortable one.

She took a deep breath. "Bea," she said quietly, "what would you do if you suspected that somebody was stealing from you?"

"Stealing?" Crumpet meowed incredulously. The two cats had not gone very far, of course. They had settled onto the grass on the other side of an untidy patch of foxgloves and daisies, conveniently out of sight but within earshot. *"A thief, in this little village? Oh, dear! Oh, poor Miss Barwick!"*

"Well, if she is making that much money from her buns and pork pies," Felicia observed in a moralistic tone, *"she's bound to attract thieves. Just like that turkey hen, I suppose. Sound asleep on her nest whilst that ratty fellow made off with her eggs. Miss Barwick is going to have to take better care of her money."*

Beatrix leaned forward. "Stealing from you?" Her eyes widened in surprise. "Stealing baked goods? Stealing money? I'm so sorry to hear that, Sarah. Do you have any idea who it is?"

50

"The same filthy rat that got the turkey eggs is my guess," Crumpet growled. *"Rats are notorious thieves, and if it's baked goods Miss Barwick is missing, he's the obvious culprit. I think I'll pay an after-hours visit to the bakery. That rat wants a bit of minding, he does."*

Sarah frowned. "Stealing from *me?* Whatever gave you that idea, Bea? It's true that I have been missing a bit here and a bit there in the past few days, but nothing to fret about."

Beatrix shook her head, looking puzzled. "I thought you just asked —"

Sarah cast a look over her shoulder to make sure that no one was listening. She leaned forward and lowered her voice.

"What I asked," she replied, very seriously, "was what you would do if you suspected that somebody was stealing from *you.*"

3
THREE SPOONS, A BROKEN ENGAGEMENT, AND A NEW BABY

Miss Potter and Miss Barwick were not the only ones enjoying a lunch out-of-doors on this fine July afternoon. A little distance away, the denizens of The Brockery have brought a picnic hamper to the rocky ledge at the top of Holly How. It is a splendid spot, for Holly How (in the Land Between the Lakes, *how* or *howe* means "hill") affords a panoramic view of green meadows and darker green fell-sides, as well as glimpses of the blue slate roofs and chimneys of Near Sawrey and the silvery glint of Esthwaite Water beyond.

From his place in the blue sky far above Holly How, the sun beamed down happily, delighted that this group of creatures had emerged to join him for an hour or two as he crossed the green hills of the Lakes on his daily journey. Indeed, the sun found it quite personally gratifying that so many of The Brockery's residents had come out to bask in the warmth of his gaze, so he encouraged the birds to sing a little louder and the breeze to blow a little less boisterously in order that the picnickers could enjoy their outing even more.

Now, in case you are new to the Land Between the Lakes and are wondering what kind of group this could be and why the sun is so pleased to see them out-of-doors at midday, I will tell you that it is made up of a quartet of badgers, a pair of rabbits, and a little hedgehog — animals who usually go out in the daytime only on very special occasions. Each and all are residents of The Brockery, one of the oldest badger setts in all of northern England. It is also by far the largest, an enormous labyrinth of winding tunnels and passageways and burrows built beneath the hill, so extensive that the farthest-flung chambers are rarely visited, if only because they are so far away that you need to carry a compass and pack a lunch.

The Brockery's badgers long ago decided that their dwelling was far too large for a single family, so they turned it into a hostelry, feeling that it was not a good thing for so many bedrooms to stand empty when so many creatures were in want of a roof. They acted in accordance with the Fifth

Badger Rule of Thumb: *It is a great pity for warm and dry shelter to be vacant and unoccupied when there are so many needy animals outside in the cold and damp.* (Badger Rules of Thumb are not strict laws but rather guidelines for personal and community behavior that badgers have adopted in order to get along in this topsy-turvy world. They are rather like the Ten Commandments, although perhaps more frequently observed.)

Over the years, The Brockery has gained a wide reputation for its generous hospitality, and it is a rare breakfast, tea, or supper that does not see the table lined with hungry animals. Some are permanent residents, whilst others are transients stopping for a night or two on their way north to Carlisle or south to Liverpool or Manchester. Sometimes unnoticed guests make free of the unused rooms and chambers, preferring to come and go as they please, taking their meals out and neglecting to sign the guest register. This is especially true of the occasional adder, who slips in surreptitiously and leaves without saying goodbye. And spiders, beetles, and worms, who tend to keep to themselves out of fear of being stepped on or mistaken for lunch — although there are very firm rules about who or what may be eaten while in residence.

Most guests, however, appreciate the hostelry's community life, observe the rules, and contribute to the extent they are able. They pay for their room and board by helping with chores, washing dishes, or sweeping the hearth. A few barter, offering, say, a half-dozen peppermint patties from the Tower Bank Arms or a small bottle of ink liberated from the Sawrey Hotel or a pair of plump marrows from the garden at Belle Green. (Animals are just like people, you know. They like to pick up souvenirs on their travels and share them with friends while they brag about where they've been and what they've seen.)

But sometimes, guests have nothing to give and are too ailing to help, like the aged ferret, nearly blind, who lived for several years in one of the best bedrooms, or the tiny orphaned squirrels, recently abandoned on the doorstep, who were too young to do anything but run in circles and squeal. These needy creatures are always welcomed and given a chance to rest and recuperate — or to grow up, as the case may be.

To manage the place currently requires a staff of three badgers: Hyacinth, the hosteller; Hyacinth's mother, Primrose, the chief housekeeper; and Parsley, the cook.

Primrose is assisted by the rabbit twins, Flotsam and Jetsam, who keep the place in tidy order, help with the laundry and the sweeping out, and run errands (rabbits are very good at this). Parsley has a kitchen helper named Honey, a pretty little hedgehog, quite a capable cook for her young age, and a dormouse named Hazel, who is exceptionally good at gathering the nuts and berries that Parsley incorporates into various dishes.

Bosworth Badger, the clan's *pater familias,* bestowed the Badge of Authority upon Hyacinth the previous year. (The Badge entitles the bearer to great respect and bestows upon her the responsibility of ensuring the safety and comfort of all the sett's residents.) Having relinquished his post as hosteller to Hyacinth, Bosworth now serves as chief recorder emeritus for the *History of the Badgers of the Land Between the Lakes* and its companion work, the *Genealogy.* Bosworth is teaching Hyacinth all she needs to know to continue with these important volumes when he is gone — a time that will come soon, he feels, for he is by now quite an old badger and has lived a comfortable span of years. This idea does not make him at all sad or fearful, for like all animals — except for we humans, of course, who are too smart for our own good — Bosworth accepts with equanimity the fact that his days are numbered.

Usually, the badgers and their helpers are busy throughout the day and well into the evening, when they finally sit down and toast their toes at the fire and relax, whilst Hyacinth reads aloud from their favorite books. This week, they are reading Miss Potter's *The Tale of Jemima Puddle-Duck* and enjoying it very much. (I am sorry to report, however, that they were not at all fond of *The Tale of Mr. Tod,* which does not portray badgers at their best. Miss Potter, it seems, is remarkably ill-informed about the true nature of *Meles meles.* There may be some badgers who, like the notorious Tommy Brock, wear dirty clothes and go to bed in their boots, but The Brockery badgers are not among that unkempt clan.)

As I say, the badgers are an industrious lot and spend most of the day doing their chores. You'd be surprised to know how many chores a badger can find to do. Their family Latin motto, engraved on the family coat of arms, hangs over the fireplace in The Brockery library:

De Parvis, grandis acervus erit

Some translate this as "Do a little bit every day, and you will accomplish a lot." Or in the vernacular of the Land Between the Lakes: "Many littles make a mickle; many mickles make a mile."

But today is Parsley's birthday, and the hardworking badgers have laid aside their tasks and are taking a half-holiday to celebrate with a picnic. Hyacinth made cucumber, egg, mayonnaise, and cress sandwiches and deviled two dozen cuckoo eggs (removed from the robin nests where clever cuckoos put them, to be hatched and fed by the mother robins). Primrose baked her famous carrot cake, and the rabbits fashioned party hats out of paper doilies decorated with crayon and bits of colored ribbon. Hyacinth invited Rascal, the little fawn-colored Jack Russell terrier from the village. He had brought a basket of snapdragons, daisies, and marigolds for Parsley, who put them in the middle of the picnic cloth for all to enjoy.

By the time the picnic was over, every sandwich, every egg, and all the birthday cake had disappeared. Not a crumb was left.

"Ah," said Bosworth, exhaling happily and stretching out full length on his back, his forepaws clasped behind his head as he gazed up at the feathery clouds that brushed

the blue sky. (I must confess that I envy him for thinking that his world is perfect and that he himself is perfectly placed in this perfect world. I do not always find my world to be as perfect as his. But then, of course, I am a human, and too smart for my own good.)

"Yes, indeed," agreed Parsley, who perfectly understood what was going through Bosworth's mind. She picked up the luncheon cloth and shook it whilst the two young rabbits and the little hedgehog dashed off to play. *"Thank you all for the beautiful birthday lunch, and especially the cake."* With a smile, she added, *"I shall have to arrange to have another birthday at this very same time next year."*

"And I shall have to learn to be more careful when Rooker Rat is around," Primrose said with a rueful smile. She put the empty cake plate back in the basket. *"I should have locked that cupboard. And put away those spoons."*

"That rat won't be around again if I've got anything to say about it," Hyacinth replied grimly. *"He is definitely on our do-not-admit list. And I intend to get your spoons back, Mother, if it's the last thing I do!"*

Two days before, Hyacinth had opened

the front door to a grimy, scruffy old rat wearing an Army veteran's khaki cap and leaning on a makeshift crutch. He was obviously in need of a wash, a bed, and a good meal. He signed the guest register as Corporal Rooker, received an hospitable welcome, and was shown to a pleasant room with a neatly made bed, fresh towel and soap, and a pitcher and basin for washing. The corporal had not said much at supper, for the poor, hungry fellow had been too busy shoveling food into his mouth. He had begged to be allowed to retire early, claiming to be completely worn out from his strenuous travels.

Meanwhile, Primrose had been planning ahead for Parsley's favorite carrot cake. She had sent Flotsam and Jetsam to fetch a bunch of carrots from Jeremy and Deirdre Crosfield's pretty little garden at Slatestone Cottage. Primrose knew that Deirdre, who was soon to be a mother, would never begrudge The Brockery badgers a few carrots, especially for a birthday cake. However, she had cautioned the rabbit twins to take only as many as were needed, reminding them of the important Twelfth Badger Rule of Thumb, which she rephrased in this way: *"When you're helping yourself in someone else's garden or larder, you must be mindful* of the others who depend upon the same food. Enough is as good as a feast, and it is a well-mannered badger (or rabbit) who leaves a fair share for the gardener and the cook."

But Corporal Rooker had apparently never heard this important maxim. That evening, after Primrose had baked and frosted Parsley's birthday cake and hidden it safely away in a cupboard, the rascally rat crept into the kitchen and helped himself. He ate most of it on the spot and carried the rest back to his guest bedroom, carelessly leaving a trail of crumbs behind him.

The next morning, Primrose discovered the empty plate and, horrified, summoned Hyacinth. The two of them followed the telltale crumb trail and confronted the thief, who was sleeping off the effects of his midnight banquet in his bed.

"I didn't do it!" Corporal Rooker protested feebly, pulling the covers over his head. "I am an innocent rat! And anyway," he added, his thin voice muffled by the blanket, "you have no proof." Rats usually find that such a defense is successful, because they have eaten the evidence. But not in this case.

"Stuff and nonsense," Hyacinth snapped. She jerked the covers off the rat. "Crumbs do not lie. You have left a trail of them from the kitchen straight to this room. And just look!

61

The bed is full of them." She narrowed her eyes and bared her badger teeth. *"Pack your things and leave, Corporal. Don't stop for breakfast — you've already eaten it. And don't bother to come back. You are no longer welcome here."*

It wasn't until Corporal Rooker had left that Primrose discovered the missing silver spoons — three of them, engraved with an ornate *B* and handed down through a dozen badger generations on her mother's side of the family. It was an appalling loss. Primrose blamed herself for not locking the silver chest, whilst Hyacinth blamed herself for giving hospitality to a thief. It wasn't until later that day that the badgers heard from one of the village cats that Rooker had been implicated in at least two other thefts: Miss Potter's turkey's eggs and Miss Barwick's bakery goods. (This is not entirely surprising, since according to the Oxford English Dictionary, the name *Rooker* has meant "cheat" or "charlatan" since the seventeenth century.)

What's more, the village cats were whispering that Rooker might not be the only rat in town, for they had caught glimpses of foreign (that is, unfamiliar) rats darting here and there through the midnight darkness. They were said to be very large rats, some even larger than the village cats — but of course, you know that cats exaggerate everything, so their reports aren't entirely reliable. Some even speculated that the village might have been invaded by a gang of organized thieves, which just shows you how far cats will go in creating a good story.

In this case, however, the cats were right. But what nobody guessed was that Rooker's real purpose for visiting The Brockery was to reconnoiter the place, with the notion that some of its far-flung bedrooms, those close to long-abandoned exits, might make a good hideout for himself and a few friends. When Hyacinth gave him the boot, he decided that it would be better if they found another place, which resulted in — Well, you'll see.

Luckily, there was still time for Primrose to bake another cake. She hurriedly dispatched Flotsam and Jetsam for more carrots (this time, from Miss Potter's garden), and baked a second cake, which was even prettier than the first. She had served it with a flourish at today's picnic.

Now, having helped her mother pack everything back into the picnic basket, Hyacinth went to sit down beside Uncle Bosworth. He was not really her uncle, but she loved him as dearly as if they were related

— as no doubt they were, for all badgers seem to be related to all other badgers, however distantly. He had been a wonderful guide and mentor and had entrusted the Badge of Authority to her — a great compliment that still made her breathless when she thought about it, for the Badge was traditionally passed on to the oldest son. Uncle Bosworth had no children, but Hyacinth had always imagined that the Badge would go to her brother Thorn. Instead, through a combination of circumstances both wonderful and frightening, Uncle Bosworth had bestowed it upon her. Hyacinth was now the first female to serve as the leader of the sett, and she tried hard to live up to the expectations that came with the position.

Rascal joined Hyacinth and Bosworth, and the trio sat quietly, gazing at the narrow green valley. Below them, the silvery ribbon of Wilfen Beck curled around the foot of Holly How. To the east, the darker shadows of Cuckoo Brow Wood climbed up Claife Heights along the shore of Windermere. To the north lay the green pastures of Holly How Farm, where a flock of Herdwick sheep kept the grass neatly clipped, and the spreading lawns and gardens of Tidmarsh Manor, where old Lady Longford waited and hoped that her granddaughter Caroline would stop lingering willfully in London and return home to the family estate. To the west rose the fells, their blue shoulders holding up the bluer sky. The animals couldn't glimpse Far Sawrey, for it was tucked away behind a low hill, but they could see the roof of Castle Cottage, some little distance away, and beyond that, the roofs of the other houses in Near Sawrey.

"I wonder how much longer the renovation at Castle Cottage will take," Hyacinth remarked, looking down at the piles of boards and stacks of slate shingles in the garden. *"It's been going on for a month or more."*

"Right you are, Hyacinth," Rascal barked. *"Three months, to be precise. And likely to be much longer."*

Bosworth sat up. *"It's taking such a great while because Miss Potter is adding on an entire wing at one end,"* he reported. *"I understand that there's to be a parlor with a fireplace on the first floor, with a large window bay. As well,"* he went on, *"some of the interior walls in the old part of the house are being torn out and the window frames replaced. Not to mention the water being laid on. It's a very big job. I don't wonder that it's taking so long."*

"The job could go much faster if Mr. Biddle's

workmen weren't such idlers," Rascal re-marked in a caustic tone. *"If you ask my opinion, he's not paying enough attention to the project. On my way up here, for instance, I noticed that they were just sitting around twiddling their thumbs, as if they didn't have the brains to get on with it themselves. And Biddle's supervisor — Maguire, his name is — was nowhere to be seen. Slackers, every one of them,"* he added scornfully.

Now, if you have ever had the privilege (or the challenge) of living with a Jack Russell terrier, you already know that he has a very strong sense of the right way to do things (his way) and the time at which they ought to be done (right now). For instance, if you and your Jack Russell always go for a walk at three in the afternoon, you will find him waiting beside the door at two fifty-seven, and if you are late, he will come to fetch you from your book and chair. If your Jack Russell has pockets, he will no doubt have a pocket watch in one and a calendar and notebook and pencil in the other. If he were a person, he would most likely be a consultant in time management.

Hence Rascal's derisive remark about slackers and lazy louts. Castle Farm is just across the lane from Belle Green, you see, where Rascal lives with Mr. and Mrs.

George Crook. The little dog makes it his business to monitor what goes on there and everywhere else in the village. But he is a devoted friend and admirer of Miss Potter, so he has paid special attention to the work at Castle Farm, which began with the repair and refurbishment of the barn and other outbuildings, then progressed to the drains and fences, and now finally to the grand old house itself (which is really a house, although it has always been called Castle Cottage). He has not always been satisfied with the way things were done: the drains, for example, were not laid exactly as he would have done. But the work was adequate, so he merely observed and held his tongue.

The work at hand, however, was quite another story, and now that the subject had come up, Rascal was more than willing to express his opinion. Bosworth gave him the chance.

"Slackers?" the badger asked, frowning. Bosworth is a diligent and hardworking badger and is always distressed to hear that someone is lying down on the job.

"Slackers," Rascal repeated firmly. *"You should see the lot, Bozzy, old chap. Only one of them — Mr. Adcock — knows what he's doing, and the supervisor — Maguire — is*

usually somewhere else. And Mr. Biddle . . ." Rascal shook his head, exasperated. *"Instead of paying attention to the job, he spends too much time at the pub, mooning around Ruth Safford."* Ruth Safford was the new barmaid, a plump, pretty widow with a flirtatious glance. She had caught the attention of half the bachelors in the village, but Mr. Biddle seemed to have an inside track. *"I tell you, it's a bloody shame."*

Bosworth disliked rough language and disliked being called "Bozzy" even more, but he didn't want to correct such a dear friend. *"I daresay it is,"* he said mildly, *"but I doubt that there's anything we can do about it."*

"What about Mr. Heelis?" Hyacinth wanted to know. *"I thought he was supposed to be looking after Miss Potter's interests. They are going to live there, aren't they? After they're married?"*

"That's what I've heard," Primrose said, coming to sit with the group. *"But there seem to be no plans for a wedding. I suppose that's why Mr. Heelis is not very urgent about requiring Mr. Biddle to get on with the work."*

"I don't think it's that," said Rascal a little defensively. He was also great friends with Mr. Heelis, who always took time out to

speak to the little dog and tug his ears lightly and find a bit of biscuit in his pocket. *"Mr. Heelis is a very busy solicitor, with clients all over the district. He can't be expected to stop by Castle Farm every day of the week and keep the men on the job. No, no — the problem lies entirely with Mr. Biddle. You know what sort he is. I'm sure that Miss Potter takes a very poor view of the situation. She doesn't much like him, either."*

The three badgers nodded knowingly. Holly How might be a tidy walk from the village, but there were always animals going to and fro, carrying the latest news and gossip. They had heard that Miss Potter had hired Mr. Biddle — against her better judgment, they suspected, for he had once worked for her at Hill Top Farm, and they had not parted on the best of terms. But that had been several years before, and Mr. Biddle's competitors had all gone out of business — strangely, some said, for there was certainly plenty of work to go around. Quite a few people had expressed their dissatisfactions with the fellow, but there were not many choices when it came to local building contractors. Mr. Biddle was one of a kind.

"If I were Mr. Heelis," Bosworth remarked, *"I fear that I should be tempted to give that*

man Biddle a sharp dressing down."

"Mr. Heelis is an awf'ly patient man." Primrose politely shooed away an inquisitive orange-tip butterfly who wanted to land on her nose. *"He and Miss Potter have been engaged for a very long time. I wonder when the wedding will take place."* Her smile was wistful. *"I think it should be a spring wedding, when all the flowers are blooming and there are new lambs in the field. That would truly be lovely."*

"P'rhaps never," Rascal replied sorrowfully.

"Never?" Primrose cried, her eyes widening. She was a romantic at heart, and obviously found this idea distressing. *"But whyever not, Rascal? Miss Potter and Mr. Heelis are perfect for each other."*

"Because there are so many people opposed to it," Rascal replied in a realistic tone. *"Miss Potter's parents absolutely refuse to let her marry. They don't want her to move here to the village and leave them high and dry in London, at the mercy of their servants."*

"It would serve them right if she did," Primrose muttered, *"for all the pain they've caused her."*

"But they're not the only ones," Rascal went on. *"At the Tower Bank Arms the other night, I heard that there are some in Mr. Heelis' fam-*

ily who are not at all happy with his choice."

The badgers rarely went to the pub and hadn't heard this news. *"Oh, come now, Rascal!"* Bosworth said, shocked. *"Who could object to our Miss Potter?"*

"I shouldn't like to say," Rascal replied reluctantly, *"since I'm only reporting what I've heard — and you know how bad humans are about gossiping. Some folks are even whispering that Mr. Heelis himself is considering breaking off the engagement. Not that I believe that for a minute,"* he added hurriedly. *"Mr. Heelis is devoted to Miss Potter. I can't think that he'd do such a thing."*

"Break off the engagement!" Bosworth exclaimed. *"Oh, surely not! Oh, dear, dear me! That would be . . . It would be . . ."* He stopped, stumped for a word that said exactly what he felt.

"A tragedy," Primrose said quietly, and folded her hands.

"Just so," said the badger, and fell silent.

Hyacinth had said nothing during this exchange, but she agreed with Primrose and Uncle Bosworth. Miss Potter might not know everything there was to know about the real lives of badgers, but she was kind and good and had the best interests of the village at heart. And not just the village, but

71

the entire Land Between the Lakes, as well. Hyacinth herself had occasionally encountered Miss Potter and Mr. Heelis on their Sunday afternoon walks in the lanes above the village and beside Esthwaite Water, surveying the meadows and wooded hillsides that might come up for sale.

Hyacinth had heard the pair talking, too, and knew that they shared the same worry: that the old farms would be sold away and with them would go the traditions of the farming life, which revolved around the farmer's sheep and cattle and fields of oats, barley, and potatoes, as well as the farm wife's garden and dairy. The Land Between the Lakes was a place where the old ways were still practiced, where turfs of peat were graved for fuel and dried bracken was sledged down the fell-sides for winter animal bedding and fodder, and where rich butter and bright yellow cheeses were made in farmhouse dairies and haver bread, made from the farmer's oats, was baked on hot iron griddles over farmhouse fires.

And even though automobiles zipped through the narrow lanes at speeds approaching ten miles an hour and noisy hydroplanes raced up and down Windermere and telegraphs and telephones brought good news and bad from the far corners of the earth, the fell farmers could still weave a tight swill basket, shear a sheep, construct a perfectly round wooden cart wheel, and rive a clog of green-stone into slates as thin as oat cakes. The farm wives still knitted the family stockings, stirred their tasty tatie pots over their hearth fires, and wore their wooden-soled clogs when they went out into the muddy farmyard to steal the freshly laid eggs from their hens. They knew that it took a quart of fair cream to make a pound of good butter, and a fresh twig of rowan in the churn to keep the fairies from turning the butter bad. And of course they knew that the heads of newborn babes should be immediately washed with rum for protection from evil, and that rum butter with brown sugar and nutmeg must be served at the christening feast.

But if the farms were sold, the farmers would have to move to the cities and holiday towns in search of work. The livestock would be sold, too, the houses torn down to make way for cottages, and the old ways entirely forgotten. Well, not quite, Hyacinth knew, for she and Uncle Bosworth were recording as many of the old practices as they could in the *History*, against the inevitable day when the Big Folk had forgotten their own traditional crafts. But she feared that Miss Potter and Mr. Heelis were right, and that the world they all loved would fall into the hands of off-comers from the city who wanted holiday cottages with a view and telephones and electric lights and metaled lanes so their motorcars wouldn't mire down in the mud.

Hyacinth frowned. It seemed as if Miss Potter and Mr. Heelis were the only Big Folks who understood this looming threat and were committed to doing something to stave it off. Clearly, Miss Potter could do more if she were living right here in the village, and Miss Potter and Mr. Heelis could certainly do more if they were married. But if Miss Potter stayed in London with her parents and Mr. Heelis got tired of waiting and looked for another wife —

Hyacinth shuddered. For all of their sakes, something ought to be done. *"Is there anything we can do to help?"* she asked. She looked from Rascal to Uncle Bosworth and back again. The animals had lent a hand — paw, rather — in many of the difficult situations the villagers had found themselves in. *"Surely there must be something that will break this stalemate and allow them to be married."*

"Right you are," Rascal said briskly. *"There must be something. But what?"*

"Yes, what?" Primrose repeated, and Bosworth echoed her words.

I'm sure that you appreciate their difficulty, as do I. But whilst the animals' hearts are in the right place, I can't for the life of me think how three badgers and a dog — however willing and well-intentioned — could think of a way to change the plot of this particular story. They're not going to do so at the moment, anyway, for they are about to be interrupted.

There was a soft *whoosh,* a flutter of feathers, and a large brown shape lurched awkwardly onto the rock beside them. It teetered dangerously for a moment and at last righted itself. All four animals turned, startled.

"Hullooo," said the shape in a hollow voice. *"Fooorgive me. I misjudged my landing. Doesn't happen often,"* it added defensively. *"Ooonly when I'm wearing these confounded goggles."*

"Oh, it's you, Owl," said Bosworth happily. *"How very nice of you to drop in. Especially at midday,"* he added, for the owl, whose habits were as nocturnal as their own, did not usually take to the skies at this hour. However, he was wearing his dark flying goggles. Although they might not promote stumble-free landings, they enabled him to go about

in comfort during the daytime.

The drop-in (as you have probably guessed) is Professor Galileo Newton Owl, D.Phil., the large tawny owl who resides in a hollow beech tree in Cuckoo Brow Wood, at the very top of Claife Heights. The Professor is universally respected for his diligent studies in astronomy, which he carries out from his treetop observatory on every cloudless night. Since he is both learned in astronomical studies and a superb flier, he has adopted as his motto the Latin phrase *Alis aspicit astra,* "Flying, he looks to the stars." He is also widely known and (I regret to say, feared) for his studies in natural history. He is particularly expert — and takes quite a personal interest — in the habits of voles, mice, rabbits, and squirrels, and knows where they are likely to be found. He regularly studies the meadows and fell-sides from the air, his great owl eyes trained on the ground, alert for any movement, his great owl talons poised to pounce. Nothing much happens that is beneath his notice, so to speak.

The Professor took off his goggles and settled his feathers. *"Whooo?"* he inquired in a genial tone.

The badger, accustomed to the Professor's method of beginning a conversation, replied, *"Quite well, thank you. We're having a picnic."*

"Actually, we've just had it," Primrose explained. *"We've been celebrating Parsley's birthday."*

The owl brightened. *"Very goood,"* he intoned. *"I say, a bit of birthday cake woooouldn't come amiss."*

"I'm sorry, Professor," Primrose said regretfully. *"I'm afraid we've finished it off. If we'd known you were coming, we would have been glad to save you a piece."* She paused. *"But do come back this evening. We're having ginger and treacle pudding for dessert. And I believe that your dragon friend, Thorvaald, will be joining us."*

The owl was exceedingly partial to ginger and treacle pudding. *"Woooonderful!"* he exclaimed happily. *"I shall plan on returning this evening, then."* He bowed to Parsley, who had joined the group. *"Please accept my best birthday wishes, my dear."* Without waiting for her reply, he turned back to Bosworth. *"I have come with news, ooooold chap."*

"What sort of news?" Bosworth asked, immediately concerned. *"Not bad news, I hope."*

I am not surprised at Bosworth's question, for there have been any number of upsets in the neighborhood in recent times.

A threatened footpath closing, a terrible accident at Oat Cake Crag, poison pen letters that nearly derailed the vicar's wedding to Mrs. Lythecoe — and worst of all, a beastly hydroplane that buzzed noisily up and down the lake, wreaking all kinds of havoc. The wretched thing was destroyed in a mysterious storm (with the help of Thorvaald, an ambitious young dragon), but not before the First Lord of the Admiralty, Mr. Churchill, had come down from London to inspect it. He must have liked what he saw, because not long after, it was reported that a similar flying machine was being fitted with guns and readied for possible war use.

War! At the thought, the old badger shuddered. A former ship's cat — a large, muscular creature with a sleek orange coat and a jaunty green mate's cap — had stopped in at teatime several days before. He had taken passage on a freighter carrying grain from Le Havre to Liverpool and then hopped a goods lorry to visit his relatives in the northern Cumbria. The cat had reported that war with Germany was now being spoken of openly in France and Brussels and elsewhere, and that everyone seemed quite keen on the prospect. But the news had sobered the animals around the table, and the thought of war had chilled Bosworth to the bone.

"Oh, nooo, not bad news at all," the owl hastened to assure the badger. He beamed. *"In fact, I daresay yooou will be delighted to hear it, I happened tooo fly over Slatestone Cottage shortly after dawn this morning, checking to see if the little rabbits in the neighbor's garden had ventured out of their nest as yet. I heard a baby cry and went tooo have a looook in the window. Deirdre and Jeremy Crosfield have a new little boy."*

"A boy!" Primrose exclaimed happily. *"How wonderful. What have they named him?"*

The Professor cast a twinkling glance at the little dog. *"I believe I overheard Deirdre call him Rascal. But please dooon't quote me. I am occasionally wrong. Not often, mind. Just every now and then."*

"Rascal?" Rascal sat up straight, his eyes wide with disbelief. *"They're calling their baby boy . . . Rascal?"*

"I wonder why," Hyacinth murmured ironically.

But of course they all knew that Rascal had been Jeremy's special friend — sometimes his *only* friend — for a good many years. Jeremy returned Rascal's affection and had even invited the little dog into the church when he and Deirdre were married. Unfortunately, the vicar had not approved

79

this idea, but Rascal had fully enjoyed himself at the wedding party, where Deirdre had tied a satin ribbon around his neck and asked him to join in the dancing.

"It hardly seems possible that our Jeremy is a dad," Rascal muttered. Embarrassed, he turned away to hide the sudden mist in his eyes. *"Seems daft, maybe, but I still think of him as a lad, rambling through the fells with his sketch book and charcoal."* He scrambled to his feet. *"Well, now. I think I'll just trot on over to Slatestone Cottage and have a quick look in. P'rhaps they have an errand or two that wants running."*

"Oh, I shouldn't," Primrose said quickly. *"Mum and Dad will have their hands full with the new babe, you know. Wait a few hours and let them get settled, and they'll be all the gladder to see you."*

"I suppose you're right," Rascal said reluctantly. *"Well, then, p'rhaps I'll go back down to the village and see who's out and about and what they're up to. Cheerio."* And off he went.

The owl put his flying goggles back on. *"I must be off myself."* He sighed. *"A pity about that cake. I shall try tooo be more prompt next year. And I shall look forward tooo this evening."* And with two great flaps of his huge wings, he lifted himself into the sky, circled once, and flew in the direction of Claife Heights.

And we shall take ourselves off, too, and follow Rascal to the village. It will soon be time for Miss Potter to meet Mr. Heelis. I don't know about you, but I would like to see the two of them together again. I don't want to miss their meeting, especially since it is to take place at Castle Farm, which (since it is the title of our book) must be an important part of our story.

4
MISS POTTER SURVEYS A MESS

[Castle Cottage] has been in such an *awful mess.* The new rooms are nothing like built yet & the old part has been all upset with breaking doors in the wall & taking out partitions. Those front rooms . . . are one long room now & the staircase is altered & we are going to have a bathroom — in the course of time — I think workmen are very slow.
— Beatrix Potter to Barbara Buxton, 1913

If Miss Potter had what we moderns would call a "pet peeve," it would most likely be day-trippers. Even in her time, there were quite a few, especially in July and August, when people hoped to escape the stifling heat of the cities by coming to the Lake District. All summer long, the coaches and charabancs were crowded, noisy motorcars chugged up Ferry Hill, and dozens of bicyclists and fell-walkers puffed along the lane. The local residents made a little money from this tourist traffic, no doubt, but they were no end annoyed by it.

And if Miss Potter could see today's traffic in her quiet little village, she would be exceedingly annoyed, for it often feels as if Sawrey is completely overrun. On a fine midsummer afternoon, for instance, you are likely to find the streets and lanes crowded with swarms of visitors, especially if you have arrived at the same time as one of the tourist buses, some of which are the size of a Sawrey cottage! But because you're a modern person, you are used to traffic and tourists and you won't (I trust) let the throngs diminish your enjoyment of this picturesque little village, which looks very much as it did in Miss Potter's day.

If you're visiting Hill Top, you will likely cross Windermere on the ferry, just as Miss Potter herself did. You will drive up Ferry Hill and through Far Sawrey. When you arrive in Near Sawrey, you will be directed by a uniformed traffic minder to put your automobile in the car park about two hundred yards from Hill Top, which is now owned and maintained by the National Trust. You will walk along Kendal Road, past Buckle Yeat Guest Cottage (do stop and admire the beautiful baskets of colorful petunias and blue lobelia and red and pink geraniums maintained by the friendly cottage hosts) and the Tower Bank Arms, where there is a wreath of pink roses blooming around the old clock above the front door.

If it's mealtime and you're feeling peckish, you may be tempted by the pub menu posted outside the Tower Bank's green-painted front door. You might consider a Cumberland sausage (supplied by Woodall's of Waberthwaite, purveyors of traditional Cumberland sausage, by appointment to HM Queen Elizabeth II), served with mashed potatoes and onion gravy. Or perhaps you would prefer the Cumbrian beef and ale stew with herb dumplings, also recommended. If you're in the mood for dessert, try the sticky toffee pudding (wonderful!). And if the day is foggy or chilly, you can toast your toes at the fire in the grate of the old fireplace or sit at the bar and warm yourself with a half-pint of fine local ale. You will find that the old pub looks much as it did a century ago, when it was the center of the village social life, a place to barter and trade, to hear the latest news, to play a game of darts or cards, and to complain about the weather and taxes.

After your visit to the pub, you will want to get on to Hill Top, where you must expect to wait for admission. The house is now a museum, and only a certain number of people are allowed to purchase tickets and go inside at any one time. While you wait, you can browse in the gift shop, admire Miss Potter's cottage garden — a delightfully haphazard jumble of herbs, flowers, and vegetables — or look over the fence toward the lovely green hill where Tibbie and Queenie, Miss Potter's Herdwick ewes, once raised their annual families of rambunctious little lambs. While you're waiting, you're sure to hear conversations in a half-dozen different languages, for children of all nationalities have read Miss Potter's Little Books and now, grown up and with their own youngsters in tow, have come to visit the place where she lived.

But I'm about to tell you something that most people don't know, for Miss Potter's *real* home in Sawrey was not Hill Top Farm; it was Castle Cottage. Hill Top was very dear to her heart, it is true. She could retreat there from London and her parents, and she wrote and drew many of her little books there. But the house itself was rather like a holiday cottage, and she was rarely able to spend more than a fortnight there at any given time.

In actuality, Beatrix Potter's real home was Castle Cottage, where she spent the last thirty years of her life. After you've toured the house at Hill Top and you're walking back in the direction of the car park, glance up the hill to the north (to your right), past the other houses in the village. The large white house at the top of the hill — slate roof, white-painted chimneys with red top hats, red-trimmed windows, and a porch with a skylight — is Castle Cottage. To get there, you will walk up the lane, past the row of cottages that used to include Ginger and Pickles' village shop and Rose Cottage and the joiner's workshop and the black-smith's forge and Croft End Cottage. At the corner, turn to the right, then turn left when you reach Post Office Meadow, and walk up the hill to Castle Cottage. Neither the house nor the grounds are open to the public. But as you stand at the gate and peek into the garden, perhaps you can imagine Miss Potter, dressed in her gray Herdwick tweeds and her old black felt hat, a woven basket over her arm and clippers in hand, coming out of the door and stepping into the green and neatly kept garden, with blooming flowers and trimmed hedges behind a stone fence.

So. That is Castle Cottage as it is now.

It did not look that way on this particular July afternoon in 1913, however. Beatrix, dressed in those same tweeds and black felt hat, is taking the same route to Castle Cottage that I have just described. But the village is not yet a tourist destination — if it were, I daresay that Miss Potter would have found another place to live straightaway! — and as she comes down the steep walk from Hill Top (the path is behind the Tower Bank Arms), there are only a few people about. Harry Turnell, the brewer's drayman, in his leather apron, shirt sleeves rolled past the elbows, is delivering kegs of beer and ale to the Tower Bank Arms. Robert Franklin, wearing his handwoven rush farmer's hat, trundles a wooden wheelbarrow loaded with two red hens and a rooster in a wooden cage. And a pair of fell-walkers in short pants and knee stockings, kitted out with knapsacks and walking sticks and pert green felt hats, are striding along as boldly as if they are setting out to climb the Matterhorn instead of merely hiking up Coniston Old Man, on the other side of Esthwaite Water.

Miss Potter barely noticed, however. She was in an exceedingly perplexed frame of mind, for what Sarah Barwick had told her as they finished lunch now lay like an ominous shadow across her thoughts. The theft of a pair of door handles seemed almost trivial enough to overlook, although she thought she really ought to do something about it.

But what? Whatever she did was bound to cause some sort of trouble — and if she did nothing, that could cause trouble, too, in the end. And not trivial trouble, either. What if she weren't the only victim? What if other of Mr. Biddle's clients were being robbed, too? Or perhaps there was no truth to the story at all. She was perfectly aware of the various ways the truth could be stretched out of shape, once it got into the village gossip mill.

She was still mulling over this problem when, in front of the village shop, she met Mrs. Regina Rosier, an acquaintance from nearby Hawkshead. Mrs. Rosier was recently retired from teaching in the grammar school there (the same school where the poet William Wordsworth, as a boy, had carved his name into the top of his desk). Dressed in tweeds and stout boots, with a wide-brimmed straw hat on her chestnut hair, a pair of birding glasses around her neck, and a camera in her capacious bag, Mrs. Rosier was obviously out to photograph birds. She was an excellent photographer and had received several awards for her fine work.

"Oh, Miss Potter!" Mrs. Rosier exclaimed, her words tumbling out breathlessly. "I am so very delighted to see you. I've been meaning to call. I have just recently learnt of your engagement to Mr. Heelis. He is such a fine, dear man, so widely respected by all. Perhaps you know that he and his cousins live very close to me, and I have heard —"

Mrs. Rosier stopped, frowning a little and biting her lip, for she had very nearly let slip what a neighbor had whispered to her, that Mr. Heelis' cousins were not pleased with his choice. "That is," she corrected herself, "I have heard that you're to be married soon. Please accept my very best wishes. I am sure you will be quite, quite happy."

As you will know if you have ever lived in one, there is no keeping a secret in a village. Word had gotten out about the engagement, and Beatrix had almost become accustomed to people's curiosity about it. She liked and admired Mrs. Rosier, whose birding skills were second to none, but she heard the slight hesitation and wondered what it meant. She didn't want to ask, though. Instead, she delivered the little speech she had been giving when people offered their best wishes.

"Thank you. We've set no date for the wedding, though. There are my parents' needs to be considered. They are elderly and my father is in ill health. And we've nowhere to live at the moment," she added in the offhand way she had practiced. She didn't want to give the impression that it was only her parents who were keeping them from marrying.

Mrs. Rosier tilted her head curiously. "Then you and Mr. Heelis don't intend to live at Hill Top?"

"I'm afraid it's rather small," Beatrix replied. "I want to keep it just as it is, as a place where I can paint and read." She had already talked her decision over with Will, who had agreed that she should do as she pleased with the house and the farm. "Mr. Biddle is renovating Castle Cottage," she went on, "where we mean to live when we marry." *If* we marry, she almost added, but didn't.

"Oh, dear." Mrs. Rosier rolled her eyes. "I fear that I've had my own unfortunate experience with our Mr. Biddle, who paid almost no attention to my instructions and made it easy for one of his workmen to —" She broke off with a sigh.

"To what?" Beatrix asked sharply, thinking of what Sarah had told her.

Mrs. Rosier shook herself. "I shouldn't really like to say, my dear. No sense in stirring up a hornet's nest, especially since nothing can be proved. But it seems that our Mr. Biddle is sweet on Ruth Safford, the barmaid at the Tower Bank Arms." She nodded in the direction of the pub. "He's probably there right now, drinking in her charms. Take my word for it, Miss Potter — if your marriage depends upon Mr. Biddle's finishing the cottage, you and Mr. Heelis had better plan to wait another year or two." She held out her hand with a bright smile. "Now, I really must get on. I'm told that a pair of great crested grebes are nesting on Esthwaite Water, and I'm off to snap their picture. Best wishes, Miss Potter. I am sure that you and Mr. Heelis will be quite, quite happy. Ta."

And with that, she hurried away.

Still wondering just what Mrs. Rosier might have been hinting at, Beatrix went on past the joiner's and Mr. Crook's blacksmith's shop, where Mr. Crook was clanging away at a red-hot iron bar while his helper pumped the forge bellows. Then, a little way up the lane, Beatrix met Hannah Braithwaite, who was just leaving Croft End

Cottage to go and have tea with Elsa Grape at Tower Bank House.

Beatrix inquired about the health of Mrs. Braithwaite's children, both of whom had been sick with summer sore throats. Mrs. Braithwaite inquired if Miss Potter had any idea when the renovations at Castle Cottage would be finished, by which she really meant to ask when the wedding would take place. Beatrix (who understood the unspoken question perfectly) replied that Mr. Biddle was not yet able to give her a completion date, and Mrs. Braithwaite sighed and said that was always the way of it, wasn't it? What with bad weather and lack of supplies and unreliable workmen who came and went as they jolly well pleased, building anything always took three times as long as it jolly well should.

Then, with the air of one who was confiding a deeply held secret, Mrs. Braithwaite added that Mr. Braithwaite had told her that Mr. Biddle had given the sack to one of the carpenters up at Castle Cottage and hadn't hired another. Which only meant more delay, she was sorry to say.

Beatrix, who was only half paying attention to this chitter-chatter, perked up her ears, for Mrs. Braithwaite was married to Constable John Braithwaite and might therefore know what she was talking about.

"Sacked a carpenter?" she asked. "Who? Do you know why?"

" 'Twas Lewis Adcock, from over in Far Sawrey," Mrs. Braithwaite replied. "Mr. Braithwaite said Mr. Biddle said t' man couldn't be trusted."

"Mr. Adcock?" Beatrix was shocked. "Why, the man worked for me at Hill Top last year. I found him not only to be a skilled carpenter but exceedingly trustworthy."

"Folks do speak well o' t' man," Mrs. Braithwaite replied with a little shrug. She hazarded a smile. "I cert'nly hope sackin' Mr. Adcock woan't delay t' work at Castle Cottage, Miss Potter. I'm sure you mean to put t' house to a good use. Will you be lookin' for a new tenant, or will you . . . ?"

She paused, inviting Beatrix to say that she and Mr. Heelis would be occupying Castle Cottage as soon as they were married.

Beatrix was tempted to tell Mrs. Braithwaite that her plans for the house were nobody's business but her own. But she left the question hanging in the air, smiled as sweetly as possible, and escaped as soon as she could, still wondering whether Mr. Adcock was Sarah's thief. It was too bad that

Sarah couldn't tell her who had sold the door handles to Henry Stubbs.

She was turning the corner when Mathilda Crook came down the lane with a basket containing a bundle of mail and a jar of currant jelly. The mail was destined for the post and the jar of jelly for the postmistress, Lucy Skead, who knew all the latest village gossip and was always glad to share what she knew, especially when she was primed with a jar of jelly or a basket of fresh buns, as Mrs. Crook never failed to be.

Beatrix, who by this time was rather out of temper with interruptions, inquired about Mrs. Crook's summer garden, and Mrs. Crook inquired about the health of Miss Potter's mother and father. Of course, what Mrs. Crook really wanted to know was whether the Potters showed any signs of either relenting or dying, in order that Beatrix could marry Mr. Heelis.

Beatrix replied that her mother was enjoying fair health and spirits during her summer holiday, thank you, and that her father was as well as could be expected.

Mrs. Crook smiled and observed that Mr. and Mrs. Potter were indeed fortunate to have a daughter who so generously dedicated her life to looking after them, and Beatrix bit her tongue to keep from saying anything even halfway truthful.

And then at last Beatrix was able to be on her way. She walked briskly up the hill until she reached Castle Cottage, where she unlatched the gate and went into the unkempt garden, surveying the scene with a heavy sigh. She had seen no point in keeping up the garden, and it was looking shamefully neglected, full of weeds and brambles. She noticed an unhappy stand of rhubarb, a climbing rose that desperately wanted pruning, and a scattering of forlorn daisies nearly smothered with weeds. There was a broken urn, pieces scattered on the ground, and nearby was a wooden bench, the slats splintered. But worst of all were the untidy stacks of boards and piles of roof slates and plumbing pipes and other building materials. Surely there ought to be a neater way to store supplies — in the barn, perhaps, where they would be out of the weather. And the rubble ought to go into the dustbin, oughtn't it? The place was a mess. Simply a mess.

Beatrix had paid a great deal less for Castle Farm than she had paid for Hill Top, and even though the buildings and fences all needed improvements, she thought it a very good buy at the price — only £1,573, not counting her investment in repair and renovation. Its twenty acres adjoined some she had already purchased and included some pastures and a pretty woods. Will, who had arranged the purchase, suggested that she allow the tenants to stay on, which she had done for a time, and their rents had paid some of the bills. But when the necessary renovations to the barns and outbuildings and drains were finished and it was time to begin on the house, she had helped them find another place. Castle Cottage was now vacant — a very good thing, she thought as she looked around, for it would be impossible for anyone to live with this construction mess and noise all around them.

Noise. Beatrix cocked her head, but if she was hoping to hear the sound of busy hammers and industrious saws, she was disappointed. There was nothing at all to be heard except the sound of men's rough laughter. As she picked her way through the littered garden and around the corner of the house, she saw them. It was well past lunching, but two workmen were sitting on a pile of rubble, smoking and trading jokes. Mr. Maguire, who was supposed to make sure that the crew stayed on the job and did the work the way it was meant to be done, was nowhere in sight, nor was Mr. Biddle.

This was most annoying, she thought, frowning. She hated confrontations, but it was time she had a talk with Mr. Biddle. There was Sarah's unsettling report about the theft of the door handles. And there were Mrs. Rosier's ominous hints of something amiss. She squared her shoulders. She had several urgent questions for the man. Their conversation must not be put off.

At that moment, the two workers looked up and saw her and elbowed one another into silence. One — a bearded fellow in a leather jerkin over a dirty blue work shirt — lifted a tin cup in salute.

"Halloo there, missus," he called. "Fine afternoon, ain't it?" Both of them burst out laughing uproariously, as if he had said something very clever and funny.

At that moment, a man came around the corner and spoke sharply to the fellows, then turned and came toward Beatrix. It was Mr. Maguire, Mr. Biddle's second-in-command, with whom Beatrix had spoken a time or two. He was a lean, sinewy man with dark hair and powerful arms, his bare sleeves rolled past the elbows. He wore brown work pants, a leather apron with pockets for tools and nails, and he carried a folded wooden rule in his hand. He looked harassed and (she thought) rather guilty, perhaps because he smelled strongly of beer and knew he should not be drinking on the job.

"Sorry, Miss Potter," he said gruffly. "The men di'n't mean nothin'." He paused, eyeing her. "Was you wantin' to go in t' house?"

"I . . . I don't suppose Mr. Biddle is here," Beatrix said uncomfortably.

Remembering what Sarah had told her, she felt stiff and awkward. Of course, Sarah herself had said that it could very well be untrue. Bertha Stubbs was very good at manufacturing news when she ran out of the real thing. Beatrix badly wanted to get to the bottom of things, which she might do by simply asking Mr. Maguire a direct question or two. But she couldn't do that without speaking to Mr. Biddle first.

"Mr. Biddle?" Mr. Maguire hesitated, then said, almost reluctantly, "Maybe I'm talkin' out of turn like, but truth is, me an' t' boys was wonderin' ourselves. He was s'posed to be here at eight this mornin'. Hasn't been heard from all day." He gave her a crooked smile. "But if you was wantin' to walk through t' house and see what's been done, I'd be glad to —"

"No, no," Beatrix interrupted him. "I'm waiting for Mr. Heelis. We'll walk through the house together. But thank you, Mr.

Maguire. I appreciate the offer."

Her spirits sinking, she turned away. The whole business was terribly disheartening. She was beginning to feel that the house would never be finished and the garden would always be a wreck. But perhaps none of this mattered, for at this moment, in her deepest heart of hearts, she had almost given up hope that she and Will would ever be able to marry. Her father might not live much longer; he was ill and required the attention of a nurse. But her mother (who was likely to live for another twenty years or more) maintained that she would always need her daughter close at hand. Will had been terribly patient so far, but heaven only knew how much longer that would last. He was younger than she by five years, a good-looking man and widely respected by all who knew him. He deserved a wife who could make a home for him. It wasn't fair to keep him waiting.

Beatrix turned to find Mr. Maguire watching her — almost furtively, she thought, and wondered if he was trying to cover up for Mr. Biddle. She almost said something, but he stepped away, gave a little wave, and went back to his work.

She looked past him at the old house. It almost seemed to be frowning crossly at her, as if it were telling her to stop this silly business of trying to pretty it up, to remedy its many glaring flaws. It didn't look much like a home, she thought bleakly. It didn't even look as if it *wanted* to be a home. Its windows were like blind eyes, the new construction at the eastern end looked like the bare bones of an emaciated skeleton, and the scabby gray limewash on its old walls was peeling away as if it were infected with a horrible skin disease.

"I am not worth fixing," it seemed to say. "I am what I am, and there's no changing me. So you might as well go away and stop wasting your time."

Her unhappy thought was interrupted by the chug-chug of a motor coming up the hill — Will's motorcycle, which he frequently rode over from Hawkshead, where he and his partner had their law office. The motor stopped, and Beatrix's heavy heart lightened at the sight of him, climbing off his motorcycle, pulling off his leather helmet, straightening his tweed jacket and his brown tie. She was glad to see him, oh, she was glad! Now that he was here, they could go through the house and make a list of what needed to be done. And she would ask him to go with her to talk to Mr. Biddle, so she wouldn't have to face that unpleasant task alone.

Beatrix walked to the gate and waited, and when Will strode to meet her, she held out her hand, putting on her best and bravest smile, although she didn't feel at all brave at the moment.

But Will was not smiling. He wore an uncharacteristically troubled look, and his brown eyes were dark. "Sorry to be late, my dear," he said, running a hand through his hair, matted and damp from the helmet. "Afraid I was delayed at the office. Have you been waiting long?"

Will Heelis was tall and slender, with the look (as one friend put it) of a "rather sweet old-fashioned English gentleman of the kind that one reads about in Dickens." His hair was brown, and even though he tried to keep it neatly combed back, it often fell across his forehead in a boyish shock. His eyes were brown and crinkled at the corners when he smiled. He was a keen sportsman and loved to fish and hunt and bowl and dance — country dancing, that is. He was one of the Hawkshead morris dancers, who put on exhibition dances at many of the local fairs. He was reserved and modest, and his shyness often kept him from enjoying formal parties and social occasions, where people who scarcely knew one another were expected to chat without saying anything at all substantial.

But Will had never been shy with Beatrix, perhaps because she was as reserved, modest, and shy as he. And because both of them were passionate about the same things, which allowed them to build a strong working relationship that, over the course of time, had ripened into an even stronger affection.

"I only just got here myself," Beatrix replied. She waved a hand at the garden. "I was looking at all this construction mess and thinking that perhaps — after we've walked through the house — you and I ought to find Mr. Biddle and have a word with him. I'm sure that the lumber should be stored in the barn, rather than out in the weather. And there ought to be something productive that these workmen could be doing, instead of wasting time sitting around." She thought of what Sarah had told her and frowned. "But there's more, Will. I had a talk with Sarah Barwick a little while ago. She said that Henry Stubbs had bought a pair of brass door handles —"

"I'm sorry, Beatrix, but I'm afraid I can't stop now," Will said apologetically. He shoved his hands in his pockets and turned away, not quite meeting her eyes. "Didn't want you to stand around wondering what had become of me. Just motored up to tell you that something's come up. Dodgy bit of business, I'm afraid — nothing for you to worry about. I'm on my way to see Wood-cock this afternoon." He took a breath and managed a crooked smile. "It would be best to delay any talk with Mr. Biddle until I am able to go with you. You'll do that, will you?" Without waiting for her answer, he added, "Sorry, my dear. Hope you won't mind."

"Oh," Beatrix said, suddenly deflated. "No, of course I don't mind."

As she spoke, she suddenly found that she minded a very great deal — but what she minded was the fact that Will had to leave. She hadn't seen him for over a fortnight, and she had been looking forward to spending this afternoon together. She stole a look at him, wondering what the "dodgy bit of business" might be and why he had to see Captain Woodcock so urgently.

"Splendid," Will replied, with what seemed to her a forced cheerfulness. "And I haven't forgotten about this evening. You and I are having dinner at Tower Bank House. I'll call for you at . . . oh, say, seven?"

"Of course," Beatrix said.

He leaned forward and brushed her cheek

with his lips. "Well, then, cheerio, my dear. I'll just clear off." He turned to go.

She stopped him with a hand on his arm. "But I really feel we must have a talk with Mr. Biddle *soon,* Will. Perhaps later this afternoon, after you've had your talk with the captain? We'd have to find the man, but —"

"This afternoon?" He shook his head. "Afraid not. Truly sorry, my dear. I have to see a client back in Hawkshead. But we'll do it soon. I promise. And I'll see you tonight." Then he was gone, hurrying out to his motorcycle, kicking it into life, and driving back down the hill with a great cloud of dust hanging in the still air behind him.

Beatrix stood stock-still, feeling herself unable to move. Will had a mild temperament and was slow to show worry or impatience. In all the many hours she had spent with him, he had never seemed quite so hurried and brusque — and evasive — as he had just now. Whatever was troubling him, it must be serious.

She opened the gate. It couldn't be . . . It couldn't be something between the two of them, could it? Between herself and Will? She thought back to the last time they had been together, in early July, when he had come over to Lindeth Howe for a brief

Sunday afternoon visit with her parents. It wasn't the first time he had called. After all, the two of them *were* engaged. And she insisted on treating it as if it were a real engagement, even though her mother and father tried very hard to pretend it didn't exist.

She and Will had made every attempt at normal conversation. But despite their efforts, her father had been mostly silent and her mother had been hostile and rude. Both had made it clear that their daughter's friend was not a welcome caller. The visit had been almost unbearably uncomfortable, and she had actually been glad when Will looked at her with a despairing sigh, said goodbye, and left. Since then she had scarcely heard from him, except for one or two short notes to explain that he was very busy with some matters at the law office and couldn't get away. She hadn't thought anything of it, for she herself had been busy with the drawings for *Pigling Bland.* But now —

Now she had to wonder. Perhaps Will was coming to realize what she had felt for some time, that there was really no use in trying to create something out of nothing, to build a future where none was likely to exist. The thought made her stomach hurt and her head ache, but the possibility had to be faced, didn't it? It would certainly be better to end the engagement sooner, rather than later, so that Will could find what he needed.

Beatrix had no heart now to go inside the house, its old life pulled out of it and spread like so much rubbish all over the garden, its new life not yet — and perhaps not ever to be — realized. It loomed behind her like a metaphor for a failed relationship, for an unrealized dream. And even if she could find Mr. Biddle, facing him in her current frame of mind was out of the question.

She went through the gate, leaving Castle Cottage and its mess behind, and began to walk slowly down the hill.

5

In the Castle Farm Barn

. . . Alice started to her feet, for it flashed across her mind that she had never before seen a rabbit with either a waistcoat-pocket, or a watch to take out of it, and burning with curiosity, she ran across the field after it, and was just in time to see it pop down a large rabbit-hole under the hedge. In another moment down went Alice after it, never once considering how in the world she was to get out again.

— **Lewis Carroll,** ***Alice in Wonderland***

It's probably a very good thing that Miss Potter did not go into the barn. If she had climbed the ladder and looked into the loft, she would have been surprised and very bewildered by what she saw. But she might have been even more surprised if she had gone into the second stall on the right, the winter home of the Cottage Farm draught horse, a big, burly fellow named Brown Billy who was spending the summer working with Mr. Jennings in the hayfield.

But Miss Potter, disheartened by her brief exchange with Mr. Heelis, did neither of these things, going instead down the hill toward the village. Since that is the case, I will take the liberty of telling you what she would have seen. She would have been very much puzzled by the stacks of lumber and other building supplies, which would have seemed to her to be a duplicate of the materials that were heaped outdoors, being spoilt in the weather. And in Brown Billy's stall, she would have noticed a great many unusual comings and goings amidst the rustling of crisp hay and the squeaking and chirping of rats.

Yes, rats. Rats with caps pulled low over their eyes, rats carrying baskets of pilfered produce and cheeses, rats staggering under heavy loads of booty. And if Miss Potter could have made herself very small (like Alice, who followed the White Rabbit down the rabbit hole and into Wonderland), I have no doubt that she, too, would have followed these rats and discovered that every one of them was going through a trapdoor in the floor under Brown Billy's manger.

Through a trapdoor in the floor? Yes, indeed, and down a wooden ladder, craftily built of willow wattles lashed with binding twine, and thence into a large cavern that had been carved out under the floor of her barn. But since Miss Potter didn't do this, we will, exercising the special privilege extended to writers and readers of stories. For as you know, we are entitled to see through walls and listen at keyholes and generally poke our noses into all sorts of odd and out-of-the-way places where real people cannot go — for example, down Alice's rabbit hole or through a trapdoor and under the floor of the Castle Farm barn.

This barn had been built over two centuries before and was in serious need of repair when Miss Potter bought it. She planned to use it to provide the cows and farm horses and pigs and chickens with a warm and cozy shelter from the snows and rains of a north England winter, so she had engaged several workmen to replace the broken slates on the steep roof, replace the rotted timbers, and strengthen the stone walls. Now, during the summer and while the house was being renovated, it was empty.

But if you have ever visited a farm, you will appreciate the fact that, while it is very easy to put cows and horses and pigs and chickens *into* a barn, it is most assuredly impossible to keep other creatures *out*. Give a mouse or a vole or even a bat the smallest opening, and the creature will enlarge it to the size of a proper front door, hang a rope bell-pull beside it, and send out hand-printed cards announcing that he (or she) will be at home every afternoon (except Wednesdays) at three. Then she (or he) will put up fresh curtains, stock the larder, set out the tea things, and receive callers.

Unfortunately, however, not all barn residents are quite so well-mannered and genteel as this. Both you and I know that the animal world contains just as many individuals of a low and despicable character (that is to say, scum and riff-raff) as does our human world. These are creatures — rats, mostly, of the vilest and dirtiest sort — who have no respect for the bourgeois niceties of bell-pulls and fresh curtains and stocked larders and would never think of inviting anybody to tea.

Oh, no, no indeed. These creatures are social pariahs, gangsters, mobsters, and desperados who live outside the law, making a career of burglary, shoplifting, house-break, bag-snatch, and assault. Give these ratty rascals the smallest opening in an otherwise respectable barn, and they are likely to turn it into a pub of the sort one finds in the slums of London and Liverpool.

Pretty soon, there will be a billiards table and dart board; somebody will install a keg of beer and set up a row of dirty glasses and a cash box; and others will bring in as many sticky buns and cheeses and cigarettes and cigars and such as they can filch from the neighborhood. Before you know it, there'll even be entertainment: concertina players and vaudeville dancers and burlesque comics, with a new and bawdier show every night. If you think I am making this up, I suggest that you read *The Tale of Cuckoo Brow Wood,* for something very similar took place in the attics at Hill Top Farm several years before the time of our story, when Rosabelle Rat invited her homeless relatives, who invited their friends and cronies, who invited any rat who happened along. It wasn't long before the entire place had been taken over and very harsh measures indeed were required to evict the interlopers.

I am sorry to tell you, however, that the gang that has moved into the hole under the floor of Brown Billy's stall in the Castle Farm barn is worse — yes, far worse — than those rowdy rats at Hill Top. The latter were merely good-time Charlies who let their unwise appetites for entertainment get the better of them. These rats are what the police call "professional criminals": hard-looking, foul-mouthed toughs whom you would never allow to darken your kitchen door — if you could keep them out, that is, which perhaps you could not. They are led by old Rooker, a wily, scruffy-looking gray rat with needle-like claws, fierce whiskers, and a reputation as a dangerous fellow and a master thief.

Yes, Rooker Rat. The same Corporal Rooker who appeared, homeless and bedraggled, at The Brockery, where he was hospitably fed and lodged. The rat who took advantage of his gracious hosts, devoured Parsley's birthday cake, and then made off with three silver spoons in his pocket. Rooker Rat. The very same.

Now, there are rats and rats. There are lovely white rats with pink eyes and twittery noses who live in a cage and feed from one's hand and are altogether compliant and agreeable creatures. Miss Potter once had a rat like this. She called him Samuel Whiskers, named a book for him, and dedicated it warmly to " 'Sammy,' The Intelligent pink-eyed Representative of a Persecuted (but Irrepressible) Race, An Affectionate little Friend and most accomplished thief."

Then there are field rats who live out their wild, free lives, roaming at large through the great woods and refusing to come near human habitation because they find us Big Folk to be too dirty and smelly (and because we harbor cats, whom field rats find to be a great nuisance).

And then there are incorrigible rats like old Rooker, who has been apprehended and hauled off to the jug (that is to say "gaol") more times than you can count. But this sort of rat never stays in prison long, for he always manages to bribe, bully, or bite his way out in very short order. Rooker will go anywhere and steal anything from anybody at any time. He is a clever rat who can appear in many beguiling disguises. He can masquerade as the innocently playful rat (sweet Sammy Whiskers) that Miss Potter enjoyed as a pet. Or the pathetically crippled Army veteran rat (old Corporal Rooker) who was welcomed at The Brockery. Or the brash, enterprising rat (Rooker the Rascally Rogue) with a cartload of goods — stolen, of course — that he will be glad to sell you if you've got a couple of spare bob about you. But beware: Rooker is also a dexterous pickpocket, so if you don't fork over your shillings, you're likely to lose them, willy-nilly.

Now, all by himself, Rooker constitutes a veritable one-rat crime wave. But he is also a first-class executive, what is called in today's common parlance a "godfather" rat. He has gathered about him a villainous crew of more than a dozen criminal specialists, each of whom has a reputation for doing one very bad thing very, very well. Some of his gang members are adept at breaking into locked pantries, closed closets, and chicken coops, whilst others are talented forgers, frauds, robbers, imposters, counterfeiters, and swindlers. Some (like Rooker and his lieutenant, Bludger Bob) are old and experienced; others (Cracksman Charlie and Jumpin' Jemmy, for example) are young rats, nimble and fleet of foot, who can outrun and outjump anyone who is fool enough to give chase. Most are male, but there are a few females: Plymouth Polly, who is very good at sniffing out the most expensive jewelry, however cleverly it is hidden in m'lady's boudoir; and notorious Newgate Nell, who has a talent for shoplifting. No shopkeeper dares to turn his back on Nell. She will rob him blind in an instant.

Rooker and his gang of reprobates have perfected the art of moving from town to town, staying just one leap ahead of the law. When they've picked a place clean, they send their scouts out into the district, looking for the richest target of opportunity. When a promising neighborhood or village is found, word is sent back, and the whole gang up sticks and moves, bag and baggage.

Their first task is to find a secure hiding place where they will be safe from discovery. It must be large enough for all of them to eat, sleep, and recreate, with adequate space to store their ill-gotten goods. It should have both a front door and a back door — several back doors, in fact, for the gang has occasionally found it necessary to make a hasty exit. The Brockery, of course, has a great many exits (more than even the badgers can count). Rooker had this in mind when he visited the place, reconnoitering it as a possibility for the gang's hideout while they invaded Sawrey. To his disappointment, however, he found that the sett was too great a distance from the village. Rats are fundamentally lazy creatures and prefer not to haul their takings very far.

But fortunately for Rooker and his felons, they quickly discovered the barn at Castle Farm, which is right at the top of the village and convenient to the cottages, the shop, and the pub. They explored the barn's many nooks and crannies and discovered that once upon a time, a very long time ago, another clan of rats had excavated a sizeable cavern under the floor of the stall that now belongs to Brown Billy. There was even a rather ingenious trapdoor over the opening, designed to look like a wooden shingle lying on the floor. When the trapdoor was closed and covered with straw, you would never in the world guess that an entire gang of thieves was living underneath the floor. And even if you did, there would be nothing you could do about it, for when the new gang moved in, they installed a latch on the underneath side of the trapdoor. If you want to get in, you have to know the secret code — a predetermined number of brisk raps, a silence, then more raps. And Thursday's code won't do you any good on Friday, because the rats change it every day.

It was from this clever hideout that the rats went out to raid the best larders, fruit and grain bins, bakery shelves, jewelry chests, money boxes, bookcases, and wine and liquor cabinets in the village. Once the Big Folks had turned down their gas lights or snuffed their candles and gone to bed, the thieves set about their jobs as systematically as any well-trained gang of workmen, making whatever forced entries were required, raiding private premises all over town, and silently departing with their loot, which they carried off to the Castle Farm barn. There they divvied up their spoils, feasted on their stolen foods, and counted their ill-gotten coins and jewels. Some of them went to bed to sleep through the day, whilst others (the more ambitious of the thieves) took only a short nap before venturing out into the daylight. They planned to keep on repeating their chicanery until Sawrey was well and truly stripped and there was nothing left to steal.

These robbers are already making inroads into the village. We have heard that Miss Potter has reported the theft of ten turkey eggs. Sarah Barwick missed a half-dozen sticky buns from her bakery, and now she can't find the leather purse with her initials stamped on it, where she keeps her earnings. There might be as much as ten or twelve shillings in it! (She has not yet got this matter quite sorted, since her accounts are so badly muddled.)

There's more, however, and the picture is not a pretty one. In the kitchen at the Tower Bank Arms, Mrs. Barrow noticed the absence of two fine cheddars and a round of goat cheese from the dairy cupboard. In the pub bar, Mr. Barrow became very cross when he took out the full can of salted nuts and found that it is now nearly empty. Both the Barrows have a tendency to blame the hired help when things get lost or misplaced, but both the kitchen maid and the bar boy protested their innocence, and of course there was no proof.

At the village shop on the other side of the Kendal Road, shopkeeper Lydia Dowling counted and recounted the sausages hanging from the overhead line that stretches across the corner above the vegetable bins and concluded that the two largest sausages were missing — or perhaps three, since she couldn't remember exactly how many there were. And as she recalled, the marrow bin was full when she shut up shop the previous evening. It now appeared to be half-empty. Where had all the marrows gone?

And at Belle Green, across the lane from the barn, Mrs. Crook was frantic, for she could not find her emerald-cut crystal pendant, the one that had belonged to her grandmother. She could swear that she put it into the rose-colored china dish on the top of her bedroom dresser (although, as a matter of fact, she had left it on the kitchen table). In the event, the pendant was in neither place, and no one in the house would confess to having seen it.

Now, as we learnt in Chapter Two, Crumpet (in her role as the president of the Village Cat Council) makes it her business to be aware of everything that happens in

Sawrey. As you will recall, she had been listening when Sarah Barwick asked Miss Potter what she would do if she suspected that somebody was stealing from her. However, at that moment, a loud commotion had erupted in the Hill Top chicken coop, and Crumpet had to rush off and see what it was. (Nothing urgent, as it turned out: Mrs. Bonnet, who is slightly myopic, had mistaken one of Mrs. Shawl's newly hatched chicks for her own and attempted to chick-nap the little one.) The brief flurry of feathery disagreement was settled by the time Crumpet arrived on the scene, and complete harmony was restored to the barn-yard.

But while Crumpet had not heard Miss Potter's answer, she had certainly heard Miss Barwick's question, and she began to wonder whether there was some serious trouble afoot. So after she left the Hill Top garden, she popped in at various cottages, asking the resident cats whether they had anything to report. She did this quite casually, because she didn't want to alarm any of her colleagues before she completely understood what was going on.

But by the time she had completed her canvass, it appeared that nearly every house in the village was missing something of greater or lesser value — a box of almond-flavored biscuits, a tin of tea, a bracelet, a book, a paper of pins, even a half-knitted sock (although the yarn and needles had been left behind). Thoroughly troubled by what she had learned, Crumpet retired to the storage shed at the foot of the Rose Cottage garden, where the Council held its weekly meetings, and began making notes on the missing items and the cottages from which they had been taken.

Now, Crumpet is a clever cat. She knew that two and two generally made four (unless decimals were somehow involved), and she could see that all these multiple pieces of evidence added up to a larger and very unsettling truth: a gang of professional thieves was at work in the village. She also knew that they must be found and caught and brought to trial as swiftly as possible.

But this task was easier said than done. For one thing, Crumpet had no idea how many thieves were at work (one? two? a dozen?) or how small or how large they might be (the size of a mouse? bigger than a breadbox?). She didn't know where they were hiding out, either. But she knew that they must be outsiders, since the village mice, rats, and voles were generally law-abiding and understood the need for cooperative co-existence. They might steal an occasional bite from a sticky bun left unattended, but they would never make off with a full half-dozen. No. There was only one creature in the whole wide world bold and brazen enough to organize and mount such a series of robberies as these.

A rat. It had to be a rat — no, a whole gang of the vile beasts — running loose in the village! Of course, it would be helpful if one of the cats had actually caught one of the thieves in the act and confirmed Crumpet's speculation. But even without a positive identification, she knew what they were faced with. What *she* was faced with, as the new president of the Village Cat Council.

The thought sent cold fright shivering up Crumpet's spine, but she knew she couldn't give in to her fear. Obviously, there would have to be a plan, some sort of organization. But what sort of organization? What kind of plan? And who would carry it out?

She found a scrap of brown wrapping paper and a pencil and began to make a list of names of those she could call on for a possible police force — printed in block letters, because Crumpet had never mastered the art of cursive. She found that her pen obstinately refused to make the lines and curves that were required, and the flourishes of a fine hand (or paw, rather) were beyond her.

But when she had printed all the names of the cats in the village (with her own at the top of the list, of course), she could only stare at them in dismay. Every one of them was as mild-mannered and law-abiding as the village mice, rats, and voles. Felicity Frummety was frightened of her shadow. Tabitha Twitchit (the former Council president) was too old and slow and anyway, she lived in the Vicarage now, although she liked to stick her nose into village business. Treacle had just produced another litter of kittens (the father, as in previous instances, was unknown); she could not be expected to leave them unless a minder could be found. Max the Manx had moved to Far Sawrey to live in Teapot Cottage, and anyway, he was a gentle soul, a lover of art and music who could barely bring himself to swat a fly. There were at least a dozen other cats in the village, but they were all similarly impaired.

Crumpet put down her pencil. Except for herself, there was no one, not a single cat, who had the strength and ferocity necessary to go up against this lot. And even though she was an unusually confident and deter-mined cat, she did just wonder whether she was up to the task. One rat, yes. Two rats, probably. A gang of rats? To be quite honest, not likely.

At this, Crumpet sighed, remembering with a certain amount of envy the Cat Who had been hired to clear an infestation of rats out of the Hill Top attics a few years before. This creature had grown into a legendary figure remembered in stories whispered around the winter firesides in the village. He was reputed to have been an exceedingly large fellow, almost two stone in weight and black as the back side of midnight, with saber-like claws and teeth as sharp as needles. He had taken the name of the Cat Who Walked by Himself (after a character in one of Kipling's Just So stories) and boasted that he was the most efficient professional ratter available for hire anywhere in the Land Between the Lakes. He had an insatiable appetite for rats, he declared, and told Miss Potter that he was not ashamed to own that he took a very great pleasure in killing as many as possible.

As events transpired, these claims proved to be true and accurate. (You can read about them in *The Tale of Cuckoo Brow Wood*.) But while the Cat Who Walked by Himself did the job he promised to do, he had not been amenable to any sort of restraint. He refused to take orders from Miss Potter, and when he set about clearing the Hill Top attics, he wreaked a horrible havoc, slaughtering the good rats (yes, there were some!) right along with the bad. That could never be allowed to happen again.

Crumpet twitched her whiskers. She was beginning to feel desperate. Something would have to be done. What? And who was going to do it?

Well. I am very glad this is Crumpet's problem, and not mine, for I confess that I don't have an idea in the world for solving it.

6

LADY LONGFORD IS AT A LOSS

Tidmarsh Manor is the home of Lady Longford, who (Lord Longford being deceased) lives there alone, clinging stubbornly to the hope that her headstrong, willful granddaughter Caroline will stop gallivanting all over the globe and hurry home to take the burden of the Longford estates from her grandmother's shoulders.

But I am afraid that Caroline Longford has no intention of doing anything of the sort. A talented pianist and composer, she has grown from a shy and unassuming girl into a beautiful and fiercely independent young woman. A young woman of means, to boot, since she inherited enough money from her father to allow her to do pretty much as she pleases for the rest of her life. And to judge from the frequent letters she exchanges with her dear friend Miss Potter (who encouraged her to apply to study at the Royal Academy of Music) that is exactly what she means to do.

This week, for example, Caroline is on her way to Prague to give a piano recital, and after that, Vienna for another recital and Rome for a holiday. Of course, things might have been different if Jeremy Crosfield had fallen in love with her, as she hoped, rather than with Deirdre Malone. But that was not to be. Jeremy and Deirdre are married now and settled at Slatestone Cottage, with a baby on the way. Caroline is fiercely determined to make the very best of her talent — and the most of her freedom. Times are changing for women, and she eagerly embraces every tempting possibility that crosses her path. Who knows what the world will offer her, or what she will do with it?

But Lady Longford, I am sorry to say, is a different story. She has not changed one iota since the day we met her, nor do possibilities tempt her. She is not a cheerful woman by nature. She continues to dress in deepest black, although Lord Longford — a generous and jolly man who enjoyed a great many friends and was as unlike his wife as it was possible to be — passed on to his reward some decades before. Some people think that living at Tidmarsh Manor has made her ladyship gloomy, for the house, built some three centuries ago at the edge of Cuckoo Brow Wood, is curtained in heavy draperies and shadowed by a row of dark yew trees. On the other hand, perhaps it is her ladyship who has darkened the house, for it would be easy enough to tear down the draperies, trim the yew trees, and bring sunlight and life into the house.

But whether Tidmarsh Manor has darkened her ladyship's gloomy view of the world or the other way around, the forbidding old place certainly matches her determined inhospitality. She distrusts most people, has almost no friends, and receives very few callers, with the exception of the vicar (who comes because he feels it is his Christian duty) and Mr. Heelis, who comes because he is her ladyship's solicitor and truly has her best interests at heart.

And if you are in the neighborhood and invited to drop in at teatime with the expectation of something nice on your plate, I'm afraid that you will be disappointed, for all you will get is bread and butter, or perhaps only a plain biscuit, and no lemon or milk with your tea. Her ladyship is reputed to be the most parsimonious person in the parish, a reputation which she enjoys and cultivates. She is not poor, of course, but she likes to pretend that she is in order to keep people from asking her for money.

It is said of her that she will not part with a shilling unless it is pried out of her cold, dead fingers, and those who know her can cite more than one instance of her attempts to cheat people out of what they are owed. And this is why she never entertains, you see. Entertaining costs money. (With such a grandmother, I think you can understand why Caroline has fled Tidmarsh Manor and refuses to return except for short visits.)

And this is why it is such a surprise to learn that, early in the previous week, Lady Longford entertained a guest. Or perhaps it is not accurate to say that she "entertained" him, because if we had gone up to the third floor of Tidmarsh Manor (where this visit took place) and peered through the open door, we would have seen her perched on the edge of a straight chair, tapping her foot impatiently and watching with suspicion as this person — a rotund, scholarly gentleman with a gold pince-nez and a pair of extraordinary mutton-chop whiskers — went about his work. Or perhaps it is not quite accurate to say that Mr. Darnwell (for this is the gentleman's name) was a "guest," for he had been invited to Tidmarsh Manor to perform a service for her ladyship, one from which both Mr. Darnwell and her ladyship hoped to profit.

There is an interesting story behind this rather unusual exercise. During his busy and active life, Lord Longford collected a great variety of *things,* obsessively and indiscriminately, most of them of no evident worth to anyone but his lordship. He collected fossils and animal bones, butterflies and moths (mounted on pins stuck into cardboard), stones and odd bits of polished wood, nails, pocket knives, string, paintings by unknown artists, carved walking sticks, and old books. Very, very old books.

Of all his collections, his lordship's books had been his lordship's passion. He kept them in a glass-fronted book cabinet in the main-floor library, where he could take out one or two every day, fondling them lovingly before he replaced them on the shelf. But when he died, Lady Longford (who could not by any stretch of the imagination be considered a lover of books) directed that the moldy old things be carted off to a dark, dusty box room at the far end of the third floor, where the servants' sleeping quarters were located. There, Lord Longford's collections were out of sight and out of mind, which was a good thing as far as her ladyship was concerned. She had no affection for fossils or butterflies or walking sticks or pocket knives, and the books were so old that she was sure they had little value. In fact, she had several times threatened to clean out the room and throw the worthless lot away, which she no doubt would have done if she hadn't been so tightfisted.

It happened that Vicar Sackett, during one of his recent duty visits, had mentioned that he was rather fond of old books, and her ladyship had mentioned that the departed Lord Longford had been fond of old books as well, although she herself could see no merit in them. (But then she does not find any merit in new books, either, since her ladyship is the sort of person who does not care to have her mind broadened in any way.) When the vicar diffidently suggested that he would be delighted to have a look at Lord Longford's collection, she had agreed. She had been thinking, in fact, that it was time to clean out that room. She ought to take one more look before she instructed Mr. Beever (the manor's general handyman) to burn the lot.

So her ladyship led the vicar up the stairs to the dark, cluttered room, where he poked about amongst the shelves, muttering this and that and making enthusiastic little exclamations under his breath whilst her ladyship began to plan how best to get rid of everything. At last the vicar asked her, hopefully, whether Lord Longford had made a proper catalog of his books.

"I am sure that he must have had a list," Lady Longford returned. She could say this with some confidence, since list-making was another of his lordship's obsessions.

"Well, then, perhaps you might look for it," the vicar suggested deferentially. He took a book from the shelf, turned several of the pages, gave a covetous sigh, and added, "Of course, one never knows, but some of these books may have value. I fear that I am no judge, but I daresay I might be able to suggest a reliable person who could appraise the collection for you."

Her ladyship (who was never inclined to take the vicar's word for anything) scoffed at the notion that the old books might be valuable, although she decided to postpone telling Mr. Beever to toss the lot on a bonfire. And as it happened, the very next day, when she was looking for something else in one of her husband's desk drawers, she came across a small notebook bound in black leather. On the first page, in Lord Longford's spidery hand, was written "My Collection of Rare Books."

Rare books? Well, now. This was news to her ladyship, who had always considered her husband's books to be merely "old" books, on a par with his old fossils and old butterflies. If somebody considered them rare, however, they might be worth a few pounds. So she sent a note to the vicar, asking him to recommend a knowledgeable person who could give her an idea of the value of the books.

A day later, the vicar replied that he had contacted a certain Mr. Depford Darnwell, an antiquarian who owned a rare book shop on Rushmore Road in Ambleside, a town at the north end of Windermere. Mr. Darnwell would arrange to call at a convenient time to have a look at the collection. For this preliminary examination, no fee would be charged. If Lady Longford decided to put the books up for sale in his shop, however, he would require a certain percentage of the price they brought.

Since this arrangement allowed her ladyship to feel that she was getting something for nothing (at least at the present moment), she saw no reason not to permit it. And that was why the portly Mr. Darnwell, his pince-nez perched on his nose and his mutton-chop whiskers bristling with pleasure, was going carefully and methodically through Lord Longford's collection, under Lady Longford's watchful eye. In one hand, Mr. Darnwell held his lordship's little black book. He was checking the list against the titles of the books on the shelves, making notes in his own little black book, and muttering under his breath, whilst her ladyship watched to be sure he didn't slide anything into one of his capacious pockets. Vicar Sackett had said that the fellow was reputable, but one could never be too sure.

The work required the better part of four hours, but by teatime Mr. Darnwell was finished. He put his notebook into his pocket, took his pince-nez off his nose, and announced in a gruff voice that in his opinion ("My expert opinion," he added severely), the books in the collection could, if offered at his shop, be expected to fetch around ten thousand pounds sterling.

"Perhaps more," he said, "if an auction were to be announced and certain collectors of my acquaintance invited. Of course, then there would be the expense of an auction, so you might consider direct sale to be more . . . profitable."

Ten thousand pounds! This figure quite took her ladyship's breath away, and she stared at Mr. Darnwell for a moment, unable to speak. At last she managed to cough out a few words. "You are sure of the amount?"

"Indeed." Mr. Darnwell inclined his head.

"The amount would be much higher — in fact, I daresay it would be ten times as much, or more — if I had been able to locate one of the titles in your husband's catalog. And if the item truly is what it purports to be, which of course one cannot be certain without actually seeing it." Mr. Darnwell lowered his voice, becoming confidential. "I wonder . . . perhaps your ladyship is keeping the item elsewhere. In a safe, perhaps, or a bank vault." He coughed. "If so, that is a good idea, for it is quite valuable. Quite."

"Ten . . . times?" Lady Longford whispered. Ten times ten thousand pounds was . . . The calculation made her dizzy.

"Just so," said Mr. Darnwell emphatically. He turned several pages in the black book. "Your husband has noted the disposal of several items in his collection by striking them through and detailing the name of the purchaser and the amount paid. There are no such notations for this particular item. I must therefore infer that it was in his possession at his death." He smiled in a cold-fish sort of way. "I shall need to see it, of course, in order to determine whether it is what the catalog listing describes. So if you will be so kind as to get it for me, or tell me where I may go to examine it, I should be most grateful."

For once in her life, Lady Longford found herself at a complete loss.

"I don't think I —" Ten times ten thousand pounds. Her mouth was suddenly very dry. She swallowed. "What . . . What is the title?"

"It is called *The Book of the Revelation of John.* It is a book that — as it is described in your husband's catalog — came from the library of Sir Robert Cotton. That is to say, Sir Robert collected it. It originally came from the monastery of Lindisfarne, by way of the Tower of London." He smiled thinly. "The Lindisfarne books were held there for some time, after Henry the Eighth confiscated the lands and treasuries of the monasteries."

Ah. The *Revelation,* revealed at last. I am sure that you have not forgotten the story that was related at the beginning of this book. In fact, you may have been wondering how all that business about the wandering monks and St. Cuthbert's coffin and Bishop Eadfrith's marvelous books was connected to our present story. Now, perhaps, you can see that it is.

But her ladyship is still in the dark, for she doesn't know as much as you and I do about the history of the book in question —

the *rare* book in question. She did know about the Tower of London, of course, and the name Mr. Darnwell had mentioned seemed vaguely familiar.

"Cotton, Robert Cotton," she mused, trying to remember if she had ever met the gentleman. "The family is from Kendal, is it?" she hazarded.

Mr. Darnwell coughed dryly. "Sir Robert Cotton is dead, Lady Longford. He died in 1631."

"Oh," said her ladyship. "*That* Sir Robert. Yes, of course. Quite."

To his credit, Mr. Darnwell did not laugh, although his mutton-chop whiskers were trembling with suppressed amusement. He cleared his throat and continued. "Sir Robert was an antiquary and without a doubt the most important collector of books England has ever seen. He lived during the reigns of Queen Elizabeth, King James, and King Charles the First. He sought out and acquired such remarkable treasures as *Beowulf, The Anglo-Saxon Chronicles,* and *Sir Gawain and the Green Knight,* along with many other early works that would surely have been lost had he not rescued them from oblivion. His library has been held in the British Museum since 1753. It is one of the museum's most valuable possessions."

"Of course, of course," her ladyship murmured, putting on a knowing air. She never liked to appear ignorant in any way. "I am to understand, then, that Lord Longford had a book from Sir Robert's library?"

"Yes, if the catalog is correct — although, strictly speaking, the *Revelation* is not a 'book,' but a codex — that is, a bound manuscript of eight vellum pages. It was produced by Bishop Eadfrith on Lindisfarne Island in Northumbria in the late seventh or early eighth century. It is a companion work to the Lindisfarne Gospels, now owned by the British Museum."

Mr. Darnwell put his pince-nez back on his nose and opened Lord Longford's notebook. He held it for her, turned a page, and pointed to an entry in his lordship's handwriting. "Here we have the title, you see: *The Book of the Revelation of John,* and the name of its creator, Eadfrith, bishop of Lindisfarne." He shook his head and said, half under his breath, "I am truly astonished at this — in fact, I confess that I find it hard to credit. The *Revelation of John* has been considered lost since long before Sir Robert's library was acquired by the museum. There was a fire in 1731, and many of the priceless items were destroyed. Or it is possible that it was stolen. No one knows."

This made no sense at all to her ladyship, and for once her need to know outweighed her need to pretend that she already knew. "Then how can you be so sure that the book my husband possessed is the book that's been lost?" she asked.

"I cannot be sure until I see it, of course. And even then, someone from the British Museum will have to make the confirmation, since the curators there are the acknowledged experts on the Cotton Library. But here is a bit of very strong evidence, in your husband's own hand." Mr. Darnwell pointed to the page again. "These letters. *Nero D.iv.* They are the code for the case and shelf where Sir Robert kept the book. It is the same case and shelf where he also kept the Lindisfarne Gospels."

Lady Longford pulled in her breath. "The late seventh century?" she asked. Her voice felt scratchy. No wonder the thing was rare — and undoubtedly of great value. "I should think that the paper would be falling apart."

Mr. Darnwell looked down his nose, severely, as if at a laggard student. "The pages of the codex are not paper. They are made of vellum — treated calfskin — and hence quite durable." He closed the black notebook. "The Lindisfarne Gospels unfortunately lack the original cover, which would of course be priceless, but even so, the book itself is astonishingly well-preserved. *The Book of the Revelation of John* was described by Sir Robert as incomplete, but it still had — at least at the time it was in his possession — the original cover."

"Ah," her ladyship said.

Mr. Darnwell lifted his head and gave her a searching look. "Do you know if your husband's book still has its cover? It would be leather, bound with gold and ornamented with precious jewels. Not large. From the description of the book held in Mr. Cotton's library, I believe it to be no more than ten by twelve inches. It is likely only about an inch or two in thickness, since the book is unfinished. There are only eight pages. Bishop Eadfrith died before he could complete his work." Mr. Darnwell's eyes glittered. "If your husband's book still has its cover, Lady Longford, it could be . . . priceless."

Bound with gold? Ornamented with precious jewels? Numbed by the thought of such a thing, Lady Longford shook her head. At last, she forced herself to speak. And for once, she told the complete truth, which she almost never did.

"I am sorry. I cannot tell you anything at

all. I have never seen the book."

Mr. Darnwell let out a long, regretful breath, and his mutton-chop whiskers drooped dispiritedly. "Oh, dear," he said. "Oh, dear, oh, dear. Then the *Revelation* is not in a safe somewhere? You're sure that your husband didn't put it into a bank vault for safekeeping?"

Lady Longford bit her lip. Recently, she had inventoried every item in the vault at the bank in Hawkshead — the property deeds, the family papers, the jewels that would someday belong to Caroline. There were no books in the vault, and nothing even remotely resembling the description she had just heard. She shook her head mutely.

"Oh dear," Mr. Darnwell said again. He straightened and handed her the black notebook. "If I were you, Lady Longford, I should have a look around — a careful look. It is entirely possible that your husband, understanding as he must have done the value of this precious book, hid it somewhere in the house." He gave her a slightly sour smile. "I also hope you will give some thought to the matter of disposing of the collection, as it is. If you decide to place it up for sale, I shall be glad to assist you."

"Of course," Lady Longford said, although

she had already made up her mind. Ten thousand pounds sterling was quite a nice sum. She would tell Mr. Darnwell that he could put the books up for sale. She might even throw in a few fossils and a carved walking stick or two.

But before she did that, she would take his advice and have a careful look around the house. She was at a loss to think where her husband's book had got off to. But it must be *somewhere.*

7

THE CONSTABLE BRINGS BAD NEWS

Captain Miles Woodcock opened the door of the library and called out testily, "Margaret, have you seen my pipe?" He waited, then, hearing nothing, called again, louder. "Margaret! Any idea where I might have left my pipe?"

Now, you and I (because we know about Rooker's gang) might leap to the conclusion that a rat had visited Tower Bank House and stolen the captain's pipe, but this is not the case. He has simply mislaid it.

"You left it beside your plate at the luncheon table," Mrs. Woodcock said, coming to her husband's rescue. She held out his pipe. "Here it is."

"Sorry," Miles muttered. "Shouldn't have raised my voice."

"Probably not," Margaret said cheerfully. "I do wish you'd tell me what's afoot, dear heart. You've been cross as a bear the past day or two. And abstracted. I hope you haven't forgotten that we're expecting guests for dinner tonight."

"We are?" Miles added hastily, "Oh, yes, of course we are. And of course I remembered."

"Of course you did," Margaret replied in a reassuring tone, although both of them knew that he had entirely forgotten that Beatrix Potter and Will Heelis, as well as Miles' sister and brother-in-law, had been asked to dinner. She eyed him, concerned. "Is there anything you want to tell me, Miles? About why you've been so cross, I mean."

"No," Miles said, turning half away. "Sorry, my dear. It's nothing to do with you."

"Good." Margaret smiled and stood on tiptoe to kiss him on the cleft of his chin. "I do hope your temper will be improved by the time our guests arrive this evening." She paused, adding, "Oh, Miles, you haven't by any chance moved our wedding photograph from the mantel in the library, have you? The small one in the miniature silver frame that Dim and Christopher gave us as a wedding present?"

"Wedding photograph?" Miles asked, taking out his pocket watch. "No, haven't moved it. Not I."

"That is very strange," Margaret said. "I can't think where it could have gotten." She sighed. "Your sister will notice that it's missing and wonder about it, I'm sure. And what I'm to tell her, I really don't know." Shaking her head in puzzlement, she went off to consult with Elsa Grape, their cook, about dessert for the evening's dinner — a damson tart, she thought, if Elsa could be persuaded. Elsa had her own ideas about desserts.

Miles looked at his watch and frowned, and went back into the library to sort through some papers. He had been justice of the peace for Sawrey for almost a decade now. For the most part he enjoyed the work, for it involved him in almost every aspect of village life. His position required him to witness certain transactions, hear complaints, certify deaths, and deal with disturbances of the peace — all of the small and large messes that people got themselves into, sometimes on purpose, sometimes not. And sometimes quite inconveniently.

Miles had not intended to become a justice of the peace when he resigned his post in Her Majesty's Army, but his experience fitted him for the work. He had served honorably in Egypt and the Sudan, where he had earned a bad knee and a case of malaria and begun to yearn for a place where one did not have to go about with a gun in one's holster and eyes in the back of one's head, and where the landscape was fog-kissed, green, and cool. Near Sawrey fit the bill rather well, for it was certainly green and cool and far enough from the alarums and excursions of the Empire to give him some peace of mind. (Of course, that was before the Germans had begun to beat their war drums and build up their war machines and the Admiralty had done likewise, to the point where the newspaper articles were making it seem that war was very nearly inevitable.) His sister Dimity had lived with him for a time, until she had married Christopher Kittredge and went off to live at Raven Hall, above Windermere. The captain had imagined briefly that Miss Potter might make a fine wife, but when he broached the idea, the lady had not warmed to it. After that, he regretfully resigned himself to living alone, with Elsa Grape in the kitchen and old Fred Phinn in the garden.

Of course, being a bachelor was all well and good, for the captain was a man who enjoyed his privacy. It was, he thought, very civilized to be able to smoke one's favorite cigar at one's luncheon table without being asked by a female to please take the horrid thing out-of-doors. But he had to concede that there were certain matters — the dinner menu, for instance, and one's collars and cuffs — that had been better managed by Dim than himself, for Elsa had a very bossy way about her and was inclined to brush off his suggestions.

And then something miraculous happened. In his capacity as a member of the village school board, Miles had frequently worked with the teacher at Sawrey School, Miss Nash. One afternoon she had stopped at his front door to ask about the repair of the school's stovepipes, and he quite properly asked if she would like to come in and have a cup of tea while they discussed it. One thing led to another, and before Miles quite knew what was happening, he found himself on his hands and knees in this very hallway, in a mess of broken crockery and spilt tea and milk, proposing to the lady, who accepted him on the spot. And so they were married and lived happily ever after.

As happily as most married couples, that is. If you had asked the captain on any given day whether he was a happy man, he would have said, "Oh, yes, very, thank you. Couldn't be happier, actually." Except that right at this moment, he was looking once more at his watch and asking himself, "Where the devil is that fellow? He should have been here by now."

As if on cue, the doorbell rang, and the captain hurried to answer it himself. "Oh, there you are, Heelis," he said. "I was beginning to think you weren't coming."

"Sorry, old man," Will Heelis said gruffly. He pulled off his leather motorcycle helmet and smoothed his hair. "I was to meet Beatrix up at Castle Cottage to go through the house. I had to tell her that I couldn't keep our appointment." He looked down at his feet, where a fawn-colored Jack Russell terrier was sitting politely. "I seem to have collected a friend. Rascal, you'll need to wait outside."

The little dog looked up, his tongue hanging out, his eyes dancing. *Really? I was hoping I could join you. I wanted to tell you that Jeremy and Deirdre have a baby boy. They're calling him —*

"No need for him to sit outside." Miles opened the door wider. "The little fellow makes himself at home in every house in town. Quite the favorite, you know. Fancies himself the official Top Dog."

"That's my title, actually," Rascal replied with some pride. *"I am the official Top Dog."* He followed Mr. Heelis into the house.

"I hope Miss Potter wasn't seriously miffed when you broke your appointment," Miles said, leading the way toward the library. He had a great deal of affection for Miss Potter, and an even greater respect, for the lady had a sharp wit and a keen eye for detail, and when she was confronted with a problem, she generally came up with a solution, and often an ingenious one. She had helped him out with several puzzling matters — mysteries, really, and some of them quite serious — that had come his way in his capacity as justice of the peace. He had been especially impressed when she solved the mystery of the baby who had been left on her doorstep — the baby his sister Dimity had adopted and who now called him "Uncle Woodcock." (You may remember this story: it is told in *The Tale of Hawthorn House*.) He had been pleased, if a little surprised, when he had learnt that she and Will Heelis were engaged.

"Not miffed, I think, but definitely perturbed," Heelis replied. "She seems inclined to speak urgently to Biddle about the fellow's delinquencies up at Castle Cottage. I had to stop her."

Miles stopped, surprised. "Biddle? Good Lord! She can't possibly have heard — You don't think she suspects —" He broke off.

"*Suspects what?*" Rascal asked, although he knew he wasn't likely to get an answer. Only a few of the Big Folks — Miss Potter, for instance, and sometimes Jeremy Crosfield — could understand him, or any of the animals. They didn't take the time.

"Suspect? No, I'm sure she doesn't," Will replied. "Not about that. She's concerned about the lumber left out in the rain and workmen who don't work. The ordinary sort of problems one has with most contractors. At least, that's the way I read the situation."

"Ah," Miles said. "She would be. Your Miss Potter is very sharp when it comes to the 'ordinary sort of thing.' In fact, I've often suspected her of being a female Sherlock. If she had been watching whilst Biddle rebuilt my stable into a garage, I daresay the rascal would have been found out sooner."

Rascal looked from one to the other. "*'Found out sooner'?*" he repeated. "*Something underhanded going on here?*"

Miles paused. "But there's some news that you may not have heard yet, directly connected to this business. Shall we ask Margaret to bring us some tea?" He looked down at Rascal. "And a little something for our friend here, as well."

"*A little something would be splendid,*" Rascal barked happily. That was the nice thing about being Top Dog. Everyone offered him a little something.

"Tea would be just the thing, I should say," said Will, sinking into a chair and pulling out his pipe. "And I have news for you, as well, which is why I wanted to talk this afternoon. It's not the sort of thing that would make for good dinner conversation — in the presence of the ladies, that is."

"Margaret just reminded me about tonight," Miles replied ruefully, on his way to the door to summon tea. "I'm afraid I had quite forgotten."

A few moments later, teacups in hand and clouds of smoke filling the air, the two men were discussing the problem which — as you have likely guessed — concerned Mr. Bernard Biddle. Rascal, having finished his little something — which proved to be a very acceptable biscuit, broken in pieces and nicely served in a saucer of milk — was settled at Mr. Heelis' feet. The dog might seem to be preparing for a nap, but he was listening with both ears. Listening was one of his jobs, and a very important one at that. How could a fellow manage the village if he didn't know what was going on?

"Yes. Well, then, what have you found?" Miles asked, leaning back in his chair. He had discovered what looked like a substantial irregularity involving materials in the building project he had hired Mr. Biddle to do and had asked Will to look into it for him. "Tell me there's nothing to worry about, and I shall feel very much better."

"I wish I could do that," Will replied ruefully, "but I can't. In addition to the stable Biddle renovated for you and the current job at Castle Cottage, he completed construction projects for three of my legal clients since the beginning of the year." Will began ticking them off on his fingers. "He built a new hay barn for Harold Grimes to replace the one that was struck by lightning. He put up a dairy for Mrs. Moore. And he constructed two outbuildings for Mr. Kirkby, at the Grange. I have spoken to each of these people confidentially and examined the invoices he gave them for the building supplies. Lumber, stone, slate, hardware, and the like." He shook his head. "The situation is clear enough, I'm sorry to say — although it won't be so easy to prove. Biddle is inflating his bills by purchasing more than is needed for the job, then apparently diverting the extra materials to his own uses."

"Ah," Rascal said grimly. "So that's what the fellow has been up to. I had him down for *a slacker, like his workmen, but he's apparently a thief. Much worse than I thought."*

"Can't say I'm surprised," Miles muttered. "I could not for the life of me see why we needed all that lumber. It looked enough to build two stables." He looked up. "You say 'apparently.' What's he doing with the stuff he's stealing, then?"

Will shook his head. "Now, that's a puzzle. A 'gert mezzlement,' as the villagers would say. I rather suspect that he sells it off as fast as he can — but I haven't been able to figure out where he's storing it until he can offload it. His office is in his house at Hazel Crag Farm. He's building an addition to the place, and if that's what the materials are being used for, I doubt it would be easy to trace them."

Miles nodded. It would be all too easy for Biddle to simply cart the goods to his own building site, where they would disappear into his construction.

"And I don't quite see how the man is keeping the lid on what he's doing," Will continued. "You'd think his workmen would get on to him, wouldn't you? Especially Maguire, who supervises the construction workers when Biddle's not around — which is a great deal of the time." He put down his cup, looking thoughtful. "Unless of course they're afraid for their jobs, so they're keeping their mouths shut."

"Or he's slipping them hush money under the table," the captain replied, puffing on his pipe. "In either case, we can't expect them to come hurrying round to turn him in."

Rascal made a noise deep in his throat. *"Maybe that's why they're not hurrying to do anything — not even pick up a hammer,"* he growled. *"They've got a bit of the dirty on the boss, and he daren't come down hard on them."*

"My thought exactly," Will replied. "I haven't talked to Biddle or any of his men yet. Didn't want to tip my hand. And there's no gossip about it — I've inquired, obliquely, and haven't picked up a word. It's all dark as the grave." He gave Miles a slantwise look. "You say there's news I haven't heard yet? What's it concerning?"

"Concerns your inquiry directly, I should think. Biddle has sacked Lewis Adcock. Constable Braithwaite told me."

"Mr. Adcock?" Rascal was shocked to hear this. *"He sacked the only workman who was willing to do the job?"*

Will blinked. "Why, Adcock's the best carpenter in the district! And he's worked with Biddle off and on for a goodly while.

What did Biddle boot him for?"

"According to the constable, Biddle said he couldn't trust the man. The sacking apparently took place yesterday afternoon and was followed up by some sort of row at the pub last night. One of them challenged the other to step outside to settle the matter — in time-honored tradition, of course. The constable happened along about that time and put an end to the fray. Sent them both packing. But not before Adcock had a fist in the eye and Biddle a cut across his cheek."

Rascal's eyes narrowed. A fight at the pub last night? *I wonder where I was,* he thought, *and why I wasn't informed.* He tried to stay on top of things like this.

But then he remembered that he had gone down to the Hill Top barn to visit his friend Mustard, Mr. Jennings' old yellow dog, and the two of them had stayed up quite late, keeping their eyes on Miss Potter's chicken coop. They had caught one rat, a sneering, filthy, foul-mouthed creature who hinted that he wasn't the only new rat in town. But when pressed for details, he spit in their faces. The rascal was sentenced and summarily executed, without uttering another word. Rascal intended to discuss this matter with Crumpet as soon as he got a chance.

As president of the Village Cat Council, she needed to know that there might be a small rat problem.

"Well, then," Will mused. "P'rhaps I shall drive down to Far Sawrey this afternoon and have a talk with Adcock. If the man knows anything about what Biddle's been up to, he might be ready to tell it. The trouble is, you see, that the evidence I've assembled is entirely circumstantial. There's just the say-so of Biddle's customers, like yourself, who object to the amount of materials they've been billed for. Once the project is completed — or nearly so — and the scrap cleared off, it's very difficult to prove wrongdoing."

"What about the Castle Cottage job? Have you checked the materials there?"

"I've had a look at the lumber that's piled in the yard and compared it to the invoices. Looks square enough to me. It's my thought that Biddle won't try anything funny with Beatrix. They had words when he did the renovations at Hill Top, you know, and she got another contractor to complete the job. She wouldn't have hired Biddle if there'd been anyone else." He frowned. "Come to think of it, we've lost several building contractors in the district in the past few years. Wonder if Biddle had anything to do with that?"

"Driving them out of business, perhaps?" Miles hazarded. He pulled his brows together. "We need to find his cache of stolen materials, Will. It's probably in a barn in somewhere."

"A barn," Rascal said thoughtfully. *"Yes, perhaps. But there are dozens of barns in the neighborhood. it would be like looking for a needle in a haystack."*

"Here's where that aeroplane that Fred Baum and Oscar Wyatt built might have come in handy," Will said with a little laugh. "We could fly around and have a look. Might be easier to spot a cache from the air."

"Aerial reconnaissance, eh?" Miles chuckled. "Don't even mention that aeroplane in Margaret's hearing, Will. My wife hated that thing with a great passion. She was delighted when she heard that it had been destroyed by that storm." He became more serious. "I daresay the Royal Flying Corps wishes they had it, though. There's talk that the Germans are developing their own flying corps. And their own aeroplanes. Fighter aeroplanes, it's said. And bombers."

"Actually," Rascal said, *"that particular aeroplane wasn't destroyed by the storm. It was destroyed by a dragon whom I happen to*

156

know quite well. He —"

"Hush, Rascal," Will rebuked sternly. "We don't need to hear that whining."

"Yes, sir." The little dog shook himself and subsided.

Will turned to Miles. "Getting back to the subject at hand, I'll go and have a talk with Adcock. Perhaps I'll turn up some information that might help us out. If so, I'll let you know." He shifted in his chair, crossing one leg over the other. "But there's something else, Miles, if you don't mind my speaking frankly about a rather personal matter. The truth is, I need some advice." He looked uncomfortably around him and lowered his voice. "I trust you won't share this with Margaret. I shouldn't like —"

"No, of course not," Miles said. "Not if you don't want me to." He grinned mischievously. "What's troubling you, old chap? On pins and needles about this upcoming wedding? Well, let me tell you that marriage is a far more delightful state than I had bargained for. You'll be all right. You'll see."

"But that's just the thing," Will said, and uncrossed his legs. "I'm afraid I *won't* see. I'm beginning to think there will never be a wedding."

There, Rascal said glumly to himself. *What did I tell those badgers? No wedding.*

Miles frowned, and Will cleared his throat. "I say, this is deuced touchy, Woodcock. Don't know quite how to get into it."

Miles gave his friend a sympathetic look. He liked Will Heelis a very great deal. In fact, he had once upon a time rather fancied him as a brother-in-law and had worked as hard as he could to spark some sort of fire between Will and his sister, Dimity. He had never understood why Dim could not seem to recognize that Will Heelis was a splendid catch who could not be faulted for character, good judgment, amiability, and temperament. Instead, she had ended up in the arms of Christopher Kittredge — well, one arm, since the fellow, a war hero, had left the other with the Boers. It was an outcome to which Miles had never quite reconciled himself, for he still preferred Will. Understood him, too, for he and Will were a great deal alike. Both of them were sportsmen, both figures of some authority in the community. And neither of them was comfortable when it came to talking about matters of the heart. The captain might not know much about what went on inside that very intimate organ, but he did know that much.

"Of course it isn't easy," he said in an encouraging tone. "Never easy for me, discussing such things. You'll just have to jump into it, old chap — it'll come. What's bothering you?"

Rascal lay down on Mr. Heelis' foot and looked up at him. *"Please,"* he said softly. *"But do take your time. These things are hard."* Rascal had no business saying this, of course, for he himself stayed away from intimate entanglements. Being Top Dog was job enough.

Thus encouraged, Will took a deep breath. "What's bothering me," he said, "is that it looks as if her parents will never come round. I was with them a fortnight ago, at that house they've taken across the lake, you see. Most wretched afternoon I've ever spent. Worse than being examined for the bar."

"Ah. Questions, were there?" Miles inquired archly. "Probing inquiries about your earnings, prospects, and the like?"

"No, worse luck. I could've managed that sort of thing. Old Mr. Potter would barely grunt — grant you, he's been ill, but he talked bright and sharp enough to his nurse. And Mrs. Potter —" Will shook his head dolefully. "Rude doesn't begin to describe it, I'm afraid. Beatrix was as embarrassed as I, but would, or could, do nothing about it, poor girl. I left as soon as I could decently get away. Felt like a traitor, leaving her to their tender mercies."

"Sorry, old chap," Miles said, puffing on his pipe. "But I don't think this is anything new, is it? They're reputed to have behaved in the same way toward that other fellow Miss Potter was engaged to. Warne, his name was. She was quite devoted to him, even after his death." He eyed his friend through the blue cloud of pipe smoke, remembering that it had been Miss Potter's devotion to Warne that had ended his own romantic intentions. She had made it clear that she was not prepared to consider another suitor. He added delicately, "I believe that she still wears his ring, in fact. You're quite sure that she is ready to —"

"Beatrix? Oh, yes, I'm quite sure." Will waved off the question. "Her engagement to Warne was in aught-five, you know. He's been dead for eight years. As for that ring, I understand her attachment, and her feelings about the Warne family, as well. I have absolutely no objection to her wearing the ring for as long as she likes, and I've told her so." He shook his head. "No, I am rather concerned about her parents, and what they are doing to her, you see. You knew she'd been ill?"

"Ill? Miss Potter?" Rascal blinked. "I hadn't heard."

"Margaret told me," Miles said. "It was serious, was it?"

"Very," Will replied emphatically. "The doctor sent her to bed for most of the spring. Influenza, and it affected her heart. But to speak frankly, I believe that it was the Potters' constant disapproval of our engagement that made her ill. She can't abide discord and hostility, and there was plenty of both in that household. I couldn't go up to London to see her, because that only made for more tension. Her parents just can't seem to understand that they've simply got to allow her to live a life of her own."

Oh, dear, Rascal thought to himself. *What complicated creatures human beings are! It's so much easier to be a dog, or even a cat. Well, maybe not a cat.*

Miles could not say what he was thinking, that most women of his acquaintance, faced with a situation like this, would simply declare that they were old enough to choose for themselves and walk out the door. Which was exactly what Dimity had done when she decided to marry Kittredge. Why Miss Potter could not do the same thing was beyond him.

Will leaned forward, his elbows on his knees. "But there's more, Miles. I . . . well,

I hate to say it, but as if the Potters weren't enough, my family is beginning to stick at the idea."

There, Rascal thought. *Now we're getting to the heart of the matter.* It was what he had heard at the pub the other night.

Miles was taken aback. "Your family objects to your marriage to Miss Potter? You must be joking!"

"I wish I were." Will dropped his voice. "The Heelis family tree is clergy-heavy, as you no doubt know. We've been high church for generations, and proud of it. Doesn't matter to me, of course, for I rarely go to service and don't set much store by religious ceremony. But several of my Anglican cousins object to the fact that the Potters are Dissenters and manifestly low church."

Miles puffed on his pipe. He had met the Heelises and knew how important their religious connections were to them. He wasn't surprised to hear this.

"It's not just religion, either," Will went on. "Another cousin has pointed out that the Potter money — and there's quite a lot of it — comes straight out of those shameful Manchester cotton mills that employed child labor. Never mind that an end was put to the notorious practice some forty years ago, or that her grandfather was enlightened enough to let his child laborers get a few months of schooling. Those mills still have a bad name."

"Ah, yes," Miles said softly, seeing the irony. As he understood it, the Potters had objected to the Warnes because the Warne money came from the publishing business. Now the Heelises were objecting to the Potters because the Potter money came from the calico mills. He shook his head pityingly. It had been his experience that when family members began to debate the relative merits of the intended's family, there was bound to be trouble.

"Yes." Will sighed. "Of course, it's ironic. And of course none of this has anything to do with Beatrix. As far as religion goes, she's fairly neutral, and as for the Potter money being tainted by what went on four or five decades ago — well, that's just plain silly. But put that together with the attitude of her parents, which is making her sick, and . . ."

He sighed again. "I think you can see my dilemma, Miles. All things considered, I'm wondering if it wouldn't be better for her if we broke off the engagement. It's putting her health in jeopardy, and I —"

"Stop," Miles commanded sternly. "Now, you look here, old man. You asked for my advice, and I'm going to give it. If Miss Potter is inclined to marry you, and if you are inclined to marry her, you must not put it off. Tell her that the two of you are going to ignore everyone else and simply go off and do the deed. Privately, by yourselves, if your families can't be supportive or give their consent." He pursed his lips judiciously. "And the sooner the better. Neither of you is getting any younger, you know."

My sentiments precisely, Rascal thought warmly. *This is the best advice Mr. Heelis is likely to get. He should take it.*

"You're right," Will said gloomily. "Yes, of course, that's what should be done. We're both adults and capable of making rational decisions about our lives — and we do, mostly. But I can't put her into that kind of position, you see. She is simply not up to choosing between me and her parents." He sighed heavily. "No, what I am asking is whether I should bow out of the picture myself, since it is our engagement that is causing her so much unhappiness. She —"

There was a loud rapping at the front door, followed by an urgent ringing of the doorbell.

"Excuse me," Miles said. He got up and stepped out into the hall as Margaret hurried past him to answer the door. Looking over her shoulder, he saw Constable Braithwaite standing on the stoop.

"Ah, Constable," he called. "Come in, come in. Margaret, could you possibly —"

"I'll bring more tea," she said, and went toward the kitchen. As she passed, she paused. "Oh, and Miles, Rose Sutton just stopped in with the nicest news! Jeremy and Deirdre have a baby boy, born early this morning. Mother and baby are both very well."

"Splendid!" Miles said, beaming. Jeremy had taken Margaret's place at the village school. An excellent young man, an admired teacher, off to a fine start in life. "We must think of a gift for them." To the constable, he said, "Well, then, Braithwaite — is there something I can do for you?"

"Sorry to bother, Captain," the constable apologized in his thick Lakeland accent. He was a short, stocky man with a florid complexion, his hair and eyebrows very blond. He wore a blue serge uniform with a shiny black belt and polished gold buttons, and a constable's hat, which he hurriedly snatched off. " 'Tis verra important, sir, or I wouldna interrupt."

"Well, come into the library, man," Miles said, "and tell me about it. Mr. Heelis is here," he added. "I was telling him about that scuffle at the pub last night."

"That's why I've come, sir," the constable said, following Miles into the room. His face was grim and set. "Sorry to say, but there's been a death."

"A death?" Miles turned, surprised.

" 'Tis Lewis Adcock," the constable said. "I was sent for by his missus, who found him in t' little shed behind their cottage."

"Adcock?" Will got to his feet.

"Adcock's dead!" Miles frowned, not understanding. "But I thought you said that he only sustained a fist in the eye last night. That you broke up the fight before either he and Biddle could injure one another."

"True, sir," the constable replied, shaking his head. "True, all true. But it wasn't t' fight that did him in, sir. He was found hangin' from t' rafters, wi' a noose around his neck, shortly before eleven thirty this morning." He glanced up at the clock on the wall. "About an hour and a half ago, sir."

There was a moment's shocked silence. Then: "A noose?" Miles asked blankly. "No chance of an accident, I don't suppose."

"Doan't see how, sir," the constable replied. "I took him down, for I felt that was right. Then I closed t' door an' left things as they was, thinkin' you'd want to come

166

straight along an' have a look for yerself." He paused. "Thought it best not to have the passin' bell rung, either, sir. In t' circumstance, that is." Joseph Skead, the sexton at St. Peter's, usually rang the bell for a death — nine strokes for a man, six for a woman, three for a child — so that everyone within earshot knew that someone had passed on. "I left young Jeremy Crosfield to guard t' shed whilst I come to fetch you. He's next door, at Slatestone Cottage."

"I see," said Miles. He went to the door and shouted, "Margaret, we've an emergency. I must be off. Forget about the tea."

"Did Adcock leave a note?" Will asked the constable. He was hoping, of course, for some word that would settle the matter — and perhaps even account for the poor fellow's motive.

"No sign of one, sir," the constable said regretfully. "I gave it a good look all round. Nothin' in his pockets or nearby. Missus said she found none in t' house. She was out for the mornin', y'see. Went to her sister's house right after breakfast to get some veg'tables her sister was givin' her and stayed to work on a quilt they was makin'. Mr. Adcock was fine when she left him, she says. When she come back, he wasn't in t' house. He often worked in t' shed — had a little workshop there — so when she'd made their lunch, she went out, thinkin' to fetch him. That's when . . ." He swallowed. "That's when she found him."

"Wretched, wretched business," Miles said soberly. "Will, you'll come with us to the Adcock place? Given what you've already uncovered, I'd like to have your eyes on this."

"Of course," Will said, all thought of his own uncertainties and tribulations forgotten. He was remembering that the Adcocks had two sons in the Army, and wondering how and when they would be notified. And wondering how Mrs. Adcock would get on by herself, now that her husband was gone. What would she do for money? Would she be able to keep her cottage? "A sad business," he said. "Very sad."

"Aye," agreed the constable somberly, and Miles nodded.

In our own day and age, I am sorry to say, deaths like that of Mr. Adcock are hardly unique events. We encounter reports like the one the constable has just brought on nearly every television newscast and in all the newspapers, but since most of us live in one place and work in another, we seldom know the victim, even if he or she lives just at the other end of the block.

At the time and place of our story, however, such events were uncommon. One can read the *Westmorland Gazette* for those years and find almost no accounts of such deaths — and only rarely a report of a violent act, except in a moment of drunkenness or high passion. Of course, bad things happened there, just as they do everywhere else in this world. People fell from cliffs and ladders, motorcars and wagons went off the road, lightning struck a farmer or a farmer's cow or a farmer's barn, or a man accidentally shot himself or someone else. And when bad things happened, everyone knew the person or persons involved and felt pity for the family's loss and worried for the survivors' welfare and gathered round to ask how they might help.

But a hanging? Oh, my dears, no! Such a thing is a highly unusual and shocking event, and I daresay one could search the newspaper for a ten-year stretch and find not a single similar instance. The news will no doubt cause a great deal of consternation in both the Sawreys, Near and Far.

8
THE VILLAGERS UNDERSTAND

As it did, of course — cause consternation, that is. News travels fast in a village, and bad news travels even faster. Word of the death of Mr. Lewis Adcock was on everyone's lips in less time than it takes to brew a cup of tea and sit down and drink it. Of course, there was good news to celebrate, too, for all were delighted to hear that Deirdre Crosfield had given birth to a little boy, and that mother and babe were both well.

But in a village, bad news is far more interesting than good news, and it was all that the villagers could think of or talk about.

"Adcock, dead?" cried an open-mouthed Lester Barrow, behind the bar in his pub, when George Crook rushed in to tell the story that he had just heard from Major Ragsdale, of Teapot Cottage, next door but one to the Adcocks'. "Well, I nivver! He was just in here last night, drinkin' his reg'lar half-pint. Hung hisse'f, dust tha say, George? Who would've guessed t' man would do such a thing! Went daft all of a sudden-like, did he, maybe?"

"I had a cousin onct," George said, remembering. "Did t' same thing. Mad as a March hare, he was."

"Sad thing, goin' mad," said Lester.

Then he and George nodded. Madness was something they could understand.

"Mr. Adcock killt hisse'f?" Bertha Stubbs repeated, astonished. She stood stock-still in the middle of the lane, frozen in her tracks where Agnes Llewellyn had given her the news. "Why, I jes' this mornin' met t' man, comin' along t' Kendal Road. Right as rain he was, an' fit as a fiddle. Lifted his hat an' said good mornin' to me purty as ye please. An' to think he's standin' face-to-face wi' his Maker reet this verra minute!" She shook her head in bewilderment. "Whatever made him do it, dust tha reckon, Agnes?"

"An' wot'll become of Mrs. Adcock?" Agnes wondered. "Sons in t' Army and no girls to take care o' her, poor thing. Mappen I'll just go home an' stir up a puddin'. She'll be wantin' somethin' sweet to dish

171

up for folk who drop in."

"I'll put on a tatie pot," Bertha said decisively. "She'll be needin' somethin' savory to go wi' that puddin'."

Their contributions determined, the two ladies went on to spread the news. I shouldn't be surprised if every housewife in the two villages contributed a dish, so that the Widow Adcock did not have to cook for quite some time.

Food and consolation was something the women could understand.

"Lewis Adcock, dead?" exclaimed Vicar Samuel Sackett, when his new wife Grace brought the word from the butcher shop in Far Sawrey, where she had heard it from the butcher when she went to buy the week's joint. "Why, he and his wife were sitting in their pew on Sunday, just as they always do. And now this? Dreadful! Appalling!"

The vicar stood up from his desk, where he had been poring over the fascinating list of books Lady Longford had sent him — books from her deceased husband's antiquarian library that she was planning to sell. Of course, the prices she was asking were far too high for the vicar, who was not a wealthy man. But the list held some truly fascinating items, and he knew other book collectors who would be interested.

"Where is my hat, Grace?" the vicar asked helplessly. (He is a dear man, but in times of crisis, he is prone to forgetfulness.) "What have I done with my walking stick? Do I need to take an umbrella? I must go and see poor Mrs. Adcock straightaway. And perhaps you will come with me, my dear. She may need someone to stay with her."

"Of course I'll come with you, Samuel," the vicar's wife said in a comforting tone. "Just let me get my shawl. And your hat and walking stick. We won't need an umbrella. Oh, and I'll take some fresh scones. They'll be wanted to serve with tea when people call."

"You're very understanding, my dear," said the vicar.

Rascal had been on the scene when Constable Braithwaite brought the terrible news to Captain Woodcock, and since he was Top Dog, it fell to him to let the other animals know what had happened. The minute he left Tower Bank House, he went straight to search out Crumpet, who, as president of the Village Cat Council, ought to be informed first.

He found her in the Council shed at the

173

foot of the garden behind Rose Cottage. She had a stub of a pencil in her paw and was staring at a piece of paper with a look of consternation. She glanced up when he came into the shed.

"Oh, there you are, Rascal," she said, relieved to see an animal she knew she could count on. *"I'm afraid I must ask you to recruit some of the village dogs for our police force. As far as cats are concerned, I've come up almost empty-pawed. What we need are several good terriers who —"*

"Police force?" Rascal was confused. *"But we have a constable. And anyway, I don't think even our Constable Braithwaite could have prevented it. He can't be everywhere at once, you know."* And he told her what had happened.

Crumpet's consternation changed to horror when she heard Rascal's astonishing news. Mr. Adcock lived in Far Sawrey and hence was not well known in their village. But he had worked at Hill Top Farm and more recently at Castle Cottage, so the village animals knew him by sight. As for taking his own life — well, that was something that no right-thinking animal would ever do, for to animals, life is very precious. Animals kill, yes, but always with a reason and a purpose: as necessary food, or in defense of oneself or one's family. An animal could never kill himself. It was unthinkable. Utterly unthinkable.

Neither Crumpet nor Rascal could understand how this might have happened.

And so it went, from one person to another and one household to another, throughout the two villages. And always, in every exchange of this terrible news, each person had his or her own idea about why Mr. Adcock had done this terrible thing. There had to be an explanation, you see, for such an unthinkable action couldn't just happen. To be understood, it had to have a cause. And everyone could think of at least one.

"I'll wager t'was losin' his place that drove t' poor fellow to it," George Crook said to Mr. Llewellyn, who had brought his big white horse to the smithy for new shoes all around. "Biddle sacked him yest'idday, ye know. Man his age, well up in years, Adcock might've figgered he'd not find other work, even though he were a reet good carpenter. Maybe t' notion drove him to despair."

Holding his horse as George Crook applied the new shoe, Mr. Llewellyn agreed. And Roger Dowling and Tom Tremblay, watching the shoeing operation, nodded their heads in sober agreement. All of these men, at some point in their lives, had known the awful emptiness of losing a place and remembered the frightening consequences that had befallen them and their families. Lewis Adcock had been past sixty and had worked as a carpenter for over forty years. If he had been driven to despair by the prospect of having no work, they understood why. Not a man amongst them could find it in his heart to cast blame upon him for doing what he did.

They understood.

But Lydia Dowling, behind the counter at the village shop, held a much darker view of Mr. Adcock's motive.

"Person'ly, I think he done it to keep from bein' accused outright of thievin'," she remarked to her niece, Gladys, who helped in the shop on Tuesdays and Thursdays. "I heard from Hannah Braithwaite that Mr. Biddle had Mr. Adcock dead to rights. He threatened to call in t' constable if Mr. Adcock didn't return wot he stole. But mappen he had already sold it an' couldna give it back."

Gladys, who was winding loose ribbons onto little cards and pinning the ends, was shocked by this news. "What did he steal?" she wanted to know.

"Who'd he steal it from?" Rose Sutton asked from the other side of the counter. Rose, the wife of the village veterinary surgeon, had come into the shop to buy a sausage, a quart of paraffin for the lamps, a package of tea, and some penny candies for the many Sutton children. She was also buying a skein of soft, hand-spun wool yarn, blue, to knit a cap for Deirdre Crosfield's new baby.

Regrettably, Lydia was unable to answer either of these questions, since Hannah Braithwaite hadn't told her. Still, the three women understood the seriousness of the situation. An accusation of this kind was a terrible thing. The stigma might linger for a lifetime and infect not only the thief, but the thief's wife and children, as well. Mr. Adcock might not have been able to endure the thought of what his friends and neighbors would say if Mr. Biddle reported his theft and charges were brought. It would have been an inescapable disgrace.

They understood.

The vicar's wife, however, had heard an entirely different story, and it had nothing to do with the loss of a job or an accusation of theft. It had to do with money, or the lack thereof, and with illness.

"The butcher says that the Adcocks have been in financial difficulties for some time," Grace Sackett told her husband, as they left the Vicarage and walked along the lane that led in the direction of Far Sawrey. The summer flowers bloomed on either side, and the skylark flew high in the blue air, saying his matins. It was too beautiful a day to be undertaking such a sad errand.

"Financial difficulties?" the vicar asked, taking his wife's arm and wondering how he had managed without her for so many years.

"Yes, I'm afraid so. Mrs. Adcock has been ill this past year, and there have been a great many doctor bills. They haven't been able to pay the butcher for over a month. He is a patient man and tries to work with people, but he's got his own family to think of. He finally had to tell her that he could no longer supply them with meat. He said she cried and begged him not to do it — she was simply desperate, for apparently they owe the greengrocer, as well." She paused, sighing. "Do you suppose that's why Mr. Adcock did what he did, Samuel?"

"I hope not, my dear," said the vicar. "I should think it a terrible thing if a man ended his life because of money. If we had only known that the Adcocks were in such dire straits, we might have been able to help."

"I don't see how," his wife replied sensibly. "We could hardly have paid their meat bill. But p'rhaps we might have found some other way to help."

"Well, we can certainly ask if Mrs. Adcock needs assistance with the funeral expenses," the vicar said. "I am sure our congregation will rally round." And then he was stricken, for he had suddenly realized that Mr. Adcock, having taken his own life, could not be buried with the full service of the Church. In the old days, the body was not permitted to be buried within the church yard, but that was no longer the case. Still, the thought of omitting the sacred service chilled him to the bone.

"I fear," he said, "that we shall not be able to perform the full rite."

His wife, however, felt quite differently. "I am very sure," she said, in her most positive tone, "that our congregation will want Mr. Adcock to be buried with the same rites granted to every deceased. It would be quite wrong to do otherwise, Samuel."

"I must consult with the deacons," the vicar muttered.

"Do that," his wife said crisply. "I am sure they will agree." She fell silent for a moment, then added in a softer voice, "The Adcocks were married for over forty years. It will be so hard for her without him." She laid her gloved hand over his, and the vicar clutched her arm a little more tightly.

They understood.

It wasn't long before everyone had heard the news. Lydia Dowling discussed her understanding of Mr. Adcock's motive (that he had killed himself rather than face an accusation of theft) with every customer who came into the village shop, whilst Rose Sutton took this news back to her husband's surgery and shared it with every client who came in that afternoon, all of whom took it home to their families. Gladys told the same story to Lucy Skead at the post office when she went to drop off the post, and Lucy told it to each one who came in for the post the rest of the afternoon and the entire next day as well.

In the smithy, George Crook told everyone who dropped in that he thought Mr. Adcock had ended his life because he had lost his place, whilst next door at the joinery, Roger Dowling offered the same opinion to his customers.

And down in Far Sawrey, the butcher was heard to say as he handed the white-wrapped packages of meat over his counter that it was a great pity that the Adcocks had fallen on such hard times that Mr. Adcock had lost heart and done himself in.

By teatime, every single person in the two villages knew exactly what had happened that day.

They all were sure that they knew exactly why.

And they all understood.

9

MISS POTTER LEARNS
THE NEWS

When we last saw Miss Potter, she had just left Castle Cottage (without looking into the barn, I am glad to say). She was feeling low and dispirited, so very low that she had entirely given up the idea of talking to Mr. Biddle about her concerns. In fact, she was feeling so very dejected that she decided that she would take a long walk, instead of going straight home. It had always been her experience that walking cured a great many ills and ailments, so in that frame of mind, she went through the pasture to Wilfin Beck, a willow-bordered stream that ran along the eastern edge of Castle Farm. When she reached the stream, she loitered along, allowing the lulling music of the little brook and the gentle melodies of the birds to wash over her, raising her spirits and lightening her mood.

It had been a dry summer so far, which was good news for the farmers who wanted to cut their hay but not such good news for Wilfin Beck, which had shrunk down to a dawdling silver trickle instead of rushing joyfully along in a high-spirited hurry down to Windermere and then on to Newby Bridge. There it would become the River Leven and flow for a short eight miles past Backbarrow, where it foamed and frolicked in a delighted dance over a rocky falls. And thence to Greenodd, where wooden sailing ships used to be built, and after that into the quiet waters of Morecambe Bay, where it is said that the tides come in as fast as a horse can run, and finally into the rolling, tumbling Irish Sea. But there was still enough water in the beck to refresh the thirsty water ouzles and the little gray dippers happily splashing in the shallows, as well as offer a drink to Miss Potter's Herdwick ewes, Tibbie and Queenie, who brought their March lambs to play along the green banks.

These ewes — the senior sheep in Miss Potter's flock — had enjoyed living at Hill Top, but now that they had moved to the Castle Farm pasture, they loved it just as well. They were "heafed" to it, as it is said in the Lakes: that is, the pasture had become their natural home. In the old days, when there were far fewer stone fences than there are now, the Herdwick sheep had been given free range upon the fell-sides and allowed to come and go as they liked, for they had an unerring sense of direction and required neither shepherd nor bellwether to bring them home again.

On their travels, Herdwicks were always encountering other Herdwicks from places as far away as Borrowdale or Dungeon Gyll or even Seathwaite Tarn, and they were in the habit of trading the latest news. The other animals always said that Herdwicks were better for the local news than newspapers, for they could tell you the name of the sheep who had produced the prizewinning fleece at the Appleby Fair, or the state of the grazing on the other side of Coniston Water, or the names of the lambs that were born to this or that ewe — information that the newspapers never carried.

Today, the ewes were all atwitter about a local birth, a local death, and a gang of thieves. They had learnt about these events from Fritz the Ferret, who lived in a bank-side burrow (very nicely appointed, for Fritz was a ferret with an artistic bent) not far away. Fritz had heard the news from his friend Max the Manx, the black cat who lived with Major Ragsdale in Teapot Cottage, which is next door to Slatestone Cottage (where Jeremy and Deirdre Crosfield's new baby entered this world early that same day) and next door but one to the Adcocks' (where poor Mr. Adcock left it). About the thieves, Fritz could tell the sheep little, except to say that he had heard that they managed to break into quite a few cottages and barns and hen coops in Near Sawrey.

The sheep were overjoyed with the announcement of the baby's arrival.

" 'Tis a joy to hear thaaat Jeremy aaand Deirdre haaave a boy," bleated Tibbie to Queenie. The two of them were acquainted with both young parents. Jeremy was a talented artist (according to Miss Potter), and as a lad, he had often sketched the Herdwicks. And Deirdre, who worked for Mr. and Mrs. Sutton, always brought the large flock of Sutton children to Hill Top Farm to admire the new spring lambs, which of course endeared her to the lambs' mamas.

"But a calaaamity for the Aaadocks," baaed Queenie in reply. She lowered her head and butted a little lamb who was playing too rough with his sister. "Why? Why would he do such a saaad thing?" Like Crumpet and Rascal, the sheep could not comprehend the idea of suicide.

"I don't suppose we'll ever know," Queenie

said sadly. *"Humaaans behave in baaaffling ways."* She glanced up. *"Oh, look, Tibbie — it's Miss Potter, come to see us!"*

And so it was. Miss Potter, walking along the footpath beside the beck, wearing a sad and pensive look. But when she saw the Herdwicks, a smile lightened her face.

"Why, hello there, ladies!" she said, as her two favorite ewes came eagerly forward to greet her. She loved these remarkably sturdy little creatures, whose ancestors had arrived in the north of England with the Viking settlers many centuries before. It didn't matter to Beatrix that their fleece was coarse and scratchy, for it could be spun into a long-wearing yarn that was perfectly suited to wool carpets and nearly weatherproof tweeds. What she liked best, though, was the Herdwicks' gentle, sweet personalities. They always made her feel better — as they did today, licking her hands with their raspy tongues, pushing playfully against her, bleating inquisitively.

"Isn't it good news aaabout Jeremy aaand Deirdre's babe, Miss Potter?"

"Isn't it saaad about Mr. Adcock, Miss Potter? Whaaat do you suppose haaappened?"

Wishing she could understand what her friends were saying and answer them back in their own language, Beatrix stroked the soft ears, pulled a few raspy burrs out of their fleece, and touched their dear, sheepish faces. But even though she couldn't make out what they wanted to tell her, the sweet sound of their voices made her feel immeasurably better, as if someone had just given her a large spoonful of feel-good medicine and a comforting there-there-my-dear kiss on the forehead. And I daresay that you and I would feel exactly the same way, for a world that has woolly sheep in it, and joyful white lambs and a wide sweep of sweet green grass and a clear, happy brook with splashing water ouzels and cheerful dippers — well, a world like that couldn't be so very bad, now, could it?

A woman's voice broke into her thoughts. "Miss Potter! Oh, Miss Potter, such good news — I have wonderful news!"

Beatrix looked up to see a familiar figure in a homespun brown dress and white apron, waving her blue bonnet as she hurried along the path, almost at a run. It was Jane Crosfield, Jeremy's aunt, an expert spinner and weaver who had produced the woolen cloth for Beatrix's new tweed suit. Jane lived at Holly How Farm, just along the path a little way.

"Hello, Jane," Beatrix said, and guessed at

the news from the look on her friend's face. "Has the baby arrived?"

"It's a boy, Miss Potter! Jeremy and Deirdre have a fine, healthy baby boy, born this mornin' quite early. I've just left 'em — mother and baby are both well," she added breathlessly. "He has his mum's red hair an' he's ever so sweet an' fat an' round — a perfect little lamb."

"A perfect little laaamb," bleated Tibbie, beaming. *"Naaaturally."*

"I think he should be called Laaambie-Pie," replied Queenie, for that was the name she had given to her lamb this spring.

"Oh, Jane, how wonderful!" Beatrix breathed. She was thrilled, although if she were quite, quite honest, she would have to admit to an uncomfortably sharp twist of envy somewhere deep down inside. Deirdre, just a schoolgirl when Beatrix had first met her, was happily married and a mother now, while she herself was still —

But this was a selfish and ungenerous thought, and Beatrix shoved it aside. "I'm walking in that direction," she said. "Would it be too soon for me to drop in?" She didn't have a gift to take — that would have to come later — but she could pick some flowers.

"I'm sure they'd be pleased to see you an'

to show off their new babe," Jane said. She paused, and her face grew serious. "You've heard about Mr. Adcock, now, have you?"

"Yes, I've heard," Beatrix said, "and I think it a great shame. Truly, I can't imagine why Mr. Biddle would do such a thing, Jane. Mr. Adcock worked for me last year, and I have found him to be —"

She was stopped by the horrified expression on Jane's face.

"Mr. Biddle?" Jane cried, her hand going to her mouth. "Oh, no! He didn't have anythin' to do with it, Miss Potter! Nor him nor nobody else. 'Twas all Mr. Adcock's very own doin', although how any man could bring himself to do such a bad thing, I doan't know."

"Yes," Queenie baaed sorrowfully. *"A very baaad thing."*

"Do such a — Whatever are you talking about, Jane?" Beatrix asked, frowning. Of course, she was thinking about what Hannah Braithwaite had told her earlier that afternoon, that Mr. Biddle had sacked Mr. Adcock, saying he couldn't be trusted. Had Mr. Adcock stolen something? What had he done?

"Why, t' poor man has killt himself, Miss Potter," Jane said, very soberly. "Mrs. Adcock found him this mornin', in t' shed at t' foot of the garden. The Adcocks live just next door to Jeremy and Deirdre at Slatestone Cottage, which is how I know about it. I saw Constable Braithwaite comin' out of Mrs. Adcock's house just a little while ago. T' constable is who told me. I went in to see Mrs. Adcock and say a comfortin' word, an' it's true."

"Killed himself?" Beatrix pulled in her breath, stunned nearly speechless. "Why, I can't believe it, Jane!"

"So very saaad," Tibbie and Queenie bleated in unison. *"Saaad, saaad!"*

Jane sighed heavily. "What Mrs. Adcock'll do now, I doan't know. Poor thing, her. Poor thing!" She lifted her apron to her eyes and began to cry.

Beatrix put her arm around Jane's shoulders, and they stood there for a few moments in a shared sadness. And then, since there really was nothing more to say, they bade each other goodbye, Jane going home to Holly How Farm and Beatrix toward Far Sawrey, no longer loitering but walking faster, now that she had a destination and a purpose.

But she was even more sorely torn in spirit than before, and not even the chatter of Wilfin Beck could help. For whilst she was delighted by the birth of a fine, healthy boy,

190

she was at the same time astonished and saddened to hear about the death of Mr. Adcock, a quiet, mild-mannered man whom she had genuinely liked. And she was wishing that she had pressed Jane for more details.

How? When? Why? Was anyone there when it happened?

But mostly why, why, why?

10

AT THE ADCOCKS' COTTAGE: THE INVESTIGATION BEGINS

Since Captain Woodcock felt that time was of the essence in the investigation of Mr. Adcock's death, he decided to drive the Rolls-Royce. But the engine didn't want to go, and it took nearly fifteen minutes of cranking and tinkering and cranking again before he could reverse the automobile out of its place in his stable-cum-garage and invite the constable to jump in beside him. Meanwhile, Will Heelis had kicked his motorcycle into life and driven on ahead, proving once more (at least to Will's satisfaction) that the motorcycle was a more efficient vehicle than an automobile.

The captain's sleek, teal-blue motorcar had attracted enormous attention when he purchased it a few years before. A few "forward-thinking" villagers had greeted it with enthusiasm, but most regarded the thing with fear and loathing. Those who drove plodding plow-horses hitched to farm wagons gloomily predicted that their animals would be stampeded off the roads by hordes of these monstrous machines, racketing along at speeds approaching an unimaginable twelve or thirteen miles an hour. Mothers worried that automobiles would spew out choking exhaust smoke, create clouds of dust, and frighten the village chickens and dogs and cats — not to mention the children. And what would happen if the chickens and dogs and cats and children didn't get out of the road? Would they be run down mercilessly, limbs mangled, lives lost forever? And why would anyone be in such a beastly hurry, anyway? The place they were going would still be there when they arrived, wouldn't it? And so on and so forth.

Constable Braithwaite waged his own war against the automobiles, flagging them down and lecturing the drivers severely about the dangers of speeding and taking a secret pleasure in the sight of a motorcar idled beside the lane with a punctured tyre or an engine breakdown. But even he had to admit that a motorcar came in handy now and again, especially when on official business. So he climbed into the passenger seat beside the captain and put his tall blue constable's hat on the floor between his feet so that the wind wouldn't blow it off his head whilst they rattled along the road to Far Sawrey. And in truth they arrived in a fraction of the time it had taken him to walk the distance, if you don't count the time it took to persuade the Rolls to start.

Will Heelis was waiting beside his motorcycle when the captain's motorcar arrived at the Adcock cottage. The constable put his hat back on, and Captain Woodcock led them up to the door, where he knocked gently. Since everyone in the district knew who he was, and Mr. Heelis as well, there was no need for introductions.

"I'm very sorry to trouble you, Mrs. Adcock," he said to the tear-stained widow, a woman in her sixties with a bent back and gray hair. "The constable and Mr. Heelis and I should like to go around to the shed now, if you don't mind."

She nodded wordlessly, and the three took the path to the back garden, where they were greeted by a tall, good-looking young man, pacing nervously. A black cat sat just off the path, under a quince bush, keeping an eye on things.

"Ah, there you are, Captain," the young man said with a relieved look.

"At last," said the cat. *"I was wondering what was keeping them."* He was Max the Manx,

a rather ironical cat. He lived next door but one, at Teapot Cottage, with Major Ragsdale.

"Likely the motorcar wouldn't go," Rascal said. He was slightly out of breath, having run the whole way from Near Sawrey to Far Sawrey, after his brief conversation with Crumpet. *"That happens a good deal of the time."*

"Motorcars," sniffed Max. *"Filthy machines. As bad as locomotives. Nothing but smoke and dust."*

"Ssh," said Rascal. *"Let's listen."*

"Thank you for keeping watch, Jeremy," the captain said, and extended his hand. "And please accept my congratulations. Mrs. Woodcock tells me that you and your wife have a fine young lad."

"My congratulations as well, Jeremy," Will said heartily. He remembered the young man as a boy, studious and more thoughtful than the other village chaps, and now grown up to be a schoolmaster, and a good one, too, much beloved by his students.

Jeremy pushed his red-brown hair out of his eyes, smiling, and shook their hands. "Yes, indeed. Born bright and early this morning, and healthy as a young horse. He has a strong pair of lungs, too, as his mother and the neighbors will tell you."

"And they've named him Rascal," the little dog whispered proudly to Max.

"I doubt that," Max said ironically. *"They wouldn't name their child for a dog."*

"But it's true," Rascal protested. *"The Professor said so."*

Max rolled his eyes. *"Oh, well, the Professor,"* he said with heavy sarcasm. *"If the owl says so, then of course it must be true."*

Jeremy lowered his voice and glanced around, making sure they were alone. "Look. I've found something out, and I feel I need to let you know about it. May have something to do with what happened here."

"Indeed," the captain said, matching his tone to Jeremy's. "What is it?"

"It has to do with that man," said the cat.

"What man?" Rascal asked.

"The visitor," Max replied. *"Here. In the garden."*

"There was a fellow here this morning," Jeremy replied. "Deirdre's friend Gilly Harmsworth saw him. Gilly is here to help with the birth, you see. Aunt Jane was here, too, but she was in the kitchen making some breakfast for me, and Gilly was with Deirdre. Gilly happened to glance out the bedroom window — it was just daylight, right after the baby was born — and saw him, coming down the path to the shed. She didn't think to mention it until I told her about poor Mr. Adcock."

"It wasn't Mr. Adcock?" the captain asked.

Jeremy shook his head. "Gilly says no. She doesn't know the Adcocks well, but she says she would've recognized Mr. Adcock. She guessed that the stranger might be one of the Adcock sons, home from the Army, in which case there was nothing odd about him being out in the garden so early. But that can't be the case. Both of the Adcock boys are soldiering in India."

"About what time would you say this was?" the constable asked, taking out a small notebook and a pencil.

"Make it six thirty," Jeremy replied. "As I said, the sun was just rising."

"Six thirty-five," put in Max authoritatively. *"I had just finished my breakfast and was beginning my morning patrol of the neighborhood."*

"And she didn't see the fellow go into the shed or leave it?" Will asked.

"I saw him go into the shed," Max volunteered. *"He didn't come out while I was in the vicinity, however."*

"Who was it?" Rascal asked, but Max could only shrug.

"She said she didn't see anything after

197

that," Jeremy replied. "The baby had been born a little earlier. As you can imagine, everyone was busy. Dr. Butters got here just in time for the birth," he added. "Mrs. Margrove had twins last night, or he would've been here sooner."

"Anything else?" the captain asked.

"I think that's it," Jeremy replied. "If you'd like to talk to Gilly, she'll be here for another day or two. To help out." He grinned bashfully. "It turns out that women are much better at looking after babies. But I suppose I'll learn."

"Oh, you'll learn, all right," the constable said gruffly, and clapped the young man on the shoulder. "Speakin' as the father o' three, I can guarantee that." He cocked his head. "And that's your babe cryin' now, I'll warrant."

"I'll be off, then," Jeremy said. "Shall I tell Gilly to expect you?"

"Do that, please," the captain replied. When Jeremy had gone, he said, "Well, gentlemen, I think we must have a look."

Built against the back fence, the wooden shed was small and dark. The only window was set in the wall beside the door, its light nearly obscured by the vine that grew over it. The square space contained a wooden workbench, a wall rack filled with carpenter's tools, and a small, unfinished piece of cabinetry on the bench. Mr. Adcock's body, covered with a muslin sheet, lay on the dirt floor. A rope noose hung limply from a rafter. A wooden crate lay tipped on its side.

"Doesn't take much to reconstruct the event," the captain said, after they had looked around. "Poor chap must have looped the rope over the rafter and around his neck, then kicked over the box."

"That's what it looks like," Rascal said to Max, as the two of them watched from the door.

"My conclusion, as well, sir," the constable said gruffly. "But what I want to know is why. Why would he do such a thing?"

"And what about this fellow who was seen in the garden?" Will put in.

"As to why," the captain said, "I suppose he might have been dejected over getting the sack. A man his age, it wouldn't be easy to find other work, especially if Biddle gave him a bad character." He looked at the constable. "Biddle told you that he wasn't trustworthy, you said?"

"Aye," the constable said. "He wouldn't give me any details, but I got t' idea that there was some sort of theft involved. A tool, maybe, or some lumber." He sighed. "I happen to know that t' Adcocks have

199

fallen on hard times. Mrs. Adcock has been sick, and there's been medicine and doctor bills. My brother says he had to tell them they'd have no more meat from him. He was sorry, but he had to do it." The constable's brother, Charlie Braithwaite, was the butcher.

"That's very sad," Will said quietly, and Rascal agreed. Animals don't have to worry about paying the butcher or the doctor, but they understand and commiserate with humans who do.

The captain became brisk. "Well, now, gentlemen, let's review the situation as we know it so far. The young woman looks out of the window at six thirty this morning and sees a strange fellow in the garden. Mrs. Adcock goes to her sister's house around nine thirty — her husband is alive and well at the time — and is gone until eleven thirty. She assumes her husband is working here in the shed, comes to tell him that lunch is ready, and finds the poor fellow dead. She summons Constable Braithwaite, who takes down the body." Frowning, he looked from Will to the constable. "Does that about sum it up?"

"I b'lieve so, sir," the constable said. " 'Tis sad, but t' facts are as t' facts are."

"One can't argue with facts," Rascal agreed.

"As long as one knows what the facts really are," Max remarked in an acerbic tone.

"Are you suggesting that there are other facts?" Rascal asked, narrowing his eyes.

"I'm not suggesting anything," Max said dryly. *"I leave that to the captain and the constable. However, there may be a rat in the woodpile somewhere."*

"What's that supposed to mean?" Rascal demanded, by now thoroughly confused.

"Just speaking figuratively, old boy," Max replied.

Will Heelis looked down at the sheeted form. "Has Butters been sent for? The facts may seem indisputable, but I'm sure this calls for an autopsy." He paused. "Especially since we don't know who this fellow in the garden was and what he had to do with the death. But perhaps Mrs. Adcock can tell us."

"Aye, t' doctor's been summoned," the constable replied, putting his notebook back into his pocket. "He was in surgery, but he'll be along when he can."

As if he had been conjured by their mention of his name, Dr. Butters himself opened the shed door and came in, carrying his scuffed leather bag. He was a tall man, somewhat stooped, with reddish hair and a gingery moustache, not quite so thin and gaunt as he had been before he married Mrs. Butters several years before. One of the most beloved men in the district, he lived in Hawkshead and had his surgery there.

"Hullo, Butters," the captain said. "Thank you for coming. We have what appears to be a suicide, I'm afraid."

The doctor looked up at the dangling noose and down at the sheet-covered figure. "A birth next door this morning, a death here this afternoon," he said, sighing heavily. "The good Lord giveth and the good Lord taketh away. Blessed be the name of the Lord." He pulled off his coat. "Well, let's see what we have here."

After a few moments of careful examination, he looked up at the three men gathered around him. "Who took this fellow down?" he asked.

There was a silence. Then, "I did," the constable admitted. "Didn't feel seemly like, leavin' him up there. He's a slight man — I could manage." He glanced anxiously to the captain, then back to the doctor. "Did I do wrong?"

"Not unless you dropped him and banged his head against something with a sharp edge," the doctor replied curtly. "And bruised his eye."

"Oh, sir, no, sir!" the constable protested horrified. "Oh, no, I didn't do no such thing! He got t' black eye from Mr. Biddle, in a fight outside t' pub last night. Dunno about t' other. His head, you say? He didn't get that in t' fight, I doan't b'lieve."

Will knelt down beside the doctor. "Why are you asking, Butters? What have you found?"

"This," the doctor said, pointing to a deep, two-inch gash in Mr. Adcock's scalp, above his right ear. He glanced up at the constable. "That's all right, Braithwaite. I'm sure you had nothing to do with this wound. But we'll need to get him to my surgery where I can examine him more closely. I want to be sure about the cause of death before I issue a death certificate." He stood up, dusting his hands. "From the look of the bleeding, I'd hazard a guess that it happened before he died — but not long before. Not, I should say, last night."

"Ah," the captain said regretfully. "That means —"

"Yes," Dr. Butters said. "It means that he was hit by something hard enough to break the skin — and perhaps render him unconscious. You might look around and see if you can find the weapon that was used."

"You don't think he might have . . . well,

stumbled and hit his head against something?" Will asked tentatively.

"I rather doubt it," the doctor replied. "But as I say, I'll have a closer look and let you know. Now, let's see what we can do about getting this poor fellow to Hawkshead. My motorcar is parked in front of the cottage." The doctor had put his old horse out to pasture the previous year and bought an automobile that occasionally doubled as an ambulance — or a hearse.

"The constable and I can handle that," Will said.

"Good," the doctor replied. "I'll have a look in on Mrs. Adcock, then. She hasn't been well, you know."

"I'll go with you," the captain said. "I want to ask her something." To Will, he said, "When you've moved the body, you might have a word with the girl — Gilly Harmsworth. Find out if she thinks she might recognize the fellow if she saw him again."

"Of course," Will said.

The captain and the doctor walked to the house. As they went, the captain told the doctor about the report of the stranger seen in the garden, adding, "I'm wondering whether you saw anyone when you were here to deliver the Crosfield baby."

"Afraid not," the doctor replied. "I can

tell you that there was neither person nor vehicle in sight when I arrived or when I left." He chuckled ruefully. "Babies seem to come just before sunrise, you know. Except for Mrs. Margrove's, of course. That lady always delivers hers around three a.m. Twins, this time."

A few moments later, they were knocking at the cottage door and apologizing to Mrs. Adcock for another intrusion. The doctor explained that he needed to take her husband's body to Hawkshead and would release it just as soon as he could. She gave her consent, and Dr. Butters excused himself to get on with the business.

When he had gone, the captain said quietly, "I wonder, Mrs. Adcock — did you happen to notice anyone in your garden early this morning? Before breakfast, that is."

Mrs. Adcock, her eyes red-rimmed, looked at him blankly. "In our garden? Why in t' world would anybody be walkin' around in our garden afore breakfast? Or any other time, for that matter."

"So you didn't see anyone? Anyone at all?"

"No, o' course not."

The captain persisted. "Did Mr. Adcock mention a plan to meet or talk with anyone today? Early or late or whenever?"

"Well, yes, he did," Mrs. Adcock said slowly. "He said he would go with me to talk to t' butcher after lunch. He had a bit of money put away, you see, and he thought we'd best use it to pay part of the butcher bill, so we could keep on gettin' meat."

The captain gave her a sympathetic look. "Besides the butcher, anyone else?" He cleared his throat. "Mr. Biddle, p'rhaps?"

She made a sharp clicking sound with her tongue against her teeth. "An' why should Mr. Adcock be wantin' to see Biddle after t' terrible trouble he's caused us?" she asked fiercely.

"What trouble is that?" the captain asked.

"Why, sackin' Mr. Adcock!" she exclaimed. "An' sayin' he was a thief! My husband nivver in t' world took nothin' that di'n't belong to him, whatever Biddle may say." She burst into a storm of angry weeping.

The captain waited until she was calmer. "Did your husband tell you what Biddle believed he might have stolen?"

Mrs. Adcock shook her head despairingly. "No more he did, for Biddle wouldn't tell *him.* Just kept pushin' him with his hand an' sayin' over 'n' over that he had to give it back, an' 'twas worth a pot of money." She looked up at him, her eyes swimming with tears. "But how could Mr. Adcock give it back when he hadn't took it in t' first place?"

"Mr. Biddle was pushing him?"

"Right. An' sayin' that if he di'n't return it, he'd have to go to gaol. If you don't b'lieve me, ask Maguire, that supervisor o' Biddle's. He was there when it happened." She reached for a handkerchief and began to mop her eyes. "I doan't know how I'm ever goin' to tell t' boys what's been done here."

Feeling that there was nothing more to be learned from the widow, Captain Woodcock said his goodbyes and was letting himself out when he encountered Vicar Sackett and his new wife coming up the path to the house.

"Ah, Captain," said the vicar sadly. "You've spoken to Mrs. Adcock?"

"Just now," the captain said, and tipped his hat to Mrs. Sackett. "She's rather broken up, I'm afraid."

"Poor thing," Mrs. Sackett said. "I am so sorry for her."

The vicar frowned. "You've been investigating, I take it," he said to the captain. "Have you come to any conclusions?" He cleared his throat. "As I understand it, this is not . . . er, a natural death. I'm asking because there will be a question about the burial service that will have to be used."

"Samuel," his wife remonstrated. "I thought we settled that."

"Easier said than done, my dear," the vicar replied. "It is not entirely in our hands, you know. Have you learnt anything definitive, Captain?"

The captain recognized the vicar's dilemma, but there was nothing he could do about it — yet. He shook his head. "The investigation is going forward. I'm afraid that is the most I can say at this point."

And with that, the vicar had to be content.

11
AT SLATESTONE COTTAGE: MR. HEELIS HAS A FEW QUESTIONS

At this same moment, on the other side of the hedge, a visitor was knocking at the door of Slatestone Cottage.

"Why, Miss Potter!" Jeremy exclaimed, answering the knock. "How very nice of you to come! Deirdre will be delighted."

"I hope I'm not intruding," Beatrix said, handing her bouquet of wildflowers, ferns, and grasses to Jeremy. "I picked these along the way. I thought Deirdre might like to have them. And of course, I want to see the new baby — if it's not too soon. If it is, I'll come back another time."

"May I come in, too?" Rascal said from behind Miss Potter's skirts. *"I want to meet my namesake!"*

"Of course it's not too soon," Jeremy assured her. "It's good to see you." He looked down. "And you've brought Rascal! Hullo, there, old chap! Come in, both of you."

"Delighted," Rascal barked, and followed

Miss Potter to the bedroom.

In a moment, Beatrix was saying hello to Deirdre and cooing over the blanket-wrapped baby the new mother held in her arms. Deirdre's carroty-red hair was caught up on top of her neck, loose tendrils curling down, and the freckles sprinkled liberally across her nose and cheeks made her look all of fourteen years old. But of course she was a young woman now, Beatrix reminded herself, and a mother — and all the more capable for having minded the young Suttons for so many years. Deirdre already had more experience at bringing up babies than many mothers earn in an entire lifetime.

Beatrix couldn't help smiling as she looked down at the cherubic face peeking out of the blanket. "He's beautiful," she said, quite honestly. She did not believe, as some people did, that all babies were beautiful, but this one certainly was. At that moment, the baby yawned and opened his eyes. "Oh, how sweet!" she exclaimed, touching the little nose with the tip of her finger. "He has his father's eyes, don't you think?"

Into her mind flashed the picture of young Jeremy as she had first seen him, a slightly built, barefoot boy, dressed in a faded blue shirt and ragged britches, with a scrap of paper and a piece of burnt coal, drawing a picture of his cat. He was grown up now, an accomplished artist, an admired teacher, and a father. Beatrix was very proud of him — although she couldn't help wishing, just a little, that he had taken at least one year at Cambridge, as both she and Major Kittredge had wanted. But if he had, there wouldn't be this baby.

Jeremy chuckled. "He has my eyes, yes, but his mother's hair." He set the vase full of Beatrix's flowers on the stand beside the bed.

"Red as a carrot, I'm sure," Rascal said. *"Tell us what you've named him."*

"See?" Deirdre pulled off the tiny knit cap and Beatrix saw that yes, indeed, little Jeremy's head was covered by carroty-red hair, the same shade as Deirdre's. The new mother looked up at her husband, her eyes wet. "He's perfect," she whispered.

"Of course he is," Jeremy replied with a smile. "He's ours. That makes him perfect, wouldn't you say?"

"And what's his name?" Beatrix asked. "I should have asked your aunt, but I was so excited I forgot."

"Rascal!" Rascal barked excitedly, and stood up on his hind legs, his forepaws raised. He did a little dance. *"They've named him after me!"*

"We're calling the dear little rascal Jeremy," Deirdre said, and dropped a kiss on the baby's head.

There was a silence. *"Oh,"* Rascal said, feeling suddenly very foolish. *"Oh, I see."*

Jeremy took the dog's forepaws in his hands and danced with him. "Now we have two little rascals," he said. "And when baby Jeremy is a bit older, you can play with him and go with us on our rambles through the woods and fells. What do you think of that, Rascal?"

"I think that's splendid," Rascal said, and meant it.

Jeremy turned back to Deirdre. "Now you must get some sleep, my dear." He bent and kissed his wife, then straightened. "I have something to show you, Miss Potter."

"I think I'll stay and watch the baby," Rascal said. *"We wouldn't want anything to happen to him, now would we?"* And he lay down beside the bed, his muzzle on his paws.

A moment later, Beatrix was standing in front of an easel that was placed near a window for good light. An array of artist's brushes and paints lay on the small table beside the easel, which displayed a large painting of a flower, its green leaves tinted with copper and faintly veined with red, its pale green, waxy petals enclosing a constellation of starry flower parts. Every part of the flower was rendered with delicate, loving attention.

"A green hellebore!" Beatrix exclaimed, delighted. "Jeremy, it's lovely!" She did not say that he was following in her footsteps, but in a way he was, for she had painted many delicate watercolors of flowers — and had then moved on to mushrooms, rendering them in exquisite detail. She was elated at the thought that Jeremy was beginning to share her passion for picturing the natural wonders of the Lakes — not the large landscapes of trees and sky that her brother Bertram liked to paint, but the tiny, hidden, secret things that people didn't see because they didn't take the time to look.

"I know it's not exactly a rare plant," Jeremy said in an apologetic tone. "But it was so striking, I couldn't resist painting it."

"It's becoming rare," Beatrix said softly. "The shady, woodsy places it loves to grow are being sold up for cottages. In a few years, there won't be many left."

"I know," Jeremy said regretfully. "That's happening to too many of our native plants. Painting them is one way to save them for the future." He brightened. "And I'm glad to tell you that I've sold this painting. It's going to the same gentleman who bought the helleborine I painted not long ago. And he says he wants to see more — to see *all* my paintings."

Beatrix clapped her hands. "Jeremy, that's wonderful," she cried. "I'm so proud of you — and so very glad that you're finding time to go on with your work. With your painting, that is." She laughed a little. "I know that you have plenty of other work, as well."

"You can say that again." Jeremy put his arm around her shoulder. "Now, come into the kitchen and have a cup of tea, Miss Potter." He grinned merrily, and Beatrix saw a hint of the young Jeremy that she remembered so well. "You can't know how wonderful it is to be able to invite you to have tea in our very own kitchen, with my wife and my new son sleeping upstairs."

In the tiny kitchen, Deirdre's friend Gilly Harmsworth, her blond hair plaited into two braids and twisted up at the back of her head, was just pouring hot water from a kettle into the teapot.

"Oh, Miss Potter!" she exclaimed, putting the kettle back on the coal range. "How nice to see you again."

Beatrix had first met Gilly when she was living with her uncle and his wife at Applebeck Farm. There, the girl had been made to work long, hard hours in the Applebeck dairy, until Beatrix helped her find another place and persuaded Gilly's uncle, Adam Harmsworth, to release her. Altogether, it had been an ugly, unhappy business and revealed the darker, exploitative side of human nature. (You can read about it in *The Tale of Applebeck Orchard.*) But in the end, things had turned out surprisingly well. Mrs. Harmsworth got what was coming to her. Mr. Harmsworth, who never really wanted to be an orchardist, sold up and left. And Gilly was still happily working for Major Kittredge and his wife Dimity in the dairy at Raven Hall, the position Beatrix had found for her. She was now in full charge of the dairy, a very responsible position for a young woman who was not yet nineteen.

Jeremy opened a cupboard and got out a plate of tea biscuits. "Gilly and I were just talking about what happened next door," he said soberly. "Have you heard, Miss Potter?"

"I ran into your aunt Jane a little while ago," Beatrix replied. "She told me. It seems very hard to believe. And so very sad. I —"

She was interrupted by a knock. Jeremy disappeared. He was back in a moment with Mr. Heelis, whom he introduced to Gilly. Beatrix caught Will's glance, and was glad that it was warm and welcoming, although there was still that sense of distance.

"Why, hello, Miss Potter," he said formally.

"Hello, Mr. Heelis," Beatrix replied.

If you wonder at "Miss Potter" and "Mr. Heelis," please remember that both Beatrix and Will are thorough-going Victorians, raised in an era when even husbands and wives called each other "Mr." and "Mrs." Beatrix and Will always call each other by their first names when they are alone or when they are writing to one another, as they do quite often. But when they are in company, except with their closest friends, they feel obliged to be formal. They might even want to hold hands and kiss in greeting, but they would never do so in public. They save those intimacies for their private moments, which I daresay makes those moments even more pleasurable. There is something to be said, after all, for pent-up longing.

Gilly put sugar and milk on the table, with cups and saucers and spoons. Beatrix noticed with pleasure that the cups were part of the china set that she had given Jeremy and Deirdre as a wedding present — along with the blue rug on the floor. It was nice to see them being used.

"I'll go look in on Deirdre," Gilly said, "and leave you to your tea."

"No, please, Miss Harmsworth," Will said, rather to Beatrix's surprise. "Actually, you're the reason for my call. Captain Woodcock wanted me to ask you a few questions, if you don't mind. About something you saw next door."

This answered Beatrix's unspoken question about why Will was here. He must be part of the investigation that the justice of the peace and the constable were conducting into Mr. Adcock's death. Although why he should be involved, she couldn't quite make out.

The four of them sat around the small table, which was spread with a blue checked cloth and centered with a jelly jar filled with daisies. Gilly poured tea and passed around a plate of chocolate biscuits. "I s'pose you want to know about the man I saw in the garden this morning," she said.

Will nodded. "Do you remember what time that was, Miss Harmsworth?"

"About six thirty," Gilly said. "A little while after the baby was born. But I'm afraid I didn't see him very well, Mr. Heelis. Not his face, that is. He had on a hat — a brown hat with a wide brim. And brown trousers, I think."

"How tall?"

She hesitated. "Medium height, I suppose."

"Bearded? A moustache?"

She shook her head, then paused. "At least, I don't think so. I really couldn't see his face. There wasn't much light, and his hat was pulled down."

"Did he go into the shed?"

"If he did, I didn't see him. I couldn't linger, you know. The baby had just come, and I had things to do. And anyway, it didn't seem important. He was just someone walking through the garden." She glanced at Jeremy, frowning. "I thought . . . didn't you say that Mr. Adcock killed himself, Jeremy?"

"That's certainly what it looked like to me," Jeremy replied in a low voice. He pressed his lips together, shaking his head. "I've never seen anything like that. I don't want to see anything like it ever again."

"The cause of death has yet to be determined," Will said quietly, and Beatrix caught her breath, hearing the implications of his short sentence. There was something more here than she had thought.

Jeremy caught it, too. He put his elbows on the table and leaned forward. "This man Gilly saw — you think he might have had

218

something to do with it, Mr. Heelis?"

"That's not clear just yet," Will replied. "We simply don't know." He turned back to Gilly. "Miss Harmsworth, I wonder — do you know a Mr. Bernard Biddle? He is a building contractor."

"I've heard his name mentioned," Gilly replied thoughtfully. "He did some building work for Major Kittredge last year, at one of the estate farms. If you're asking me whether he was the man in the garden, I'm afraid I couldn't say. I've never laid eyes on him." She lifted her head alertly. "I think I hear the baby crying. If you don't have any more questions, Mr. Heelis —"

"No," Will said quickly. "Thank you. But if you remember anything else — anything at all — be sure and let Captain Woodcock or Constable Braithwaite know at once, will you?"

Gilly nodded, smiled at Beatrix, and left the room. A few moments later, Beatrix and Will took leave of Jeremy and left, too. They paused at the gate.

"I must apologize for my abruptness earlier this afternoon," Will said a little stiffly. He scanned Beatrix's face, looking for reassurance. "Is it . . . Are you all right?"

"I'm all right," she said with a small smile. "I just wish things didn't have to be so complicated. And I'm very sorry for Mrs. Adcock. I must stop in and tell her so." She hesitated. "But I really do have to speak to Mr. Biddle about one or two important things, and I'd rather not do it alone. I wish you would come with me. Will you?"

"No," he said, and then added, rather more urgently than the question seemed to call for. "And I don't want you seeing him, either, Bea. Not until I can go with you. Please. Promise me."

She frowned, wondering why he was so positively negative. "Is this because of what happened to Mr. Adcock?"

"No — at least, I don't think so. It's . . . It's as you say, Beatrix. It's complicated." At that moment, the constable and Captain Woodcock came around the Adcock cottage, and Will took a step away. "I'm sorry. I have to go now. Don't forget about dinner this evening with the Woodcocks. I'll see you at seven."

With that, he was gone.

And Beatrix had not promised.

12
THE SECRET LIFE OF BERTRAM POTTER

My news is all gardening at present, & supplies. I went to see an old lady at Windermere, & impudently took a large basket & trowel with me. She had the most untidy overgrown garden I ever saw. I got nice things in handfuls without any shame, amongst others a bundle of lavender slips . . . Mrs. Satterthwaite says stolen plants always grow, I stole some "honesty" yesterday, it was put to be burnt in a heap of garden refuse! I have had something out of nearly every garden in the village.
— **Beatrix Potter to Millie Warne, 1906**

Beatrix dropped in at the Adcocks' cottage to pay her respects to the widow. But Vicar and Mrs. Sackett were already there, and just about the time she arrived, Bertha Stubbs knocked on the door, clearly itching to know what had happened. So Beatrix said what she had come to say (and meant from her heart) and didn't linger. Mrs. Adcock would have all she could do to cope with Bertha Stubbs, who was the worst gossip in either Sawrey.

Back at Hill Top, Beatrix tried to settle down to work at the project she had left when Sarah Barwick knocked at the door, some hours before. She sat down and looked at the table in front of her, sighing. It was littered with galley proofs, her drawing supplies, and the last pen-and-ink illustrations for *Pigling Bland,* to be pasted into the galley. She was hoping to get the drawings completed as soon as possible, so she could post the finished package to Harold Warne. His most recent letter had been rather urgent, because the catalog had announced the book for October, so that children could have it for their Christmas.

But now that she looked at what was yet to be done, Beatrix wasn't sure that she could meet the deadline. It seemed that something was always getting in the way. Her father's illness, her mother's constant demands for attention, the need to run back and forth from Hill Top to Lindeth Howe, where her parents were spending the holidays. Not to mention the constant delays in the work at Castle Cottage, where she and Will had once dreamed of living out their lives together.

And in her lowest, darkest moments, that dream seemed utterly impossible. She now felt that it would be kinder to release both of them from it: Will, so that he could get on with the rest of his life; herself, so she could stop being pulled between two impossible poles. It was bad enough when she had been torn between her parents and her books and her farm, all competing for her full attention, her consideration, her devotion. Now, it was her parents, her books, her farms (for there was more than one) — and Will Heelis. There simply was not enough of her to go around, especially with this book deadline hanging over her head like an ominous cloud.

Beatrix put her elbows on the table and covered her eyes with her hands, feeling unspeakably weary. How many books was it, now? It was hard to keep track. Twenty-one or twenty-two, depending on whether she counted that first private printing of *Peter Rabbit* twelve years ago. She had spent a full year sending the manuscript out to one publisher after another and getting back nothing but curt rejections, until she had got so impatient and out of temper with the process that she had taken matters into her own hands and published the book herself.

To everyone's surprise, it had sold over four hundred copies. And then Norman Warne had read it and liked it and had urged his brothers to publish it. And the rest — as her brother Bertram liked to say, with a slightly envious smile — was literary history. Everyone, and most especially Beatrix, had been astonished by the public's apparently insatiable eagerness for bunny books.

Beatrix rubbed her smarting eyes with her fists. Well, literary history or not, she was dreadfully behind with this particular project — and the way she was feeling, she was glad she hadn't yet proposed another one. Perhaps it really was time to stop. In some ways, she hated the idea, but in other ways it seemed incredibly liberating. Yes. Yes, indeed. This book ought to be the last — especially given the problem of getting paid for her work.

While Norman was alive, there had never been any financial difficulties. Her royalties were always paid promptly and in an orderly way. But after his death, the accounting system at Warne seemed to have broken down. The payments had become increasingly erratic, and the royalty statements that accompanied the cheques were either incorrect or incomplete. She frequently had to send them back with questions that were almost never adequately answered.

The situation seemed to be getting worse, too — to the point where she had started keeping track of what was owed her. In fact, she was going to have to write a letter in the next day or two, asking about some money that was owed her. She hated to think it, but she was beginning to feel that she couldn't trust Harold Warne — Norman's brother, and now her editor. Something was going on there. What, she had no idea, but it was making her very uncomfortable, to the point where she sometimes found it difficult to do her work.

She dropped her hands and blinked until her vision cleared. Even though she had rushed the drawings, she felt they were good. She picked up the painting of the two little pigs, Pigling and his lady-friend Pigwig, standing beside the grocer's cart, which she had drawn from a photograph of Mr. Preston and his horse Blackie, who came round three times a week to deliver the village wives' orders. But the suspicious grocer was laying a trap for the pigs, and the two little friends were lucky to escape with their lives.

And escape they did. It was the perfect ending to a get-away story, the dream of a child's life. Boys and girls — especially the ones who dreamed about escaping from restrictive parents and starched collars and nursery puddings — ought to like it very much.

Beatrix looked for a moment at the last drawing, which she had just started to sketch. The two little runaway pigs, Pig-wig released from her imprisonment, were finally free, dancing ecstatically to a tune played by a trio of rabbits whilst the sun set over a lake.

She chuckled sadly. It wasn't just little children who dreamed of getting away from their parents and from all the rules and restrictions that kept them from doing what they most wanted to do. Wouldn't it be wonderful if she and Will could simply clasp hands and run away? They would be free at last, and together. Together, forever and ever. They could dance to their own lovely tune, and nobody else's.

But she knew better, of course. Running away and living happily ever after was a fairy story. Her little book was a fanciful tale about pigs, written for little children. She and Will were grownups with obligations. Running away wasn't an option. Not now, not ever.

There was a hard, bitter lump in her throat. After a moment, she pushed back her chair, put on her garden gloves and her wide-brimmed straw hat, and went out to the garden. If she was too disheartened to work with her paintbrush, she could work with her trowel. Perhaps an hour's weeding in the sunshine and clear air would relieve her mind so that she could get back to the book.

Outside, she took a deep breath, looking around, finding pleasure in the untidy tumble of flowers, herbs, and vegetables. Unkempt and unattended, the garden hadn't amounted to much when Beatrix bought Hill Top, but she had worked on it over the seasons, turning it into a lovely, informal cottage garden. She had hired quarrymen to build flagstone walks and stone walls between the garden and the Tower Bank Arms (her next-door neighbor). The wall nearest the house sheltered a wooden beehive, and another was a "warm wall" — a west-facing wall of stone and brick along which she had planted a grape vine. She'd only got three bunches of grapes (the climate was really too cold, this far north), but the kitchen garden provided vegetables and herbs, the apple orchard yielded plenty of apples, and flowers bloomed everywhere.

As for plants, they had come from many

generous people: a bundle of lavender slips and some violets from an old lady on the other side of the lake, some saxifrage and moss roses from Mrs. Taylor at the corner cottage, phlox from a man who lived on the road to the ferry, and honesty from the village rubbish heap — as well as lilacs, rhododendrons, and fuchsia from a plant nursery in Windermere, and black currants and gooseberries and strawberries. She loved them all dearly, every plant, each one. If ever she and Will had a garden at Castle Cottage, she thought, she would divide many of these wonderful plants and move them there, or take seeds and plant them. If ever, if ever —

With a bitter ache of longing in her throat, Beatrix pushed the thought away. Really, there was no point in planning a garden at Castle Cottage or even in wishing for one. If the house could somehow be magically finished and ready for someone to live in it, she'd have to find a new tenant. As long as her mother and father had their way, there would be no wedding. No wedding, and no garden. Viciously, she shoved a trowel into the earth and began to dig.

A half hour later, Beatrix was leaning over the lettuces, tugging on a stubborn weed, when she heard footsteps behind her.

"Hullo, Bea," a man's voice said, and she straightened and turned, thinking for an instant that it might be Will.

But it wasn't. A slender, handsome man with a thin dark moustache stood at the garden gate. A little taller than she, he was dressed in a neat dark suit and vest, a red tie, and a tweed cap. He pulled the cap off his dark hair and held it in his hands, giving her his usual charming smile.

"How is my favorite sister?"

"Bertram!" Beatrix exclaimed happily. "Why, what a wonderful surprise! I had no idea you were coming. Have you been at Lindeth Howe with Mama and Papa?"

Her brother gave an exasperated chuckle. "For the past three days. I wanted to come over and see you yesterday, but the parents kept finding things they wanted me to do, or subjects they thought we should talk about. You know how they are." He glanced at the weeds she held in one hand. "I'm interrupting your work."

"No matter," Beatrix said with a warm smile, dropping the plants onto the pile beside the path. "Weeds can wait. I'm delighted to see you. Let's go put the kettle on, and I'll make tea." She stripped off her gloves, thinking that she hadn't seen Bertram since the Christmas holidays in London. And he hadn't been here at Hill Top for over a year. She was very glad that he had come.

"First this," Bertram said, and unexpectedly folded her in his arms.

She leaned against him for a moment, enjoying the strength of his embrace. Their mother and father had never been fond of "demonstrations," as Mrs. Potter called them. They preferred cool handshakes and restrained formal greetings. They almost never indulged in a warm hug — in fact, they rarely even touched. And Beatrix and Bertram had lived apart for years, Bertram at his little farm in the south of Scotland, Beatrix with their parents in South Kensington. They shared some important interests in common, but they rarely saw one another and their lives were very different. Beatrix often felt as if she barely knew her brother.

But Bertram is not a minor character in our story. In fact, while I don't yet know all the details, or exactly what is likely to happen, I understand that he is going to play a very large — and completely unexpected — role in the course of future events. I think we shall have to get better acquainted with him, so we won't be completely taken by surprise by the way things turn out in the end.

Beatrix was six years old when her baby brother was born, and she had always looked out for him. This was especially important for both of them, because these two very Victorian children did not see as much of their mother as modern children do. In fact, if the Potters were like other families in their social class, the children saw their parents for an hour at teatime and another brief while at bedtime, and that was all.

But Beatrix and Bertram had each other. They lived in the same third-floor nursery, were cared for by the same nursemaid and nanny, and had their lessons in the same schoolroom from the same governess, Miss Hammond. As privileged upper-class children living in London, they didn't go outside to play, the way country village children did, and they had no playmates or friends.

But their lives were never boring — oh, no! Beatrix's journal from her growing-up years is full of visits to the British Museum (where she was fascinated by a fine collection of illuminated manuscripts), the Kew Gardens, and all the many London art galleries, where she saw exhibits of the best painters, as well as the classics. In Oxford, she went to the Bodeleian. On the way to Edinburgh, she saw the Holy Island of Lindisfarne. They visited Brighton, Edinburgh, Manchester, Falmouth, Portsmouth, Torquay, Wales, and the Lakes, as well as a great many other places.

And every August, when the London streets began to sizzle, the Potters packed up their children, the butler, the cook, the maids, the governess, the coachman, the coach, *and* the horses and went on holiday until October. In those early years, they went to Dalguise House in Perthshire, in the Scottish Highlands. There, the children could roam through what seemed like enchanted woodlands along the River Tay, identifying wild birds and searching out their nests, catching rabbits and hedgehogs and voles and bats to take back to London to live in the nursery with them, and sketching birds and animals and trees. They studied everything from leaves to lizards and sketched and painted and drew all that they saw. And as it turned out, they both had an unusual gift for drawing.

For children of their social class, art was a hobby to be encouraged, but Beatrix and Bertram seemed never to have thought of their art as a hobby. Both of them took their art seriously, and both became serious professional artists. As an adult, Bertram painted large landscapes of dark and rather gloomy wildernesses topped by dark skies and tinged with a decidedly Romantic melancholy. (When you visit Hill Top Farm, you will see several of Bertram's paintings, framed in gilt and hanging in the upstairs rooms.) Unfortunately, he couldn't seem to interest buyers in his art.

Beatrix, on the other hand, was an accomplished miniaturist, painting plants and the small animals she loved to collect — rabbits, mice, guinea pigs, frogs, and even beetles and tiny insects — as well as fossils, fungi, and lichen. And when Peter Rabbit became popular, she was able to earn quite a respectable sum of money from her art.

But while Beatrix mostly thought of herself as a happy child and young woman, Bertram did not have the same experience. Beatrix was educated at home by a governess. But boys of the Potters' social class were always sent away to school, so Bertram was packed off to The Grange, at Eastbourne, and three years later, to Charterhouse, in Surrey. A slight, delicate child, he had a woeful time of it. He was taunted by bullies, he couldn't make friends, and he wasn't very good at his studies. He would rather paint than do anything else. The headmaster's reports made Mr. Potter scowl and mutter under his breath, while Mrs. Potter dabbed her handkerchief to her eyes and complained that no one understood her dear son, who would surely do better if he just had another chance. It's not clear how many chances he got. But he came home without taking his exams (Beatrix mentions some sort of dreadful disgrace in her journal but doesn't elaborate) and was then sent back to Eastbourne to prepare for Oxford.

But Oxford was as big a disappointment as Charterhouse had been, for Bertram, a good-looking boy with a certain shy charm, clearly preferred his social life to his studies. Beatrix worried about her brother, for there was a streak of alcoholism in the family, and she feared — with good reason, it turns out — that Bertram had inherited it. But perhaps drinking was the only way the young man could rebel against the father whom he could never please and the mother who eternally hoped that he would improve. Always intensely attuned to the emotional climate in the family and continually hoping that everyone would be happy, Beatrix did what she could to shield her brother from the worst of their parents' displeasure. She got into the habit of being in the middle, and that's where she stayed.

After his failure at Oxford, Bertram left home. First, he went abroad, as did many other young men. When he came back, he began taking long sketching trips to the Scottish border country where he and Beatrix had spent so many happy months as children. About the same time that the little books became popular and Beatrix began escaping into her new career as an author and illustrator, Bertram escaped, too, but more literally than she did. He bought a small farm called Ashyburn near Ancrum, a pretty village in the south of Scotland, and began spending all his time there, painting.

He was painting, yes. And he (like his sister a few years later) was farming.

But most important of all, Bertram Potter was hiding a secret, a calamitous, truly momentous secret. For in 1902, this only son of the wealthy, socially conscious Rupert and Helen Potter had secretly married a pretty, penniless young woman named Mary, whose background and family connections, it is fair to say, were not those that the Potters would have chosen. In fact, Mary Potter had worked in the textile mills and as a maid in her aunt's boarding house. Her father was a wine merchant.

Now, you and I are used to working for

our livings, so the idea of having a job in a textile mill or a boarding house presents no special problem. In fact, it may seem quite admirable to us that Mary was able to look out for herself instead of depending upon her family. But the Potters, who saw themselves as creatures of a different order altogether, did not share this view. Bertram knew that his father would be apoplectic at the very idea of his throwing away his life on such a marriage, and his mother would suffer one of her attacks and have to be put to bed for a week. Or more.

I think you can see where this is going. Lacking the courage to tell his parents what he had done, Bertram simply pretended he hadn't done it. Nothing could be simpler, actually. He saw his parents as little as possible, coming to join them for a few days during their annual country holiday and taking the train up to London once or twice a year. Of course, he never invited them to his farm — and one wonders what he would have done with his wife if they had turned up there unexpectedly.

But then, he and Mary were probably pretty safe. Mrs. Potter never visited her son's farm, for the same reason she refused to come to Hill Top: Ashyburn was too remote, too primitive, and too dull for her refined taste. It was a very good thing that Bertram and Mary Potter had no children. A child — especially a boy — would have been an enormous complication.

Well. This is a sorry business, as I'm sure you will agree. Parents who attempt to control their adult children's lives. A daughter who is forbidden to marry the man she loves because he is too common. A son who runs off and marries the woman he loves, no matter that she *is* common, but hides the whole business from his parents as if it were a sordid, backstreet affair — and drinks too much, to boot.

In our day, the Potter family would be labeled highly dysfunctional, and long-term individual and group therapy would be recommended. In Beatrix's day, it would merely have been said, as Tolstoy famously wrote at the beginning of *Anna Karenina,* "Every unhappy family is unhappy in its own way."

Beatrix had known about Bertram's marriage for some time, and even though she was horrified by the thought that he had hidden something so important from their parents, she had faithfully kept his scandalous secret to herself. She cared very much for her brother and would never find fault with him for choosing to marry the woman he loved: people ought to have that freedom.

But Beatrix was a straightforward person who was deeply troubled by lies and deceit and tried to practice truthfulness in her own life, whatever the cost. She hated the idea that Bertram was living a lie, and while she told herself that she wasn't bitter about what he had done, I'm sure her feelings were terribly complicated. Her brother was leading the life he had chosen — and if he had been honest with his parents, perhaps her own situation would have been different. But he hadn't, and it wasn't. If there was some secret bitterness in the recesses of Beatrix's heart, I for one am not going to blame her for it.

Now you know as much as I do about Bertram Potter and his marriage, which he has kept a secret for over ten years now. With this in mind, let us follow Beatrix and her brother into the house, where they are going for their tea.

While Bertram looked over the drawings for her new book, Beatrix got out jam and bread and cheese and poured tea. Then they sat down to eat, enjoying each other's company just as they had enjoyed their nursery teas so many years before.

Bertram glanced around with a puzzled look. "It's very peaceful here. And quite lovely, Bea. But I don't see any construction. Papa said you were rebuilding something or another. Adding on new rooms."

"Up the hill, at Castle Cottage," Beatrix replied, cutting a slice of cheese. "It's the farm I bought several years ago — another twenty acres. A house, a barn, and some much-needed pasture for the sheep. I'm enlarging the house." She met Bertram's eyes and spoke her heart. "Mr. Heelis and I would like to live there someday. In the present circumstance, that hardly seems feasible, but we can hope."

"Ah," Bertram said gravely. "Yes, of course. I see." He knew about her engagement, of course. She had told him in a letter, and they had discussed it at Christmas.

"I've explained all this to Mama and Papa," she added, "and more than once. But of course, they're not in favor of my marrying, so they choose not to listen when I tell them about Castle Cottage." She gave a wry chuckle. "But construction always takes forever. Perhaps they've just forgotten."

Bertram's echoing chuckle held a note of bitterness. "Oh, they haven't forgotten, Bea. You know better than that. They're only pretending not to remember. That way, they can keep it from happening."

She nodded, wondering if she should confide all her misgivings about the engagement. But she was used to keeping things like that to herself. So she picked up the teapot. "More tea, dear?"

Bertram nodded, and she poured another cup. "Of course," he went on, his voice taut and angry, "the parents have never listened to either one of us. They only hear what they want. If it's something *we* want, they simply ignore us. They are the only ones in the family who count for anything."

Beatrix didn't answer. Bertram had said all this to her many times before. It was a frequent complaint of his.

"Well, enough of that," he said, cutting his usual tirade unexpectedly short. He stirred in sugar, then looked at her, frowning a little. "Mama said you were ill this spring."

Beatrix lifted her shoulders and let them fall. "It's true, Bertram. I felt wretched all during March and April. I was in bed most of the time." She gestured at the papers on the table. "That's why I'm so behindhand with this book. It should have been finished by now."

"Your illness. It was physical or — ?" He didn't finish the sentence, but she knew what he meant, and she answered the question he hadn't asked.

"It was both. Mama and Papa don't make any secret of the way they feel about my engagement. It was all very under-the-table, of course, rarely out in the open — except when the post brought a letter from Mr. Heelis. That always provoked some mean remark or another. But then I caught the flu and couldn't seem to shake it." She managed a small laugh. "I'm much better now, though. Truly, Bertram. I am always better when I can get out of London."

"You don't look quite well yet, I'm afraid." Bertram raised his cup and added, so softly that Beatrix almost didn't hear him: "How you've stood to live with Mama and Papa all these years, Bea, I'll never know. It must have been pure hell."

Her brother's words surprised Beatrix. While he often talked about the way *he* felt about their mother and father, he rarely seemed to take her feelings into account.

"Well, I wouldn't call it 'hell,' " she replied, "although it's not been very pleasant. But whilst duty may be an old-fashioned concept, it's still important — at least to me." Hurriedly, because she hadn't meant to sound critical, she added, "And since I don't see any changes on the horizon, I just go on, day to day, doing what has to be done." She smiled. "You know, stiff upper lip, soldiering on, all that sort of thing. We all have to do it, in one way or another."

The silence lengthened. Then Bertram put down his cup with a sharp clatter. "I say, Bea," he burst out. "Do you truly want to marry Heelis?" When she didn't immediately answer, he added urgently, "Come now. You must tell me the truth."

Surprised by his question, she kept on staring at him. "The truth? Yes, Bertram, I do. I don't think it's going to happen, but I want it from the very bottom of my heart."

He looked away. "He seems a decent sort," he muttered.

She blinked, surprised again. "You've met him?" Bertram had not been there when Will called on the Potters, first in London and again in that awful visit just a few weeks ago.

"I haven't met him, no." He raised his eyes, clearly embarrassed. "I . . . I made inquiries, that's all. Wanted to see what kind of a situation you might be getting yourself into." He paused and added, in a reassuring way, "The men I talked to had nothing but praise for him."

"Well, I should think so!" Beatrix exclaimed hotly. "Mr. Heelis is admired by everyone who knows him. Really, Bertram — I don't understand why you would do such a thing. If you had wanted to meet him, all you had to do was ask, and I should have been glad to arrange it. I —"

Bertram raised his hand. "I know, I know. I just wanted to assure myself that you were doing the right thing. That Heelis had a good character, and all that. That he would make you happy."

The right thing! Well, I don't know about you, but I find that remark insufferably patronizing. Who is Bertram Potter to decide whether his sister is doing the right thing? What if he had thought it was the wrong thing? What if he decided that Will Heelis' character fell a little short? Or suspected that Heelis could not make his sister happy? What would he have done then? Lined up with his father and mother in opposition to the marriage?

Beatrix sat back in her chair, folded her arms, and said the first thing that came to her mind. "None of the family made inquiries into Mary's character before you married her." But the angry words were no sooner out of her mouth than she regretted them. It was perhaps the worst thing she had ever said to him, and she was sorry.

Urgently, she put out her hand. "No, Bertram, please. Forget I said that. It wasn't fair. I do apologize."

"None of this has been fair," Bertram said in a very low voice. "I've behaved badly. Mama and Papa have behaved badly. You've been a saint. I don't see how you can bear *any* of us."

Struck by the genuine feeling in her brother's voice, Beatrix leaned forward and took his hand. "Oh, I'm no saint," she said with a little laugh. "But you know my philosophy." She quoted something she had once written to a friend. "Believe there is a great power silently working all things for good, behave yourself, and never mind the rest."

"Ah, yes," Bertram said. He squeezed her hand and released it. "Well, you have certainly behaved yourself, my dear." He drew himself up with the air of someone who was making a declaration. "And now it's my turn."

Beatrix frowned, not understanding. "Your . . . turn? Your turn for what?"

"It's very simple, Bea. I love my wife, but I have hated myself every day for the past eleven years. I have betrayed Mary and myself — and you. I have left you to carry the lion's share of the burden at home. I have been a wretched coward."

This was all very true, Beatrix thought wryly, although his recognition was coming a little late. No, not a little late. Eleven years late. But there was no point in saying so, and recriminations were no help.

"I *am* their only daughter," she replied evenly. "And for good or ill, it's a daughter's responsibility to do what she can for her parents."

"Yes, and you've been doing that forever!" Bertram slapped his hand on the table. "That's why I say it's my turn, Beatrix. You're right — I can't do anything about taking care of them, given the circumstance." He upended his cup, drained it, and pushed his chair back. "But I can be a man at long last. I can tell them the truth. About Mary. About our marriage."

Beatrix's heart seemed to stop. "Oh, no! No, you can't, Bertram!" she exclaimed in sheer terror. "Not after all these years! They will never get over it. It will destroy them."

"Better to destroy them than to destroy you and Heelis," Bertram replied stonily. "They've got to be made to change their minds."

Beatrix bit her lip. Bertram had inherited his stubbornness from his father, and you could never get anywhere arguing with him. But perhaps logic could prevail. She pushed down the panic and focused on keeping her voice level and reasonable.

"I don't see how telling them about Mary is going to make any difference to me, Bertram. They'll be furious at you. Papa will threaten to disown you, and Mama will scream and probably faint. But none of that will alter their attitude toward *my* marriage. If anything, it will only make things worse. There will be arguments and tantrums and demands for attention. And anyway, it seems to me that —"

She stopped. She wanted to say that his decision was a selfish one, that he was only trying to make himself feel better, trying to seek forgiveness, perhaps even trying to redeem himself in Mary's eyes. Poor, poor Mary, whose husband was too frightened of his parents to publically acknowledge the woman he loved and had married.

All that was true. But she could tell by the look on her brother's face that he had already made up his mind — and he was as stubborn as she was. At this point, nothing she could say to him would make a single bit of difference.

He laughed harshly. "Make things worse? Well, maybe it will. If it does, I'm sorry, truly. But maybe it won't. And anyway, how could things be any worse than they are now?"

There was enough truth to that to make

her chuckle helplessly. "Well, I suppose one might say that. But I just can't see why you should want to upset the applecart, that's all." Especially when she was the one who had to pick all the apples up and put them back where they belonged.

He stood and shoved his hands in his pockets, looking down at her. "I don't know what is going to happen, Bea. But I did think it was important to see you and explain, before I did it. Look, dear. I really think you should be there. I plan to make my confession on Sunday afternoon, just at teatime. My date with destiny, you might say," he added, with a crooked, self-mocking grin. "And then I shall go back to Scotland on the earliest possible Monday train."

"*I* should be there to hear your confession?" Beatrix suppressed a wild, half-hysterical giggle. Of course. Bertram would tell them and then — having cleared his conscience — he would escape to his farm and his wife, leaving her to clean up the mess he was leaving behind. He only wanted her there to help defend him, to stand between him and Papa and Mama the way she always had. She usually gave in to his requests — he was, after all, still her brother. But not this time. This time, he would have to fend for himself.

She took a deep breath and straightened her shoulders. "This is your confession, Bertram, not mine. If you are determined to tell them what you've done, you will have to face the music all by yourself. I will not be there to help. And that's all there is to it."

Bertram was used to getting his way with Beatrix, and he gave her a surprised look, judging her strength. Then he gave it one last try. "You won't change your mind?" he asked plaintively. "I'm sure I should feel so much more confident if you were there, lending me courage."

Beatrix heard the wheedling tone and chose to ignore it. "No, I won't change my mind. But I will certainly wish you well — even though I don't think it's a good idea. In fact, I think it is a singularly *bad* idea." She stood up and brushed her lips across his cheek. "I'm planning to go back to Lindeth Howe on Monday at teatime and stay through the end of the week. By that time, I expect the fuss will be over. You will have told them and left," (she did not say *escaped,* but she thought it) "and they will have settled down, and everything will be as dull and boring as it usually is."

She didn't expect any such thing, and both of them knew it. She was only saying it to make him feel better, for of course Papa and Mama would never get used to the idea that Bertram had married without their consent or even their knowledge.

And worse, oh, much, much worse, they would use his secret marriage as yet another reason why *she* should never marry. Their son had betrayed and deserted them. She could never be allowed to leave them. No, never, never, never.

"Dull and boring," Bertram repeated. Obviously hoping for the best, he seemed to accept what she had said. "Well, if you won't come, you won't," he said in a resigned tone. "But I do hope you understand why I'm doing this, Beatrix. It's for you and Heelis as much as for myself and Mary. I hope it will change things for you."

Beatrix managed a smile. "I hope so, too," she said as warmly as she could.

But she knew it wouldn't. Changing her parents' minds would be like moving a pair of mountains.

And moving mountains was impossible.

13
CAPTAIN WOODCOCK
GOES FISHING

Whilst Bertram Potter was alarming his sister, Captain Woodcock was embarking on the next stage of his investigation into Mr. Adcock's death. Constable Braithwaite had gone off to Hawkshead with Dr. Butters and would bring word when the doctor finished the autopsy and had written his report. Will Heelis had ridden his motorcycle back to Hawkshead to keep an appointment with a client. So the captain was carrying on the investigation alone.

Mr. Bernard Biddle kept his office in his house at Hazel Crag Farm, between Near Sawrey and Hawkshead. A large sign, visible from the road, announced that this was the office of BERNARD BIDDLE, CONTRACTOR. The captain motored up the curving driveway and stopped his Rolls-Royce in front of an imposing stone house with a fine view of Esthwaite Water, built against the side of a hill.

As the captain got out of his motorcar, he saw that a wing was being added onto the house — the new construction that Will Heelis had mentioned. He stood for a moment, watching a pair of carpenters going about their tasks. He suspected that this was where those missing building supplies were ending up — perhaps some that had come from his very own stable. He shook his head, frowning. But if that was true, there would be no hope of tracking them, since one sawn board or one shingle or slate looked pretty much like another.

The captain's knock at the front door was answered by the housekeeper, a round-faced lady in a plain brown dress and white apron, stern and unsmiling. The captain remembered hearing that Biddle's wife had died several years before. As she was ushering him into the office, he asked in a kindly tone, "Your name, ma'am?"

"Framley, sir. Mrs. Framley."

"Thank you. Well, then, Mrs. Framley, do you live in?"

She seemed surprised by his question and answered it hesitantly. "No, sir. I live in t' cottage up t' hill. I come in days."

"What time of the morning do you usually come in, then?"

Another hesitation. "Six, most days. Mr.

Biddle likes an early breakfast, all but Sundays. I doan't come Sundays. Sundays he does for hisse'f."

"Today?"

She was backing toward the door. Clearly, she did not want to talk with him, and he thought he knew why. " 'Twas elev'n today."

"Eleven, eh? Why so late, Mrs. Framley?"

"Mr. Biddle said I could, sir." Hurriedly, she added, "I'll fetch him." She turned and fled.

The office was a medium-sized room, very plain but neatly outfitted with shelves; a table that served as a desk, its surface littered with papers; and two wooden chairs, both stacked with papers. A large and handsome pike, stuffed and mounted, hung on one wall, and under it a half-dozen photographs of Biddle at various lakes in the district, displaying his fine fishing catches, all large fish. Beside the photos there were a half-dozen blue and red ribbons from various angling competitions, and as many plaques. The captain glanced at them, remembering that Biddle had quite a local reputation as a fisherman.

On the opposite wall, there was a framed map of the district. The map had several pins stuck into it, representing, the captain surmised, Mr. Biddle's current construction projects. Hands in his pockets, he was studying it when Mr. Biddle himself came into the room.

"Well, now, Cap'n Woodcock," Mr. Biddle said energetically. He was a sizeable man with burly shoulders, a florid, pockmarked face, and a stubbly brown beard and a moustache. There was a fresh cut across his cheek. "How's that stable workin' out for ye? Got 'ny complaints?" He rubbed his hands together. "Always like to hear from a customer, one way or t' other. Praise or complaints, but hopin' for praise, o' course."

"Good afternoon, Biddle," the captain said, not answering the questions. Without being asked, he removed the papers from one of the chairs and sat down, crossing his legs.

After a brief hesitation, Biddle went behind the table, removed the papers from that chair, and sat down as well. "Well, then, Captain," he said with a careless air. "Somethin' on your mind?"

The captain, who had spent a great deal of time in Military Intelligence when he was in Egypt, always enjoyed fishing for information. Over the years, it had got to be quite the game with him. He let Biddle's question rest for a moment, like a trout fly briefly suspended on the surface of a calm pool, then ignored it and cast one of his own.

"I say, Biddle, that's a nasty cut you've got on your cheek. How did it happen?"

Biddle raised his hand to his cheek as if to hide the cut, then dropped it. "Ah, that," he said dismissively. "Nothin' important. Been hurt worse many a time. Got kicked in t' face once by a horse. Bad, that was. Verra bad. This ain't nothin'."

The captain gave his question a casual twitch. "A fight, was it?"

Biddle eyed him nervously, as if he were trying to decide what and how much the captain knew. "Bit of a dust-up," he allowed. "Nothin' serious."

"The constable called it a fight," the captain remarked. He took his pipe out of his jacket pocket. "Apparently the other fellow caught your fist in his eye."

"Aye." Biddle grinned crookedly. " 'Twas only a small disagreement. As I said, nothin' important."

"I understand that it happened after you sacked the man," the captain went on. He pulled out a tobacco sack and filled his pipe, moving with slow deliberation. "Lewis Adcock, was it?"

"Aye," Biddle admitted after a moment. He fumbled in his pocket for a crumpled cigarette pack, shook one out, dropped it on the floor, picked it up.

"You remarked to the constable that you thought he was untrustworthy."

"Well, and so wot if I did?" Biddle was truculent. He struck a match to his cigarette and puffed on it. "I hired 'im. I paid 'im. I sacked 'im. I've got a right to discharge a fellow who can't be trusted, doan't I?"

The captain let the question float for a moment while he tamped the tobacco in his pipe. Then he rejected it for one of his own. " 'Can't be trusted,' he repeated thoughtfully, taking matches out of his pocket. "He stole something, did he?"

Biddle nodded shortly. His eyes were wary now.

The captain struck a match to his pipe, and pulled on it. "At Castle Cottage? That's where he was working, I understand."

"Aye," Biddle said slowly, shifting in his chair. "Aye. Castle Cottage. Miss Potter keeps a close eye on things, she does. Can't have a thief on the job, now, can I?"

"What did he steal?"

Biddle leaned forward and tapped his cigarette into the ashtray. "I say, Cap'n Woodcock, wot's this all about?"

"What did Lewis Adcock steal?" the captain asked, now more sharply.

There was a moment's silence as their

eyes met. At last Biddle's glance slid away. "It was a tool. Aye, a tool. A . . . carpenter's level, y'see. Didna cost much, but a man can't allow his employees steal him blind, now can he? Let Adcock get away with it, next thing you know, they'll all be doin' it, ev'ry man of 'em." He shook his head sternly. "Nobody can be trusted these days, seems like."

The captain considered this for a moment. He would lay a quid that Biddle was lying. Adcock might have stolen something, but it wasn't a carpenter's level. Lewis Adcock had practiced the carpenter's trade for years and could be presumed to have a full set of his own tools, like those in the shed behind his house. Perhaps he had been involved with the lumber and materials theft that Heelis had identified and Biddle had found out about it.

But if that was the case, why hadn't Biddle gone to the constable with the accusation? And why hadn't he acknowledged the theft in answer to his questions, just now? More likely, it was the other way around. Adcock had stumbled onto Biddle's thefts and had threatened to tell the authorities what he knew. Biddle couldn't incriminate himself by revealing that, so he concocted the lie about the tool.

The captain turned his pipe in his fingers, examining it. Without looking at Biddle, he said, as if to himself, " 'Nobody can be trusted these days.' " He let out his breath. "Well, I can certainly agree with that. Seems that theft is epidemic hereabouts, especially on construction sites."

Biddle stiffened.

The captain continued to muse aloud. "Reports of building materials being stolen. Lumber disappearing. Slates and supplies, too." He looked straight at Biddle. "Do you know anything about that?"

"No," Biddle said edgily. "Haven't heard it m'self." He frowned, now alert. "Building materials, you say? Sounds serious. Sounds like somethin' I should know about."

"I should say so." Then, abruptly, before Biddle could take the interrogation in that direction, the captain cast another question. "Where were you this morning at six thirty?" That was the hour at which the man had been seen in the Adcocks' back garden.

There was a silence. "Six thirty?" Avoiding the captain's glance, Biddle put out his cigarette in the ashtray. "Why, I was right here at home, I was, eatin' my breakfast. Eggs, bacon, porridge. Why?"

"Who can testify to that? Your house-keeper, I assume."

Biddle's nostrils flared. "Wot's all this in aid of, Cap'n? Wot's all these questions for?"

"Can your housekeeper verify that you were here in this house at six thirty this morning, Biddle?" the captain repeated steadily.

"Nay, she canna!" Biddle replied in a testy tone. "Her old dad's sick wi' t' influenza, so I give her a half-day holiday to walk over an' see him."

"That was very generous of you," the captain said dryly. And very convenient, he thought. "What time did you leave this place this morning, then — after you had your lonely breakfast?"

Biddle slapped the desk with his hand. "I woan't say another word 'til you tell me wot's it about, Cap'n!"

The captain pinned him with his gaze. "Lewis Adcock is dead."

"Dead?" Biddle's mouth fell open. There was a silence. Then: "Oh, aye? Dead, y'say? How? All I give him was a poke in the eye," he added defensively. "Not hard enough to hurt a flea."

"Wasn't the poke in the eye that killed him." The captain blew out a stream of pipe smoke, letting the silence ripen. "It was the rope around his neck."

"T' rope?" Biddle asked, as if dumb-

258

founded. He raised his hand to his cheek as if remembering Adcock's blow, then dropped it again. He swallowed. His eyes had grown very large. "You mean to say that Lewis Adcock . . . hung hisself?"

"That's what it looks like," the captain acknowledged. "Well, then, Biddle. What time did you leave this place this morning? Where did you go?"

Biddle swallowed again. "I left near about eight. I went to . . . to Castle Cottage. I was there most of t' mornin'. Until noon. Noon I went to t' pub to have my dinner."

"And the men on the job will verify that?"

"Aye." Biddle nodded awkwardly, but his hands were clenched on the desk. "Aye, o'course they will. I'll just tell 'em to get in touch with you an' —"

"Good," the captain said, and made as if to rise from his chair. "But you needn't bother to tell them. I will go straightaway and ask each of them, this afternoon. If they can vouch that you were on the job all morning, you're home and dry."

"I thought . . . I thought you said he hung hisself," Biddle said, and his voice cracked.

"I said that's what it *looks* like," the captain replied with careful emphasis. "Dr. Butters is conducting an autopsy."

Biddle stared at him. "You mean, there's

some question?"

"There's always a question until after the inquest," the captain replied casually. "In the meantime, it's my job — and the constable's — to make sure that all the facts are ascertained. And it is most certainly a fact that you accused Adcock of thieving and that the two of you fought the night before his death. Who's to say that you didn't finish the job you started?"

"But I —" Biddle sat stone still.

Captain Woodcock stood, then bent over and knocked his pipe out into the ashtray. In a businesslike tone, he said, "The day isn't getting any younger, Biddle, and both of us have things to do. I am going to drive to Castle Cottage and ask your men to corroborate your alibi."

Biddle held up his hand, shaking his head. "No need, Cap'n," he said in a low, sullen voice. "T' truth is that I didn't go to t' job this mornin'."

"Oh?" The captain sat back down again. Perhaps they were getting someplace at last. "Well, then. Where did you go?"

"I went . . . fishin'."

"Fishing." The captain blinked, not quite sure he had heard properly. "Did you say *fishing*?"

"Aye." Biddle nodded emphatically. "It's

260

t' truth," he added in a gruff voice. "God's truth. I swear it."

Now, the mounted fish and the ribbons and plaques on the wall attested to Biddle's reputation as an expert angler. And it is true that occasionally one of the residents of the Land Between the Lakes will decide that what he or she needs most of all is a holiday and make up a packet of sandwiches and cheese and an apple and disappear for a glorious, carefree day of fell-walking or bird-watching or some other loitering pursuit. But for the most part, the villagers and farmers and other folk are a hardworking lot who keep their noses to the grindstone, so to say, all week long, and save their recreation for the week's end. To hear Biddle confess that he had gone fishing on a Thursday morning when he should have been at work was surprising, to say the least.

"I see," the captain said, recovering himself. "Well, then. Fishing where?"

There was a silence, as if Biddle wasn't sure he wanted to answer. "Moss Eccles Tarn," he finally said in a resentful tone. "And no, nobody saw me. I was by m'self, all alone. And if I wasn't," he added enigmatically, "I wouldn't tell ye who was with me. Ye'll just have to take me at my word. I was fishin', and that's the first an' last o' it."

Well, now. I must confess that we have arrived at a gert mezzlement, as the villagers like to say. Was Biddle alone, or wasn't he — and why the mystery? And a second mezzlement, as well, for the captain (himself an experienced angler) is quite sure that, had Biddle sincerely wanted to catch fish, he would have done much better in a rowboat on Esthwaite Water, where he would have had a good chance at large char and even larger pike. Moss Eccles is a small, out-of-the-way lake to the north of the village that is known to be stocked with brown trout, and some of the villagers managed to pull their dinners out of the water occasionally. But in the captain's opinion, it is a rather tame place for a sportsman of Mr. Biddle's reputation to go fishing, and I must concur. In fact, I can't think of a single good reason for him to do so.

Captain Woodcock sighed and gave it one more try. "Well, Biddle, I don't suppose there's any use asking, but I will. It is common knowledge that the job at Castle Cottage is lagging well behind schedule, and that Miss Potter finds the delay provoking and troublesome. I have heard that the workmen themselves do not seem to feel a proper urgency, and now I learn that the building contractor himself goes fishing on a Thursday morning, rather than encourage them to get on with the job. P'rhaps you will be so good as to tell me why this is the case."

But now Biddle had his back up. "No, sir, I woan't say." Biddle's mouth took on a firm, hard set. "What I did or didn't do this mornin' has got nothin' wotsomever to do with poor Adcock's hangin' hisself. For which I am as sorry as the next 'un, but that's not here nor there, neither one." He stood up, his face by now very red and his voice loud and decidedly passionate.

Well. I don't know about you, but I am surprised, and so is Captain Woodcock, who is not accustomed to having his questions answered in such an unambiguously negative tone. But wait! Mr. Biddle has not yet said all he's got to say.

"So no, sir, Captain, sir, I am *not* goin' to tell you why I went fishin' on a fine, bright Thursday mornin' when I could've been on the job, settin' an example for t' men. 'Tis good enough for ye to know that I *did* go fishin', and that I went fishin' at Moss Eccles Tarn, and that I brought home three brown trout, and that Mrs. Framley is goin' to fry 'em up for my supper. If ye please, ye can go round by the kitchen and ask to see 'em. And now, sir, I have work to do an' you do, too. So I'll wish you good day."

And that, the captain saw, was the end of that, and there was no point in asking any more questions — at least, at this moment. As he left, however, he did take Mr. Biddle's suggestion and stepped around the back of the house to the kitchen, where Mrs. Framley was kind enough to show him three smallish brown trout, very fresh, laid out to keep cool on the marble slab in the dairy room, awaiting their appointment with the frying pan. According to Mrs. Framley, the fish had been there when she arrived back from her old dad's, who was better today, thank you verra much, and even better yet for enjoying an unexpected visit from his daughter that morning. And wa'n't it sweet of Mr. Biddle to suggest that she go?

But as the captain remarked to himself, getting into his motorcar and driving down the lane, one fresh brown trout looked pretty much like another. There was no telling whether these three had been caught in Moss Eccles Tarn this morning or purchased from the fish vendor's boy, who always drove his blue-painted cart through the village at eleven on Monday and Thursday mornings.

And if the captain doesn't know, I'm sure
I don't, either.

14
CRUMPET TAKES COMMAND

At the same hour that Bertram Potter was on his way back to the ferry and his date with destiny at Lindeth Howe, and Captain Woodcock was investigating the three brown trout in Mr. Biddle's kitchen, Crumpet was marshalling her forces. Or rather, she was attempting to, but without a great deal of success.

Throughout the afternoon, the gray cat had continued her survey of the village, gathering more reports of mysterious break-ins, petty kitchen and dairy thievery, and even a case of grand larceny. (Mr. Leach's grandfather's gold watch and fob was missing from its hook on the walnut bureau mirror in the bedroom at Buckle Yeat Cottage, where it hung when Mr. Leach wasn't wearing it.) And Sarah Barwick was still tearing her hair out over her bakery accounts. When she finally got them unscrambled (which might not be for another week or two), it would be seen that she was missing at least twelve bob from her cash box.

Well. When all these misdemeanors and felonies were tallied up, they made for a frighteningly long list. Crumpet felt that she did not need a Sherlock Holmes to tell her that the village had been inundated by a crime wave of unprecedented proportions, and that she — as president of the Village Cat Council — should most assuredly have to do something about it. And since she was the *new* president, and this was her first significant challenge, whatever she did should be exceptionally fine and outstanding. (If you are thinking that this is an abrupt departure from the more . . . shall we say, sedentary style of her predecessor, Tabitha Twitchit, you are correct. Crumpet is out to make her mark on the world.)

So she had called an unusual meeting of the Executive Committee of the Council in the shed at the foot of the Rose Cottage garden. It had proved rather difficult to get the committee together, since Tabitha Twitchit (who still served on the Executive Committee) had to come all the way from the Vicarage, and Treacle — a motherly orange tabby who lived just across the lane at the Llewellyns' — had to ask Felicity Frummety to mind her kittens. This small group obviously wasn't the police force Crumpet knew she needed, but perhaps it could function as a decision-making body.

"Well, then," Tabitha Twitchit said cattily. Tabitha was a plump, elderly calico with an orange and white bib, who — even though she was no longer president — still fancied herself in charge of things. *"What's it all about, eh?"* She scowled. *"I should like to remind you, Crumpet, that during my tenure as president, I never, ever called a meeting of the Executive Committee before teatime. It just isn't* done." With a resigned sigh, she examined a paw. *"Although, of course, you're new to the presidency, so allowances must be made. Do remember, though, for future reference. No meetings before teatime."*

Yes, indeed: sedentary. The older Tabitha got, the lazier she became. I daresay that both you and I have been acquainted with a great many such cats. There is such a one sitting on my foot as I write these very words.

Crumpet narrowed her eyes. *"I do not believe, Tabitha,"* she retorted, *"that during your tenure as president, the Council ever faced such a dire and dangerous dilemma as the one that confronts the village now. We have to come up with a workable solution,*

268

and quick, before we are completely over-whelmed!"

"*I sincerely hope,*" Treacle put in plaintively, "*that this won't be a very long meeting. I need to get home as quickly as I can. Felicity was the only minder I could get on such short notice, and I'm not at all sure I trust her with those kittens. She means well, but she's never been a mother and has no idea of the mischief a kitten can get up to when nobody's looking. What's the problem, Crumpet?*"

"*Don't worry, Treacle,*" Tabitha said in a comforting tone. "*Whatever it is, I'm sure it isn't nearly as 'dire and dangerous' a dilemma as Crumpet is making it out to be.*" She gave a scoffing meow. " *'Overwhelmed,' indeed. Our friend has always been prone to exaggeration, you know. The worse a thing looks, the better she likes it. A regular kitty Cassandra.*"

"*Cassandra?*" Treacle looked around, puzzled. "*Cassandra? Who's she? I don't believe I've met her.*"

"*I have never understood this personality quirk myself,*" Tabitha went on reflectively. "*Personally, I am very much a realist. I like to see a thing entirely as it is, without any exaggeration. I make it a rule never to cry wolf unless I myself have seen the paw prints and smelt the horrid creature. I am speaking* metaphorically, of course," she added with a superior sniff. *"We have not had wolves here in my lifetime. And in the absence of proof, I should have to say that our Crumpet is making a 'dire and dangerous' mountain out of an innocent little molehill."*

This did not sit well with Crumpet. *"Well, as far as metaphorical wolves are concerned,"* she replied hotly, *"I will tell you that —"*

But whatever Crumpet was about to say was drowned out by the deafening rattle and clatter and pot-banging at the back door of Rose Cottage, to the accompaniment of shrill female shrieks. It was young Mrs. Pemberton, who with her husband and infant daughter had recently moved into Rose Cottage. (You may remember that this was the cottage where Grace Lythecoe had lived with Caruso the canary before she married Vicar Sackett and moved to the Vicarage.)

Hearing the racket, all three cats rushed to the shed door, to see brave little Mrs. Pemberton on her back stoop with a broom in her hand.

"Out!" she cried, swinging the broom so hard that it nearly pulled her off her pretty feet. "Get out of here, you dirty, nasty, wicked creature! Out!"

And across the garden, with a perfectly

calibrated insouciance, sauntered the largest rat Crumpet had ever seen. He was very nearly as large as herself, with a sleek gray coat and neat paws, and a long, proud tail. He was carrying a cheese over one shoulder. A string of dried peppers was draped like a scarf around his neck. Balanced on his head, like a rakish brown hat, was a raisin-studded scone.

Now, the cats could not have known what this rat portended, but I am sure that you do. For this was no other than Jumpin' Jemmy, one of Rooker's boys, and the fastest rat in the pack.

Crumpet stared at the rat. The rat stared back. And then, incredibly, the filthy fellow gave her a broad, tantalizing wink and a seductive grin that showed crooked yellow teeth.

"Ah, kittee, my leetle love," he crooned in a phony French accent. *"Come, my sweet, let us rrrun away together. I'll even show you where old Rooker's rat gang lives!"*

At that moment, Mrs. Pemberton looked up and saw the three cats sitting in the shed doorway, staring with stunned amazement at the rat.

"Get him!" she shrieked. "You lazy, good-for-nothing cats, get t' wretched beast! Kill him!"

Perhaps you have been in a similar situation. You have opened the kitchen door and seen a mouse, or even large rat, helping himself to a cupcake or chewing open the corner of a package of pasta. And nearby, washing her paw or looking up at the ceiling or humming a little tune, sits your cat. Your lazy, good-for-nothing cat. So I am sure that you know exactly how Mrs. Pemberton felt about the members of the Executive Committee of the Village Cat Council.

But Crumpet was made of sterner stuff than her colleagues. Stung by the words "lazy" and "good-for-nothing" and infuriated by the rat's bold wink and insulting taunt, she snarled, unsheathed her claws, and leapt into action. The rat glanced casually over his shoulder without a trace of fear. Then, at a speed that Crumpet found utterly astonishing, he ran straight for a gap between two boards in the back fence and darted through, still carrying his ill-gotten gains. Crumpet, chagrined, flung herself at the top of the fence but could not quite scale it. With an ignominious *whump!* she thudded to the ground.

In the backyard of the village shop next door, Lydia Dowling had been pinning up damp tea towels on her clothesline. Now, hearing her neighbor's lamentations, she rushed to the fence.

"What's wrong, Mrs. Pemberton? What's happened?"

"It's a rat!" Mrs. Pemberton cried. "A huge, horrendous, hideous rat! He's been into my cheeses, an' he's made off with t' very best one! And a scone an' my peppers, too." Her voice rose even higher. "And just look at those worthless cats — three of them! They sat there like dunces an' let t' beast get away! They're not worth t' food we feed 'em."

"We were taken by surprise," Crumpet replied defensively, as she limped back to the shed. *"I don't think you understand what we're up against, Mrs. Pemberton. This is going to require a concerted effort. Effort and planning. And troops, as well. Troops who are a match for the enemy."* Her right shoulder hurt horribly and she was sure she had sprained it, attempting to leap that fence. *"But at least I tried,"* she added, glaring at Tabitha and Treacle. *"You lot didn't even budge. I call that cowardly, I do."*

"He was HUGE," Treacle retorted with a shudder. *"Revolting! Disgusting! And I have to put my kittens first, don't I, Crumpet? If I had been injured or killed going after that rat, who would take care of my babies?"*

Tabitha smiled a lazy, Cheshire-cat grin.

"You were frightfully brave, Crumpet. But I'm sure you don't expect a dowager cat of my years to actually chase a rat. You are so much younger and faster on your feet than I am, and you obviously gave that filthy fellow a run for his money. But fleet as you are, even you couldn't catch him, now, could you? So you can't expect me to do it for you."

"I am so sorry," Lydia Dowling condoled, leaning her forearms on the fence. "I wonder if it's t' same filthy rat that stole t' sausages from t' shop last night. And marrows, too — half a bin of 'em!"

"And Hannah Braithwaite told me this morning," Mrs. Pemberton said, "that something pulled the lid off her pickle crock during t' night an' stole every last one of t' little cucumbers she was savin' to make sweet pickles with."

"It's an invasion," Lydia said darkly. "That's wot it is. They probably came in on a lorry or in the back of t' brewer's cart." She shook her head. "Rats are bad trouble. And our village cats're all too fat an' lazy to do anything about 'em."

"Well, something's got to be done, Mrs. Dowling," Mrs. Pemberton replied in a determined voice, "or us woan't have a single cheese left. Nor pickles nor scones, neither." She raised her broom and pointed it at the cats. "An' you fat, lazy beasts doan't need to look for any treats from me," she cried. "Not until you take charge of those rats. An' that's a fact, that is! A pure fact."

"Wot a grand idea, Mrs. Pemberton," Lydia said approvingly. "We must all stop feeding t' cats. When they get hungry enough, they'll kill t' rats an' eat 'em. We'll tell everybody in t' village. No food for cats 'til t' rats are gone."

"*No food?*" Treacle cried. "*I'm a nursing mother. If I don't eat, how will I feed my babies?*"

"*Let them eat rats,*" Crumpet growled. "*And you, too.*"

"*My goodness,*" Tabitha muttered under her breath. "*No supper? I certainly hope they don't hear of this at the Vicarage.*"

"*Wouldn't hurt you to miss a meal or two,*" Crumpet retorted sharply. Tabitha had gained several pounds since she'd resigned the Council presidency and moved to the Vicarage.

"No food," Lydia said in a definitive tone, and left the fence.

"No food," Mrs. Pemberton agreed heartily, and went back inside and shut her door.

"*Oh, dear,*" Tabitha cried.

"*Yes,*" Treacle meowed piteously. "*My*

275

babies will starve!"

"*Can't you see?*" Crumpet shrilled. "*Forget food! Food is a minor consideration! That rat is the proof you were asking for, Tabitha. I am no Cassandra. I did not exaggerate. Those rats have broken into nearly every cottage in the village, taking food, valuables, even money — anything that the beasts can carry off.*"

Tabitha cleared her throat. "*I suppose we do have a problem,*" she said reluctantly.

"*Indeed we do,*" Crumpet replied. "*We must recommend a plan to the Council. But we have to take our resources into account. The village cats are in no position to take action. They are simply too weak and untrained. And lazy.*" She did not add "Like the two of you," but the accusation could be read in her manner. She looked from one to the other. "*Well? I'm open to suggestions. What sort of plan do you think we should recommend? If we need a police force — it looks to me like we do — who should we recruit?*"

There was a long silence, during which nothing could be heard except for the loud buzzing of a fly trapped against the window. Somewhere in the distance, thunder rumbled.

Treacle cleared her throat. "*I'm sorry,*

Crumpet," she said apologetically, *"but this sort of thing just isn't my line, you know. I simply must get home to my kittens. You and Tabitha have much more experience of these matters than I do. Whatever you decide to do, you can count on my support."* She left without another word.

Tabitha cocked her head. *"It must be nearly teatime,"* she said, *"and I'm sure I hear thunder. The Vicarage is quite a long walk, and I hate to get my fur wet. But do let me know when you've organized some sort of effort, will you, Crumpet? And please tell the Council that I wholeheartedly support whatever action you recommend. If it's raining, I probably won't come to the meeting."*

She walked to the door, adding carelessly, *"Oh, and I don't recommend trying to scale fences. You're not all* that *young, you know."* And with that spiteful remark, she was gone.

Crumpet was still sitting in the dusky twilight of the old shed, smarting at Tabitha's last remark, when Rascal pushed open the door and came in. He had just come from Jeremy's house. He was still somewhat chagrined at the thought that the new baby was not to be called Rascal (with a capital *R*) and only rascal (with a small *r*, and prefaced by the words "sweet" and "dear" and "little").

"I thought you were having a meeting this afternoon," he said, looking around the empty shed. He gave himself a shake, spraying drops everywhere. It was beginning to rain, and his coat was a bit damp. "Where is everybody?"

"They left," Crumpet said bitterly. "Tabitha and Treacle got a glimpse of the kind of horrid creature we are up against, and they were so frightened they bailed out." She reported on Mrs. Pemberton and the piratical rat who had sauntered across the back garden, as well as all the other break-ins and robberies around the village. "It's a crime wave," she said. "Old Rooker's gang, the rat told us. Something's got to be done, Rascal. And whatever it is, it has to be soon!"

"You're right," said Rascal in a thoughtful tone. He sat down on his haunches. "Mustard and I caught one of those fellows last night, in the Hill Top chicken coop." He told her about the sneering, filthy, foul-mouthed creature that he and the old yellow dog had captured and executed. "We thought he might be part of a gang, but we couldn't wring anything out of him." He paused, assessing the situation. "Well, old girl, I'd say we're in a bit of a bind, wouldn't you?"

Crumpet heard Rascal's "we" and was im-

278

measurably heartened at the thought that somebody was on her side. She had been feeling abandoned.

"A bit of a bind is right," she said. "This is a brazen enemy. We are under attack. It was very bad last night — thefts all over the village — and I shouldn't be a bit surprised if it's even worse tonight. And if we don't catch them quick, they'll get dug in, and it will be even harder to get them out of here."

"I wonder where they're holed up," Rascal mused. "Since they're carrying off the stolen property, they have to have a hideout somewhere close by. Did you get any hint of that, when you were asking around about the thefts?"

"No. But I didn't ask, either," Crumpet admitted, wishing she'd thought of it. Somebody might have been able to give her some information. "But when you stop to think about it, there aren't too many suitable places in the village. It's hard to say how many of these rats there are, but judging from the number of thefts, I'm guessing at least a dozen. I don't think a gang that size could slip into any of the cottages without attracting the Big Folks' attention."

"You're right. But a barn is a different matter," Rascal said. "They're full of holes and cubbies and places where rats can hide."

"Exactly," Crumpet said. "Felicia Frummety is frightened of her shadow. Perhaps this gang has moved into the Hill Top barn."

"Not there," Rascal asserted. "Mustard may not see as well as he once did, but there's nothing wrong with the dear old fellow's sense of smell. There are no rats in his barn."

"Well, there's the Llewellyn barn at High Green Gate," Crumpet said. "And the barn at Belle Green."

"Not at Belle Green," Rascal barked firmly. That was where *he* lived. And even if he had been so careless as to overlook a bunch of hooligan rats holed up in his barn, the cow and pigs and chickens would certainly let him know about it.

"Well, then, that just leaves High Green Gate and Castle Farm," Crumpet said thoughtfully. "And the stable at Tower Bank House."

"What about that old ramshackle barn behind the post office?" Rascal suggested. "They might be there. Or in the shed behind Courier Cottage, where Mr. Sutton puts his extra patients when he doesn't have enough room in the surgery." Mr. Sutton was the village veterinary and a good friend of all the animals.

"Right." Crumpet sighed. *"I know what we ought to do, Rascal. We ought to set up an overnight surveillance at every single one of these places and find out where the rats are hiding. Then we might be able to come up with some sort of effective battle strategy. But there aren't enough animals to manage the surveillance, let alone conduct the war."* She sighed again, despondently. *"Right now, there's just you and me, Rascal. And we can't be everywhere at once."*

"Well, you're definitely right on that score," Rascal replied, *"although you mustn't forget that I'm a terrier, and rats and foxes and such are my speciality."* He got up and stretched, forelegs first, hind legs after. *"But I think I have an idea about a few friends who might help out. Let me do some checking, old girl, and I'll get back to you."*

"But who?" Crumpet asked. She picked up the list of names she had discarded earlier and glanced through it. *"I've tried and tried, and I can't think of anybody who —"*

"Later," Rascal said, on his way to the door. *"Don't do anything until you hear from me."*

15
RATS!

I once had a white rat called Sammy . . . a dear; but he was a bit of a thief. I used to find all sorts of things hidden in his box. Once I found a stick of red sealing wax & some matches, just as if he had intended to write a letter and seal it carefully.
— **Beatrix Potter to a child named Dulcie**

Whilst Crumpet and Rascal were trying to come up with a plan, the rat in question — Jumpin' Jemmy, who had stolen Mrs. Pemberton's best cheese, peppers, and scone — had made his way through the back gardens and shrubbery and up the hill to the Castle Farm barn, where Rooker had installed his gang of rats.

When the rats took up residence in Miss Potter's barn a few days before, the hideout was a dismal place, just a large cavern under the floor, with a trapdoor in the roof but no special amenities. It hadn't stayed that way, however. Old Rooker's gang was energetic, innovative, and well organized. They were used to moving into a place and making themselves at home. In this case, they had done some additional digging, so now their hideout under the barn floor featured a suite of quite comfortable rooms: one large room for rest and relaxation, a bunkroom, and a smaller room for a headquarters, where Rooker could meet with his lieutenants.

In fact, it was all quite cozy, especially the headquarters room, which was carpeted with a large piece of woven fabric from Bertha Stubbs' sewing box. There was also a map table fashioned of a smooth strip of board set up on large wooden spools. It was lighted by a hanging oil lamp fashioned from a small bronze cup taken from the village shop and the chain from Mr. Leach's gold watch. The watch itself, properly wound and hung on the wall, served nicely for a timepiece.

And of course, since these were thieves, there was a large bowl for the deposit of the money they had stolen and the empty silver snuffbox (taken from Mr. Dowling) for the deposit of jewelry. Mrs. Crook's crystal pendant was there, along with a several rings, a set of studs, and a gold locket. The badgers' silver spoons were there, too, waiting to be traded or sold.

Indeed, that would be the fate of most of the "hard goods," as the rats called the money, jewelry, and other fine trinkets they picked up. Sully the Screed (a screed, in their parlance, is a writer or scrivener) kept the gang's account books, carefully noting what each rat brought in and giving him credit for his booty. Once the rats had established themselves in an area, they contacted members of the local underworld (there always is one, you know) and began to sell and trade. Every so often, Sully sat down and counted up what they'd brought in, then divvied the proceeds equitably, every rat getting his share of the profits, based on what he had contributed. Even edibles were counted, since the provisions kept the gang going strong. *"An army travels on its stomach,"* Rooker was fond of saying. *"We ain't no diff'rent from an army, boys."*

In the bunkroom, along two walls, there were tiers of bunk beds where the rats slept when they were off duty. The beds were padded with wads of soft cotton pulled from village mattresses and yarn and half-finished socks taken from knitting baskets all over the village, and there was a rug on the floor made from Mrs. Crook's dishcloth (which she has not yet missed).

In the common room, there were tables where the rats could play cards and eat and drink, a few makeshift benches, and a couple of upholstered chairs stolen from Mrs. Braithwaite's daughter's doll house. There was a dart board on one wall and a long shelf where food and drink were set out as soon as they were brought in by the foragers. They had sausages and marrows from Lydia Dowling's village shop, nuts from the pub bar and cheddars and goat cheeses from the pub kitchen, sticky buns from the bakery. There were meat patties and pickled pigs' feet and ham croquettes (stolen from Elsa Grape's larder), and apples and pears and nuts and raisins. The air was thick with cigarette and cigar smoke, several of the rats were singing a raucous ditty, and from the corner could be heard the clink of a game of pitch-and-toss.

There was a celebratory mood in the headquarters room, too, where Rooker and three of his henchmen were gathered around the table, under the overhead lamp. They were passing around a bottle of red wine, and chunks of cheese and pieces of scone littered the table. (Rats are not known for their tidy eating habits.) Jumpin' Jemmy had just brought in the loot he had stolen from

Mrs. Pemberton's kitchen, along with a report on the three cats who had watched him from the shed.

"One was old, one was fat, and only one — gray, with a red collar — looked halfway fit." He gave the self-congratulatory chuckle of a rat who was mightily pleased with himself. *"Ye should've seen the look on the gray cat's face when I tossed her a wink and a few choice words. She thought she'd come after me, too, she did, but I squirted right between the boards of the fence."* He hooted. *"An' her too big to squeeze thro' the gap an' not near nimble 'nuf to hop over the top."*

"Well, if that's the top quality of cat hereabouts," Firehouse Frank said judiciously, *"we've lucked into a sweet spot to hang out for a while, boys. Fat cats, old cats, slow cats — just the kind o' cats we like to see."* Frank, like Jemmy, was a young rat, but he'd had a bad run-in with a tomcat in a dark alley and was lucky to get away in one piece. He wore a rakish black patch over his right eye — quite a handsome beast, I must say, if a bit piratical.

"Aye, but did ye hear that Big Bill Bolter got nabbed last night?" Rooker asked somberly, puffing on a long-stemmed clay pipe. *"Worst luck fer 'im, I'm afeard. He's gone, boys. Big Bill Bolter's gone."*

"*The devil ye say!*" cried Jumpin' Jemmy, suddenly sobered. He picked up the bottle of wine and tipped it up. "*Where'd it 'appen? 'Oo done it? Not a cat, was it?*"

"*'Appened at the chicken coop at Hill Top,*" Rooker replied. "*Him and Nick the Knife was there, with their eyes on a tasty little yellow chick they thought to snatch for a midnight meal.*" He reached for the bottle, shaking his rattish head. "*Nay, 't weren't no cat, Jemmy. 'Twas two dogs did fer 'im. But Nick said Big Bill held loyal an' true right to the end. Never chirped on us, not a word. Wouldn't say where we're holed up, although they twisted 'is tail 'n' ears right off 'im, poor old sod.*" He lifted the bottle. "*'Ere's to Big Bill, boys. No finer rat never lived than Bill.*"

"*No finer rat!*" they echoed, as Rooker drank. There was a moment's silence as they reflected on the bravery of Big Bill Bolter, who had loyally refused to yield up their whereabouts. They were used to losing one or more of their number every now and then — rats who chose to live an outlaw life lived on the razor's edge. But the loss was always felt with a pang, and a sharper one, this time, given the appalling violence of Bill's end. And there was the terrible thought, in every rat's mind, that *he* might have been in that chicken coop when the dogs came. Would *he* have died so valiantly, without chirping on his pals?

"Two *dogs, ye say?*" Firehouse Frank asked nervously. "*We got us a dog problem, do we?*"

"*Nick says that one of 'em — the big yellow dog — is so old 'ee could barely see,*" Bludger Bob replied, tipping his black felt bowler to the back of his head. Bob, a scrawny brown rat with one missing front tooth, had been with the Rooker gang longer than any of them. His opinion was always listened to with respect. "*It's the other we got to watch out for. Rascal, 'is name is. A Jack Russell.*" He said this deliberately, looking around the table to make sure they took his point.

"*Uh-oh,*" said Jumpin' Jemmy.

"*Them Jack Russells is allus trouble,*" Firehouse Frank agreed very seriously. He took out a packet of tobacco and a packet of papers and began to roll a cigarette. "*They never know when to quit. Stubborn as the devil hisself.*" He had tangled with one once, and the encounter had seared itself into his memory. "*Any more terriers in town, Bob?*"

"*Not that we've heard.*" Bludger Bob handed Firehouse a match. "*Mostly, just old slow dogs, tho' there's a few young sheep-*"

dogs, without any trainin' or interest in rat-catchin'." He shook his head. *"Don't seem like we'll run up against any we can't handle. But pass the word to keep a close eye peeled for that Rascal. Nick the Knife says 'ee's trouble with a big* T."

"Well warned, then." Rooker straightened up and glanced from one to the other of the rats around the table. *"Yer all set to go out agin tonight and clean up, boys?"*

"Yessir," the rats answered in an eager chorus. *"All set, sir."*

"I got my eye on that bak'ry," Jumpin' Jemmy asserted. *"The lady wot runs it never locks her cash box. And 'er sticky buns ain't half-bad, neither."* He elbowed Frank with a playful grin. *"Ye can go with me if ye want, Firehouse. Wouldn't mind somebody watchin' the door for me, now, would I?"*

"Not me," Frank replied warmly, pulling on his cigarette. *"I'm headed for the pub. I'll be glad if ye can go along wi' me, Bludger Bob. Between the kitchen and the bar, there's work for two an' then some."*

"I'm yer man, Firehouse," said Bludger, with a conscious irony. He yanked his bowler hat down over his eye, rubbed his paws together, and grinned evilly. *"We'll clean 'em out, we will. Won't be nuffin left fer*

289

breakfast when we gets finished with 'em."

"Looks like rain out there t'night," Jumpin' Jemmy added, grinning. "It'll keep the folks in by their fires. 'Speshly the cats an' dogs," he added.

"Aye," Rooker agreed. "Rain is right for the likes o' we." He knocked the bowl of his pipe onto the floor. "One more thing. If ye see somethin' ye fancy — plate or a picture or fine tool — and it's too big to be dragged through the trapdoor, don't let that stop ye. Ye can stash yer swag under that pile of hay on the floor up there." He nodded in the direction of the ceiling of their hideout. "The barn ain't in use right now, so nobody's goin' to find it."

Rooker was led to say this because his rats were in the habit of dragging in swag of various sizes. Some of the booty — rings and studs, for instance — was quite small, whilst some of it was larger, such as the cream jug that Firehouse Frank had lifted from Mrs. Braithwaite's sideboard and the miniature silver frame containing the wedding photograph of Captain and Mrs. Miles Woodcock that Bludger Bob copped from the Tower Bank library. The photograph was obviously of little value, Bob thought, but the silver frame might be worth as much as a crown. (Actually, Dimity Kittredge had paid double that at the expensive shop in London where she'd bought it. There are all kinds of thievery.)

Or the very curious book that Rooker himself had stolen.

Now, it must be said that our larcenous friend is not much of a book reader (his taste runs to racing forms, theater playbills, and sensational penny-sheets). But even if he were a reader, he could not have read this unusual book. It wasn't written in English, and even though the letters looked tantalizingly familiar, he couldn't make heads nor tails (so to speak) of the words. It wasn't printed on paper, either, as most books of his acquaintance were. The letters appeared to be written in ink (some of it slightly smudged) on soft, supple pages that felt very much like (Rooker shuddered) animal skin. One or two of the pages contained no writing at all, but only a brightly colored design that looked something like a Turkish carpet.

It was not the pages of this book that caught Rooker's attention, however, nor was he particularly interested in what was written on them, or who wrote it, or when. What had attracted him (and the reason he had nicked the thing in the first place) was its remarkable cover, which was devised of leather and hammered gold and studded with what looked to Rooker like rubies and emeralds and sapphires. Of course, they might be just bits of polished glass, but Rooker didn't think so.

Rubies and emeralds and sapphires, indeed! And unless the old rat missed his guess (which he almost never did, for he had the eye of an accomplished thief), this curious book would be worth quite a bit in the underworld art market.

Which was why he had hidden it under the pile of hay on the floor of the Castle Farm barn.

16
SPEAKING OF BOOKS . . .

When we took leave of Lady Longford at the end of Chapter Six, she had been nearly bowled over by the news that her husband's collection of moldy old books was worth the tidy sum of ten thousand pounds sterling. But as you will recall, Mr. Depford Darnwell, who appraised the collection, made it clear that this amount did not include the *Revelation of John,* which was listed in Lord Longford's book catalog but was not on the shelves with the rest of the collection. Mr. Darnwell had informed her ladyship that even though the book was unfinished and consisted of only eight pages, it might be ten times more valuable than the collection as a whole. Where was it? Might he see it? Her ladyship, chagrined, had to confess that she had never seen the book and knew nothing about it. It had apparently gone missing.

Remembering this (and putting two and

two together), perhaps you have concluded that Rooker Rat has broken into Tidmarsh Manor and stolen this valuable book. But I must tell you, straight off, that this is not what happened, so that you will not waste your valuable time attempting to follow this particular red herring.

But is it not true, you quite reasonably ask, that the book hidden under the pile of hay in the barn at Castle Farm is the very same book that Lady Longford is searching for?

Yes, indeed. It is the same book — or at least I feel that it must be, for Mr. Darnwell has said that there is not another such book in the world, except for the Lindisfarne Gospels, which the British Museum holds firmly in its proprietary grip and which you can see if you visit the museum. And which Beatrix herself had seen on numerous occasions when she visited the museum with her father and Bertram — had seen and admired and no doubt remembered.

Well, then, I hear you asking, if Rooker did not steal the book from Tidmarsh Manor, where did he get it? You will learn the answer to that question in good time, if you will contain your soul in patience for a little longer. Or at least I think you will, for stories generally provide the answers to important plot puzzles, of which this is certainly one.

Therefore, we shall return to Lady Longford and the missing book.

Her ladyship is particularly anxious to find it, I am sorry to say, not because she values the *Revelation* as an object of art and rare antiquity but because of what Mr. Darnwell has said it will fetch when it is sold. And she has another reason, too, even less laudable than this. She is deeply and painfully mortified by the idea that something that belongs to her has disappeared and cannot be accounted for. You may be acquainted with people like this, who have an exceedingly strong proprietary sense and value a thing not because it is fine or beautiful or ancient or otherwise desirable, but chiefly because it is *theirs.*

This is the case, I am sorry to say, with Lady Longford, who is not only chagrined that the book has gone missing but is deeply annoyed at poor Lord Longford, whom she suspects of having carelessly mislaid it.

Now, when Lady Longford began her search, she had the idea that the book would be found quickly and without a lot of trouble. She began by searching the rooms adjacent to the third-floor box room where the books were kept, then extended the search to the servants' sleeping quarters and the old nursery and schoolroom, unused for many years, all on that same floor. Did she search the servants' bureau drawers? Yes, quite naturally she did, for didn't the rooms belong to her, and the drawers, and the servants, as well? And after that, she moved up yet another flight of stairs, to the dark and dusty attics.

I daresay you are laughing up your sleeve at the futility of all this rummaging around, for you know where the book is — and that it is not at Tidmarsh Manor. But Lady Longford does not know this and is driven by an extraordinarily intense and greedy desire to find it. She is not doing any of the searching herself, of course. She is merely supervising the work that is carried out by Maud Bloomsdale, the upstairs maid. But she is supervising very carefully, making sure that Maud does not "accidentally" slip the book or anything else (a cuff link, say, or a silk handkerchief or a tortoiseshell comb) into a pocket of her frilly white apron.

However, whilst this search was conducted both expeditiously and intensively, it was carried out under a substantial handicap, for Lady Longford stubbornly refused to tell Maud Bloomsdale what they were looking for. When Maud asked, her ladyship would only say, "Never mind, Maud. I shall tell you what we are looking for when it has been found." She did condescend to add that the object was some ten inches by twelve inches and perhaps an inch thick, from which Maud might have inferred that they were looking for a box or a stack of papers or a piece of wood or even a book. But beyond that generality, her ladyship would not go.

Now, this meant that the contents of every bureau drawer and shelf and every nook and cranny in every room (and of every box and bag and bundle in all the attics) had to be turned out onto a table, and when her ladyship had gone through it, it must then be put back in its proper place. Since Tidmarsh Manor contained twenty-two upstairs rooms, that was a great deal of turning out and putting back, as you can well imagine.

In the course of this, a number of things were found that had not previously been known to be lost, such as the lavender lace fichu that her ladyship had worn with her going-away costume some fifty years before, and the polished turtle shell that her ladyship's great uncle had brought home from the Galapagos Islands, where he had voyaged on the *Beagle* with that awful Mr.

Darwin, in 1831. Oh, and also found was the silver-backed mirror that Lady Longford believed to have been stolen by the last upstairs maid but one, who had been accused of and summarily discharged for the theft. (I am very sorry to tell you that her ladyship was not discomfited by the discovery of the mirror, as you or I might have been, nor did she feel at all guilty for having falsely accused an innocent servant. In fact, she had forgotten all about the incident and was merely pleased to have the mirror back again.)

But the attics were finished, and the third-floor servants' rooms and the second-floor bedrooms, and no book had been found. All that was left was the main downstairs rooms, the great dining room, and the drawing room. And when all these were done and still nothing had been found, there was only the library remaining. This was the hardest room to search, of course, for there were floor-to-ceiling shelves on three walls, all of them lined with a great variety of books. Yes, books. Books of all sizes and dimensions.

It was by now beginning to dawn upon on her ladyship that her deceased husband might not have simply mislaid his valuable book. Instead, he might have deliberately hidden it, although why he should do such an inconsiderate thing (and especially why he should not have told her about it!), she could not begin to guess.

But if he *had* hidden it, what better place than his library? He might have tucked the precious book inside some larger volume, or perhaps behind a row of volumes. Which meant, of course, that Lady Longford had to see that every single one of the thousands of volumes in the library was taken off the shelves and opened in front of her, to be sure that it did not contain the book she was looking for.

At this important juncture, a spanner was tossed into Lady Longford's works, for Maud Bloomsdale's mother fell ill. Old Mrs. Bloomsdale lived alone and had no one to care for her, so Maud naturally asked Lady Longford for a few days' holiday. To which request, her ladyship quite naturally said no (which is what she always said when one of the servants asked for time off), and required Maud to choose between her employer and her mother.

To Maud's everlasting credit, she chose her mother and then went home to care for her, leaving Lady Longford to look for another upstairs maid. (Please don't worry about Maud. I am pleased to tell you that, after her mother was well again, she was hired by Mrs. Kittredge at Raven Hall, which is a far better and kinder situation at a far better and more rewarding salary than she could ever have earned at Tidmarsh Manor.)

But since Maud was now gone and her ladyship did not trust the young tweeny — a girl named Lucy — to carry out her search, she had no other choice than to ask Mrs. Beever. So the very next morning, Lady Longford summoned her cook from the kitchen and ordered her to report to the library at two every afternoon for the next three days.

When she heard this request, Mrs. Beever felt decidedly uneasy. She was a round-faced, plump, and cheerful lady who had cooked at Tidmarsh Manor for many years and felt most at home in the kitchen.

"An' what'll your ladyship be wantin' me to do in the library?" she asked uncertainly.

Lady Longford waved a hand at the shelves (for they were in the library whilst this discussion was going on). "We will be searching every book and each shelf. The task should take, I estimate, about four days. You will remove the books from the shelves and show them to me. Then you will dust and replace them."

Mrs. Beever was taken aback, and never being one to keep silent, she said what came first to her mind. "Well, mum, if ye'll forgive me for sayin' so, couldn't t' job wait until t' new maid comes? If it's only takin' down and dustin' books, I mean. If I'm dustin' books in t' library, I woan't be cookin' in t' kitchen, for I canna be in two places at once. Supper is bound to suffer, as well as t' next day's dinner. An' t' plums are comin' on this week. Who'll make t' jelly, if I'm dustin' books?"

"The job is important," her ladyship said sternly. "It cannot wait."

"Aye, mum," Mrs. Beever said. She paused, recalling what Maud had told her, that her ladyship was frantic to find something she had lost and was turning out the whole house in the hunt for it. "If ye'll pardon me askin', are we lookin' for the same thing that you an' Maud were lookin' for?"

Lady Longford drew herself up to her full height. "What we are looking for is none of your business, Mrs. Beever," she said ferociously. "All that is required of you is to be here at two this afternoon to look for it. Is that understood?"

And with that, Mrs. Beever had to be satisfied. But that night, after spending the entire afternoon in the library, she told her husband, " 'Tis a gert mystery, what we're lookin' for. She woan't even tell me, just has me pull out book after book and open each one on the table in front of her. Mayhap she's huntin' for a piece of paper."

"A letter, mebbee?" Mr. Beever hazarded. He frowned. "Or money? Could be money."

"It's crazy," Mrs. Beever said, shaking her head. "Mayhap she doan't even know her own self what she's lookin' for. Daft as a brush, the woman is."

"Daresay she'll know it when she sees it," her husband said in a comforting tone. "An so'll you, Mrs. Beever."

"But what if we doan't find whatever it is, an' she starts accusin' folk of takin' it?" Mrs. Beever asked worriedly.

"Borrowin' trouble nivver pays," Mr. Beever cautioned, but he looked worried, too.

So for the next two afternoons, Lady Longford and Mrs. Beever went through all the books in the library. Mrs. Beever was required to clear an entire shelf at a time, baring the wall behind the books. Then she brought the larger books to the table where Lady Longford sat. Her ladyship would open each book in three or four places, then close it again, to be dusted and returned to the shelf.

In this way, they went through all the volumes in the library. They found a five-pound note tucked between two pages in Gibbon's *Decline and Fall,* and four-leaf clovers, and a shoestring that had been used to mark someone's place, and odd bits of writing, lists and notes and even several letters. But none of this seemed to be what her ladyship was looking for.

They finished the job on the day that news of Mr. Adcock's death was making its way around the village. Mr. Beever had carried the tidings to Mrs. Beever, who knew Mrs. Adcock from the parish committees they served on and was deeply saddened. Mrs. Beever took the news to Lady Longford, who only pressed her thin lips together and said, "Well, it was Adcock's choice, wasn't it? Nobody made him do it. I suppose he simply decided that his life wasn't worth living."

Mrs. Beever had to literally bite her tongue to keep from snapping a bitter reply, and began dusting the empty bookshelf with such ferocity that the dust flew into the air, sending her ladyship into a violent sneezing fit — quite a satisfactory fit, as far as Mrs. Beever was concerned, even though she had to endure a scolding for it.

By the end of the afternoon, the last book had been examined and replaced on the shelf. Her ladyship sat forward in her chair and folded her hands with a scowl, speaking sternly.

"Well, now, Mrs. Beever, I have arrived at a conclusion. This entire house has been searched from top to bottom as carefully as possible, and the object for which I am searching has not been found. So I must presume that it has been stolen." She had the grace to add, "Not that I am accusing you or Mr. Beever." They had been with her for so long and had been so earnest and unimaginative that she could not picture them as thieves, and in this case, I must assure you that her ladyship is right. The Beevers are as honest as the day is long.

"But there have been other servants in the house," her ladyship added, "and you yourself have been acquainted with each of them. In your opinion, who might have stolen it?"

Mrs. Beever had been preparing herself for this question. "Well, I s'pose 'tis possible," she said unwillingly. "But I canna say more until I know what might've been took."

Lady Longford hesitated, still reluctant but feeling that it was now necessary to reveal what she was looking for. "It is a book," she said at last, "a very old book that Lord Longford acquired a very long time ago. So now I must ask you who might have had the opportunity to steal this thing."

"A book!" Mrs. Beever was astonished, for she could not fathom why anybody would want to steal a book, especially an old book. She wrinkled her nose. "Well, there've been three or four tweenies. But what they'd want with a book, I canna guess. Anyway, they're seldom left alone long 'nough to make off with anythin'."

Mrs. Beever was right, for the tweenies (who worked both upstairs and down) were either in the kitchen with her or working with the upstairs maid. They slept upstairs and could have crept into the box room and taken the book when the rest of the household was asleep, but Mrs. Beever did not think of that.

"Who else?" Lady Longford asked.

"There's been four upstairs maids over t' past years," Mrs. Beever said. She counted them on her fingers. "Mayhew, Brandon, Lamont, and t' last one, Maud Bloomsdale."

"Brandon!" Lady Longford seized on one of the names. "Brandon. Sally Brandon. She lives at Castle Farm with her mother and father, I believe. Did I not discharge the girl for theft?"

Mrs. Beever nodded uncomfortably. Sally Brandon was the unfortunate young person who had been accused of stealing Lady Longford's silver-backed mirror — falsely and tragically, as it now seemed.

"Well, there you have it!" Lady Longford exclaimed triumphantly. "Once a thief, always a thief. It was Sally Brandon who took the book! I'm sure of it!"

"But Maud said that t' mirror was found," Mrs. Beever reminded her ladyship. Half under her breath, she added, "So Sally Brandon wa'n't a thief after all."

No thief, she thought sadly, but without a character from Lady Longford and with rumors of thievery swirling all around her, poor Sally had not been able to get another place in the village. She had married the eldest Crawley boy, who then lost his arm in a mowing accident. The two of them had disappeared into the maw of London. Lord only knew where they were now, or what they were doing.

"Nonsense," Lady Longford replied crisply. If she heard the barely concealed accusation in Mrs. Beever's tone, she ignored it. She also ignored the supreme illogic in her own reply. "Of course Sally

Brandon was a thief. The fact that the mirror was discovered means nothing. She could have taken a half-dozen other items and not been found out. I am quite sure that she took the book." Her ladyship lifted her chin. "Tell Mr. Beever I want the phaeton brought round. I shall drive at once to Castle Farm and demand that the girl return Lord Longford's book."

Mrs. Beever tried not to roll her eyes. "But t' Brandons have been gone for quite some time," she said. "Sally got married an' her an' her husband went to Lunnun, an' nobody's heard from 'em since. Her mum's dead. Her dad got married again and went to Canada."

Lady Longford's eyes narrowed to slits, and her bosom began to heave. "You're telling me that Sally Brandon got away with my book and I'll never get it back?" Her voice rose shrilly in the course of this sentence, and by the time she reached the question mark at the end, she was shrieking. "Summon the constable! Fetch Captain Woodcock. I want that girl found and my book returned!"

By this time, Mrs. Beever was deeply offended. Righteously offended, she felt, and her sense of affront on Sally's behalf gave her courage. She drew herself up, standing

307

like a rock, chin up, fists on hips, elbows out at right angles, the image of stalwart dignity and offended justice.

"I am tellin' your ladyship that Sally wa'n't no thief," she said staunchly. "Whatever happened to t' book ye're lookin' for, Sally Brandon didn't take it."

This is quite wonderful, isn't it? So admirable of Mrs. Beever, defying Lady Longford's terrible wrath in defense of a vulnerable young woman.

But I am very sorry to say that Mrs. Beever — who can usually be counted upon as a very reliable judge of a servant's character — is completely wrong about Sally Brandon. For when that slight, pretty young girl of sixteen found herself accused of theft and realized that she was about to be sacked for something she did not do, she did something she would not have otherwise done, not in a million years.

She crept into the small, dark box room where Lord Longford's collections had been willy-nilly dumped on the shelves and thrown on the floor and took the *Revelation of John.* Like Rooker, Sally didn't care how old the book was or who had made it, and she had no interest in what was written on its pages, for she herself rarely read anything but penny-dreadfuls and lending-library romances. She couldn't have read it, anyway, because it was written in Latin.

What's more, she had no idea — none at all! — that the thing had any value. She merely thought that the cover was pretty, with all that gold-colored metal and the bits of sparkling green and red and blue glass that looked like emeralds and rubies and sapphires. Of course, she knew that the metal couldn't really be gold, and those couldn't really be jewels, for if they were, the book would be enormously valuable and would be locked up in the family safe, away from thieves. But it wasn't. It was lying on a dusty shelf, along with broken butterflies and dirty old rocks. Nobody knew it was there. Nobody would know if she took it.

So Sally, no thief at heart but accused of being one, became one.

And the book? It went back to Castle Cottage with her, carried away in her little bundle of underwear and stockings and the apron Lady Longford required her to buy out of her meager earnings. She put it under her bed and forgot about it in all the flurry of efforts to find new work. Then she fell in love with the eldest Crawley boy and forgot about everything else in the whole wide world, which I am sure you understand from your own experience.

And then one day her little brother Dickey looked under his sister's bed and found the book, and he, too, thought it was pretty, with all those bits of glass stuck all over it. Dickey had chiseled out a little hidey-hole in the inner wall of the tiny corner room where he slept, where he hid his three precious marbles and the broken knife blade he'd found in the lane and the star-shaped brass decoration that had fallen off Captain Woodcock's horse's bridle. It was in this hidey-hole that he tucked the book for safekeeping. And then, not a week later, tragedy struck. Dickey's mother died, and he was summarily shipped off to live with his grandmother in Carlisle. He didn't have time to take his pretties with him.

And now (having put two and two together again) I can hear you cry once more, with a note of triumph and great glee: "Oh, now I have it! Rooker Rat found the book that Sally Brandon stole and her little brother Dickey hid in his hidey-hole in the wall! That's how the *Revelation* got into the pile of hay on the floor of barn!"

But once again, dear reader, I must tell you that this is not what happened. And once again, I must beg you to be patient, for there are several more twists in the story of the *Revelation.* We will untwist them in

310

good time.

But in the meantime, we are going down to Hill Top Farm, where Miss Potter is also thinking about a book.

And her book, too, is unfinished.

17
MISS POTTER AND MR. HEELIS
SPEAK FROM THE HEART

I am rather disturbed at that cheque not having come — is there going to be any delay in keeping to the plan of settling the 1912 account, & beginning to pay the 1913 account in October? . . . I am not short but I am spending money on building, and I ought to cut my coat according to my cloth! When one knows there is money overdue one is tempted to spending.
— **Beatrix Potter to Harold Warne, 1913**

After Bertram left to go back to Lindeth How, Beatrix sat very still for a very long time, turning things over in her heart. Her brother's quixotic decision might help him feel better about his deception, for making a clean breast of things usually did improve one's state of mind. She certainly could not blame him for wanting to do that. But his revelation would completely and utterly destroy their parents. When she arrived on

Monday, things would be in a terrible state. Her mother would be hysterical, her father would be furious. However would she cope? Just the thought of it made her head hurt.

But it wasn't Beatrix's way to sit around and fret. Bertram was going to do whatever he was going to do, no matter how unwise she thought it. Anyway, there were other, more immediate things she needed to attend to. The unfinished book, still just a litter of partially completed pages on the table in front of her. She had to finish it as soon as possible, or the children would not have it by Christmas. There was the letter that she ought to write to Harold Warne, inquiring about the missing royalty cheques. And the invoices for building materials that had arrived in Saturday's post from Mr. Biddle, which she had put in a stack on top of the oak dresser against the wall. She had bills to pay, although if the royalty cheque didn't arrive soon, there might not be enough money to cover everything.

Characteristically, Beatrix chose to do the most unpleasant thing first. She sat down, picked up her pen, and drafted the letter to Harold Warne. The few sentences — especially the phrase "money overdue" — seemed curt, and she frowned at them. Was there a less offensive way to remind him that she was still waiting for the payment he had promised her last year? But perhaps it was better to be direct. Beating around the bush never got her anywhere with Harold, who seemed to turn a deaf ear to her concerns about reliable accounting and timely payment. She often wondered whether he treated Warne's other authors in the same cavalier way, or if he was careless with her accounts because he considered her — his brother's former fiancée — to be one of the family. Familiarity breeding contempt, as it were.

She put the letter aside to finish and recopy later and turned to glance at the grandfather clock in the alcove beside the stairs. The clock's graceful hands and lovely painted face told her that it was not quite six. Will would be here at seven, and she had to change for dinner with the Woodcocks and Kittredges. There was just enough time to have a look at Mr. Biddle's invoices — and now was the right moment to do it, too, with Sarah Barwick's question still echoing in her mind. "What would you do if you suspected that somebody was stealing from you, Bea?" and the thought of those brass door handles that Henry Stubbs had bought.

She turned and went to the oak dresser,

which displayed on its shelves some nice old pieces of Staffordshire blue willow earthenware and a pair of antique portrait bowls. She picked up the invoices and carried them back to the table, pausing to pour herself a cup of hot tea. Then, still thinking about what Sarah had told her, she sat down with a pencil and paper and began making a list of the building materials, by category: lumber, slate, flooring, window frames, window glass, nails, hardware, and so on, with the amount she had been billed for each.

A little later, she got up and fetched the notebook where she had filed the other invoices — the ones she had already paid — and added those items to her list. As she worked, something caught her attention. And then another thing, and another. She stared down at the items, noting the initials on each one. She went back over the list once again, but she could see that there was only one conclusion to be drawn. She put her pencil down with a heavy sigh. Only one. And now that she understood the situation, what should she do about it? What *could* she do?

The cuckoo clock cleared its throat — hesitantly, as if reluctant to interrupt her — and struck once. She glanced up, startled.

Half past six already. She pushed her chair back and got up, stretching stiffly. She had better go upstairs and change for dinner.

To Mrs. Potter's often (and loudly) expressed dismay, Beatrix was not a "dressy" sort of person. The Potters frequently entertained and Beatrix always helped serve as hostess, but even when she was younger, she had resisted her mother's attempts to choose stylish costumes for her. A simple dark dress or a trim woolen or serge skirt and a tailored blouse with a tie or a modest bit of lace — these were much more to her taste than expensive materials, tiers of ruffles, and yards of ribbon, even for parties. Tonight, for the party at the Woodcocks', she put on her blue silk blouse, which Will said was just the color of her eyes, and a gray wool skirt. She applied a comb to her flyaway brown hair and managed to bring it at least partially under control.

Still holding the comb, she stared for a moment at herself in the mirror, wondering what handsome Will Heelis, who was admired by all who knew him, could possibly see in someone as plain as she. And then she remembered his remoteness earlier in the day and thought once again that perhaps he had decided to break off their engagement. After that disastrous session with her parents, he might have come to share her feeling that there was no use in waiting for a future that might never happen, a feeling that was even sharper now that Bertram had made up his mind to tell their parents about his marriage.

She put down her comb, pressing her lips together and trying to swallow the sudden large lump in her throat. William Heelis was a gentleman through and through, and gentlemen did not break engagements. If left to his own devices, he might go muddling along forever, feeling miserable but unable to bring himself to do anything about it. Something so decisive, so definitive, would have to be up to her. And Beatrix knew that what had happened this afternoon, here in this very house, had changed everything: Bertram's announcement of his marriage would make her own marriage impossible. She should tell Will that they must break it off. And she should do it tonight, before they went out to dinner together.

She took a deep breath and squared her shoulders, looking straight into her eyes in the mirror. Yes, that's exactly what she should do — break it off. Of course, telling Will before they went out to dinner would make for a terribly awkward evening. But if she left it for later, she might lose her nerve. This constant seesawing tug between hope and apprehension was too painful to bear. A clean break would be easier for both of them, wouldn't it? And it would surely be better to end their engagement sooner rather than later. The longer they went on together, the more deeply they cared for one another, the harder it would be to go their separate ways.

Beatrix sighed. She was wishing now that she had not begun the construction work at Castle Cottage, which she had romantically imagined as the house of their dreams. Really — that was so silly, so foolish. Not only would the house never be finished, but she and Will would never live there together. The thought broke her heart.

She took another breath, leaned forward, and spoke earnestly to her mirror, rehearsing what she knew she had to say. "Will, dearest, dearest Will, I cannot go on causing you so much pain and unhappiness. You know my heart: it's yours forever. But Bertram told me today that he intends to make a clean breast of his secret marriage to Mama and Papa. But I know them, and I know that his confession will only make them more stubbornly opposed to our marriage. I cannot ask you to wait and hope for something that will never happen."

Yes. That was what she had to say. She rehearsed it once more, so that she would get all the words right. "Will, dearest Will . . ."

But on her third rehearsal, the words stuck in her throat and she dissolved into helpless tears. She was mopping her eyes with a very wet handkerchief when she heard the knock at the door. Two raps, a pause, a third. Will's knock.

She went slowly and reluctantly down the stairs, her heart beating, feeling as if she were going to her execution. And then she opened the door.

Of course, Beatrix was right. Will Heelis *was* considering breaking off their engagement — although not for the reasons that Beatrix imagined. If you will remember, you and I were eavesdropping on the conversation in the library at Tower Bank House when Will told Miles Woodcock that he was desperately worried about Beatrix's health. He was wondering whether he should break off the engagement (although true gentlemen never do anything like that!) and free Beatrix from the terrible tug-of-war that was making her physically ill.

Miles, of course, had advised him to simply pack up Miss Potter, bag and baggage, and make for the nearest church. "And the sooner the better," he had added sternly. Miles spoke with the confident voice of a happily married man, although if truth be told, he himself had delayed marrying for many years and was not sure even now exactly how he had come to propose to his wife. All he knew was that he was very happy about it, however it had happened. (You can read the whole story, which is really quite amusing, in *The Tale of Applebeck Orchard*.)

But even though Will desperately wanted to take his friend's advice, he could not, for he absolutely refused to put Beatrix into the dreadful position of choosing between becoming his wife and remaining her parents' dutiful daughter. He had promised her, over and over again, that he would be content to wait until she could come to him with an easy heart, free of all other considerations.

This was still true, of course, and always would be. He was willing to wait. Indeed, he would wait for her until the end of time, if that's what it took, for Will Heelis was a romantic where matters of the heart were concerned, and Beatrix Potter was and would always be the love of his life.

But while Will was content to be led by his heart, he was very much a pragmatist. As a solicitor, he had trained himself to understand and evaluate cause and effect. He understood what sort of predicament Beatrix was in, how true she was to her duty, and what a terrible toll was being exacted upon her by this intolerable, unbearable conflict of loyalties. He knew how desperately sick she had been during the spring, and he understood the reasons for her illness, for he could read them between the lines of her letters to him, just as clearly as if she had spelled them out. And he had been entirely serious when he told Miles that he felt he had to break their engagement, for *her* sake. It would tear his heart in two, but he could live with a broken heart, if it restored Beatrix to health.

Which is why, when Will Heelis stands now on the stoop at Hill Top Farm, his hand raised to knock at Miss Potter's door, he fully intends to tell her that he wishes to be released from his promise. It is a hard, hard thing, the hardest thing he has ever done in his entire life. It is also a *despicable* thing, a thing that no gentleman worthy of the name should ever consider! But he knows he must do it, and he must do it now, before he is a minute older, because if he puts it off, he won't do it at all. He screws his courage to the sticking point, rehearsing in his mind the words that he has already practiced a dozen times or more, words that he will begin to utter the minute Beatrix opens the door.

"My dearest dear," he will say, "I have come to the sad conclusion that we cannot go on as we are. I am yours and will forever remain so. I will never love anyone in this world but you. But I am afraid for your health, which is endangered by your promise to me. And my fear for you is tearing me apart. For both our sakes, I must ask you to release me from my promise to marry you."

There. Those are hurtful words, and he knows how much pain they will cause, how they will wound. But he has thought the whole thing through in his lawyerly fashion, and this is what he is determined to say. He fixes the speech firmly in his mind. "My dearest dear, I have come to the unutterably sad conclusion that we cannot go on as we are —"

The words taste bitter, and he swallows. "My dearest dear, I have come to the unutterably sad conclusion —"

He swallows again. "My dearest dear, I have come —" and he mutters the rest of it, fast, under his breath.

Enough. He has it now, by heart. He raises his hand and knocks. One, two raps, a pause, a third. He hears hesitant feet on the stairs, and at last the door opens.

And there she is, in that beautiful blue blouse that is just the color of her eyes, and her brown hair (impossible to comb, she complains) is loose and unruly around her face. Her eyes — those remarkably blue, blue eyes — are red-rimmed and wet with tears, and his heart lurches painfully. He finds that he has just enough courage to reach for her hands, as if he were a swimmer sinking into the sea and she the only hope of rescue.

"My dearest dear," he says, and then discovers to his horror that he has forgotten everything else he meant to say. But he can remember it all later. Now, at this moment, he finds that he doesn't want to talk at all. He only wants to pull her into his arms and hold her against his heart, and then to lift her face to his and kiss her lips.

And so he does, and so does she, and so they do.

For a moment, there is only silence, the silence of two people kissing. I am sure you have heard that silence before and know what it means and why they should not be interrupted. You wouldn't want somebody interrupting you when you were busy kissing your favorite person in all the world, now, would you?

So we will just stand here respectfully for a moment, a few steps away from the scene of the action, although you may avert your eyes or turn your back, if you prefer. But I have watched people kissing in the movies and on television a great many times and must confess that I rather enjoy the experience. And since Beatrix and Will have no idea that they're being watched, they're not likely to be embarrassed — at least, not by us.

Finally, still holding hands, the two step apart. Or rather, they pull themselves apart, with the abrupt and guilty self-consciousness of people who are suddenly aware that they did not intend to do what they have just done.

Or (to state this more precisely) that they have just done something that they fully intended *not* to do, which, in this case, is to kiss one another with passionate abandon, as if they had never kissed before and would never kiss again.

And, with a jolt, they simultaneously realize that they had better get on with whatever it was that they had meant to say before this happened, without any more delay.

So naturally Will recalls the words that he had practiced at the very same moment that Beatrix remembers the lines that she had rehearsed, and they both speak at once.

"My dearest dear," he begins. "I have come to the unutterably sad conclusion —"

"Will, dearest, dearest Will," she says, "I cannot go on causing you so much pain —"

They stop. Both of them are covered with consternation, of course, and so they try again. And again, in unison.

"Regrettably, I have come —"

"I really cannot go on —"

Now, this may strike you and me as funny. But we're not the ones who are trying to say what must be said. And they're not smiling, so we shouldn't either.

Will takes a deep breath, feeling that if he doesn't say what he has come to say right at this very moment, it will never get said. But he's already forgotten what he had rehearsed, so he has to improvise. Since he had the gist of it firmly in mind, however, that should not be a problem. He is, after all, a lawyer, and has trained himself to speak before the bench, extemporaneously, when that is necessary. All he has to do is marshal his facts, gather his thoughts, and all will be well.

So he opens his mouth and hears himself say, quite clearly and distinctly, "I would give anything if we could run away and get married tomorrow, Beatrix, and have the whole ridiculous wedding business over with so we can get on with our lives together, the way we're meant to do. But I know we can't do that, for all kinds of reasons, none of them good but all of them . . . well, compelling. So I can only tell you that I love you very, very, *very* much and I will never, never let you go. I'm in this for as long as it takes, and I hope you are, too."

And then he stops, struck dumb with astonishment. That wasn't what he meant to say, not at all! What happened to his stalwart and ungentlemanly determination to plead for release from his promise, for her dear sake? What happened to his worry for her health? He still feels it, oh, yes, he *feels* it. And gentleman or no, he certainly had every intention of breaking off their engagement.

But while intentions are all well and good, they sometimes falter when it comes time to put them into action, as I'm sure you understand. How many times have you fully intended to do one thing — you've thought

326

it all through, planned out each move very carefully — and then found yourself doing something entirely different, if not entirely opposite? You were surprised by what happened, I am willing to wager. It wasn't what you intended at all.

Or rather, that is not what you intended with your *head.* Your heart had a different plan all along and only waited to reveal it until the moment when you opened your mouth and said what you really meant to say. And personally, I suspect that your heart waited because it didn't want your head to get in its way.

Thus it is with our Will, who is not only surprised but completely confounded by what has just happened — and is of course stuck with it, now that the words are out there, hanging in the air between them, alive with significance. He can't very well bow his head and say, "Oh, dear, that's not what I meant at all, Beatrix. What I meant to say was 'Our engagement is obviously a terrible mistake that is making you desperately sick and making me feel wretchedly sad and guilty, so if you don't mind very much, dear girl, let's just call the whole thing off.' "

And Beatrix? She is entirely prepared to say — well, you know. But now that Will has offered his spontaneous and heartfelt pledge, she can hardly say, "Well, of course that's entirely wonderful, Will, and I appreciate it very much, but I've already made up my mind that you must not wait for me. Our engagement is hopeless and our marriage will never happen and I'm breaking it off."

That would be mean and churlish of her, and Beatrix (who often accuses herself of impatience and ill temper) is never mean and churlish.

So even though Beatrix knows very well that she and her dearest love will never in this world be able to marry, she can only take his hand and raise it to her lips and say, with the utmost simplicity and sincerity, "Thank you, my dear, from the bottom of my heart. I love you and I will always be as true to you as I am able."

"Well," Will says, and smiles. "That's good. I'm glad." Then, remembering what he had come to do and suddenly seeing the funny side of this ridiculous business, he begins to chuckle. And then to laugh.

Beatrix, not quite seeing it yet, is not amused. "What's so funny?" she asks stiffly.

"I am," Will says, grinning crookedly. "Sometimes I am just downright silly. I'm amazed that you haven't laughed at me, too, dear heart." He puts his hands on her shoulders and bends over and kisses the tip of her nose, then holds her close against him.

"There," he says softly, his cheek against her hair. "That's better. Much better."

And of course it is. He has been utterly foolish to think that he could ever give this woman up, no matter what obstacles might be thrown across their path. Somehow, in some way, they will muddle through together. Her parents won't live forever. And in the meantime, they have each other, and their time together, and it is enough. Almost enough, anyway — although he is fully aware that even if he were granted the privilege of spending the rest of his life with this remarkable woman, it wouldn't be long enough.

And Beatrix — who knows that she can't tell Will what she had meant to say, and what she had rehearsed until the words had made her cry — finds herself pulling back a little and glancing at the clock and saying, in a surprisingly calm voice, "We still have some time before we have to go to the Woodcocks'. Would you like a cup of tea, Will? There's something I want to show you."

Will glanced at the unfinished pictures and the stacks of papers on the table where

Beatrix had been working. "It looks like you've been busy," he says. He finds it very odd that he can speak in an ordinary, everyday tone after the emotional hurricane he has just weathered. "Working on the book?"

"I should be," she replied ruefully. "But I was working on something else." She pulled out a chair and put a sheaf of papers in front of him. "Sit down, please, and I'll get the tea." Over her shoulder, she adds, "Look at the items and the amounts and tell me what you think."

Five minutes later, he was scowling at her penciled figures. "You're sure about this, Beatrix?"

"I've double-checked it, and then checked it again. The invoices aren't exact duplicates, but there's enough overlap so that I can see that I've been double-billed for nearly half of the materials at Castle Cottage." She sat down on the other side of the table. "And it's not just the numbers — that's circumstantial. There's evidence. Sarah Barwick says that Henry Stubbs bought a pair of brass-plated door handles that were meant for Castle Cottage." She took one of the invoices off the stack and pointed to an item. "Probably these."

"That wretched Biddle!" Will exclaimed,

looking at the invoice. "I took a quick look at his materials list, and I didn't think he'd doctored it." He picked up his teacup and drank. "I thought he was too smart to try his little game with you, but it looks like I was wrong."

"Biddle?" Beatrix asked, frowning. "His little game?"

"Yes, Biddle," Will said, putting his cup down. "He cheated Captain Woodcock and three of my clients. Harold Grimes, Mrs. Moore, and Mr. Kirkby, at the Grange." His voice hardened. "It's this very same swindle, Beatrix. Materials double-billed, half of them not delivered — or delivered and stolen. It's hard to tell."

"So I'm not the only one," Beatrix said mildly.

"Right. But in this case —" Will gave her a grin. "To tell the truth, I am delighted to hear that Henry Stubbs bought your door handles. If that turns out to be true, it's all the evidence we need to nail Biddle."

"But I don't think it's Mr. Biddle," Beatrix said, frowning. "I've had my problems with him over the years, and I know that he is not the best and most attentive manager in the world — especially these days, when he has other fish to fry. But I don't think he's a swindler."

Will pulled his brows together. "Not Biddle? Then who the devil is doing it, Bea? And what's this about 'other fish to fry'?"

Beatrix picked up one of the invoices and pointed to a very small initial in one corner. The initial *M*. "These bills are initialed by Mr. Maguire, Will. And Sarah said that Bertha Stubbs told her that it was Mr. Maguire who sold the door handles to Henry Stubbs. Sarah wondered whether he might have stolen them from Castle Cottage and thought to warn me about it. But looking at these invoices, I'd say that the problem is bigger than a pair of brass door handles."

"Maguire?" Will sat back in his chair and blew out his breath. "Maguire!"

"Don't you think that makes sense?" Beatrix asked. "He's in charge of ordering materials and supplies on Castle Cottage. Mr. Biddle has several crews at work on various projects and divides his time among them. So it would be easy for Mr. Maguire to take whatever he wants and simply put in a duplicate order. I'm sure he's counting on people being too busy to check their invoices. And he's probably counting on Mr. Biddle to be too . . . distracted."

"Yes, that makes sense," Will replied thoughtfully. "Maguire, eh?"

Beatrix took a sip of tea. "It was imprudent of him to sell those handles here in the village — and especially to Henry Stubbs. Henry's wife, Bertha, is the biggest gossip in town. Henry hadn't had those handles for half a day before Bertha was telling all her friends that both her front door *and* her back door were about to have new brass handles, which her husband had bought at a very good price. Two for the price of one, she said." She chuckled wryly. "But Mr. Maguire isn't from Sawrey. He probably had no idea that Bertha's door handles — *my* door handles! — would soon be the talk of the village. It was a reckless mistake."

"I see," Will said quietly, thinking about everything that Beatrix had said and what he had learnt from his clients — and several other things as well. A picture, and not a pretty one, was beginning to emerge.

"Yes, I do see." He narrowed his eyes. "What's this about Biddle having other fish to fry, Beatrix?"

"Other fish?" Beatrix laughed. "Why, haven't you heard? Mr. Biddle is sweet on Ruth Safford, the new barmaid at the Tower Bank Arms. In fact, he's spending most of his time at the pub, just to be near her." She leant closer and lowered her voice theatrically. "I know, because Mrs. Rosier told me so."

Will laughed helplessly. "Gossip," he said, and threw up his hands.

But he knew very well that there was almost always more truth in gossip than anyone suspected, and that the wisest man in any village was the man who kept his ear to the ground.

18
MRS. WOODCOCK GOES MUSHROOM HUNTING

I'm sure that you have hosted many dinner parties and will readily understand what has been on Margaret Woodcock's mind for most of the day. She had to make sure that every minute trace of dust was removed from every flat surface in the library, the drawing room, and the dining room. She had to oversee Elsa Grape's sometimes erratic cookery. She had to make sure that the table was correctly laid with the wedding china, crystal, and silver. And she had to cut and arrange the flowers for the table and the other rooms. It had been a very busy day — especially when she considered how much time those mushrooms had cost her.

And then there was the question of what to wear. Margaret knew that Miss Potter would likely wear a blouse and skirt, that her sister-in-law Dimity always wore something very sweet and simple, and that the hostess must never be dressier than her guests. So she finally decided — for sentimental reasons — on the same pink-and-white crepe de chine blouse that she had worn on the day that the captain proposed marriage to her, with a flounced gray skirt, and a lovely pink-and-white cameo on a gold chain around her neck, a Christmas gift from her husband. In my personal opinion, this was a happy choice, for the pink of the blouse reflected the pink in Margaret's cheeks and complemented the rich brown sheen of her hair.

Finally, it was time to fuss at her husband, who (still wearing his smoking jacket) was standing in the library doorway, reading a message that had just been delivered by Constable Braithwaite, who had ridden his bicycle over from Hawkshead and was now on his way home to his supper.

"Miles," Margaret said sternly, "you really must get dressed, my dear. Our guests will be here in another half hour."

There was no answer. Frowning intently, the captain was engrossed in what he was reading. Margaret tried again.

"Miles, *please*. I've laid out your fresh shirt and tie and jacket. Whatever it is you're reading, it can surely wait until after our guests have gone."

Miles looked up at her, his forehead creased. "It was murder," he said in a hard voice.

Margaret blinked. "Murder?" Her hand went to her mouth. "Who? What? What in the world are you talking about?"

Miles held up the paper in his hand. "The constable just brought this from Dr. Butters. It's his autopsy report. Adcock was struck above the right ear, hard enough to render him unconscious. And then the poor fellow was strung up like a dead fish, in an effort to make it look as if he had committed suicide." He pulled in his breath. "Damn!" he exclaimed. "Damn and blast!"

"Oh, dear," Margaret said faintly, and the captain recollected himself.

"I'm sorry, Margaret," he said apologetically. "I ought not to swear. And I oughtn't to have upset you with this." While the captain kept his office in the library, he always tried to separate his professional work as justice of the peace from his family life. He wasn't always successful, however, for his wife was an active participant in village life and often knew as much as he did about what was going on.

"I was just thinking of poor Mrs. Adcock," Margaret said sadly. "Her boys attended Sawrey School, you know, when I first taught there, years ago. She was always most conscientious, wanting to be sure that they behaved properly and always did their lessons. This will be so hard for her. But no more difficult than the alternative, I suspect. Suicide is an ugly thing." She took a deep breath and let it out again. "Murder! Who could have possibly —"

"Biddle," the captain muttered, half to himself. "It was Biddle, that's who it was. That's the only answer."

"The man who renovated our stable?" Margaret cried, clasping her hands. "That's terrible! Why would Mr. Biddle do such a horrible thing? Why would *anybody* do it?"

"Adcock must have got on to Biddle's swindle with the building supplies and threatened to tell the constable," her husband said. "Maybe Adcock even tried to blackmail him."

"Mr. Biddle, a swindler?" Margaret asked breathlessly, her eyes growing large.

"A swindler and a murderer." The captain shook his head. "Fishing," he said with a snort of disgust. "Well, he's going to find out that fishing is no alibi at all, when I get through with him. I know how to make people talk." Which is true, for (as we noted earlier) the captain had been in Military Intelligence, and he prides himself on his interrogation skills. We should probably not inquire too narrowly into details of means and methods, but I have no doubt that, given enough time with Mr. Biddle — or anyone else, for that matter — the captain could wring out a confession.

"Fishing?" Margaret asked. "That's his explanation — his . . . alibi — for where he was when Mr. Adcock died?"

"Yes. Would you believe it, my dear? Adcock was killed sometime between ten this morning, when his wife last saw him, and eleven thirty, when she found him dead. When I questioned Biddle this afternoon about his whereabouts for that hour and a half, the man had the temerity to claim that he was fishing at Moss Eccles Tarn. Fishing!" Captain Woodcock exclaimed, and smashed his fist into his palm. "All alone, he said. Ha! If that fellow was fishing, I'll be a monkey's uncle."

Margaret squared her shoulders. "Oh, but he was, my dear. Although he was not alone. And he wasn't fishing when I saw him." She cleared her throat. "That is, not exactly."

Astonished, the captain stared at his wife. "He wasn't . . . what? When did you see him? Where?"

"Well, you know that we are having stuffed mushrooms as one of our starters," Margaret said briskly. "Or perhaps you didn't know. But yes, we are, although I could not be sure of getting any good ones — the greengrocer in Hawkshead has had none at all for nearly two weeks, and I was on the point of deciding that I should plan on something else, some of those lovely tinned Morecambe Bay shrimps, perhaps, put into ramekins and served with toast points, or —"

"Margaret," her husband barked. He did not appreciate feeling like a monkey's uncle and was perfectly willing to take it out on her. (If you are married, perhaps you understand his reaction. I know I do.)

She took a deep breath. "Yes. Well, anyway, Elsa told me that Hannah Braithwaite's eldest boy had been up to Moss Eccles and had found a great many fine mushrooms on the south side of the lake, under that lovely large oak tree." (This is very near the spot where Bailey Badger was rescued from near-incineration by his young dragon friend. You may remember the story from *The Tale of Briar Bank*.) "I was wanting a walk anyway," Margaret continued, "so I took a basket and went up to the tarn — it really isn't that far, you know, scarcely a mile. And when I got there, I found the mushrooms, just where Mrs. Braithwaite's eldest boy said they were, near the oak tree, and quite a nice lot of them, growing very well. I filled my basket quite easily and —"

The clock struck, interrupting her. Margaret's hand went to her mouth. "Oh, dear! It really is time to dress, Miles. Our guests will be here in a very few moments and you're still —"

"Not yet," the captain said, very firmly. "I must hear this. Get on with it, Margaret. You filled your basket and —"

Margaret sighed. "I filled my basket and turned to look across the lake and that's when I saw them. Mr. Biddle and his . . . friend." She was blushing. "They were . . . kissing. Oh, quite properly," she added hurriedly. "It was very sweet, really, Miles. The old green rowboat that people use there was moored at the edge of the lake, and they had been fishing in it, and then he started kissing her and she wasn't objecting, not one bit. In fact, I'm sure she was enjoying it." She smiled. "I had heard he fancied her, but he has been a widower for a while, and somehow one does not think of an older man as a suitor for —"

"Margaret," the captain said in a warning voice. By this time he was very serious indeed. "*Who* does Mr. Biddle fancy? Who was in the rowboat with him? And what

341

time was this?"

"What time? Oh, dear. Well, I'd say around ten or a little after. I left here at nine fifteen and . . ." She glanced up and saw her husband's frown and added quickly, "It was Ruth Safford who was with him."

"Ruth Safford?" Miles asked blankly.

"You don't know her? She's the new person Mrs. Barrow hired at the pub a few weeks ago. She helps Mr. Barrow behind the bar when he's busy and works in the kitchen with Mrs. Barrow when he's not. She's pretty, in a mousy sort of way, and rather shy, but very fetching. I should think she would make a good wife for Mr. Biddle, although I'm sure Mrs. Barrow will be put out about it, since she's just got her trained and —"

"Margaret." The captain put both hands on his wife's shoulders. "You mean to tell me that you are corroborating Biddle's alibi for the time of Adcock's murder?"

"Well, yes, I suppose I am," Margaret said, rather flustered now. She did not like the look on her husband's face. "That is, if poor Mr. Adcock was killed this morning. I first saw the two of them around ten — and they were still there when I left, about fifteen minutes later. I mean, it's at least two miles from the tarn to Far Sawrey, isn't it? I hardly see how Mr. Biddle could be kissing Ruth Safford at ten fifteen, and be murdering Mr. Adcock at . . . what time?"

"His wife found him dead at eleven thirty."

"Eleven thirty. Well, then, my dear, I don't see how it could have been done, do you? But you don't need to take my word for it. If Mr. Biddle won't tell you all about it, I'm sure that Ruth Safford will."

"Yes," Miles said glumly. "Yes, she probably will. I shall have to see her right away. She works at the pub, you say?" He was turning away, as if to go.

"Oh, no," Margaret said, grasping his arm in alarm. "Not now, Miles! You need to get dressed right away. Our guests will be here any —"

She was interrupted by the peal of the doorbell.

19
"We Few, We Happy Few, We Band of Brothers"

When we last saw poor Crumpet at the end of Chapter Fourteen, she was at her wits' end. She had been trying to come up with a plan to deal with the renegade rats who had invaded the village and were stealing the villagers blind — and not having any luck. Crumpet knew what ought to be done, of course, and what ought *not* to be done. For instance, it would be utterly foolish to expend a great deal of energy in attempting to stalk and kill individual rats, one at a time. It would be far better to set up surveillance at the half-dozen or so places where the whole gang of rats might have their hideout and watch to see where they were coming from. Once the location of the headquarters was pinpointed, she could come up with a feasible plan of attack.

But who could manage the surveillance? More importantly, even if it was known where the rats were holed up, who could she send in to rout them out? The cats in the village were completely undependable. They were either too old and fat (the venerable Tabitha Twitchit) or too full of delicate sensibility (Felicia Frummety) or too soft-hearted (Max the Manx) or too maternal (Treacle, with her kittens). There were other cats, of course, a great many of them, but they all fell into one of these categories. There were also plenty of village dogs, but most were lazy, undisciplined creatures or superior hunting dogs who would never condescend to take orders from a cat. They might obey Rascal, but Crumpet was the president of the Cat Council and felt that she had to take overall responsibility for this effort. It wasn't something she could delegate.

And, like any good general, she instinctively knew that launching untrained, unprepared troops into the field was inviting disaster, especially with such formidable foes as Rooker's gang. She could depend only on herself — and Rascal, of course, who knew exactly what ought to be done with a bad rat. His great-grandfather on his mother's father's side had been a small but fierce rat terrier who had gained an enormous notoriety in rat pit fighting in Liverpool. His master had won a great many wagers by betting that his terrier could kill a dozen rats in three minutes. Rascal was confident that — once he found where the filthy creatures were hiding — he would do his great-grandfather's memory proud. He'd slaughter the whole lot of 'em in less than three minutes!

But first the rats had to be found, and there were only Crumpet and Rascal. It was physically impossible for the two of them to be everywhere at once. Despairing, Crumpet had said as much to Rascal.

"Well, you're definitely right on that score," Rascal had replied ruefully. He cocked his head. *"But I think I have an idea about a few friends who might help out. Let me do some checking, old girl, and I'll get back to you."*

Crumpet picked up the list of names she had jotted down earlier and glanced through it. *"Who do you have in mind?"* she asked, feeling hopeless. *"I've tried and tried and I can't think of a single cat who —"*

"Later," Rascal said, on his way to the door. *"Don't do anything until you hear from me."*

We last saw Hyacinth at the end of Chapter Three, where she was deeply annoyed at herself for not keeping a closer eye on The Brockery's silver spoons, which had been bagged by the wily Rooker. In fact, she had spent the entire day fretting about the theft, getting angrier and angrier and vowing to retrieve those spoons, although she couldn't think how in the world she was going to accomplish this. For one thing, she had no idea where to find the thief. For all she knew, Rooker might be in Ambleside by now, or on his way to Carlisle. He might even have ridden a lorry to Morecambe Bay and taken ship on a freighter, with The Brockery's spoons in his pocket, to be gambled away in one card game or another.

Hyacinth was an honest badger and felt guilty that the theft had occurred on her watch — and right under her nose, too. So she made a full confession in the *History,* in which she took note of all events of local importance:

Visited by a thieving rat named Corporal Rooker (disguised as an Army veteran), who not only ate every crumb of Parsley's birthday cake but made off with three silver spoons, which I (Hyacinth Badger) had not properly secured.

And then, scowling mightily and wielding her pen as if it were a sword, she had added:

Said rat will be tracked down and

brought to justice, as soon as I am able to figure out how. In the meantime, I hope he doesn't think he's gotten away with this reprehensible behavior!

The afternoon and evening were busy at The Brockery, with a great many animals signing the guest register and requesting supper and overnight lodging. It was summer, you see, when animals are frequently on the move — going on holiday, changing residence, or visiting friends and relations. But this particular evening looked to be damp and unseasonably chilly, with rain clouds draping themselves like a diaphanous shawl around the shoulders of the fells and curling familiarly across the surface of Esthwaite Water. The animals who might otherwise have spent the night camping out in the woods or the meadow decided to find shelter from the gray drizzle and came knocking at The Brockery door.

When Primrose checked the guest register, she saw that there would be nearly two dozen diners at the supper table, including a few old friends who had dropped in at teatime to wish Parsley a happy birthday. One thing had naturally led to another, and the friends found themselves invited to stay to supper and the night, an invitation which all were glad to accept, for as the evening wore on, it looked increasingly damp outdoors, a very good night to sit around the fire and tell stories. Most animals don't like to get wet unless there's a good reason for it — unless they are ducks or fish, of course, or otters, none of which make a habit of dropping in for tea at The Brockery.

A wet, chilly evening is also a good evening for a pot of soup, so Parsley made a very large kettle of cream of potato soup, using the contributions brought by several of the guests: potatoes, onions, celery, bacon, and a beautiful chunk of cheddar cheese. She also baked a large pan of buttery hot buns and for dessert, made a lovely ginger and treacle pudding, which is the badgers' all-time favorite. (You'll find Parsley's recipe for this pudding in *The Tale of Applebeck Orchard,* along with a note about the whys and wherefores of treacle.)

Because of the season and the weather, the guests around the long, narrow table in The Brockery's dining hall were more numerous and varied than usual. Bailey Badger and his guinea pig companion, W. M. Thackeray, had come over from Briar Bank, on the other side of Moss Eccles Tarn. Bailey was a bookish badger whose days were spent managing the Briar Bank library he had inherited from Miss Potter. Thackeray (his full name was William Makepeace Thackeray, after the author of *Vanity Fair*) was a handsome guinea pig whose silver-streaked black hair was very long and covered both ends of him, so that it was hard to tell whether he was coming or going. A well-read animal, Thackeray had once belonged to a collector of rare books and after that to Miss Potter, who had brought him to the village. (His story is too long to tell here: you shall have to read it for yourself in *The Tale of Briar Bank,* where you can learn how Thackeray escaped and was taken in by Bailey Badger.)

Accompanying Bailey and Thackeray was their dragon friend, Thorvaald, who was visiting Briar Bank before flying off to investigate an erupting volcano in Indonesia. Thorvaald had spent quite a few centuries dozing in a rear bedroom of Bailey Badger's sett, where the dragon had been assigned to guard a treasure. Now, he was commissioned to look into volcanoes by the Grand Assembly of Dragons, who were convinced that all volcanoes must be the underground residences of friends who ought to be on their mailing list. So far, Thorvaald had explored more than a dozen volcanoes without finding a single dragon who would give him a postal address. But the Grand Assembly refused to take no for an answer, and Thorvaald certainly didn't mind flying around the world on the Assembly's expense account.

When he visited The Brockery, Thorvaald, a smallish dragon and still quite young, as dragons go, was always careful to mind his tail and bank his fires, although on chilly nights, his badger friends were glad of a little extra warmth for their cold paws. This evening, the dragon, at the foot of the table (where it was easier to manage his tail), was deep in conversation with his dear friend, Professor Owl. The owl rarely came visiting underground but had made an exception when he heard that Thorvaald would be there and that Parsley was planning to serve ginger and treacle pudding. The dragon and the professor had become fast friends after they vanquished the Water Bird (in *The Tale of Oat Cake Crag*) and saved the residents of the Land Between the Lakes, both animal and human, from being buzzed into insensibility by the frantic hydroplane that cruised up and down Windermere, making a noise (as Miss Potter had put it in a letter to her friend Millie Warne) like ten million bluebottle flies.

As usual, Bosworth Badger sat at the head

of the table, as befitted his status as the sett's senior badger. To his right sat Hyacinth, although she kept jumping up and down to fetch this and that from the kitchen, as did both Parsley and Primrose, who were seated nearby. The other guests had taken their places on benches and chairs up and down the table and were busily attending to their bowls of soup and hot buns, which were occasionally replenished with fresh supplies.

Since the evening's crowd is a large one, we won't bother to take attendance. If we did, we might have counted a trio of rabbits who had stopped in to get out of the wet (rabbits detest wet paws); a clutch of chattering voles; a pair of bouncy red squirrels, friends of Hyacinth's and frequent guests to tea; a fox with a badly torn ear (not the same fox who seduced Jemima Puddle-duck — nobody knew where that fox had gone or what he was doing these days); several hedgehogs (it's difficult to count hedgehogs because they keep changing places and they all look alike); and Bailey Badger and Thackeray, his guinea pig friend. Last (but never least, of course) there was Fritz the Ferret, who had come over from his den in the west bank of Wilfin Beck to sketch Bosworth. Fritz, an accomplished artist, was painting the old badger's portrait, which would join the other badger family portraits hanging on the walls in The Brockery's library.

Oh, and there were as well eight or nine stoats and weasels, insalubrious creatures who gave off a bouquet of unsavory odors and muttered amongst themselves in their unintelligible tongue. This crew was assigned to the far end of the table, nearest the dragon — a good place to put them, because they were wary of Thorvaald and behaved with a little more civility when he was near enough to scorch them. Stoats and weasels always go everywhere fully armed (they like to carry large sticks, slingshots, and pockets full of stones), but Hyacinth had required them to leave their weapons out on Holly How, beside The Brockery's front door. But weapons or not, they have hair-trigger tempers, and fights occasionally break out.

Now, this may seem to you like an odd and unlikely congregation of animals, especially since many of them would (under other circumstances) prefer to have one another for supper or a snack, rather than sit in neighborly companionship around the dining table. But when animals stop in at The Brockery for a meal and a night's lodging, they are expected to set aside their culinary preferences and abide by the Badger Rule of Thumb that states that every guest deserves a place at the table where he or she can eat undisturbed and unafraid. This is why a rabbit can sit between a fox and a ferret and eat and laugh and tell stories without the slightest apprehension. (I for one am of the opinion that life with our fellow man might be a great deal more peaceable if the badgers' rules were extended to the world as a whole.)

And all are welcome, friends and natural enemies alike, to share their stories. In fact, it is widely agreed among badgers that animals are story-making creatures and live by their tales and the tales they have learnt from the generations that preceded them. Everybody knows that an animal's story is one of the most important things about him or her, and it is appallingly rude to criticize it, no matter how wanting in art it might be. Indeed, it is one of the Badger Rules of Thumb (the eighth, I believe) that one's stories are as vitally important to one's self-esteem as the state of one's fur or the length of one's whiskers and ought to be admired in much the same way. So the dining hall was buzzing with the companionable sound of animals sharing stories whilst they shared their evening meal.

The badgers and their guests were on their second bowls of soup (the weasels might even have been enjoying their third — weasels have no table manners) when the front doorbell rang. Parsley got up to fetch another bowl, and Flotsam (one of the twin rabbits who work at The Brockery) went to answer the bell. She was back in a moment with Rascal.

"Why, hullo, Rascal!" Bosworth boomed happily, delighted to see his friend for the second time that day. He was always of the opinion that the more animals there were around the supper table, the more stories would be shared and the more interesting the evening would be. *"I hope you haven't eaten your supper yet. Sit down and have a bowl of Parsley's potato soup."* To the other twin rabbit, he added, *"Jetsam, be a good girl and get our Rascal a chair from the library."*

Rascal, who had run all the way from the village to the top of Holly How, was very much out of breath and still rather damp, even though he had given himself a good shake in the hallway. But he managed to wheeze, *"Don't mind if I do, thank you very much,"* and accepted the chair that Jetsam placed between Bosworth and Hyacinth.

When he was seated, Rascal glanced

around the table, doing a quick mental inventory of the guests. He was surprised — and then very pleased — when he saw the weasels and stoats, who were growling and grumbling amongst themselves.

"Looks like you have quite the crowd this evening, Bozzy," he said.

"It's the wet," Bosworth remarked, genially overlooking Rascal's use of his nickname. *"Most of our friends were looking for a dry place to spend the night."*

"Might be the chill, too," Hyacinth added politely. *"Surprising, for July, don't you think?"* She paused. *"Is it raining very hard, Rascal? Down here, you know, it's hard to keep track."*

Bosworth smiled happily. The great advantage to living underground was that the climate was always the same: comfortable and dry. It might be snowing, sleeting, raining, or blowing a gale around the top of Holly How, but none of that perturbed The Brockery's weather. As far as the badger was concerned, it was the very best climate in the whole wide world.

"Raining just hard enough to get one thoroughly wet," Rascal replied with a crooked grin. But he hadn't come to trade pleasantries about the weather. He thanked Parsley for the bowl of creamy soup and the hot bun that she set in front of him, although

he didn't begin eating right away. Instead, he leaned toward Bosworth and spoke urgently, in a low voice.

"We need help in the village, Bozzy, and I've come to ask for volunteers. There's a big job to do. It may be dangerous, and it needs to be done tonight. May I tell everyone about it?"

"I'm sure it is important, dear boy," Bosworth replied, *"and of course you may tell us all about it. But you must eat your soup and hot bun now. You can share your story while we are eating our dessert."*

The old badger was following the family tradition that bad news always tastes better if it is served along with dessert. Bosworth guessed, and rightly, that Rascal's news was not likely to be good.

Rascal knew this, of course, and understood that when he was at The Brockery, he ought to play by the badgers' rules. So he ate his soup and his hot bun — both were very good — and waited as patiently as he could.

Finally the soup was gone. The ginger and treacle pudding made its appearance and was handed round. Bosworth picked up his spoon and took the first bite. Then he rapped his spoon upon his glass.

"Please listen, everyone." He spoke in a voice that carried to the foot of the table.

"Our friend Rascal has come up to Holly How on this rainy night to bring us an urgent message from the village. Lend him your ears, please."

At Bosworth's words, all the other animals stopped talking and looked up with interest — all, that is, except the two squirrels, whose noses were deep in their puddings, and the smallest hedgehog, who was licking butter off a scrap of bun he had found on the floor.

"It's rats," Rascal said tersely. *"A horrid gang of them. They've moved into the village, and they're threatening to take it over."* He looked around the table, trying to catch everyone's eye. *"We need to boot them out just as quickly as we can, before they settle in and rob the villagers blind. That's why I'm here. Crumpet and I need your help."*

The largest hedgehog looked up, his eyes wide with alarm, his teeth chattering. *"D-d-did you say r-r-r-rats?"* It is well known that hedgehogs are very much afraid of rats — but then, hedgehogs are terribly timid. They are afraid of almost everything, including their shadows, which is one reason why you will rarely see them out-of-doors on a sunny day.

"Rats, eh?" The fox — who called himself simply Foxy — leaned forward, his amber

eyes narrowed. *"I've just come over the fells from Ravenglass. The town was invaded last month by a plague of rats that came by ship from London. You don't happen to know the name of your rat gang, do you?"*

"It's not my *gang,"* Rascal replied. *"It's Rooker Rat's gang."*

"Rooker!" Hyacinth exclaimed. *"That filthy old rat! He had a meal and lodging here and helped himself to Parsley's birthday cake and three silver spoons, which of course we didn't know, or we wouldn't have let him go."* She scowled fiercely. *"If I get my paws on that wretched beast, I'll wring his scrawny neck — I swear I will. I want those spoons back!"*

"Now, dear," her mother said in a soothing voice. *"Let's not get excited. I'm sure we can manage without those spoons. I don't want anyone to get hurt."*

"Rooker Rat." Foxy shook his head. *"Well, you've got a jolly hard job cut out for you, I must say. That's the gang that took over Ravenglass. They're a rough lot, one and all."*

"Perhapszs there iszs sszomething I can do." At the end of the table, the dragon spoke up hopefully. *"A little szmoke? Szsome sziszzsle?"* The steam was beginning to hiss out of his nostrils and curl around his head like blue smoke, the way it always did when

he was excited. The dragon had not had a good fight since that stormy night when he and the Professor had tackled the Water Bird. He was obviously eager for another and already stoking up his fires.

Parsley put down her spoon, looking worried. *"But the rats should be the cats' problem, Rascal. Why can't Crumpet and the other cats handle it? And this is really a village matter, isn't it? Why have you come to us?"*

"The Brockery is connected to the village, don't you think, Parsley?" Bosworth asked, gently but pointedly. *"We visit the village gardens often enough. The potatoes in your soup were from Mrs. Crook's potato patch, weren't they? In time of need, it seems to me that we ought to be good citizens and do our part."* Of course, the old badger was remembering the Third Rule of Thumb, also known as the Aiding and Abetting Rule: *One must always be as helpful as one can, for one never knows when one will require help oneself.*

"That's all very true, I suppose," Parsley said reluctantly, although you could tell from the look on her face that she didn't much care for the idea of doing her part. *"But I still don't understand why the cats can't do it."*

Rascal sighed. *"It's a most awfully awkward*

situation, I'm afraid. With the exception of Crumpet, the village cats are either too old, too fat, too dainty, or they're nursing kittens. They just aren't up to the job."

"Nor were the Ravenglass cats," Foxy said in an ominous tone. "Overpowered in one night, they were. Three or four killed in an awf'lly bloody fight. Ordinary village cats are simply no match for that beastly lot."

An apprehensive murmur ran around the table. One of the voles fell into a coughing fit and had to be thumped on the back. The smallest hedgehog burst into noisy tears and was comforted by his brother.

"Anyway," Rascal went on, "I told Crumpet that I'd try to round up a few volunteers who could help us find out where the rats are holed up and then . . . And then do whatever we have to do, I guess." He looked around the table. "We don't need very many animals — six or seven ought to do the trick. Of course," he added hastily, "if more want to come, that would be capital."

"If I know those rats, you're going to need more than six or seven." The fox cleared his throat. "However, you can count on me."

"And on me," Hyacinth announced.

"Oh, no, dear," Primrose said urgently, her paw going to her mouth. "This will be much *too dangerous. Rats aren't as large as bad-gers, of course, but —"*

"These are," the fox put in. *"Well, not quite as big as badgers, maybe, but they're the big-gest rats I've ever seen. Bigger than some cats. And fierce."* He rolled his eyes. *"My aunt, but they are fierce!"*

"You see, dear?" Primrose said to Hya-cinth. *"These rats are big and fierce and they bite terribly, and their bites can cause terrible infections. Let the males do this job. You don't need to —"*

"But I *wear the Badge of Authority, Mother,"* Hyacinth reminded her in a quiet but firm voice. *"I am responsible for ensuring the safety and comfort of The Brockery's resi-dents. Rooker and his crew may be content to stay in the village now, but there's nothing to keep them from coming here. If we don't fight them now, we may have to fight them later — on our own home ground. And besides,"* she added grimly, *"I want those spoons!"*

Bosworth put a gentle paw over Prim-rose's. *"She's right, you know,"* he said. *"It's her job. You have to let her go."* He glanced at Rascal. *"Who else might you find helpful, Rascal?"*

Rascal looked down the table, his glance going from one animal to the next. *"Well, in* addition to Hyacinth, there's the fox, Thor-vaald, the Professor —"

"Whooo did yooou say?" the owl inquired, looking down his beak. "I?"

"Yes, sir," Rascal said. He always spoke deferentially to the owl. "I know how fast you are when you swoop down out of the sky to catch voles and squirrels and —"

There was a chorus of high-pitched squeals, as the two squirrels and several voles abandoned their chairs and dove under the table.

"Sorry to alarm," Rascal said apologetically. "But if you could come with us, Professor, I'd be personally grateful. And you stoats and weasels —"

The group of animals at the end of the table stopped muttering amongst themselves and stared at him with narrowed eyes. "What-t-t's that-t-?" asked the weasel-in-charge, in his clicking, chattery voice. "You're ask-k-king us t-t-to volunt-t-teer to rout-t-t out-t-t rat-t-ts?"

A rat-tat-tat chorus of excited weasel and stoat voices rose around him. "Rout-t-t out-t-t rat-t-ts! Rout-t-t out-t-t rat-t-ts!"

"Are you sure about that, Rascal?" Bos-worth asked, concerned. "Weasels and stoats can cause more problems than they

363

solve, you know."

"*I am asking them,*" Rascal replied staunchly, "*but only as long as they behave themselves and take orders.*"

"*I'll szsee to that,*" the dragon hissed, glaring down his smoking snout at the weasels and stoats, who flinched under his fiery gaze. "*If you don't behave, you weaszsels and stoatszs, you'll anszswer to me!*"

"*Very good,*" Rascal said. "*I saw their weapons outside the front door. Thorvaald, please see that they're appropriately armed.*"

Bailey Badger had been listening silently, but now he raised a tentative paw. "*I'll go,*" he said. Bailey was a bookish badger, but he was strong and stout and had no fear of rats. "*Briar Bank is on the other side of the tarn, but we still consider ourselves a part of the village. I feel it an obligation.*"

"*I'll go, too,*" Thackeray squeaked.

"*No, Thackeray,*" Bailey said, shaking his head. "*You're much too small.*"

Thackeray pushed his hair back and turned his beady black eyes on Rascal. "*I know I'm small, but I'm brave. Will you have me?*"

When the question was put that way, Rascal had to say yes, even though he had misgivings. "*As long as you promise to stay out of the way," he added in a cautioning tone.

"*Anyone else?*" Bosworth asked, adding apologetically, "*I'd be glad to volunteer, too, but I'm afraid I'm a little too old to be of much use.*"

Rascal gave the badger an understanding nod. "*You've done your bit in your time, old friend. Remember the raid on the badger-baiters in the barn behind the Sawrey Hotel a few years ago? You organized that, you did, and carried it off in grand style.*"

"*Ah, yes. I was a young chap then,*" Bosworth said with a reminiscent smile. "*And reckless, very reckless. But it was a worthy cause.*" His glance went to Primrose, who nodded, her eyes misty. Badger hunters had pulled Primrose and her two young badgers, Hyacinth and Thorn, out of their sett at Hill Top Farm and carried them off to face some horribly fierce dogs in a violent badger-baiting. All three would have been killed for sport if Bosworth and his animal friends had not mounted a rescue, as you will recall from *The Tale of Holly How.*

Bosworth looked down the table toward the owl. "*As I remember, Professor, you sent us off on that dangerous expedition with a rousing speech. Do you remember?*"

"Dooo I remember?" intoned the Professor, lifting his wings imperiously. *"Of cooourse I remember! It is my favorite dramatic monologue. Revised by myself,"* he explained to a nearby stoat, who was watching him with a gaping mouth. *"King Henry's famous St. Crispen's Day speech. Delivered tooo his troooops before Agincourt and thereafter immortalized by Shakespeare."*

"Well, then," said Rascal, who also remembered the occasion, *"p'rhaps you'd be willing to recite it again."* He looked around, feeling proud of the group that was assembled. *"After all, we are setting off to do battle with an invading army. It isn't quite like Agincourt, but perhaps it is close enough."*

"Of course," replied the owl without hesitation. He hopped up on the table, whilst around him the smaller animals rolled their eyes at one another and one or two covered their ears with their paws, protesting that they should not have to listen to Shakespeare, of all things, when what they really wanted to do was to finish their puddings.

But when the owl began his speech, the entire assembly fell silent, and even the squirrels and the voles crept out from under the table, for the Professor spoke with his best Shakespearean intonation and an admirable fervor, although with quite a few of his own revisions, to fit the occasion. The speech went on for quite a while, but the animals found the recitation stirring, and every one of them was deeply touched. By the time the Professor had got as far as *"No winter's night beside the fire . . ."* the animals' eyes were wet and many were sniffling and reaching for their pocket handkerchiefs:

Nooo winter's night beside the fire shall
    e'er gooo by,
From this day tooo the ending of the
    world,
Without our story told, and we in it
    remembered:
We few, we happy few, we band of
    brothers;
For he tooonight whooo sheds his blood,
    whatever kind
Of animal he be, shall be my brother!

And with that, a great sigh gusted around the table and then a mighty cheer erupted, the animals applauding and thumping each other on the back and saying how marvelously brave everyone was to go off and fight those filthy rats, and shaking paws and dancing and chanting Highland war cries and singing "It's a Long Way to Tipperary" and generally urging themselves and one another to do something splendidly brave and glorious, the way soldiers do when they're getting ready to go into battle.

Hyacinth waited for a lull in the noisy rabble-rousing. *"Excuse me,"* she said firmly, *"but shouldn't it be 'We band of sister and brothers'?"*

"Whooo?" asked the owl.

20
A Dinner Party at Tower Bank House

At the very moment that the animals in The Brockery are being inspired to battle by the stirring words of Professor Owl, Captain and Mrs. Woodcock, Miss Potter, and Mr. Heelis are enjoying their dinner at Tower Bank House. Unfortunately, the Kittredges were not able to come, because little Flora Kittredge had developed a very bad cough that afternoon. Her mother would not leave her, and Major Kittredge would not come without his wife, so at the very last minute, they had sent an apologetic begging-off note. Disappointed, Margaret had hurried to remove their place settings from the table and rearrange the chairs. She was sorry that Dim and the major couldn't come, but it would mean that the evening would be a little less formal and certainly more fun. Miles and Will were not only friends but hunting and fishing companions and always easy together, while she and Beatrix were

369

fast friends.

Beatrix and Will arrived under the shelter of Will's big black umbrella, for there was an intermittent rain. Margaret thought that Beatrix was looking exceptionally pretty tonight, with a fresh color in her face and tendrils of brown hair escaping around her cheeks and her eyes as blue as her blue silk blouse. The four of them settled comfortably in the sitting room, where they enjoyed a glass of before-dinner sherry and the stuffed mushrooms, which were very tasty, Margaret decided, and certainly worth the trouble of gathering them.

But despite her best efforts to keep the conversation focused on pleasant dinner-party topics, the talk quickly turned to something that was obviously on the minds of the guests. Will reported what Beatrix had discovered when she compared the items and charges in the invoices for the Castle Cottage construction materials. Then Beatrix reported that Henry Stubbs had bought a pair of brass door handles — handles that she thought must be the "extra" pair that had been ordered for Castle Cottage — from Mr. Maguire.

Miles raised his eyebrows. "From Maguire?"

"The construction supervisor at Castle

Cottage," Will told him.

"Yes, yes, I know the man," Miles said. "Maguire supervised my stable renovation." Frowning, he looked narrowly at Will, then at Beatrix. "You say those invoices have Maguire's initials on them. You're thinking that *he* is the source of our little criminal problem — and not Biddle?"

Beatrix tilted her head, studying him. "You had concluded, Will tells me, that Mr. Biddle was the one who was doing the double-billing."

"It seemed logical," the captain said, a trifle defensively. "After all, Biddle *is* the owner of the construction company."

"But not an owner who pays a great deal of attention to what his men are doing on the job," Beatrix remarked. "As I have learnt to my distress," she added wryly. "I have often thought that Mr. Biddle's workmen are left to get on with things as whim and whimsy take them."

"That may not be good business practice," Will said with a crooked grin, "but it isn't a crime."

Margaret put down her sherry glass. "You mean, Mr. Biddle is not a swindler after all?" She leaned toward Beatrix and said, in a confiding voice, "Earlier today, my husband was insisting that he was."

371

The captain gave Margaret an injured look. "I was speaking from the knowledge I had at the time."

"I thought so, too," Will defended his friend. "In fact, all the evidence I dug up seemed to me to point directly at Biddle, and I told Miles as much. It wasn't until Beatrix showed me the initials on those invoices that I even considered another possibility." He turned to the captain. "I think you need to talk with Maguire as soon as possible, Miles."

"But not tonight, please, dear," Margaret put in hurriedly. "At least, not until after dinner. And do remember that it's very wet. Perhaps tomorrow?"

"But I do agree that it should be soon," Beatrix replied. "You may take my invoices as evidence." Her handbag was at her feet, and she reached into it, pulling out a sheaf of papers and laying them on the table beside her. "I imagine that Henry Stubbs will be glad to tell you who sold him the door handles — Sarah Barwick says he is quite proud of his bargain."

Margaret chuckled. "I am sure he is. Henry Stubbs is always glad of a bargain."

Beatrix nodded. "Oh, and when you question Mr. Maguire, Captain, do please try to find out where he is hiding my duplicate construction material. Since I have paid for it, I should like to have it back. I'm quite sure it isn't at Castle Cottage — although," she added thoughtfully, "I have not looked in the loft at the barn. I suppose some of it might be there."

Miles glanced at the invoices and shook his head. "Our Miss Potter does it again," he muttered ruefully.

"I'm sorry?" Beatrix asked.

As Will laughed heartily, the captain had the grace to look apologetic. "I just meant that, once again, you have pulled a rabbit out of the hat. It was quite an admiring remark, believe me. I don't know how you do it."

"Miles," Margaret said in a rebuking tone, "whatever can you be talking about? Hats? Rabbits?"

The captain ducked his head. "Sorry. Didn't mean to be offensive. It's just that I have often suspected our Beatrix of being a female Sherlock Holmes, and now I am quite sure. Quite, quite sure."

"I can hardly lay claim to that kind of detective skill," Beatrix said, frowning a little. "There's nothing very Holmsian in reviewing invoices from one's construction site, I should think. And no sleight of hand, either. It's all very straightforward. One does not like to be billed twice for the same thing."

"Miles," Margaret said, now very serious, "I think you should tell them the rest of it." To Beatrix and Will, she added, "Just a few moments before you arrived, Constable Braithwaite brought a message from Dr. Butters."

Will spoke sharply. "From Butters? Was it the —"

But he was interrupted by a light tap at the sitting room door. Elsa Grape put her head through and announced, in her bluff, peremptory way, that dinner was served in the dining room. Further conversation on the subject was suspended until they were seated, the soup — tomato bisque — and fresh bread had been served, and Elsa had closed the dining room door and returned to the kitchen. And even then, they all spoke with hushed voices. Everyone knew that anything Elsa heard left her lips and flew straight into the ears of two dozen of her very best friends.

Will immediately returned to the question he had begun. "The message that the constable brought. It was Butters' autopsy report, regarding Mr. Adcock?"

"It was the autopsy report itself," the captain said.

"And?" Will prompted.

"It wasn't Adcock's doing." Miles glanced at Beatrix, as if to assure himself that she would not be offended at hearing this tragic business discussed over the soup. "He was struck above the right ear, hard enough to render him unconscious. The rest of it was apparently meant to make the death look like suicide." He sighed. "The vicar, at least, will be relieved."

"I'm sure," Beatrix said sympathetically. "Reverend Sackett must have been worried about the burial, poor man."

"He was, yes," Miles said. "Very much. But this does leave us with a question. An urgent question."

"Indeed." Will put down his spoon. "Who? And why?"

"Quite naturally, I thought first of Biddle," the captain replied. "He had a motive, I believed. Adcock had learnt about his thefts of construction material and planned to tell, or was asking for money to keep quiet, or something like that. And when I questioned Biddle this afternoon about his whereabouts at the time of Adcock's death, he gave me what I thought was a cock-and-bull story about going fishing at Moss Eccles. He implied that he might have been with someone but wouldn't say who."

"Moss Eccles?" Will asked in surprise. "Why, Biddle is an expert angler. He's won quite a few competitions. What under the sun was he doing at Moss Eccles? The fish in that lake hardly present what I would consider an angling challenge."

"Exactly," Miles said. "Moss Eccles, on a Thursday morning, when everyone else was hard at work? With a companion he preferred not to name? You can see why I thought it was a trumped-up story. But then Margaret informed me —" He paused, looking at his wife. "Tell them, my dear."

Margaret put down her soup spoon. "Well, you see, I saw him."

"Saw Biddle, you mean?" Will asked in great surprise.

"At Moss Eccles?" Beatrix asked with interest.

"Exactly. I went to gather mushrooms for tonight's starters, and there he was. Fishing, from that old green rowboat that's kept up there. He wasn't alone, though. He was with Ruth Stafford, the pretty barmaid at the pub. They were" — Margaret felt herself blushing — "kissing."

"Ah," Will said, and cast a laughing look at Beatrix. "It is as you said, Bea. Biddle had other fish to fry."

"Three of them," the captain said thoughtfully. "Three brown trout."

"Beg pardon?" Beatrix asked.

"After I finished interviewing Biddle, I went round to his kitchen," the captain explained, "and there they were. Three fresh brown trout. Evidence, I now suppose, of his morning's fishing."

"But not the only evidence, surely," Beatrix replied. "I imagine that Miss Safford will be glad to testify to Mr. Biddle's whereabouts, even if he prefers to play the gentleman."

"No doubt," Miles replied. "Which leaves us —"

"With Mr. Maguire," Beatrix said.

"I suppose it does," Will said thoughtfully.

Beatrix shivered. "And to think that I spoke with the man this afternoon!"

"I don't quite see —" Margaret began.

But Elsa came in at that point to remove the soup and convey the golden-brown roast duck, stuffed with sage and onions, as well as a dish of braised ham and spinach. She was followed by the tweeny carrying the vegetables: new potatoes and peas in a cream sauce, vegetable marrows, baked tomatoes (a rather bold recipe from *Mrs Beeton's Book of Household Management*), and salad. When the food was served round and the two servants had left, Miles looked at his wife.

"Mrs. Grape doesn't wait until the bell is rung?" he asked plaintively.

"Mrs. Grape is a law until herself," Margaret replied, which was entirely true. She put a fork into her tomato to see if it was baked through, and was glad to see that it was. Baked tomatoes were new to her, but if Mrs. Beeton thought they would do, she was sure they would.

"As you were saying, Margaret," Beatrix prompted. "You don't quite see —"

"I don't quite see what Mr. Maguire has to do with Mr. Adcock's death," Margaret said.

"It's possible that Adcock found out that *Maguire* was the one who was stealing construction supplies," Miles explained. "Which would give Maguire a motive for wanting Adcock dead."

"Don't forget about Gilly Harmsworth," Beatrix said to Will.

"Gilly Harmsworth?" Margaret asked, puzzled. "Who is she?"

"She's a friend of Deirdre and Jeremy," Beatrix replied. "She was helping with the birth of Deirdre's baby early this morning. She looked out the window and saw a strange man in the Adcock garden."

"Ah, yes." The captain was thoughtful. "If

Miss Harmsworth could identify the man she saw —" He did not have to finish his sentence. Everyone knew what he meant.

"But this doesn't explain why Mr. Biddle sacked Mr. Adcock," Beatrix said thoughtfully. "He told Constable Braithwaite that the man couldn't be trusted. And there was a fight, too."

"I asked Biddle about that," the captain said, working on his roast duck. "He said Adcock stole a tool — a carpenter's level, which struck me as fishy."

"Three brown trout," cautioned Margaret.

"Well, yes," Miles replied. "But doesn't it seem odd that an experienced carpenter should steal a common tool that he must already possess?"

"He must have taken something else, then," Margaret mused. "I wonder what it was."

"Or Mr. Biddle thought he did," Beatrix said thoughtfully, "which is not quite the same thing." She tasted the stuffing. "Margaret, whatever Mrs. Grape's shortcomings, she certainly makes a fine onion and sage stuffing. Do you suppose she would give me her recipe?"

"I'll ask, but I'm sure it's Mrs. Beeton's," Margaret said. "Elsa and I live and die by Mrs. Beeton. Do you have the book?"

"I'm afraid not," Beatrix said ruefully. "Mama's cook keeps one in the kitchen at Bolton Gardens, of course, and I've looked at it for menu ideas. But I don't have a copy of my own."

Margaret leaned toward her guest with a teasing smile. "Perhaps you ought to have one for a wedding present."

Beatrix laughed a little and slanted a look at Will, who was now engaged in a deeply serious conversation with the captain, speculating about what might or might not have been stolen. "I'm sure I should," she said. "I certainly haven't had much practice as a cook. And I'm definitely not up to stuffing a duck." She looked down at her plate and added ruefully, "Or even tomatoes. Perhaps I won't need it, though. I'm afraid the wedding will never take place, Margaret."

"Oh, dear," Margaret said with sincere compassion. Beatrix was the first person she had told when she and Miles became engaged, and she had been among the first in the village to hear about Beatrix's engagement to Will. She knew that the Potters stubbornly opposed this match, just as they had opposed Beatrix's earlier engagement, and she knew how painful this whole episode had been for Beatrix. "Has something happened?" she ventured sympathetically.

Beatrix put down her fork. "Bertram has decided to tell our parents about his marriage to Mary," she said, very low.

Margaret — who knew that Beatrix's brother had been secretly married for a decade — understood the implications of this at once. "Oh, dear!" she exclaimed, this time more fervently. "That's going to upset the applecart, isn't it?"

"I'm afraid it will," Beatrix said with a sigh. She leaned toward Margaret. "I just learnt about this today, from Bertram himself. I haven't told Will about it yet. I thought . . . well, I thought I would wait until it has happened and then let him know the outcome. My parents are going to be in a terrible state, of course. I dread what's to come." She sighed, her eyes dark and troubled. "I hope you won't mention it to anyone, not even the captain. He might feel obliged to tell Will."

"Of course," Margaret said. "Not a soul."

At the end of the table, the captain broke off his conversation with Will and raised his voice. His eyebrows were pulled together, and he wore a serious look. "Will and I are agreed that we must speak to Maguire tonight, Margaret. We shall leave directly after dessert. Will tells me that the fellow lives on this side of Hawkshead, so it's only a few miles."

"Oh, dear!" Margaret exclaimed, for the third time in just a few moments. "Are you very sure, Miles? It's getting late. And it's raining!"

"We're sure," the captain said. "And a little rain isn't going to hurt us. I daresay we won't melt."

"And it's only going nine now," Will added, glancing toward the dining room windows. "The sun won't set for another fifteen minutes, and the sky will be light for several hours."

Margaret sighed. That was true. At this time of year, twilight lingered long past sunset. On a clear evening, one could sit outside in the garden and read the news-paper until bedtime, if the gnats didn't drive one indoors. "Well, if you must, then of course you must," she replied bravely. "But I hope you'll be very careful."

"Perhaps," Beatrix suggested, "you might take the constable with you."

"We shall do that," the captain replied. With a grim satisfaction, he added, "We may be able to make an arrest, you know. I should certainly like to get this dreadful business wrapped up."

Will cast an apologetic look at Beatrix.

"I'm sorry. I hope you don't mind, Bea. It's rather an unusual situation, and it seems that I should be involved, since I managed the investigation into the theft of the construction materials."

"Of course I don't mind," Beatrix said resolutely. "I don't like the idea any more than you do, Will, but the man must be confronted. And the sooner the better."

"Well, then," Margaret said, "now that you have decided what you are going to do, shall we set the subject aside and talk about something else? Something a little less . . . well, worrisome? More nicely suited to the dinner table?"

"Of course, my dear," her husband replied in a reassuring tone. He turned to Will. "I read in the Sunday *Times* that the Kaiserliche Marine has just commissioned the first German U-boat powered with a diesel engine. There are plans for several more just like it, apparently. Kaiser Wilhelm and his gang are spoiling for war." He raised his fork, brandishing it in the air like a weapon. "I tell you, Heelis, if I were Churchill, I wouldn't waste a minute. I'd send the Royal Navy over there to clean up that nest of filthy rats!"

"Miles!" Margaret exclaimed, nettled.

"What?" the captain asked, looking up.

"What did I say?"

Margaret looked at Beatrix and rolled her eyes. Beatrix shook her head, and both women began to laugh.

21
THE LOST IS FOUND, OR
REVELATION REVEALED

The men excused themselves immediately after finishing Mrs. Grape's damson tart, not even staying for the customary coffee, port, and cigars. Beatrix and Margaret walked with them to the porch and watched them drive off in Miles' Rolls, on their way to pick up the constable. It had stopped raining, the air was fresh and cool and deliciously rain-scented, and the sky was beginning to clear. To the west, the sun had already slipped below the horizon, and the clouds over the fells were tinged with orange and lemon. The sky itself had a pearly quality, the promise of a lingering summer twilight.

After the men were gone, Beatrix followed Margaret into the sitting room where they sat with their after-dinner coffee and a few sweets, talking in a desultory way about community matters — Jeremy and Deirdre's new baby, the fête that was coming up in a few weeks, the plan to renovate the school-house, and the possibility of hiring a village nurse, a project that Beatrix had long had in mind. Dr. Butters was wonderful, but he was just one person, and the people he cared for were scattered across a dauntingly large district. A nurse would be an enormous help to him — and to the villagers.

But neither Beatrix nor Margaret spoke of the thing that was on both their minds: what might be happening with Miles, Will, and the constable. Would they be able to find Mr. Maguire? What would they learn? Would their interview end in an arrest?

After a while, the conversation grew more and more haphazard, punctuated by longer and longer silences. Finally, Beatrix glanced toward the window and said, "I wonder — would you like to go for a walk, Margaret? It's not that late, and there's plenty of light left."

Margaret jumped to her feet. "What a splendid idea, Beatrix! I'm longing for a breath of fresh air."

Beatrix smiled as they went to the door, thinking how very different village people were from Londoners. In the city, two women would not venture out in the evening unless they were going somewhere specific — to the theater, to a party — and even then, they would have to take a cab or the family coach and would feel much better if a man accompanied them. They would never just go walking, especially not after the sun had set. That could be dangerous, even in the best neighborhoods, and of course, people might talk. Here in the village, there was no danger. No one thought anything of two women going out for a walk in the twilight.

A few moments later, Beatrix and Margaret were walking slowly along the Kendal Road in the direction of the village. When they reached Sarah Barwick's bakery, they turned left and went along the main lane, past the village shop, the blacksmith, and the joinery. They were enjoying the quiet sounds of the evening — a dog barking urgently in the distance, a baby crying nearby, small scurryings here and there in the shrubbery, the soft swish of a tree branch against a wall, the quiet drip-drip of a gutter. The lane was deserted. People were indoors, finishing their dinners and gathering around their fires.

"You know, I haven't been up to Castle Cottage for quite a little time," Margaret remarked, as they walked slowly up the street. "Shall we walk there? I would very much like to see what you've been doing to the house and to hear more about your plan for it."

"Of course, if you would like," Beatrix said. "As a matter of fact, after I mentioned the barn at dinner tonight, I've been thinking about it. I suppose it's possible that at least some of the 'extra' material I've been charged for might be stored in the loft. Mr. Maguire would never imagine that I would look there." She sighed a little, thinking once again that she had been foolish to try to renovate the old house. "As to my plan, well, perhaps the least said about that, the better. I've learnt that plans don't always work out the way we hope."

Suddenly something scurried across their path, a large, furry creature with a very long tail. Startled, Margaret gave a breathless shriek and stepped back. Then she laughed, embarrassed. "Just a rat," she said. "Sorry, Beatrix. I'm not one of those women who faint at the sight of a mouse. But I do think it takes a bit of cheek for a rat to be out and about in the lane before full dark, don't you?"

"I do, indeed," Beatrix said. "I'm glad that the village hasn't had a rat problem since that awful time we had to clear them out of the attics at Hill Top. I —"

She stopped. Another rat, even larger than

the first, had just flashed past them, its lips pulled back from yellow teeth in what looked like a taunting grin.

"Just look at the size of that fellow!" Margaret exclaimed, turning to watch the rat as it skipped into the shadows. She added, "You know, Elsa Grape was complaining this afternoon that something — she thought it must have been a rat — made off with a half-dozen carrots she had put by for tonight's dinner and a couple of crumpets from her bakery box. We must be —"

A third rat careered around the corner of Croft End Cottage, darted across the front stoop, and disappeared through a hole in the fence.

Beatrix finished Margaret's sentence. "We must be in the middle of an invasion. What a pesky nuisance. We shall have to get the cats to do something about it."

"Oh, those cats!" Margaret exclaimed with scornful disdain. "I have never in my life seen such a lazy lot as these village cats, Bea. I doubt that there's more than one or two who are capable of dealing with a plague of rats." She shuddered. "I daresay traps are in order, but from the size of those beasts, I'm not sure that what we have will do the job. We'll have to get bigger traps!"

They were walking up Stony Lane now,

toward Castle Cottage, which rose like a gray ghost at the top of the village. As they walked, a delicious scent wafted from the roses along the lane, and Beatrix pulled in her breath appreciatively, already feeling somewhat better, under the spell of the quiet evening. She was still apprehensive about Will, of course. If Maguire had been responsible for poor Mr. Adcock's death, he was clearly dangerous. But three strong men — Will, the captain, and Constable Braithwaite — ought to be able to deal with him.

By this time, they had reached the gate that opened into the Castle Farm barn lot, across the road from Belle Green. The sky had deepened to a darker blue in the east and the stars were beginning to glitter over Claife Heights, but the western sky was still streaked with sunset-tinged clouds and a silvery light filled the air around them, transforming the landscape into something not quite real, something out of a fairy tale. Beatrix glanced up as a dark shadow glided overhead, wings stretched out and motionless in the soundless, sweeping flight of a large tawny owl, the largest in the Lakes. It was rare to see one so near the village.

"Look, Margaret!" she exclaimed. "An owl! Perhaps it's the one who lives in the beech at the top of Claife Heights."

Margaret looked up, too, as the owl dipped his wings and dropped lower over the village rooftops. "Oh, how beautiful!" she breathed, and then added practically, "Let's hope he has an appetite for rats."

Beatrix chuckled, agreeing. "If we could count on that owl, we wouldn't need those traps."

She lifted the latch on the wooden gate and they went through, threading their way between piles of building materials and heaps of plaster and lathes and slates that had been removed from the house. The bare ground was slick and muddy from the evening rain, and Beatrix found herself wishing for her pattens — the wooden-soled shoes that she and other farm women wore when they went outdoors. She had worn her town shoes for the dinner party, and they were going to get unspeakably dirty.

Just as Beatrix was thinking that perhaps this wasn't such a very good idea after all, she saw Rascal, her favorite village dog, trotting purposefully around the corner of the old stone barn. As she and Margaret approached the barn, he looked up and saw them, then ran forward.

"Miss Potter!" he barked loudly, planting himself firmly in front of the barn door, stiff-legged. *"What are you doing here? And*

Mrs. Woodcock, too! Don't you know how late it is? Why, it's almost dark! Go home, both of you! Go right home, now! Shoo!"

"My goodness," Margaret said mildly. "Why, look at him, Beatrix. He's trying to chase us away."

Surprised at the flurry of urgent barks, Beatrix went toward the little dog. She often wished she understood what the animals were saying — and sometimes she thought she almost did.

"Whatever in the world is the matter, Rascal?" she inquired.

"What's the matter?" Rascal shouted, dancing up and down in front of them. *"What's the matter? The matter is that you're not wanted here tonight, Miss Potter! Hostilities are about to get under way! A battle! A war! All animals must stay out of the barn — and that includes you!"*

I am sure that Beatrix would have responded differently if she had truly understood what Rascal was trying to tell her. But she didn't, I am sorry to say — which just goes to show that even our dear Miss Potter, who understands quite a lot about animals, does not know everything there is to know. She bent down and patted the little dog's head gently. "But this is *my* barn, Rascal. And I am going inside. Right now."

"No!" Rascal shrilled. *"No, no —"*

But Beatrix was grasping the door and pulling it open just wide enough for herself and Margaret to slip through. Over her shoulder, she said, "Hush, Rascal. We've had enough of your noise. Now, go away."

But Rascal had already gone. He had seen a very large rat slinking around the corner of the barn, and he was off to do his duty, as a fierce, brave terrier-warrior should.

It was dim and dry and musty inside the old barn, with the scent of dust and musty hay in the air. Beatrix was aware of a faint rustling in the hay — rats, she assumed, and thought that it might be a good idea to set several rat traps right here in the barn. She looked up. Overhead, the barn roof rose into the shadowy twilight like a cathedral ceiling. A wooden ladder was propped against the edge of the open loft, about a dozen feet above the floor.

Beatrix touched Margaret's sleeve. "Would you mind holding the ladder for me? I'm going to climb up to the loft and have a look. It should be empty. If it isn't —"

"Are you sure, Bea?" Margaret asked, eyeing the ladder worriedly. "It looks a little unstable."

"Let's give it a go." Beatrix went to the ladder. She positioned it firmly, and as Margaret held it, she began to climb, one rung at a time. A few moments later, she could see into the loft, an area about twenty feet by twenty feet — and stacked with lumber and other building materials. She puffed out her breath. "I've found it, Margaret!" she cried excitedly. "I've found the materials that Mr. Maguire has stolen. Some of it, anyway."

She turned to look down at Margaret. As she did so, she caught a glimpse, out of the corner of her eye, of something large and dark, about the size of a badger. And then, to her surprise, she saw — or thought she saw — a fox. And a — a weasel? And a stoat? She twisted around, shifting her weight, trying to see better. Was she imagining this? Was she —

"Beatrix!" Margaret called. "What's the matter? What are you doing? You —" She broke off with a shrill scream. "Help! The ladder! It's tilting! I can't hold it!"

The next instant, the ladder was slipping sideways and Beatrix was falling, with Margaret's scream loud in her ears. I am sure that she would have been badly injured if she hadn't fallen into a pile of musty old hay that had been heaped up in the corner. The hay cushioned her fall, but the wind was knocked out of her, and for a moment, she was too stunned to move.

"Beatrix!" Margaret cried, rushing over to her. "Bea, are you all right? Speak to me, Bea! Say something."

"Pfft," Beatrix said, sitting up and spitting straw out of her mouth. "Pffoey!" And then she sneezed. "Achooo!"

"Oh, thank heavens," Margaret gasped. "You're all right!"

"More or less," Beatrix said dizzily, rubbing her shoulder. "Did you see that badger? And the stoat? And the weasel?"

"Badger? Stoat? Weasel?" Margaret leant over, peering anxiously at her. "No, I didn't see a thing. Are you . . . Are you sure you're all right, dear Bea? You haven't hurt your head, have you?"

"No, just my shoulder." Beatrix struggled to stand up but fell back. "And I'm afraid I've turned my ankle." She put her hand down to steady herself. Feeling something hard under the straw, she pulled it out. "What's this?" she asked, holding it up.

Margaret stared. "Why . . . Why, it's our wedding photograph — in the silver frame that Dimity and Christopher gave us as a wedding gift! What in the world is it doing here?"

But Beatrix was too busy digging in the hay to answer her. "Look at this!" she said in a wondering tone, holding up a silver cream jug. "And this!" She held up a monogrammed leather purse. "It has Sarah Barwick's initials on it!" She fished through the straw again and pulled something else out. "What on earth — ?"

But I'm sure that you've already guessed.

It is *The Book of the Revelation of John,* created many centuries ago by Eadfrith, bishop of Lindisfarne. It has been hidden under the hay by Rooker Rat, who planned to sell it on the underworld art market.

And just where did Rooker get this precious book?

Why, he stole it from Mr. Biddle, of course!

And Mr. Biddle — where did he get it?

Well, if you will recall, Sally Brandon stole the book from Lord Longford's collection and brought it home with her to Castle Cottage. Her little brother Dickey hid it in his hidey-hole, along with three marbles and a broken knife-blade and the star-shaped brass decoration that had fallen off Captain Woodcock's horse's bridle. Mr. Biddle found it when he was surveying the tear-out work that needed to be done at Castle Cottage.

Of course, he recognized at once that the book was of value, at least as far as the gold and silver and jewels were concerned, and knew that he should show it to Miss Potter, since he had found on her property and understood it to be hers by rights. You would have done that, wouldn't you?

But I am sad to say that Mr. Biddle's greed overwhelmed his good sense, which happens all too often in this world — and not only that, he was not terribly fond of Miss Potter and knew that she had employed him only because she could find no one else. So he put the *Revelation* with his jacket and canvas lunch bag, intending to take it home with him and show it to a book dealer of his acquaintance named Depford Darnwell, who might give him as much as a hundred quid for it. (I am sure that Mr. Darnwell would have been delighted to do this, since he has already told Lady Longford that the book is worth a great deal more than a hundred quid.)

And that is where Rooker Rat discovered the book, when he was rummaging through Mr. Biddle's lunch bag, looking for an apple. Rooker, a clever rat with an eye for value, made off with both the apple *and* the book.

And what happened when Mr. Biddle discovered that the book he had stolen had been stolen from him? Why, he blamed Mr.

Adcock, naturally, because Mr. Adcock had been working in the same room where Mr. Biddle had put his jacket and lunch. And Mr. Adcock quite naturally refused to confess that he had stolen anything, because he hadn't. And then Mr. Biddle sacked Mr. Adcock and they got into a fight at the pub and —

But you know what happened after that.

And now, here is our Miss Potter, who has fallen off the ladder in her barn and tumbled into the pile of hay where she has discovered all manner of stolen goods: Hannah Braithwaite's cream jug, Margaret's wedding photograph, Sarah Barwick's monogrammed leather purse, and —

And she is holding the *Revelation* in her hand, staring down at it wonderingly. She opens it, sees the decorated Latin lettering and the gorgeously illuminated pages and breathes, "The Lindisfarne Gospels!" For as a young girl, Beatrix had many times visited the British Museum, where she looked closely at Bishop Eadfrith's gorgeous Gospels and admired (as a young artist naturally would) the lettering, the illuminations, and the brilliant colors. And because she is an artist, she recognizes this same lettering, illuminations, and coloring when she sees it again.

"Beg pardon?" Margaret says, now thoroughly confused and convinced that Beatrix had indeed fallen on her head.

Beatrix pulls in her breath, stammers, and finally manages to say quite breathlessly, "Margaret, I have no idea how this book got into the barn. But I have seen another, very like it, in the British Museum. It's very, very old. And enormously valuable."

"Well, I don't know about that," Margaret replies in a matter-of-fact voice. "But I do know that you have just had a bad fall and you've likely hurt your head as well as your shoulder and your ankle." (She thinks this, I am sure, because Beatrix believed that she had seen a badger, a stoat, and a weasel, when most people who fall on their heads simply see stars.) "I am taking you home right this minute for a cup of hot tea, some arnica liniment, and bed." She holds out her hand and adds sweetly, in the tone she has so often used for her schoolchildren, "Don't argue with me, dear. Just come along."

And Beatrix suddenly found that the idea of a cup of hot tea, arnica liniment, and bed sounded just about perfect. She went with Margaret without a word of complaint.

Now, you and I know that Beatrix really *did*

see a badger, a stoat, and a weasel. In fact, she might have seen a half-dozen weasels and stoats, if she'd had a moment longer to look — oh, and a cat, of course. The badger was Hyacinth, the cat was Crumpet, and they were hiding in Brown Billy's stall where, after an hour's surveillance, they suspected that Rooker's gang was holed up.

No, that's wrong. It wasn't a matter of suspecting any longer, for as they kept watch in the shadows, they had seen several rats — including an immense gray creature that they thought must be Rooker — emerging from a trapdoor in the floor under the manger. Their strategy discussion was interrupted when Miss Potter and Mrs. Woodcock entered the barn, and then Miss Potter climbed the ladder and fell off and Mrs. Woodcock rushed to her rescue and several moments later, the two women left, Miss Potter leaning on Mrs. Woodcock for support.

Breathing a sigh of relief that Miss Potter was not terribly injured, they returned to their discussion of strategy.

"I'm in favor of taking them on right now, here in the barn," Hyacinth said grimly. *"If some are still loose in the village, Rascal and the other animals can pick them off when they try to get back here to their headquarters. And*

the fewer there are down there in that hole, the easier it will be to destroy them."

Crumpet shook her head bleakly. *"Destroy them? I don't know how you're going to do that, Hyacinth."* She gave the badger a measuring glance that took in her substantial girth. *"I certainly can't squeeze through that trapdoor, and you're bigger than I am."*

Hyacinth gave a wry chuckle. *"Of course I am. And both of us are bigger than that weasel over there."* She nodded toward a dark corner, where a weasel was snuffling through the hay, looking for mice. *"And that one there."* Another, in the other corner. *"But while they may be smaller than we are, they are* fierce. *Believe me. And the stoats are just as fierce as the weasels. In fact, I think we'll send the stoats down first. They love nothing better than a good fight. What do you say?"*

"I say YES!" Crumpet cried excitedly, thinking that she hadn't heard such a good suggestion since the beginning of this horrible episode.

So the stoats went first, slamming the trapdoor after themselves so that rats could not escape. Through the floor, Crumpet and Hyacinth could hear the satisfying sounds of terrified squeals and cries of *"Mercy! Mercy, please!"* and the sound of furniture being overturned and crockery broken and things flying around.

And then there was silence.

And then the trapdoor opened, and one after another, the weasels and stoats came out. One of them dragged up the limp body of Jumpin' Jemmy, another the carcass of Firehouse Frank, and both dead rats were thrown on the floor for everyone to see. The stoats and weasels themselves were bloody, a few ears had been bitten and fur torn, but — to an animal — they were proud of their victory.

"We rout-t-t-ed those rat-t-ts!" the weasel-in-charge announced, in his clicking, chattery voice.

And the stoat-in-charge echoed him. *"We rout-t-ted the rat-t-ts! Rout-t-t out-t-t rat-t-ts!"*

"Congratulations!" cried Hyacinth and Crumpet, with one voice. *"Thank you for your help!"*

But of course it wasn't over. Throughout the village that night, rats were spotted, attacked, and speedily slaughtered — by Rascal and the fox, by the Professor, by Bailey Badger, and of course by the weasels and stoats, who weren't quite ready to go home and be peaceful. The dragon, too, did his part, with a little help from his friend Thackeray. Riding on Thorvaald's broad shoulders, the guinea pig looked down and saw Rooker, who was trying to escape by sneaking west along the Kendal Road. He alerted Thorvaald, who dove down out of the sky, with Thackeray holding on for dear life, and incinerated the wretched rat on the spot.

In this way, and in a matter of only a few hours, the Rooker gang was completely eliminated, and the animals could all go back to The Brockery and celebrate their victory — which they did, of course. They had a grand party that lasted well into the night.

If the villagers had been out and about while all this carnage was going on, they would have been astonished by the battles that were waged, the blood that was spilled, and the anguish that was caused — anguish among Rooker's rats, that is. But like quiet, well-behaved Big Folks, they kept indoors until the next morning, when a few of them were greatly surprised to find their stolen treasures (Mr. Dowling's silver snuffbox, Mrs. Crook's emerald-cut crystal pendant) on their stoops, returned with the compliments of the animals of The Brockery. They were also astonished when they saw the numerous carcasses of dead rats that littered their lanes and back gardens.

"Whatever do you think?" young Mrs. Pemberton said in great wonderment to Lydia Dowling, as she carried three dead rats to her rubbish tip. "Do you suppose it was t' cats did 'em in?"

"Doan't hardly see how our fat, lazy cats could've killt all these rats," Lydia Dowling said, adding two more carcasses to her own tip. "But if they were t' ones who done it, I'm glad to take back everything I said about 'em."

Mrs. Pemberton nodded. "Think I'll put out an extra bowl of milk," she remarked.

Watching from the doorway of the shed at the foot of the Rose Cottage garden, Crumpet smiled.

22

AN ASTONISHING
TURN OF EVENTS

By Sunday, Beatrix's wrenched ankle was much better, but it had been an exhausting week, and she was glad for the chance to rest and relax. The sun was bright, the sky was a crystalline blue, and the air was deliciously scented with summer roses, so she spent an early hour in the garden before coming indoors and settling down to *The Tale of Pigling Bland.* The work went well, and she finished another drawing — Pig-wig and Pigling running across a bridge together — that she would insert into the galley proof at the end of the book, to illustrate the last paragraph: "They came to the river, they came to the bridge — they crossed it hand in hand — then over the hills and far away Pig-wig danced with Pigling Bland."

There were still three or four pen-and-ink drawings to complete and in a few weeks she would have the proofs to check and correct — that would take several days. But happily, she could finally see the end of the project, which had seemed to stretch out interminably. She could hope, now, that *Pigling Bland* would be published on schedule, in October.

Would it be the last of her little books? If she had her way, she rather thought yes, all things considered. It was so hard to find time for sketching and painting, and her dealings with Harold Warne were almost always uncomfortable, one way or another. But the farms would certainly continue to need money — for drains, barn repairs, fences, livestock. It would be difficult to give up the books, if only because there were so many places to put her earnings. Now, if Mr. Warne would just pay what was owed her . . .

She pushed that unfinished thought away. She would have to deal with it sooner or later, but the day was too lovely to spoil it with unpleasantness about money. It was time to clear the table for Sunday dinner.

Will had fallen into the regular practice of riding his motorcycle to Hill Top Farm on Sundays, so that he and Beatrix could eat and take a quiet country walk together. Mrs. Jennings had cooked an especially nice dinner for today: roast lamb with mint sauce;

new potatoes; spinach and marrow; a garden salad with onions, cucumbers, and tomatoes; sliced bread and butter; and an apple pie with wedges of yellow cheese.

As Beatrix set the food on the table, she reflected with a warm contentment that every part of the meal came from Hill Top, from its sheep and cows, its garden, and its orchard. If war came, as Captain Woodcock seemed to think it might (or rather to hope that it would!), there would likely be plenty of food here at the farm and in the rest of the village. Of course, London was a different matter, because so much British food was imported now — lamb from New Zealand, beef from Australia, wheat and maize from Canada and the United States. It was frightening to think that an enemy blockade of ships or those terrible new U-boats might reduce the nation's food supply. But surely Mr. Churchill would send out the Royal Navy and —

It was another disquieting thought to be set aside. Beatrix picked up her shears and went out to the garden to cut some pink and white roses for the table. She was settling them into a bowl when she heard Will's tap on the door and went happily to answer it. Pulled into his tweedy and tobacco-scented embrace, she could forget for a few moments about everything else. She could almost pretend that they had crossed the bridge to happiness together, hand in hand, and everything had been settled at last.

But that was not going to happen, she knew. And in spite of all her resolution to push away unhappy thoughts, one hung like an ominous cloud over all her present happiness. Today was the day that Bertram intended to confess his secret marriage. And tomorrow afternoon, she would go back across the lake to Lindeth Howe, where she would be bombarded by her parents' anger the minute she walked through the door. And worse, they would adamantly refuse to hear another word about *her* being married. She desperately wanted to confide in Will, but she knew it was better to wait until Bertram had done what he was going to do and the consequences were clear. Then she would tell him and release him from their engagement. By that time, even he would have to agree that their marriage would be entirely out of the question.

Will pulled out her chair so she could sit down at the table, then took his place opposite. "There's news, Bea, about Maguire. The Kendal police apprehended him at his brother's home in Kendal late yesterday, thankfully without a fight. Tomorrow, he'll be brought over to Hawkshead and arraigned." He gave her a crooked grin. "Miles said to convey his thanks — he says that you've done it again, and he is grateful."

Beatrix let out her breath. Her fall from the ladder in the barn had put an end to her dinner-party evening, but Will and Captain Woodcock had been out for several more hours. They had returned empty-handed, for when Maguire heard them knocking at his door and realized who they were, he went out the back window. The constables and police authorities in the neighboring districts had been alerted, and this was the outcome. Maguire was in custody, without a fight.

"I'm very glad," Beatrix said, deeply relieved. "And glad that there was no more violence. Has he . . . Has he confessed to Mr. Adcock's death?"

"Yes, and to the theft of the construction materials, as well — which turns out to have been the motive for the killing. He told the police that Adcock had found him out and threatened to go to the constable with the information about the thefts. He went to Adcock's workshop early that morning and waited for him, hoping to persuade him otherwise. When Adcock refused, Maguire picked up a piece of lumber and hit him. The rest — well, he said he panicked. All he could think of was trying to hide his crime." He shook his head. "Such a pity."

"Poor Mr. Adcock," Beatrix said softly. "And Mrs. Adcock, too. But perhaps she will take some comfort in the knowledge that her husband was doing the right thing." She added, "Sarah Barwick told me that the villagers are asking for contributions to help with Mrs. Adcock's bills."

That was one of the things she loved about Sawrey. The villagers might carry petty grudges and gossip unmercifully about their friends, but they genuinely cared for one another. When one was in want, the others were glad to pitch in, even when their own pockets were nearly empty. And while Mrs. Adcock's loss was immeasurable, help from her friends and fellow villagers would go a long way toward easing it.

Will nodded. "Oh, and I ran into Vicar Sackett in Hawkshead, and we talked about the book you found in the barn at Castle Farm. He told me that he was the one who recommended to Lady Longford that she have her husband's collection appraised."

"Yes," Beatrix said. "That's what he told me yesterday, when we talked." By this time, Beatrix had discovered that the *Revelation*

410

had belonged to Lord Longford, although she still did not have a clue as to how it might have come to be buried in that pile of hay in the barn. Even the remarkable Beatrix Potter doesn't know *everything.*

"He asked me to pass along a suggestion." Will buttered a slice of bread. "He thought we ought to try to persuade Lady Longford to sell or perhaps even to give the *Revelation* to the British Museum, where it could rejoin the Lindisfarne Gospels." He chuckled wryly. "Of course, it won't be the easiest thing to do. Her ladyship is never inclined to be generous. But perhaps she can be convinced that the book really belongs to the British people, rather than hidden away in the library of a private collector."

"I've been thinking about that myself," Beatrix said. "The book belongs in the museum. And she might be willing to donate it — especially if the museum would give a reception in her honor and the *Times* would publish an article about the find, with her photograph." She chuckled. "Her ladyship can often be persuaded with the promise of a little public attention. I'll be glad to help encourage her, Will."

They had finished the main part of their meal, and Beatrix was just cutting the pie when a shadow darkened the window and there was a knock at the door. When she opened it, she was surprised to see her brother.

"Bertram!" she exclaimed. "What are you —" She bit it off and smiled. "How good to see you."

He set down the leather valise he was carrying and took off his hat. Looking over her shoulder, he glimpsed Will sitting at the table.

"Ah, Bea," he said, "I'm sorry — I'm intruding on your dinner."

"Not at all," Beatrix said, stepping back. "Come in — you're just in time for pie and coffee. And you can meet Mr. Heelis." She smiled, teasing. "I think you already know something about him, don't you? Will, this is my brother, Bertram."

"Ah, Potter!" Will exclaimed, getting up and coming forward to shake hands. "Very good to meet you, at long last! Yes, do come in and have dessert with us, won't you?"

Beatrix cut three pieces of pie and three wedges of cheese and put down another cup and saucer. Glancing at Bertram's valise beside the door, she said with some surprise, "You're going back to Scotland today? I thought it was to be tomorrow."

"Yes, today," Bertram replied, taking a chair. "To tell the truth, it was a bit uncomfortable around Lindeth." He ducked his head. "I've told them, Bea. I couldn't stand the suspense, so I did it yesterday, instead of waiting until today. And believe me, it wasn't easy."

Will turned curiously to Beatrix but said nothing.

Beatrix sighed. Confronted with it now, she had no choice but to explain. "Bertram has told Mama and Papa about his marriage," she said to Will. She caught his suddenly sharp glance. He understood the implications without any further explanation. To Bertram, she added, "I'm sorry it was so difficult. I don't need to ask about their reactions."

Bertram picked up his fork. "Well, I could only do my best. As you can imagine, Mama flew into hysterics. Papa was absolutely apoplectic. Mama said she never wanted to see me again, and Papa vowed to disinherit me — not a shilling of his precious money will ever be wasted on me. It was hours before they were calm enough to discuss the matter rationally." He forked a bite of pie.

Beatrix looked up in surprise. "Discuss it rationally? They were able to do that?"

"More or less," Bertram replied. "Although not without continuing recriminations, of course," he added ironically.

"Of course," Beatrix replied. "Those can go on for weeks. And probably will."

"Which is why I elected to go back to Scotland a day early." Bertram put his fork down and looked from one to the other. "But I did want to come over and tell you that you and Heelis have their permission to marry."

Permission to marry. The words seemed to hang in the air over the table, shimmering. *Permission to marry . . . to marry . . .*

Beatrix swallowed. She opened her mouth, tried to speak, and found that her throat was so dry and her tongue so thick that she could not utter a word.

But Will wasn't speechless. "Say that again, Potter," he commanded sharply.

Bertram pushed his empty plate back and put his hand over Beatrix's. "You and Heelis have the parents' permission to marry," he repeated slowly and distinctly. "You may marry now, soon, or at a time of your choosing." He laughed a little. "Although if I were you, I'd do it soon. Or at least make a public announcement, so they can't somehow change their tune."

"But why . . . how . . ." Beatrix managed.

"They were completely flummoxed by my announcement, that's how," Bertram replied. "They were so flummoxed that when I told them that they had to let you live your own life, they agreed." He gave her a wry grin and released her hand. "Maybe they were afraid that if they denied you, you and Heelis would take a leaf from my book and marry in secret. So they chose the lesser of two evils."

Will leaned forward, his face a study in astonishment, delight, and uncertainty, all three at once. "Their permission?" he asked urgently. "You're *sure* about that, Potter?"

"Absolutely sure," Bertram said. He drained his coffee cup. "But just the same, I suggest that the two of you go over there tomorrow or the next day, together, and tell them when you plan to do it. To marry, that is."

"We'll go today," Will said, pushing his chair back. "Get your hat, Beatrix."

Beatrix got up, too, protesting. "But Will, I —"

"No buts," Will said sternly. "I'll ask Woodcock if we can borrow his Rolls. Potter, if you're taking the afternoon train, you'll be going back on the ferry. You can ride with us."

Beatrix put out her hand. "But I'm not ready, Will! I have to think! I have to —"

"Hush," Will said, and put his finger

across her lips. "I've waited long enough for this, Beatrix — long enough for *you.* Don't make me wait a minute longer than I have to."

And when he put it that way, Beatrix could only agree.

23
WEDDING BELLS

I'm sure you want to hear all about the wedding, don't you? Imagining this wonderful event, I felt it would be delightfully appropriate if Miss Potter and Mr. Heelis were to be married at St. Peter's Church in Far Sawrey, by the Reverend Samuel Sackett, with the Woodcocks and the Kittredges and the Braithwaites and Lady Longford and all their village friends in attendance, dressed in their very best. The church would be quite crowded, but I'm sure that everyone would find a place.

As to the weather, the ceremony would take place on a beautiful autumn day — perhaps a Saturday afternoon — and the sun would be so charmed by the event that he would shine from sunrise to sunset without allowing a single cloud to cross his beaming face. I do not imagine that Mr. and Mrs. Potter will attend the wedding. After all, they are not fond of the village and they know almost nothing of the villagers — and this is not exactly the happiest of events for them. They are indeed gaining a son, as the saying goes, but they are losing a daughter. That is, when Beatrix is married, she will be living with her husband in Sawrey. She will no longer be at her mother's beck and her father's call, and they will miss her devoted attentions. But of course, they are free to come if they choose. I am sure that everyone would welcome them.

Now, then. Thinking about the wedding party, I felt that Mrs. Woodcock would most likely be Miss Potter's choice as her matron of honor, and that Mr. Heelis would ask Captain Woodcock to be best man — that would be fitting, don't you think? The bride might be dressed in a lovely white lace-trimmed gown with a flowing white tulle veil caught by a cap of silk flowers trimmed with pearls, and her matron in pink. (Mrs. Woodcock looks so well in pink.) Both would carry bouquets of pink and white lilies from the Hill Top gardens, with fresh ferns and rosemary and trailing ivy. The groom and groomsman would wear handsome morning coats and fresh boutonnieres of tiny white flowers made and presented by the bride.

Before the ceremony, I'm sure that Mrs.

Grace Sackett (accompanied on the organ by Miss Rebecca Randall) would offer a memorable rendition of "Oh, Promise Me." And after the wedding, there would be a lovely reception at Major Kittredge's Raven Hall, and of course all the villagers would be invited. Sarah Barwick would bake and decorate a tiered wedding cake — a culinary masterpiece — whilst Mr. and Mrs. Barrow (from the pub) would provide hams and cold tongue and salads and many other delightful refreshments. The great hall would be decorated with bouquets of wildflowers gathered from the surrounding countryside by the village children, under the direction of Deirdre and Jeremy Crosfield. Lady Longford (who had allowed Miss Potter to persuade her to donate *The Book of the Revelation of John* to the British Museum and was now quite proud of her generosity) would be asked to offer the first toast, which would then be followed by such a round of toasting as the village has never before seen.

And when the toasting is finished, the wedding couple and their friends would be serenaded by the Village Volunteer Band (Lester Barrow on trombone, Mr. Taylor and Clyde Clinder on clarinet, Lawrence Baldwin on coronet, and Sam Stern on the concertina), and perhaps Mrs. Heelis would be persuaded to dance with her new husband, whom everyone recognizes as the very best dancer in all of the Land Between the Lakes. Mrs. Regina Rosier of Hawkshead would photograph the entire occasion and would present an album of her photos to Mr. and Mrs. Heelis, so that the wonderful event could be remembered forever, just as it happened.

And as the autumn afternoon wears on into a cool autumn evening, all the creatures of the Land Between the Lakes would undoubtedly creep out of the woods and fields and gather outside the windows to watch the Big Folks celebrating the marriage of their friends. Rascal and Crumpet and Tabitha Twitchit and the other village cats would be there; and those dear badgers from The Brockery and Briar Bank, with Thackeray and the dragon, of course. Professor Galileo Newton Owl has flown in from his beech at the top of Claife Woods. Hyacinth, Primrose, and Parsley have organized the animals to pick baskets of tiny blossoms, and when Mrs. Heelis and her new husband step out of the front door, they step onto a delightful carpet of wildflowers, brought as a special gift by their woodland friends.

Meanwhile, down at Hill Top Farm, the barnyard animals would no doubt be holding their own celebration. Mustard the old yellow dog and Kitchen the cow and Mrs. Heelis' three favorite hens, Mrs. Boots, Mrs. Bonnet, and Mrs. Shawl, as well as all the Puddle-ducks, and of course the pigs and Tibbie and Queenie and their multiple lambs — well, what can I say? They are all delighted that the wedding has finally taken place and look forward to seeing Mrs. Heelis every day, rather than just on the days when she manages to escape from London and her parents.

And then I believe that Mr. and Mrs. Heelis would borrow Captain Woodcock's blue Rolls automobile and drive off by themselves, perhaps to the Magical Isle of Somewhere, where they can be together, alone, and enjoy a blissfully quiet few days, walking along a glittering beach and sitting before a roaring fire and toasting one another's health with glasses of bubbly. And kissing and holding one another close and in general behaving exactly like a devoted couple on their honeymoon — and all the more happy a honeymoon for having been delayed for so very long. After a week or two of these intimate pleasures, they would return to the village and take up their everyday lives as a married couple, to the welcoming applause of all their friends.

Ah, yes. That is how I imagine it, or nearly, and I imagine you did, too. It is entirely lovely and exceedingly romantic, isn't it?

But it isn't what happened.

What happened — I mean, what *really* happened — was a great deal simpler, if less romantic. The wedding of Beatrix Potter and William Heelis took place on Wednesday, October 15, in London, at St. Mary Abbots, a large church not far from the Potters' home. The church, which counted many socially prominent Londoners among its parishioners, boasted a vaulted, cathedral-like nave, elaborate stained-glass windows, and an ornate marble-and-wood altar with a carved Florentine crucifix. It seated seven hundred worshippers.

But except for the wedding party of six — seven, counting the officiating curate — the vast church was empty. Mr. and Mrs. Potter attended, as did Beatrix's friend Gertrude Woodward (also an artist and a scientific illustrator) and Will's cousin, Lelio Stampa, an Oxford don. Beatrix is thought to have worn the same outfit she wore for the wedding photograph her father took the previous day in the family's garden: a gray tweed suit woven of Herdwick wool, a dressy blouse with a lace jabot, and a flower-trimmed, broad-brimmed hat. William wore a suit.

Make of all that what you will. What I make of it is that sensible Miss Potter wanted to become Mrs. Heelis with as little fuss and as few feathers as possible, and that her parents — for their own reasons — were glad to have it over and done with and did not wish to invite their friends. There was a brief announcement in the *Times* and a longer and more admiring story in the *Westmoorland Gazette.* The writer began, "In the quietest of quiet manners two very well-known local inhabitants were married in London. None of their friends knew of the wedding, which was solemnized in the simplest form, characteristic of such modest though accomplished bridegroom and bride."

And the honeymoon? The Magical Isle of Somewhere, the beach and the bubbly?

No. Sorry to disappoint. The newly married couple returned to Sawrey by train on the day after the wedding. At the Windermere station, they collected Beatrix's wedding present, a young white bull, which they took on the ferry back to Hill Top Farm. Beatrix also brought pieces of her wedding

423

cake from London to share amongst her village friends. She would perhaps have invited them to their home, but Castle Cottage was not finished. (Are you surprised?)

But that hardly mattered, I am sure, for at last Beatrix had found her dearest love, and Will had married the wife of his dreams, and the two of them did what all married couples, in every story, should do:

They lived happily ever after.

HISTORICAL NOTE

Stories don't always end where their authors intended. But there is joy in following them, wherever they take us.

— Beatrix Potter

The story of Beatrix Potter is surely one of the most remarkable stories of an entire generation of British women, and I count it an enormous privilege to have traced its outlines over the nearly ten years I have worked on this series. From *The Tale of Hill Top Farm* to *The Tale of Castle Cottage,* the books have followed the course of Miss Potter's life from the 1905 death of her fiancé, Norman Warne, to her marriage to William Heelis in 1913. I have tried to paint an accurate picture of her real life during those pivotal years and to give you some idea of the many forces that shaped her choices and actions. (Not all of the things that happen in the books are real, however:

for example, I made up *The Book of the Revelation of John,* which appears in this story. The Lindisfarne Gospels, of course, are real, and even more beautiful than the fictional *Revelation!*)

Many things changed in the years immediately after Beatrix's October 1913 marriage to her beloved Willie. Beatrix's father died in May 1914. His will bequeathed £35,000 each to Beatrix and Bertram, with the rest left in trust to Helen Potter, to be divided at her death between the two children. (The Potter estate was valued at the modern equivalent of some eleven million dollars.) This meant that Beatrix's financial situation was secure and that she no longer had to create books in order to support her farms. After a period of indecision, Mrs. Potter agreed to come to Sawrey, where she moved into a house not far from her daughter — not nearly far enough, probably. Eventually, she closed the house in Bolton Gardens and moved back across Windermere to Lindeth Howe, where Beatrix visited often.

But all of these family difficulties were overshadowed by the war, which began in August 1914. It was a wrenching experience that changed every British citizen's life and robbed the nation of nearly a million of its young men. For farm families, it was a terrible time, for labor shortages and the government's conscription of horses made it hard to plow the fields, and food, medicine, and even coal were in short supply. Bertram tried to enlist but was rejected for health reasons. He died in 1918 of a cerebral hemorrhage at his farm in Scotland — a devastating blow for Beatrix, who corresponded regularly with her brother and loved him dearly.

Between her farms, her family obligations, and the challenges of a nation at war, the years were so busy that there was no time for art. Shortly after her marriage, Beatrix thought of doing a book called "The Tale of Kitty-in-Boots," but Harold Warne was not enthusiastic about it, and she dropped the idea. Her next publication was *Tom Kitten's Painting Book,* a reissue of an older book with a few new drawings and no story text.

But it wasn't just a lack of time and energy that held her back. For years, there had been problems with the payment of her royalties, and by 1917, the publishing company owed their star author a great deal of money. In April of that year, Harold Warne, Beatrix's editor and Norman's brother, was arrested for a series of forgeries amounting to some £20,000, resulting from his bad management of a fishing business he had inherited from his mother. Harold pled guilty and was sentenced to prison, and his brother Fruing took over the company. Beatrix, not just Warne's bestselling author but its largest creditor, helped the firm to stay afloat by producing *Appley Dapply's Nursery Rhymes* and *The Tale of Johnny Town-Mouse,* both of which were greeted with pleasure by reviewers. About *Johnny Town-Mouse,* the *Bookman* gushed happily: "Miss Potter need not worry about rivals. She has none."

And of course, while she was dealing with all these publishing upsets and demands, there were the continued challenges of the war years, as well as epidemics of measles and influenza in the village and periods of dreadful storms, floods, and rains, which ruined harvests and caused great suffering. In June 1918, William got his call-up papers, but his age (forty-six) and a bad knee kept him at home, much to everyone's relief.

But finally, the awful war was over. Mrs. Heelis could turn her attention to farming, to her sheep, and to the project that she and Willie had long discussed: acquiring more Lake District property in order to protect it from development. In 1924, with Willie's legal assistance, she bought the

2,000-acre Troutbeck, the area's most spectacular hill-farm, and five years later, the Monk Coniston Estate, some 4,000 acres of fell and tarn, with several farms and cottages. In the heart of the Lakes, Monk Coniston was a land of incomparable beauty, and the Heelises' purchase protected it from being carved up into small parcels and used for holiday estates. Again, it was Willie who handled the legal and financial details, while Beatrix undertook the management of the far-flung property. The purchase had been made with the help and cooperation of the National Trust, which bought half the land. Beatrix and Willie kept the rest, to be deeded to the Trust upon their deaths.

In the 1920s, Beatrix produced two more books, the last of her three-decades-long career: *The Fairy Caravan,* published in America by Alexander McKay (who journeyed from Philadelphia to persuade her to do it); and *The Tale of Little Pig Robinson,* published simultaneously in America and England. But she was also busy with her own farms and especially with sheep breeding: her Herdwick ewes were acknowledged to be the best in the district. She collected pieces of fine old furniture (some of which can be seen at Hill Top) and did her best to influence local zoning boards to preserve the vernacular architecture of the area.

Beatrix's relationship with her mother had never been comfortable or happy, and Mrs. Potter — who lived on at Lindeth How, amusing herself with needlework and canaries — seemed to become even more demanding and querulous as the years passed. She did not approve of her daughter's love of farming, her countrified and often careless appearance, or her conservation work on behalf of the National Trust. She refused to donate any of her substantial wealth to the Trust or to any other charity, which meant that much of her estate, as Beatrix wrote to her cousin Caroline, would "simply be wasted in death duties when she has hoarded it up." Healthy to the end of her life (in spite of being so frequently indisposed), Mrs. Potter died in 1932. She was ninety-three. To a friend, Beatrix wrote simply, "I am glad she is at rest at last."

The last decade of Beatrix's life was a busy and mostly happy one, with her animals, her farms, and the far-flung properties she owned and managed. She had come to terms with her age. To a friend, she wrote, "Do you not feel it is rather pleasing to be so much *wiser* than quantities of young idiots? . . . I begin to assert myself at 70."

But the late 1930s brought fear of another war and of Hitler, the "brutal, raging lunatic," as Beatrix called him. She was soon getting out the "dark curtains, rather motheaten," which she had saved from the blackout days of World War I, and stocking up on sugar and biscuits for her two "spirited and affectionate" Pekingese.

The new war brought renewed challenges. "Crops have been a struggle," she wrote, and markets were difficult: "I had more than three tons of wool to sell." Her gardens produced vegetables, her hutch rabbit meat, and her cows milk, so the Heelises did not go hungry. But even though she kept busy with work, she was more frequently ill and fretted about having to spend time in bed with a cough when she would rather be up and about. She was hospitalized for serious surgery in 1939, recovered and was active for several years, then fell ill again with the familiar bronchitis. In the last months of 1943, she could look out of the window of her bedroom in Castle Cottage and across the garden to Hill Top, which she still loved with all her heart.

And that is where she died, with her beloved husband at her side, on December 22, 1943. Willie died eighteen months later. And not long after that, the National Trust, honoring their stewardship, announced the Heelis Bequest of some 4,300 acres, including fifteen farms, 500 acres of woodland, cottages, and houses, and funds for maintaining them. It was a magnificent gift. Linda Lear, Beatrix's biographer, has written of her, "Through her passionate and imaginative stewardship of the land, she challenged others to think about preservation, not just of a few farms or fells, but of a regional ecology, of a distinct farming culture, and of a particular breed of nimble-footed grey sheep."

When she was sorting through family letters years before her own death, Beatrix wrote to a friend that all the stories of illness and dying — the subject matter of most of the letters — left the wrong impression. "The milestones are all tombstones!" she wrote. "But the record of the cheerful jog trot round of life between them is not well kept." I hope that, as you have read through the Cottage Tales, these small stories, light and whimsical as they are, reflect something of that "cheerful jog trot" that was Beatrix Potter Heelis' wonderful life.

Susan Wittig Albert
Bertram, Texas, October 2010

RESOURCES

Denyer, Susan. *At Home with Beatrix Potter,* New York: Harry N. Abrams, Inc., 2000.

Hervye, Canon G. A. K., and J. A. G. Barnes. *Natural History of the Lake District.* London: Frederick Warne, 1970.

Lear, Linda. *A Life in Nature: The Story of Beatrix Potter.* London: Allen Lane (Penguin UK) and New York: St. Martin's Press, 2007.

Potter, Beatrix. *Beatrix Potter's Letters,* selected and edited by Judy Taylor. London: Frederick Warne, 1989.

Potter, Beatrix. *The Journal of Beatrix Potter, 1881–1897,* transcribed by Leslie Linder. London: Frederick Warne, New Edition, 1966.

Potter, Beatrix. *The Tale of Mr. Tod.* London: Frederick Warne, 1912.

Taylor, Judy. *Beatrix Potter: Artist, Storyteller*

and Countrywoman, revised edition. London: Frederick Warne, 1996.

GLOSSARY

Canna. Cannot.

Dost'a. Do you.

Gert. Great.

Grave. To cut, as to cut turf or peat.

Haver. A bread made of oats.

Mappen. May happen, perhaps.

Metal paving. Metaled lanes that are paved roads.

Mezzlement. A mystery or puzzlement.

Pattens. Traditional Lake District women's shoes, wooden soles, leather uppers.

Rive. To cut.

Tatie pots. A potato stew.

Wigging. Dressing-down, lecture, chiding.

RECIPES

PARSLEY'S EGG MAYONNAISE, CUCUMBER, AND CRESS SANDWICHES

4 eggs, hard-boiled, finely chopped and
   mashed
4 tablespoons mayonnaise
1 tablespoon mild mustard
salt, to taste
freshly ground black pepper, to taste
16 thin slices of firm white or whole wheat
   bread, crusts removed
2 cups fresh baby mustard cress or garden
   cress

Mix the eggs, mayonnaise, and mustard
together and season to taste. Spread half of
the slices of bread with the egg mixture and
layer fresh mustard or garden cress on top
of each one, reserving some cress for gar-
nishing. Place the remaining slices of bread
on top, and cut each sandwich diagonally
into four triangles. Arrange the sandwiches

on a platter and garnish with the remaining mustard and cress.

PRIMROSE'S CARROT CAKE

Badgers love carrots in all forms, but especially in cakes.

2 cups flour
2 cups sugar
2 teaspoons baking powder
2 teaspoons baking soda
1 teaspoon cinnamon
1/2 teaspoon nutmeg
1 teaspoon salt
4 eggs
1 1/2 cups vegetable oil
3 cups grated carrots
1/2 cup nuts

Mix together all dry ingredients. Beat eggs and stir in the oil. Combine the wet and dry ingredients. Add carrots and nuts. Pour into three greased 9-inch layer pans. Bake at 350 degrees for 25–30 minutes.

Frosting

1/2 cup butter, softened
4 cups confectioners' sugar
1/4 cup evaporated milk

Combine all ingredients and beat with an

egg beater until of spreading consistency. (Modern cooks will be glad to use an electric mixer.)

CUMBRIAN BEEF AND ALE STEW WITH HERB DUMPLINGS

A favorite in the Lake District, especially on a gray and rainy day. Serve with a hearty salad for a one-dish dinner. And please don't leave out the parsnips.

2 pounds flank steak, chopped into chunks
salt and freshly ground pepper, to taste
3 tablespoons flour
2 tablespoons cooking oil
3 red onions, chopped
3 slices bacon, chopped
3 sticks of celery, chopped
3 tablespoons minced fresh rosemary
5 cups Newcastle Brown Ale or other dark ale
1 cup water
2 parsnips, peeled and chopped
2 carrots, chopped
4 potatoes, peeled and chopped

Dumplings
2 cups flour
3 teaspoons baking powder
2/3 cup butter

1/2 teaspoon salt
pepper, to taste
2 tablespoons minced fresh rosemary
water

Season the beef with salt and pepper and toss with flour until coated. Heat the oil in a frying pan and brown the beef. Transfer to a large kettle, along with the rest of the flour. Place over medium heat, add the onions and bacon, and cook until the onions are translucent. Add the remaining ingredients. Bring to a boil, cover, and reduce to a simmer while you make the dumplings.

Work the flour, baking powder, butter, salt, pepper, and rosemary together until they are crumbly, then add just enough water to make a dough that is not sticky. Form golf ball–sized dumplings and drop these into the stew, pushing them under the liquid. Cover the pot and simmer for 2 hours. Serves six.

STICKY TOFFEE PUDDING

This North Country dessert is said to have been developed in 1907 at The Gait Inn in Millington in the East Riding of Yorkshire, although the Udny Arms Hotel in Newburgh, Aberdeenshire, claims to be the pudding's birthplace. Like other English puddings, it is a moist, fruity cake topped with a sauce instead of a frosting.

1 cup plus 1 tablespoon all-purpose flour
1 teaspoon baking powder
3/4 cup pitted dates, finely chopped
1 1/4 cups boiling water
1 teaspoon baking soda
1/4 cup unsalted butter, softened
3/4 cup granulated sugar
1 large egg, lightly beaten
1 teaspoon vanilla

Toffee Sauce
1/2 cup unsalted butter
1/2 cup heavy cream
1 cup packed light brown sugar
1 cup heavy cream, whipped (for topping)

Preheat oven to 350 degrees. Butter a 10-inch round or square baking dish. Sift the flour and baking powder together into a small bowl. Place the chopped dates in a small bowl; add the boiling water and baking soda and set aside. In a medium bowl, beat the butter and sugar until light and fluffy. Beat in egg and vanilla. Beat in the flour mixture in two or three additions. Add the date mixture to the batter and fold with a rubber spatula until blended. Pour into the greased baking dish. Bake until set and firm on top, about 35 minutes. Cool in the baking dish.

In a small, heavy saucepan, combine butter, cream, and brown sugar. Heat to boiling, stirring constantly. Boil gently over medium low heat until mixture is thickened, about 7–8 minutes. Set aside.

Just before serving, preheat broiler. Spoon about 1/3 cup of the sauce over the pudding, spreading evenly. Place pudding under the broiler until the topping is bubbly, about 1 minute. Spoon into dessert dishes and serve immediately, drizzled with remaining toffee sauce and topped with a generous dollop of whipped cream.

Mrs. Beeton's Sage and Onion Stuffing (for geese, ducks, and pork)

It was Millie Warne who gave the new Mrs. Heelis her copy of *Mrs Beeton's Book of Household Management,* a classic of domestic literature that every proper British bride of her era longed to possess. It included a table of wages for domestics, instructions on "How to Bleed," and a remedy for toothache that required a shilling and a piece of zinc. But while some of Mrs. Beeton's instructions may be dated, her recipes for such traditional British foods as sage and onion stuffing are truly timeless, whether or not you dispense with the egg.

4 large onions
10 sage leaves
1/4 pound bread crumbs
salt and pepper, to taste
1 1/2 ounce butter
1 egg

Peel the onions, put them into boiling water, let them simmer for 5 minutes or rather longer, and, just before they are taken out, put in the sage leaves for a minute or two to take off their rawness. Chop both these very fine, add the bread crumbs, seasoning, and butter and work the whole together with the yolk of an egg, when the stuffing will be ready for use. It should be rather highly seasoned, and the sage leaves should be very finely chopped. Where economy is studied, the egg may be dispensed with.